W9-BQU-012

THE TRUE LIFE ADVENTURES OF

IRENE

IN WHITE TIGHTS

A NOVEL BY
LYNN DOIRON

Lynn Doiron

Water
street
press

Designer Credits
Cover art by Mark Bartman
Interior design by Typeflow

Library of Congress Control
Number: 2016936485

Produced in the USA
ISBN 978-1-62134-280-9

Acknowledgments

The author wishes to thank her children and the many people who shared their time and support during the adventure of writing this book. In particular, the author wishes to thank Karin (Lowe) Runyen, Buddy Lowe, and the inspiration for this fictionalized work, Irene Lowe. Additional thanks and acknowledgments of their patience and expertise are herein offered to past and present members/attendees of Emerging Poets, Poetry Circle, Maggie Flannigan-Wilke, Lavonne Westbrooks, AWP Writers Conferences, Santa Barbara Writers Conferences, Meredith College's "Focus on Form" summer workshops, the crew of Lynn Vannucci's "Beat the Book," and my agent, Elizabeth Trupin-Pulli.

The author is grateful for the existence of New York City's East Side Tenement Museum, Atlantic City's Steel Pier Museum, Prospect Park's Botanical Gardens, and the docents who brought history to life.

Author's Note: Variations on the spelling of Chinatown/ China Town and abbreviations of Pennsylvania to Penna., Penn, and PA are intentional and based upon newspaper articles, essays, historical works and printed research materials which appeared during the particular eras the fictionalized characters occupy in the novel.

Lynn Doiron

Part I

he's not loving the Texaco cannon
she's about to climb into.

Damn Wil. Wilbur Johns, her youngest
brother, who could kill her with his carelessness; the brother who fancies himself
the next Sandoval, Strongman of the Century; the brother
who poses, flexes his muscles in the moments when he ought
to have a care for her safety; the idiot brother who failed to
warn her when he lit the cannon's fuse for the morning act;
the same brother who will attend the fuse-lighting when Foster gives him the nod.

At the moment, ringmaster Foster gargles some potion to
enhance his Irish tenor voice. He's a little man, as they so
often are, these barkers who sell tickets to folks with loose
change and a deranged or misplaced curiosity about lunatic-
daredevil acts—the acts desperate people will undertake to
buy bread or keep a roof over their heads. While he gargles,
Irene waits—rib-sore and hungry as six horses. Watching
him through a break in the cabana's curtained back entrance,
she eyes his fabulous curling moustache, newly amazed
the waxed and hard-looking tip-ends fail to break when he

strokes them. His velvet-frock coat is worn through the nap in places, eaten away by time and velvet-eating moths or silverfish or whatever it is that takes something rich and makes it less. Black-lapelled, the coat fits like the skin on an orange; his white jodhpurs are nearly as snug. She is tall and meagerly fleshed. Spangles adorn her white jumpsuit; inside the cabana, out of the watered-down sunlight, her spangles seem as opaque as fish scales scraped free of carcasses by fishermen on the docks.

She notes Foster's boots. Calf-high and meant to be black, they wear a glaze of graying brine. When he struts before the stands, he will have donned his black bowler and be carrying a black cane he will wheel in audience-encompassing arcs to reel the attentions of a paying crowd to the cannon and Irene's burst upon the stage.

She can't see Poseidon Park's small band from the cabana enclosure. Hearing them is enough to know how they busy themselves. Less than half in number to the band at the Steel Pier over in Jersey, members tune their instruments—tuba, trumpet, cymbals, an accordion, a drum—while the leader in a white hat with a short red feather center-front turns a thin baton in his hand. Dull brass buttons march in sets down the front of his white coat. The grind is the same with every show.

Poseidon Park's bleachers are less an arena, less stacked, less filled, less everything than Atlantic City's Steel Pier. The water looks the same, receives her with the same hard slam as it does off the Jersey shore, yet Irene finds a herky-jerky quality to this venue, this ocean. Even though it's the same ocean—it's smaller, has less depth. The show world she's known for (how long?) better than fifteen years seems to be shrinking. Nearing thirty, she was fourteen the first time she sent her wages home to Olive. *Sixteen years!* She does not wonder about, or question, Olive's decision to allow a daughter to tour with Dottie Clay and her Nymphs at such a young age, nor does she wonder where Dottie Clay is these days: Dottie is on tour with her Nymphs. New Nymphs, Irene is certain. No one, except perhaps a sister or mother, is interested in paying to watch aging mermaids.

The tuba groans like a broken frog of Goliath proportions and the accordion wheezes as Irene smoothes her slipper ribbons and Foster continues his gargling routine. Dottie could be in Cuba for all Irene knows or cares. Irene is at Poseidon Park, the dream child of some joker with bigger plans than his pocketbook. It is a small-potatoes venue where what was shiny and new at the onset of '28 went dull by later that year and duller yet on Black Tuesday of '29. Not since the Spanish Flu pandemic of '18 had Irene found the business so sick. She shrugs, feels another pinch of pain in her ribcage as Foster dons his bowler and offers the nod she's been dreading.

He moves from her line of vision. She thinks about Pal, that poor old black dog, and if he knew what was coming before Wilbur ended his whining. She thinks about Bucky rewarding piglets, bottle-feeding them with warm milk, over at the pig slide where ball throwers hit a paddle and the squealers come sliding down a chute. He's wearing a bald cap under a pointed dunce hat with red balls, blue triangles painted on under brown eyes, a red mouth that always smiles, even when the mouth underneath is frowning. He's wearing the clown's ruff trimmed in red, and the white blousy clown suit that hides the contours of his bulldog-ish build. He has no way of knowing as yet, but Bucky will bottle-feed more than piglets by early June. Irene smiles inside the dim cabana, all of her straight white teeth showing.

She holds her hand to her ribcage; an Ace bandage is hold‑ing her in, keeping her tight, under the spangles and under her skin. She thinks about Buddy, her nephew, waiting off‑shore in the dinghy. He will row her back into shore. She will find him another puppy to love. It won't be Pal. There could ever only be one Pal. But she will force Olive to accept a new dog—she will hound Olive until she gives in.

The band quiets.

"Boys! Girls!" Foster intones, and Irene can imagine nei‑ther boys nor girls in attendance on such a bleak day.

"Prepare yourselves for Madame Alexie M.!" he shouts, as if calling out Irene's stage name is equal to announcing Iron Man Lou Gehrig at a World Series game. "The One, The Only, Little Girl Human Projectile! Born of Vikings! Born with the wild gray seas of warriors in her veins!" At times Foster's voice is less distinct and Irene knows he is turned away, addressing an opposite tier, or the ocean. "Cut her and she will bleed Valor! Ladies and gentlemen, she will bleed Adventure from her fearless Nordic Heart!"

When Foster ends his pitch, she will sweep out, her drape furled to hide all but her head. The scattered patrons in the stands will see red billowed by breezes off the Atlantic; the satin will ripple like a live flame; the blue stars spangling her ginger hair will sparkle. Come next summer, under a real sun, before real crowds, with real children in the stands—she will be brilliant!

Real children, she thinks. *I carry the start of a real child.*

She will strike a pose, once she leaves the cabana, and raise her arms up and out, unfurling the red fabric like the wings on white butterflies she once chased in fields on the farm. A stron‑ger sun will glint off the blue stars, but not this sun, not today.

Exposed, she will turn left and then right with shallow

bows. No one will notice her smile is built on a grimace, and what spectators there are will seem to breathe as a unit, emitting one great awe-filled gasp.

Jesus, she thinks, grits her teeth.

Here is Irene's final moment alone, here in this striped cabana, the solo star of a suicidal act — save the small fish of a beginning baby inside. Her hand goes to her mouth, rests on her lips as she remembers — she is not alone, not solo.

Any second now Foster's endless introduction will end with a nod toward Wil, her muscle-headed dolt of a brother, signaling him to whirl away the red circular drape, expose the Human Cannonball cannon. The drape will be handed inside the cabana for Irene to don, to furl herself inside. She won't wear the red long. At the age of eight, she learned capes were for play-acting *before* the actual dive. The lesson nearly killed her.

That dive was from a platform built in a sycamore tree. She wonders if it's still there, every nail holding strong, the wood slats Budd and Edison hammered in place no more weathered by time than they were when she was a fiery girl. Her last dive from the platform was then. As Foster continues his spiel, Irene doodles sycamore branches on the edge of a lined pad of paper she keeps in the cabana for writing letters to Flo in California, or Nessie in Williamsport. She's better with postcards, a quick *Wish you were here! Love, Stick.* It's been a long time since any member of her family used her nickname, but she still signs off "Stick" when she writes.

She's never gone back to the Williamsport farm; she's never made another dive from the platform her brothers built above Loyalsock Creek or swam there again; she's never again sat on the dock at Yostel's pond, feet dangled into the water when the pond level was high and dangling yards above the surface at summer's end; she's never stood again to skip back to the land, then, running for all she was worth to the end of the dock, leapt to sail like dandelion fuzz, knees clutched into a cannonball scrunch to enter with the greatest splash her balled-up young body could make.

I will take you there, she thinks, palm pressing her abdomen.

Sometimes her flights over Poseidon Park's stands hint of that kind of freedom, of an invisible something out before her, or behind, that if she can latch onto the tail of whatever it is, it will carry her off. Sometimes, eyes closed, she can see the valley below Neversink Mountain, a river winding its way that she cannot recall the name of (Mae would know, or would've known, when Mae still knew of things); other times, the valley is different, the valley of the Susquehanna, the valley of Loyalsock Creek, the broad backs of Joseph's draft horses, Jake and Pearly, seen from above as her mind circles above the farm where she ran as a girl; Nessie hanging wash on the lines, stopping to look up and see her little sister Irene on an updraft, adrift like a red-tail hawk on the look-out for what she needs; or, another time, Nessie climbing into a wagon, wearing an ivory gown on her way to the church to marry that boy, the one with prospects of having his own farm. Sometimes, her body a shock-absorbed throb during those split seconds of flight, Irene sees Olive bent with a hoe in the garden, five-year-old Wilbur attached to her leg, his curly red hair like a hazard light shooting off rays of sun. Another time she finds Flo with paper dolls on the porch step. Or Mae scattering feed for the chickens.

Irene's older brothers seldom occupy these moments. An oddity, she thinks. Budd and Edison were her heroes. Mae and Flo may have claimed the boys built the platform in the sycamore tree for them as well, but Irene knew it was hers. Mae would've vomited all over her shoes before reaching half such a height; and Flo, petite and tiny, hoity-toity Flo, would've never climbed where her bloomers might be exposed to boys down below. No. It had been hers, this aerie above deep water where the creek's flow crook-necked back on itself like the neck of a resting black swan. The plank floor might just as well have been made of marble or gold, it felt that good to Irene's bare feet — never mind the splinters Olive teased out with a red-hot needle once they festered and Irene developed a limp. It had been *hers*, this platform her brothers built.

Back then, the whole wide world had been hers. She'd put on shows, happy to entertain a sparrow or squirrel if no family was about. A tablecloth with two ends tied off at the neck was her cape. Nearly hung Irene to her death when it snagged on a twig too big to break. If the knot hadn't let go, let her plummet feet-first into the deep — she most likely would've died in 1907.

Foster winds down his spiel: "Ladies and gentlemen! Allow me to introduce The Magnificent Madame Alexie M.!"

Then she's before them, out of the cabana with a view of the stands, mostly empty; she could fire a cannon and miss every stiff there. She smiles. It's a practiced smile, a smile for the sparse crowd, their hands hidden in pockets, shoulders pinched, most of them men. None wear summer straw boaters. Brimmed fedoras are pulled down as far as ears will allow. From the look of these Everyday Joe's, they need a big smile coming at them from someone; hers will have to do. She spreads the red satin cape as if about to take flight, offers the butterfly pose, bows toward the tiered stands, toward Wilbur who stands beside the cannon, and toward Foster in his red-velvet coat. Releasing her grip on one edge of the cape, she frees the fabric to fly out from her body like the Stars-and-Stripes stretch and roil from poles on government buildings in the seaboard cities she's toured. The onshore breeze carries it. There's no rain—she's thankful for that. She bends again with a stitch of pain, an unplanned bow, then chucks the halo of stars for a white bathing cap—Russian royalty to snub-nosed rocket in a jiff.

Her smile is the last thing the spectators will remember, and blown kisses from both hands that pause, imperceptibly, as she lifts them to fetch the kisses and blur tear tracks—tracks she will not allow Wilbur to see. She's blown a lot of kisses, shown a lot of white to Nervous Nellies she'll never meet, or meeting them, forget them as fast as the miles of iron tracks she's blown over in the past. A hand on the cannon's mouth steadies what might have turned into a wobble.

Stripes of every leftover paint known to Poseidon Park circle the cannon—lavender near yellow, gray next to green, a pink she recognizes from the pig chutes bang-up to a sickly brick-red. The narrow color bands, not precisely lined off, make her dizzy. She takes two steps up a short ladder and slips, feet first, inside. Turning from her back to her stomach, she tucks her arms close-in, feels the cannon's launch pad hard against the soles of her leather-bottomed slippers, white satin tops like a dancer's, wide ribbon laces crisscrossing to tie-off around her ankles.

"A drum roll, please!" Foster shouts.

The band responds and Wil, if he is attentive, brings the whistle to his lips as he lights the fuse.

The fuse hisses and spits. She braces. Weather allowing, three times a day, seven days a week, she waits for Wil's final whistle, the signal that should arrive simultaneously with his pull of a lever to release the spring-loaded thrust. The thrust will come with a force to catapult Madame Alexie M. over the stands and into the Atlantic. Smoke plumes from the fuse will dissipate into the shore wind, the stench of black powder will settle — neither having a rat's ass to do with the cannon's operation.

If it's forty today she's a monkey's uncle, and the water will, more than likely, be about that. She shivers, waits. When the whistle comes, she'll leave no bone unlocked from a braced rigidity. A second ticks by and another.

It's not her idea to be billed a Russian princess or a Viking warrior. Foster's done that — given her a fictitious past, passing her off for a season as a cousin of the slaughtered Romanov royals. She knows his thinking: there's a chance, if she fails to resurface, of giving spectators a new tragedy, one they can witness, tell stories, say, *I was there; I saw her fly, then, she never came back.*

Seconds are adding up. *What gives?* She'd climb out, but if she starts out as the signal comes, as Wilbur pulls the lever, no telling what body parts would fly.

Earlier, after the first act, after the "mishap," with the pain of what she hoped was only a rib, she'd moved on Wil, landed a blow Jimmy Slattery, the new light-heavyweight champ, would've been proud of. She'd felt righteous rage and then something akin to shame, followed by anger for feeling the shame. If she felt pride in the moment, it had sunk like a stone. She's not proud of plenty of things.

Olive's never come to one of her cannon shots, never offered an Atta Girl!

That's OK, that's OK. Olive's not big on burlesque or the paint Irene wears to doll up for the stub holders or how she sometimes has to sleep with strangers on trains, not to say Irene's big on the stranger bit either, or sitting inside cannons waiting for Big Six to get his act together, hoping he's not zozzled, not blotto again, knowing, even if he is, Olive will figure a way to take his side.

Baloney to all that, Ma, Irene thinks.

She's not proud Olive's seen her black and blue body now and again down the years, of the watery look in Olive's eyes almost, but not quite, tears.

When she landed the Slattery blow that morning, she'd said, "What the hell, Wil? You callin' the curse on me or something? Why was I in there so long?"

"What long?" he'd said. "Two seconds, maybe three. What's the beef?"

"Ten, more like," she'd said. "What if I'd relaxed? What then?"

He'd chewed on a matchstick, offered a casual glare.

"You're the Dumb Dora who climbs in there, you tell me what." Then he'd said, "Butt me," and Irene fished a Lucky Strike from her pack.

"Wil," she said in a voice she wished she'd had more control of, her hand on the Zippo lighting him up, "don't do that again. You could kill me, you know?"

WILBUR LIKES HIS costume well enough. The tight-fitting knit shirt with its red and white stripes circling around his chest and arms shows off his muscles well enough; the wide belt cinching his waist gives him the look of a pirate and he likes that well enough, too. His problem isn't the costume; his problem is not enough attention. Not enough respect. Foster's monotonous spiel goes on and on.

Wil tosses away a frayed matchstick and draws out a new one. His problem is *women*—his mother, Olive; his sisters— particularly Irene. They have, or ought to have, ought to *know,* their places. They ought not head the family, as Olive had taken on by moving them from farm to city. They ought not, as Irene has taken up, headline Poseidon Park's main seaside act. He picks a splinter from his tongue, examines it. *Madame Alexie M. my ass,* Wilbur thinks, as the drum roll goes on and on.

His problem is he was born the last of nine children. And sickly. That sickliness — as his mother had previously lost two babies to disease and spindly weakness — that sickliness made for a smothering mother Wilbur finds hateful and hurtful of his chances for *true success.*

Wilbur's problem is he's a father now, has a wife and a son, and the attention he ought to have the baby boy's getting; he's no longer the star of the parlor at Olive's St. Terence Street boardinghouse brownstone. He'd gained a little ground, once Olive let it be known Irene wasn't so welcome. He *is* the man of the house at the brownstone, which would count a deal more if there weren't this baby of his and Honey's getting the lion's share of attention.

He gnaws the matchstick, considers the crew minding three-legged stools up at the Clover & Jug Pub. He imagines himself there, inside, his eyes adjusting to the near-nonexistent lighting, the heads of the regulars turning his way and some mugs lifted toward his entrance. His teeth, exposed now as he grins about his pleasure of being recognized, clench harder on another new matchstick. The match disappears with some long-practiced tongue action and just as quickly reappears. *Set 'em up,* he'll say to Joe, the barkeep, and the mugs will tilt his way again.

Leaned into the cannon on Poseidon Park's stage, Wilbur nods, just as he'll nod toward his drinking crew, acknowledging their acknowledgement of his beneficence.

INSIDE THE CANNON, one second seems a year long. Irene's forgotten the rib. The snare drum continues its roll; she can feel the sound through her palms pressed against the cannon's curvilinear cold, the current of sound waves sensed through her hands. If she can feel this, then surely her little fish in its cushy red prison feels the buzz, too, of something about to happen, the hubbub outside echoing inside. *When you make your break, little one,* Irene thinks, *I will teach you to swim.*

A millennium has passed since she climbed inside. What *are* you doing, Wil? She doesn't believe he means her harm. But sometimes, sometimes she thinks he'd like to teach her, the Dumb Dora, a lesson.

CLAD IN BLACK overcoats and dark fedoras, spectators seated at Poseidon's ocean-side venue seem little more than ink splotches against the sea-salted gray of the tiered benches. If any among the paid attendees grow impatient with the continued drum roll they keep their frustrations tethered, offer no grumbling, no shows of discontent. They've arrived like birds on a wire—one by one—to rest where they've lit, observe or ignore their surroundings, the arrival of the next bird, and the next. Unlike birds, only one among them will take flight when the Texaco cannon propels Madame Alexie M. in an arc toward the ocean. They are grizzled and gray, even the younger among them, worn with defeat the way those who have lost all but everything of what kept them alive—whether love or money or power.

Earlier, Moses Cheung, a Chinese-American teacher from Williamsport, Pennsylvania, seated himself on the bottom-most tier nearest the entrance/exit. Pulling the length of his

dark coat around his thighs, lowering his thin, almost inconsequential frame to the grayed bench, and tucking his hands
within his pockets once he was seated, he had, according
to habit, made himself as unobtrusive as possible. The first
to arrive, he stared at his shoes then looked seaward, not-
ing a boy in a small wooden boat at some distance. The boy
appeared as shades of gray—his jacket a deep charcoal, his
hair and face the pale shades of a dove.

Ten minutes later, the arrival of a second spectator
momentarily surprised Moses. If Phoebe had noticed, she
would chide him for his surprise. He straightened, squared
his shoulders. His Phoebe could be pensive, if not down-
right peevish, when he slumps or tilts his head, lowering the
remains of a damaged ear until the slick sheen of its mended
surface nears his shoulder. He'd been focused on the mono-
chrome still life of the boy in the boat, and that had triggered
the memory of late summers with Phoebe, their strolls near
reservoirs for Williamsport farm herds. A smile appeared
on the undamaged side of Moses's face. Her name, Phoebe,
derived from the Greek, meant *bright/pure* and was associated with the moon in Greek mythology. Of late, their shoreline strolls or strolls along other familiar paths occurred as
the moon waxed into fullness and eventually waned to a fingernail crescent of brilliance. Thus the smile Moses wore.
Thoughts of Phoebe invariably brought the same.

Poseidon Park was a detour. On the way to make his con-
fessions, Moses had been calm to the point of near numbness,
unseeing, but aware of obstacles: trunks and travelers and
those pedestrians meeting friends or loved ones as they dis-
embarked from the train. A broadside advertisement pasted
to a wall outside the station brought Moses here. Although
weathered, the upper edge losing its grip on the wall, the

advertisement was of a magnificent woman wearing a head-dress of blue stars.

During the distant days of his recuperation—days when he'd become ambulatory if not fully recovered, days when he ached to be useful—he had ventured out after nightfall into towns near the areas John Latterby engaged for his circus, paste bucket in tow, rolled broadsides in hand. In those days, more than two decades ago, The Latterby Brothers' Circus crisscrossed the Midwest and Eastern Seaboard with Moses on board and on hand, his presence known only to a few. He'd been nursed, often in the presence of his magnificent Phoebe, her ostrich-plumed headdress shivering above his head as she brought him back from the dead.

This detour from Moses's set-upon itinerary is, thus far, a disappointment. The bench where he sits blisters white paint, planks warp to curl at the ends, the orchestra (tuning up as paying patrons straggle in) plays with a vigor as lackluster and bedraggled as the plume on the conductor's hat. Beyond the bandstand, the cannon—painted in diverse colored stripes—extends its length for several feet at an upward tilt. At present, it targets Moses, the gaping hole—no larger than a bowling ball from his viewpoint—ominous. The magnificent woman depicted in the broadside will be shot from that hole, from that narrow cave crafted by man.

Moses shifts his gaze back to the sea. Invisible in this inclement weather, a horizon exists beyond the boy in the boat, way beyond to islands and other countries. Places Moses will never see rise on the far side of the ocean's wide highway, towns smaller than Williamsport with schools full of children and teachers who listen with two good ears, with faces a wife could love. Trees blossom there. And deaths occur. It is possible, sitting on the warped bench in the salted

October chill, to imagine his uncle did not die in London, that his father still lived, that he'd never felt the fires of hate, Phoebe's tentative touches, or the dreamlike weightlessness of mending, of sensing he was healed.

Now the ringmaster appears near the cannon. He differs little from the ringmasters used by the Latterby Brothers' Circus; he is more rotund, less tall, squashed inside his ill-fitting attire, and, if possible, more dramatically flamboyant, but to little effect. From the few dozen seated in the stands, no murmurs of interest are heard. Yet he continues, impassioned, Moses believes, by the sound of his own voice, and, Moses realizes, not altogether dissimilar in his gestures from those flourishes of sincerity sometimes offered from the Lutheran pulpit in Williamsport. Not that Moses recalls any mention of Vikings during his rare church visitations — then again, was not Jesus himself something of a Viking? A courageous voyager out to conquer a sea of men (and women), a fisher of souls, of netting the hopeless (and hopeful) by faith? *Aiyee*, Moses thinks — *faith*. For a moment a face from old dreams pauses within his head, brings an involuntary shiver not induced by the cold. In his pocket he fingers the key to his release. Phoebe's bright and pure image replaces the other. Moses will free himself, find peace and, to achieve this, he will locate a confessor. He will hand over the key.

As the ringmaster struts, Moses waits, avoiding the stage, the dark hole of the cannon that stares his way like a singular lifeless eye socket, focusing instead on the small boat and the boy gently bobbing out on the water. He surmises the boat is there for the rescue of the magnificent woman — Madame Alexie M. — pictured on the broadside.

Finally, Madame Alexie M. appears on stage. She is taller than his Phoebe but not slimmer. She has a certain flair for the dramatic, unfurling her cape in a blaze of red, but not Phoebe's flair. Removing her headdress, she tosses kisses toward Moses in the stands, kisses as hollow as the cannon into which she lowers her body. Gone from view, , Madame Alexie M. awaits her fate.

As a louder drum roll begins, Moses rises and unobtrusively makes his exit.

Funeral Flowers

COTTONWOOD, ARIZONA

Fall 2007

he chrysanthemums never had a chance. Rose of Sharon's grandfather, Wilbur Johns, had been a man who trimmed hedges and cut back perennials for the cost of a few rounds with his friends at the local watering hole so his wife, Sharon's Grandma Honey, wouldn't throttle him with her stares over good money spent on less than good things; and his son, Lincoln Johns, Sharon's father, wouldn't lecture him on the ways of the good book. But whatever his faults, Wilbur had known his perennials, biennials, and shrubs.

Beyond the gardening and cultivation tidbits she'd picked up from him, Rose of Sharon had done her Internet research and knew the chrysanthemums would fail: Arizona's growing environment *was not* Carpinteria, California's. Mums grown in a coastal climate wouldn't take to Cottonwood, Arizona's high desert. The giant bird-of-paradise plants — one for Wilbur and one for Honey, each planted at their passing, if she'd uprooted them, yes, they might've had a chance. But she hadn't. She had uprooted the chrysanthemums.

In Arizona, her patio is flagstone and the French double doors, white when she moved in, are orange. On most evenings the sky above a low-walled fence is nearly as intense, nearly as vibrant as the freshly painted woodwork. Of course the sky dies, first out of blue and then into a neon flame before paling to lavender. She would kill for yarn that exact pink/blue/gray and fancies knitting a cloche, mittens, and a scarf in these shades of approaching night. For this she needs patterns.

She turns on a light to find what she needs in the third bedroom—a room dedicated to projects and organized (without a bed to interfere with space) alphabetically.

ART—stretched canvasses, brushes, an easel for travel and an easel for home; *How To Draw The Human Form, How To Paint Realistic Flowers,* and other books are immediately to the left of the door. To the right of the door: WOOD—carving tools, whittling books, a length of wood chain carved from a single piece of wood. KNITTING—needles, yarns, a shelf of magazines, plastic-zippered bags with incomplete projects are located opposite the door. She finds the book and the page with hat, gloves and scarf within minutes.

Her master-suite closet is organized by color, texture, and season. Bathroom shelves hold salves for her feet on the bottom and the perfect variety of products to maintain the sheen and controlled aspect to the sway of her straight, white hair on the top. Thick white towels occupy the middle shelves.

Returning to the dining area, she flips a switch and three pendulum lights wash down on the table. The table is painted blue-green; she's hit the corners, randomly, with a sander, taking the surface down to cream-colored pine. Ladder-back chairs—two to a side and one at each end—are individually red, blue, yellow, pink, green, and purple. The purple, nearest the orange double-doors, is placed for the contrast Rose of Sharon finds complimentary and satisfying. Neither surface allows the other one to be forgotten.

Beyond the patio wall the low sky is pale gray; a heavier blue sits on the ashy emptiness, pushing what light there is to another place. As a girl she watched this horizon disappear into darkness. Her family lived near Sedona the year she entered the second grade and her mother, Appleonia, tucked her into bed with stories about the people of the red rocks. Sharon dreamed about them. Their brown dogs, whistling corn and yellow squash moved through her dreams; even the knobby gourds had legs and green tendril arms. In Appleonia's stories, an Indian pony with a travois pulled the sun to a place where it could set up camp for the night. *Good night, Sun. Good night, ponies. Good night, God,* they used to say— Appleonia and Rose of Sharon.

Below the sky the chrysanthemums sit in their pots. Funeral flowers, they were sent as condolences when Appleonia died and, a couple months later, Lincoln. They are just as dead now, her mother and father in their graves, the mums in their pots, as they were when Sharon settled her eyes and thoughts upon them. Dead is dead. She remembers the pattern book in hand—a better occupation than staring at reminders.

What is it about light, or the absence of light, Sharon wonders, *that brings what I miss to the forefront?*

Then, on the fourth pane down from the top on the right she notes unmistakable smudges. The heel of a palm? The smudge is hers. Whose, but hers, could it be? But it doesn't look like a palm, or the heel of a palm. She tilts her head. *It looks like giant lips,* she thinks, *like someone has left a kiss on the fourth pane down.* A hurried kiss, one that smeared, made the lips, the imprint of the lips, well—she considers, brings her head back upright—made the lips grotesque. Human, but grotesque. They are not Teddy's lips. He was fine-lipped. She used to wonder, still wonders, how such thin lips, hardly a line when he was deep into concentration, pruning the bonsai or gleaning Dear Abby for ways to handle prickly situations—she used to wonder how they, his lips, could be so . . . she tries to think of the right word and stands to retrieve the Windex from under the kitchen sink.

It is not the same sink where she stood washing yellow yolks from breakfast plates with a view to the ocean in Carpenteria, seldom looking up, intent upon specks of yolk, when Teddy would suddenly be there, behind her, arms circling, pressing up beneath her all but non-existent breasts (amazing, the milk Bet pulled from those breasts! that they were actually functioning tools, a means to nutrition, and could satisfy a newborn—a stunning achievement, she'd thought at the time). Not the sink where Teddy held her close, closer and closer until they were one four-legged, two-headed presence. No. It is not the same sink as that, but when she has withdrawn the Windex from under this sink with a window over it and glimpses, out there, beyond the flagstone, bougainvillea pushing a dark tide of fuchsia blooms along the crown of the wall— it *feels* like the same sink. She has the same ache in her privates, an area Teddy and Rose of Sharon, depending upon Sharon's mood and propensity for intercourse, sometimes referred to as Frau Blucher (oh, how they'd laughed at Cloris Leachman's part in *Young Frankenstein*); an ache in the form of an empty ping that comes on like a throb, as if a tooth has gone missing and the hole it has left doesn't know how to heal.

Ping! She takes the paper towels in hand and unrolls a square and another.

"Rosie," he would say, "Let me help you."

The ping travels to her heart. No one called her Rosie but Teddy.

In grade school some had called her "Of."

"Hey, Of," they'd say and laugh. She was a preposition. Ha-ha. Not a noun or proper noun, not the action a noun might take. Or a word, a place, a noun might connect to, but a "connector." Between one solid thing and the next. Rose "of" Sharon, that's what they'd named her. It wasn't as if Lincoln and Appleonia Johns read Steinbeck; they weren't readers of thick books. Zane Grey—yes. Those slim gray books with black titles: *Riders of the Purple Sage, The Rainbow Trail.* The Holy Bible, of course. She eliminates "Rose of" when signing letters or papers with the exception of deeds, licenses, Bet's birth certificate. Her retired dependent's military ID has the whole noun-preposition-subject in place.

Moving from the sink to the smudged windowpane, she thinks, *It's not as if Mom's name was Sharon. I am not "of" any "Sharon"; I am "of Appleonia."*

The Windex spritzes out with three squeezes. Her circular swabs make the customary squeaks clean-glass-being-polished makes. The smudge is not on the inside. She can afford the extra, the uselessly sprayed solution, but waste, of any kind, rankles.

It is September and Teddy's been sprinkled onto the foil glimmer of the Pacific, dissolved, or settled into the sediment of the ocean's floor, since the millennium change. Eight years. Eight years, and yet, she thinks, Teddy's death seems closer than Lincoln's or Appleonia's—both gone less than a year. Why is the old passing, Teddy's death, the one that feels new? Almost fake? She loved her parents, she did, still does, but— and this was especially true once Teddy stopped taking the organ-transplant rejection drugs—but, one way or another, she'd resented their "couple-ness." Or their longevity. Or their ever-increasing ailments with the ever-increasing cures medical science kept providing.

"I coveted them," she says to the window. She has cleaned all but three of the already-clean inside panes. "God damn it!"

If she believed in "thou shalts" and "shalt-nots" beyond a reasonable set of guidelines to live by, she might worry about hell. But she doesn't believe. Not literally. Not totally. Despite how she's been raised, Sharon will never be "Sharon of God." *By the same token,* she thinks, watching the back of her hand and the verdigris veins popping up from exertion, *I am tattooed with memorized verses of who and what I am or should be and am not.*

She makes a mental note to find some appropriate memorial plant, a cactus or succulent, maybe a jade plant or two, for her parents the way Lincoln had planted the birds-of-paradise for his father and mother. *Yes,* she thinks, *it's the least I can do.*

She should move to the outside and get at that smudge someone has left. *She* has left—there is no other possibility except that it's there by her own doing. The closest neighbor is a pinprick of light, a porch light left burning, acres away; the road to Sharon's is rutted, and nobody—save the postman when he has a package from Bet to deliver—ever ventures near.

She studies the grotesque smudge. Too high for a stray dog or coyote to manage—not with their lips. Paws? Maybe. Maybe the culprit is coyote, The Trickster. Beyond the window, the patio is full-on dark except for light thrown from the pendulum fixtures. If she steps into the dark and there is a coyote or bear (does Arizona's high desert have bears?), will she have the presence of mind to get back inside before they attack? What if there is a heaven and they won't let her in? *What about that, huh?* She'd be gnawed out there by god-only-knows what—possibly for days.

Past the smudge, past the pane, she notes her shadow. Her presence makes a figure, a jagged shape on the flagstone. Flat and uneven on the varying stones, elongated to reach other shadows, the darkest recesses of her walled yard—she is a giantess. Near the potting shed, clay pots with dead sticks of chrysanthemums are little more than one chunky smudge of dim clay set next to another; tomorrow, she'll dump their contents. That they died so quickly is no surprise—not given the heat in Cottonwood, her inattention to watering.

She doesn't wonder if she will survive this high desert; she will be sixty in November and is reconciled to living interminably. She did not pass with Teddy's death, as her father had managed to do within a few short months of her mother's. No. She will continue on and on.

In the glass pane her reflection is framed by orange-painted grids; her white hair seems the color of Teddy's ashes—a little yellowed, a little singed without any traces of having been burnt. The white blouse she wears is the same reflected color of death; she can barely tell where her hair ends and the blouse begins. Uncomfortable, she looks from her image to what surrounds. Reflected in the numerous panes are a hodgepodge of saturated colors, like daubs squeezed from oil tubes onto an artist's palette.

This bright lair she's created asks her to stay inside—but the smudge is there—on the dark side. Windex in hand, she levers the handle down and the door swings out.

Launched

**rene keeps her** head down, chin tucked. Time is an abstract. Time has nothing to do with now. There are no second hands, no minutes ticking past—not for Irene and not for her baby. She will be here, hunkered in, waiting, and then she will not. Time will reappear; second hands will sweep past, minutes and hours will again rack up until the third act.

Will there be a third act?

If she survives this one, will she climb back inside for the next? *They'd put us in the slammer for the duration, right fish? It'd be some fun, telling folks you were born in a jail cell. Nah, that'd burst your Grandma's bubble about the Johns family name for good and ever.*

Irene breathes against the cannon's interior; her breath rebounds, warms her face. There is a judge in a New York courthouse, probably sitting in chambers fingering the black folds of his robe, running his dry hands down the lists of Whose Life Can I Futz Today.

He'd futzed hers, right enough, a couple months back. Who'd a thought Poseidon Park's big cheese would level a beef about her No Show with the cops? *Huh, fish? Who'd a thought it? What was it he said?* "Is this not your signature here on the contract, dear woman." *Dear woman, my ass.*

Irene lets her chin touch the cannon wall. *Here's another fine mess you've gotten us into,* she tells herself, wishing she sat at the Bijou, wishing she could laugh at Stan and Ollie. She will ask Bucky about going back a fourth time. She will explain to him that he'd laughed so loud the other three times she couldn't hear what'd been said. *I'll tell him that. He likes when I blame him for what's got nothing to do with him. Makes him laugh.*

But then, Bucky laughs at most everything. He even laughed when he came to visit her that night she'd spent in jail for breaking her contract, for being a "no-show." He's the one made the crack about a "fine mess" that time. She'd smiled at his chuckle and he'd poked at her through the bars. "Hell's bells, Irene," he'd said, like he didn't know what to say or do. He'd laughed again, not all out, but like *what else could he do?* Not a damned thing; they didn't have two nickels to rub between them. Truth was, she'd got to laughing right with him.

Besides, she'd been on the inside before. Back in '18. And not just for bailing out Wil, not just front-desk cajoling some beefy sergeant to let her baby brother go free. The money Olive had put up for his bail, for damages from one barroom brawl or another, was sinful, a waste.

Wil manning the whistle was all Olive. All Olive—trying to keep her babies employed.

Rats to that! Irene thinks.

She exhales and her breath ricochets back. She wants to shout, "You dunderhead! What gives?" but knows where he stands at the back of the cannon, knows her voice will dissolve into the drum roll, knows he'll never hear her, not while she's inside. She'd yell anyway, but yelling would take away from the body tensions she can't afford to weaken.

Maybe the slammer's the answer. She might learn something, like she had the first time around. Easy to remember the date, Armistice Day, 1918. And the crime was no crime at all. They'd called it "Contempt of Decency and All that is Morally Right." *What did they know? Nothin'. They didn't know nothin'.*

The whistle blast comes. Irene leverages every muscle. *Every thing. They knew everything.* If I'd listened. If I'd only—

The impact comes like a train slamming into the soles of her feet, all the cars of her spine jamming one into the next, and she's airborne over the stands, dark hats blur men's heads; faces turned upwards seem like gray dimes in the light. Then, the water, a great hard fist—the fist of a fighter who has survived since the beginning—slams Irene broadside. The rib she's grieved the whole day long bends as surely as a clean jackknife off the sycamore platform of childhood. *Is my cape caught?* "I'm not wearing a cape!" burbles forth.

Her voice is where nobody hears. She goes down and down, bubbles loosed from her white-spangled costume breaking loose, floating up through Atlantic currents. Should she try to alter her descent? Or let weight and velocity take their course? She is slipping—an assemblage of parts like train cars gone off a trestle caboose-first, engine last. Her mind is the engine and her engine wants her feet to react, propel her up, break this descent through shafts of daylight cutting the current with wide slanted bars.

Her eyes open, close; the moment to fight hasn't come. Tiny specs she thinks of as ocean dust hang suspended as she passes; they seem lit with an inner light. There is an increasing density; the light bars are less pronounced, less like the light in the corridor to that first jail cell.

The darkening water is as drab as the matron's clothing had been, a liquid blend between iron and light. She had imitated the matron's stolid pace, placed each boat-sized foot down with a certainty before placing the next. It had been a day of parades, Armistice Day—a day of celebrations. No one applauded in the jail's corridor. No one laughed. The matron had offered an unpleasant grin as she stood aside for Irene to enter the smallish pen.

"Good for you," the matron had said. "That attitude'll serve you right in here." Hard and compact as a short icebox, the matron put a spin on the words so they seemed the opposite of what she meant—and slightly personal; as if she owed Irene for some past injury she'd done her, as if locking the cell door settled some debt.

Irene, hardened by five years of touring with Dottie Clay's troupe, stuck out her tongue, as if ten again, when the matron turned to go, and called out, "Ducky!"

She believed someone would come to post her release. After all, Olive had posted for Wil's release when he was arrested at barely fifteen for a street fight. She would surely post for Irene. But who would bring the money down? Not Wil. He'd give the money to some bum before he'd give her a hand. Never mind she was the one Olive sent to the station house to free him up. No, never mind that.

Olive wouldn't come. Oh, she'd want to, right enough. She would. But set foot inside a police station? Not on her life; not on anybody's life. Not even when the crime wasn't a crime.

What had she done, after all? Dallied in the dressing room, put off changing or donning a robe to cover the altered men's one-piece maillot? An oversight, sure. Irene freely confessed to that—but no crime. Mermaids needed *sleek*, not soggy skirts. She'd been slower in changing than the other five girls in Dottie's aquatic act, that's all.

Olive wouldn't come. Irene knew this as sure as she knew where she sat on the cot behind bars. Even before she'd figured out the personal nature of the jail matron's gibe, that the matron *knew her*, knew Irene. Worse yet—the matron and Olive attended the same Methodist church!

Irene had only half-suspected Olive wouldn't personally arrive to post her bail. Once she'd placed the matron's face in church mode, she knew she wouldn't be seeing her mother that night.

Irene respects Olive's faith. She's no faker; neither is Irene. If she were, she might've tried to hide the fact she thinks church is a hill of beans—all those psalms and sermons sliding off one another to bang into somebody else's beliefs. Out of respect for Olive, Irene's attended church when she's off the road. At least she had done—when she still made the brownstone her home—back in 1918.

Once that matron's face clicked into place, Irene settled into the cell, stretched out on the cot, pretty damned sure she'd be there for the night. She'd never been inside a jail cell before; the truth was, she liked new adventures and this— lumpy cot and all—qualified as an "adventure." The truth was she'd got caught in a man's swimsuit with skin showing down the sides where Dottie Clay's costume manager had cut away fabric and reconnected front and back with X's for some girlie-show appeal. And the final truth was if she hadn't spent that night in jail she'd never have heard the lady a few cells down yammering on about *pessaries* and how they could keep a girl from growing a baby inside.

With equal weight Irene owed Olive, the icebox matron, the officer who cuffed her and brought her in, the judge who condemned her, and the holier-than-thous who thought skin was an unpardonable sin—she owed all of them for what she'd learned from the pessary lady. And what she learned was how everything from dung to chopped grass to wool to sea sponges wrapped in silk with little pull cords to remove them could plug off what might make a baby.

Did Olive know she'd had a hand in eliminating so many grandchildren that might have sprung from Irene, but for that long ago night in a cell down the way from a woman who knew it all? Would it have mattered, to anyone, if Olive did know?

Continuing her descent, lungs ready to burst, Irene blames Wil's delay with the signal whistle. The delay messed with an internal clock she relies upon, a subconscious countdown as she descends that is absent today. Both she and the little fish she's begun to feel moving inside, the little fish Olive is not aware of, are on nature's downward course. She would smack Wil but good, land him another blow, but he's safe and dry near the empty cannon on shore.

Tired of sinking and done with it, she commands her knees to bend. Her ankles respond; feet push in unison; dolphin kicks propel her into the light.

"You okay, Aunt?" Buddy asks the way someone might ask a stranger on a street corner who leans too heavily against a post or a wall. Men known to Irene seldom treat her like a lady. Twelve-year-old Buddy is hardly a man, not just yet, but he knows his aunt as his chum, his pal. Sitting with a basket of needlework in her lap or fussing with a lattice crust on a peach pie might garner dainty attentions for some, but if Irene put her hand to such nonsense, friends and family would bust a gut laughing.

"That uncle of yours," Irene sputters, "never liked me much. I need you to man the cannon in the third act."

"He won't like it," Buddy says. His jacket is dark from ocean spray and his round face is chaffed by cold to the point his freckles have sunk out of sight. He faces her as he rows, his expression concentrated, stern beyond his years.

"You look like—" Irene starts, looks away, starts again. "Don't worry about him. He'd like it less if I died."

On shore, Irene climbs from the dinghy, takes the ladder up to Poseidon Park's stage and reclaims her role as Madame Alexie M. of the Nordic heart. Her rib pings with each curt-sied bow. Damp ginger curls hang limp when she sweeps the white bathing cap from her head and smiles, smiles, smiles.

In the cabana, Wil rolls a cigarette. His feet are on the dressing table, crossed ankles showing below the hem of white-cropped pants, sprinkles of tobacco on his tight, striped shirt. The wide seaman's belt he wears for Irene's act straddles the chair arm, but that's as far as he managed before putting his feet up.

If he hears Irene come through the door, he doesn't show it. She lifts his feet with both hands from the small table cluttered with make-up and blue stars and swings them away. Tobacco and cigarette paper fly from his hands. He's stand-ing, fist raised.

The back of his hand is freckled and hairless. The yellow knobs of his knuckles aim at Irene, who says, "C'mon, little man . . . gimme your best shot." His eyes leave hers for the door behind her.

She doesn't turn. "Whoever's there—this is private."

"It's me," Buddy says.

"Bitch," Wilbur says, pushing past her and shoving past Buddy.

"Did you let him go?" Buddy asks.

"He left on his own. Now, could you give a girl some privacy? I gotta change out of this suit."

"Are you okay, Aunt?" Buddy says, turning away without walking.

"What did I tell you? Go on. Get."

The zipper goes slower when wet and Irene grunts an obscenity or two before the brass edges disengage and the front of her white-spangled jumpsuit parts. She pulls one arm out, then the next, lets the whole of it puddle around her ankles, stands on the wood planks with nothing but the Ace bandage holding her middle in place.

"Okay," Buddy says, "But, Aunt—"

"But nothing. Outta here. Go on! Get, before they arrest me again. This time for corrupting the innocent mind of a minor." One of her ear-to-ear smiles is there, as if she's shared a joke about her less-than-wholesome future.

Buddy, facing the exit, grins. Irene watches his profile. He shares her father's smile even when half that smile is turned away. When Buddy's young face had grown stern out in the boat as he rowed her to shore, she'd seen her father as he must've looked in his youth. And Buddy, too, in that moment, as he would look at fifty.

JOSEPH JOHNS HAD passed the fifty-year mark when he traveled to upstate New York in 1913. His little "Stick" was debuting with Dottie Clay's Aquatic Nymphs and he'd taken it into his head he should be there. Four years had elapsed since Olive's desertion of the Williamsport farm in 1909, since Olive's desertion of Joseph.

During those years, he slept in different rooms each night,

moving from one to the next in the empty farmhouse—with the exception of the kitchen and the room he had shared with Olive. The kitchen had offered no floor space for a pallet and the table, while it was sturdy and more than long enough for his six-foot frame, seemed a cruel place to bed down. Nor could he fall asleep in the bed he'd shared with Olive. Despite her desertion, he heard her even breathing there at his back. The one night he'd tried, Olive's warm breath on his shoulder had caused him to turn from his side, sure he would find her cotton gown and soap-scented skin. The moon had been three-quarters full, lighting the jungle-leafed wallpaper. When he found her missing, he'd felt as if they, the leaves in the patterned paper, might somehow liquefy, might turn into watery sand, and by morning he would be gone, sucked inside and lost, just as the yellow touring car had sucked his family off in clouds of road dust.

"Sleep, my child, and peace attend thee, all through the night." Joseph had talked the words, almost unintelligibly, in the room where Wilbur and Flo slept. Whether he spoke the lyrics to soothe himself or bridge the distance to wherever his family might have been on their journey was uncertain.

"Guardian angels God will send thee, all through the night." His first night alone in the house, Joseph bedded down in Budd's cot on the screened front porch; it was nearest to the screened door where, if they should, for whatever reason, decide to return, he would hear the hinges whine open. *Soft and drowsy hours are creeping. Hill and dale in slumber sleeping. I my longing vigil keeping . . . All through the night.*

The next day, the first Sunday after his first night alone, Joseph arrived at church early. It was his habit to arrive early every Sunday; he couldn't enter the house of God until the doors opened for all the worshippers, but he believed that being there, outside the Methodist church for a half hour, or even an hour beforehand, gave him a personal nod from God to quietly exit before the final prayer. There were chores on a farm, even on Sundays, that God understood. And because Joseph Johns was often lax about staying at what Olive referred to as "the necessary tasks" throughout the week, there were always a certain number of leftover "necessaries" for Joseph's Sundays.

There was, on this initial Sunday morning after his family abandoned him, an oddness in the air—not *in the air* so much as *within* his fellow parishioners. He was, after all, a Lycoming County commissioner. He had, as such, shaken the hands and held the babies of all of the brethren who attended his church, not to mention the attendees of other churches in Lycoming County. He had laughed at their jokes, commiserated with them over losses, fixed loose planks in the walkways outside their stores. He had helped to identify drainage problems along the roadways, brought petitions before the county supervisors about whatever the citizens needed to petition—from Lucy Jenkins's crazed bull that no fence could hold, and the desire of neighbors to see the bull made into pot roasts, to bridge repairs.

But on this Sunday, of all Sundays, there seemed to be an invisible barrier built around Joseph Johns. There were nods and nervous smiles—but no hand was placed on his shoulder; no humor shared, no wit, no sorrows.

From the last pew and his normal aisle seat, Joseph watched the heads of his neighbors bow in prayer and come back erect. He stood when the others stood, said "Amen!" when the others said "Amen!" He stayed, uncharacteristically, through the final prayer. If he'd been the sole occupant of the last pew, he would've entered the flow of exiting worshipers about midway between those still going and those already gone. But the Henriksons, with their two young boys, were on his right, and although no one pressed against him to file out into the aisle and out the church doors, he'd known it was the natural thing for occupants of the last pews to do—last in, first out—an unwritten rule of pews. As a consequence, Joseph was first to exit.

"I hope you enjoyed the sermon, Mr. Johns," Pastor Nielson said as he shook Joseph's hand in passing.

Joseph did not have the least idea as to what the sermon had been about. "Yes," he said, continuing to hold the pastor's hand though the shaking had ended. Both men nodded, their hands parted, and three steps later he was off the church stairs, solid earth underfoot, wondering, *Where do I go now?*

His invisible fencing—like a barbwire corral, hardly bigger than a horse stall—moved along with him as he took hesitant steps across the churchyard, the corral stopping when he stopped, moving on again when he moved. He flinched when Marion Rathke's palm weighed on his shoulder.

Mr. M. Rathke had not been Joseph's teacher, but he had taught Olive and six of their surviving children. He would've taught Wilbur in the coming year if Wil hadn't left in the automobile with the others.

"You must miss them sorely," Marion offered.

"Yes," Joseph said.

"Come by . . . come by the school when you get the time, when you have the time. I have some work your girls left behind. Florence's and Irene's. Sorry, I don't have anything from Mae's years with me. And Edison. Well, you know how he was with his homework."

Joseph looked at the schoolmaster. It was only a brief look, his eyes circling the immediate area as if looking for one of his missing children among the diminishing worshippers.

Marion understood the look Joseph shared, hasty as it had been: Joseph Johns did not have a *clue* about how Edison had handled homework. That Edison's recitations of assigned memorizations failed, decisively, with nearly the same frequency as Irene's half-hearted attempts, would've surprised their father.

"Well, I'm there, at the schoolhouse, most mornings. Sometimes into the afternoons. I find it the most congenial place to work." Marion paused, already missing the workplace he'd occupied for better than two decades. "I will miss it when the new term begins. How I envy the young man who will replace me."

Joseph's stare had been blank and not directed at Marion. An awkward moment passed. Marion squeezed Joseph's shoulder, offered a final pat, and "Stop by, Mr. Johns. I will set the girls' papers aside. They'll be waiting for you."

Joseph's attention was brought to bear with Mr. M. Rathke's last words.

"Waiting for me?" he said. "Yes. Perhaps so. At the farm. They may have forgotten it's Sunday."

But Mr. M. Rathke, whose hearing was poor, had already turned away, and Joseph had spoken more to himself than another. He watched his children's teacher move away, watched as Mr. M. Rathke stopped, turned, and offered one last nod before continuing on in the direction of the house where he roomed. Where Mr. M. Rathke turned to wave was, Joseph thought, where an invisible gate must have been hinged to the invisible fencing. He'd started home then. They could be waiting. Olive could have had a change of heart.

This wasn't the case. They didn't return. His oldest, Nessie, married and settled in at a farm within a day's ride from his before Olive's desertion, had informed him of Irene's job: "Our little Stick is a nymph."

"A what?"

"An *aquatic nymph*. She'll be touring with Dottie Clay. Diving and swimming exhibitions. Mother sent this article. Stick's debut is the last Saturday of this month. Upstate New York. Have you heard of this place?"

Joseph hadn't, but he found his way there, left his fields and cows to the care of a neighboring boy and stood hatless among the throngs of people watching young women leap from a high rocky point, arms spread, backs arched—beautiful swans, they entered the water with barely a splash. They took his breath away. Who among them was his little Stick, he couldn't fathom a guess. She'd been ten the last time he saw her. Of course she had grown over the course of four years.

After the crowd thinned and Joseph found Dottie Clay's curtained changing area for her girls, he stood face-to-face with his daughter. His little Stick wasn't little. She'd grown tall, perhaps as tall as Edison had been the last time Joseph saw him. Face tilted in recognition, Irene's smile had widened from ear to ear. Had there been words expressed between them? Joseph couldn't recall. She was there with her smile— and then she was gone. A train to catch. A ride to somewhere. And he went back to his Williamsport farm.

How YOUNG WE *all were*, Irene thinks as she unwinds the bandage from her ribcage. It's been sixteen years since she stepped away from her father, pulled and pushed by fellow nymphs, urged to hurry lest they miss the train to

Baltimore—or wherever the hell they'd been bound. He'd been soft-faced and jowly, a sheen of gray whiskers covering his cheeks. Yet even he must have been slim and round-faced, much like Buddy, in his youth. *Will Buddy grow soft-faced and jowly like Joseph? I think yes*, is her answer.

"And you, little fish," she says out loud, one hand on her tummy, "you will most likely be freckled, and, if we're lucky, will grow fat and jowly, too, as I'm hoping to do."

All we need do is get through our third act. Or—

Irene considers the Ace bandage hanging in damp spirals to the floor. "Or, we could blow this joint. What do you think?"

The first time Irene left the drawer closed on the bed-side table and the diaphragm idle inside that drawer was on account of forgetfulness. *When did I ever want a kid? Never! That's when!*

The second time, she was sober, as focused as hitting her mark when the whistle blew. Knowing she carried a little bit of herself inside, this new little fish swimming around, bumping her interior walls—changed who she was or may have been. Life works its name on the long tunnels that run her with its fins or fingers or toes. Hell, she doesn't know. All she knows is this baby has left, continues to leave, messages tickling along her internal highways, scratching hearts and arrows and *True Love Forever* on the bark of whatever makes her—her. She is the platform, the sycamore, the tree. Little fish will leap—given the chance. Little fish wants to survive.

"Good," Irene says to the cabana's empty space. "We're agreed. No more whistles. No more fodder for cannons. No more job for Wil. Sorry, Honey. And sorry, too, for your baby boy, Lincoln. I've done all I'm going to do."

Mending

There are things as interminable as life; waiting for a doctor to appear is one of them.

The two fractures, one to each ulna, are "looking good; knitting well," the doctor had said, and she will be "OK" in "no time" but should "wear the braces," especially the one for the right, where the break was closer to the wrist, as much as possible; she wouldn't want to "stress the process," he'd cautioned, and so she asked, "Can I resume sweeping, mopping, everyday housework?" His answers to that: "Not just yet," and "old bones take longer to mend," and "let's see where we are in another week."

Well. It is another week. Rose of Sharon wears a paper gown over her bra so the doctor can examine the rake wounds left in her side. He is not the same doctor she met on her first or second visits to the clinic.

"Doctor Pena," he says. "Mrs. Brown?"

Rose of Sharon nods, acknowledging her name.

Dr. Pena thinks she might be a virgin to doctors' offices. She wears a stricken look, as if he approached with a long hypodermic syringe and will draw out her brain matter at any moment. Her hair is sleek, but the kind of white he's read about in horrific books, the kind that results from fright, some trauma so great in nature as to cause hair follicles to forget to pigment new growth.

Seated on the end of the paper-covered examining table in the waffled paper gown, she is rigid; the only bends in her body occur at right angles: stiff back down to buttocks; stiff thighs out to knees. From there, her denim-covered legs hang. The pale blue running shoes point downward as if she is a sprinter on her mark in Velcro-fastened tennis shoes. Dr. Pena has the keen impression his patient might jump from the table and bolt out the door, save herself from a syringe he doesn't carry, save herself from the round-cornered plexiglass medical chart he holds.

"Let's see," he says. She does not flinch as he sets down the chart and says, "May I?" He parts the paper gown where it comes close to closing along her spine. She has a very straight spine; she has good muscle tone in her back for someone her age. He says, "You have good muscle tone in your spine for someone your age."

Dr. Pena has seen a lot of poor spines, folds of skin hanging off poor muscle tone and crooked vertebrae. "Sixty, is it?"

Rose of Sharon does not answer his remark.

He checks the wounds indicated on her chart. "Look-king good," he says; he wonders if it will matter to her that the two small wounds will heal with little scarring but doesn't ask.

"A paper bag," Sharon says. She finds breathing next to impossible and her vision is stippled with tiny black dots. She is no virgin to clinics, to doctors' examining rooms, to ICUs or Emergency Rooms, to claustrophobic waiting rooms with vending machines holding stale crackers and white-chalky Snickers bars. She has been here a hundred thousand times. She has attended the before and after of two liver-transplant procedures with Teddy, carotid artery clean-outs for her mother and later her father, numerous stents inserted in each; she's given birth, for chrissake, been there for stitches when Bet's knee ripped open after a skate-boarding incident. It's the disinfectant, odors of alcohol, spinning her head, sucking out breathable air.

"Here," he says. She covers her nose and mouth and takes what air the bag contains. It fills and empties, fills and empties, and he is lowering her to the papered table, saying, "Better?"

She nods. At least she won't fall on the floor. Eyes closed, she sees all the machines attached to Teddy, lights blinking. She can't hear the beeps, the steady beeps, because at some point the beeping stopped.

Coming back to herself, she's embarrassed. Panic's replaced by how she must appear to this child of a doctor who can't possibly be thirty, who probably doesn't need to shave every day, but does, perhaps with the prospect in mind of thick-ening what beard growth he has, the way Teddy had, in the early years, before they were married, in high school, when every boy did, when every boy tried to get past the peach fuzz of adolescence and into manhood, the way finally going all the way had carried her out of girlhood into another place. How foolish she must look to this (what was his name?), she looks at his badge, Dr. Pena. How silly and old. How foolish.

She has not felt this shaken about her own presence since that consultation with a third grief therapist the year after Teddy died, the one (finally a woman!) who'd told her she wasn't promiscuous but simply—she'd said "simply"—"reconnecting with life." And here, Sharon had thought at the time, she'd believed herself on a suicidal bent, throwing herself into the beds of near strangers—a mechanic at the Jiffy Lube, a Country Swing dance instructor, the bartender at the Country Swing dance-lesson venue, the meter reader for Southern California Edison—none of whom she could label with a name.

Where she had sought out counsel to save her from taking her own life via some stranger who might strangle her after a climax, or infect her with HIV, she hadn't been suicidal at all. She'd been "reconnecting."

Reconnecting? Out of the question. Teddy was dead. She never went back to that therapist—or any other.

Of course, she'd felt stupidly foolish after her mishap with the hose and the rake. The pain of it all, her useless arms. That neighbor (she can't remember his name—Tim? Or Jim? Was it Slim?) who'd kept apologizing. Something to do with the rake or those damned dead mums. She recalls the horror on his face, a lean face in need of a shave—a shocked sort of innocence in his eyes—a look Rose of Sharon couldn't quite shake.

As she leaves Dr. Pena's office wearing the removable braces she'd come in wearing, he asks, "You're sure you're feeling OK?"

"Yes, except for these." She lifts her braced arms and offers a look she hopes expresses some humor, some "Oh well, at least it's not my neck . . ." communication.

He does not smile. The door closes. *What to do?*

She did better while Lincoln still needed her—shopping and doctors' appointments, keeping her mother's herbs alive in his window, the succulents from shriveling on his patio. But her father is dead now. She has moved from coastal California to Arizona. She has moved away from the cemeteries she hated to visit (there's just something about walking all over the dead), and what tasks she *could* set her hands to, she can no longer do—not with braces on both arms, not without stressing the mending process going on, underneath, at the bones.

What to do? She walks two doors down and into World Travel. *Bet won't mind a visit,* she thinks; she hopes.

Elizabeth Appleonia Brown is the only child of Teddy and Sharon, a daughter Teddy thought it would be a grand thing to send off to a college bearing her name, his name, Brown, for her education. She had left, everything having been pre-arranged before his death, the year after, in 2001. Now, seven years down the line, Bet works in the foreign land of Pennsylvania with her master's degrees—one in Art History and another in Library Science—as assistant to the Art History Librarian at Bryn Mawr College. Foreign as Pennsylvania is, no passport is needed to visit.

Sharon's become something of a pest with visits to her daughter. She knows this, but purchases a ticket to PA anyway. Then she calls Bet with her cell, asks if it's OK. *Of course it's OK.* Isn't that what Bet said?

Once home, Sharon lets herself in at the back gate and crosses the flagstone patio. The iron rake, nearly new and still boasting grass-green painted tines, is safely stored in the shed; the pots of dead chrysanthemums wait to be dumped in the mulch bin—there are things she can do and things she cannot.

Twenty years earlier, Teddy had observed that her night vision wasn't so good. And what had she done? Rolled her eyes at him and asked how he thought he could know how she saw things, at night, or any other time, and had felt, she remembers, vexed that he should presume to know, to dictate, how the world might appear to her.

Pausing, she rethinks the rake incident, the fractured arms, her numb fingers pushing 9 and 1 and 1, the siren screaming across the acres to the neighbor's pinprick of light, how the paramedics had collared her neck and made her lay down on a board. She is fuzzy about the neighbor; what is his name? She is so very bad with names. She'd decided that first week after to take him a coffeecake, the one she is good at, the one with pecans and a sinful amount of butter. His family (does he have a family? And if he does, do his children have Gary Cooper blue eyes?) should like that.

But how had the rake gotten there? I didn't take it out, so I couldn't have left it out and if I didn't leave it, then how was it there?

She looks down. *How was it here,* she corrects her thoughts, *to trip over? Or was it the garden hose?* Another mystery, that. She always coiled the hose back into the hose pot, to keep it out of the way, to avoid accidents. She'd never broken a bone, not one until then. *Did the neighbor move it? The hose, the rake? Was the window smudge made by him? Why would he kiss her window?* At least with the hose she knew she did use it; she might've forgotten; she might've imagined she'd put it away.

None of it matters, she supposes. Something alarmed her, made her step forward and back and somehow or other she was airborne. Her landing, stopped by her hands from a full face-plant, required two casts. No coyotes came. Now that, she thinks, would've mattered.

SHARON PACKS, CALLS a taxi. It won't be cheap but seems necessary to get her suitcase lifted into the car. She'll take the shuttle to Flagstaff, and from there, the flight to Philly.

She's tried, she has, tried very hard to make it through this mending process on her own. Her colorful home is a disaster; paper plates have become her best friends and worst enemies: she hates eating off paper. Mornings now find her jaws aching from grinding her teeth through the night.

Bet's graciously said she can stay through Thanksgiving, even Christmas, if she wants. She's stopped the paper; set up timers to turn lights on and off inside and to start the drip system twice a week; she's put a forward on her mail. She double-checks window and door locks and pulls the drapes to overlap. The taxi is overdue. And then it is there.

A week before Thanksgiving Bet says, "How strange it will be without him this year."

"It's strange every year without him," Sharon replies.

"Every year?"

Sharon glances up to find Bet's questioning look, gives her head a quick toss, almost as if it's laughable. "Oh. You mean my dad, not yours."

"Yes, Mom, I meant Grampa Lincoln. But you're right about Daddy." Bet has Teddy's bristly hair, straight as a German shepherd's and the same muzzle-brown color of tan. She keeps it cropped in a near buzz-cut; she is a feminine tomboy, a no-nonsense woman with little time for frills; a tall, slim, young woman who has inherited her mother's small breasts and cleft chin, her father's hair and brown-brown eyes. That hair, Sharon thinks, will never be sleek, never be white. At least she can't picture Bet with white hair. Blue? Yes. Been there, done that. But not white.

Who, after all, can picture their children aging, growing bent and prone to broken bones, bald, or gray, jowls lower than chins, with teeth they take out at night and soak in Polident? Sometimes Sharon wonders what Teddy would think, to see her now, a woman who will begin to draw off his social security within the next few months, a woman who looks, for all the world, like a woman who has been left out on the desert to bleach bone-white in the sun, sere and wrinkled, a mapwork of tiny veins breaking fresh paths to a new age spot here, another there. This is, after all, what we hope for, she's thought — to age, not die — to continue waking up on the right side of the grass, see a sunset so gorgeous you want a hat made out of that exact sky, and a scarf, a long scarf, one knit with angora you can pull through your fingers and *feel*. Yet, watching Bet sort through the day's mail, Sharon cannot imagine her old anymore than she can imagine Teddy past fifty-one.

"Who's this?" Bet asks, waving an unopened envelope her way.

"Who's who?" The envelope has the shape of a greeting card, is nearly a perfect square, and Sharon says, as she knees the seat cushions on the sleeper sofa further back so the faces of each are in perfect alignment, "Not Christmas cards already! Who's it from?"

"Don't know. It's been forwarded, twice. California to Arizona, Arizona to here. The postmark's Brooklyn. St. Terence Street? Who do we know in Brooklyn?"

Sharon shrugs. "Nobody?"

"Didn't Grampa have a cousin who lived in Brooklyn?"

The card is not Christmas but condolence. There's an embossed lighthouse on the front, a tiny blue sailboat on the horizon. Sharon's heart pinches up. She does miss Lincoln Johns — not because he had been in any way close to a friend, but because he had been in every way the patriarchal father: a gentle, if firm, guide to a "right way" of living.

"Does that say 'Budgy J'?" Bet asks, tilting the envelope as if to do so could make the writing more legible. "Grampa's cousin, do you think?"

"I don't know." She tries to be more careful since the mix-up about who would be missed at Thanksgiving. "Grampa, my dad, he had an uncle named Buddy, I think."

"Did he live in Brooklyn?"

"Maybe." Sharon shrugs.

"My God, Mom, he'd be older than old to be alive and sending out condolences. Maybe you've confused the relation to Grampa? A nephew maybe or younger cousin?"

"Bet, what possible difference can it make whether the sender is uncle or cousin? I never knew him. We never met. I'll send Budgy J, whoever he is, a thanks." She's made the sofa as perfect as a second-hand sofa can be made to be—all cushion cords perfectly aligned, all the loose potential for sat-upon wrinkles smoothed to non-existence. Four bright throw pillows purchased at Pier 1 since her arrival are arranged for the best contrasts. "And that'll be that," she offers, smacking the air from one of them, well-pleased with her efforts.

She sits in a hard chair at the small dining table. She stands. "I'll put a pot on for tea. Want some?"

"You should look him up, Mom."

"Who?"

"Budgy J—of Brooklyn. He's family, however old. Give him a call."

With not the least intention of calling a stranger, she answers, "Sure. Did you say yes on the tea?

Thank God for Velcro, Pigeons, and Little Girls

BROOKLYN

February 2008

uddy's brownstone on St. Terence Street is near Prospect Park, where he feeds pigeons. Children talk to him there, the small ones, and he listens. He doesn't trust icy walks and wears black Velcro-strapped tennis shoes with good tread; for a week he thanked God almighty for the inventor of Velcro, and he's never regretted, nor thinks that he ever will regret giving up the struggle to tie laces with fingers thickened by age and arthritis.

There are many things Buddy does regret. Who can live ninety-one years and not suffer pangs of remorse about one situation or another—though he's no dunce about it. He's got a pretty good handle on how, if you adjust one little slip-up God made here, a dam could break over there, or a hole open up in the ground and, even if there were only pigeons pecking around that hole for what he'd left them, and they were all that the ground swallowed up . . . Well.

This girl of Lincoln's calling him after the holidays—Rose of Sharon—what a lark it was to hear her voice the first time! He finds it odd she doesn't want to be called by her whole beautiful name, or Rose, another beautiful name all by itself. Odder yet, she wants to be called Sharon—a fine name, yes, but so plain when compared to the others. They talk often now, a half hour and longer each time, and he has, he admits, wondered if she talks so much because she's a chatterbox like he's been accused of or if she's more lonely than she cares to let on. If he'd stayed in touch with Lincoln, he might have known her as a little girl; he might've met Lincoln's wife, Appleonia. Another wondrous name!

A little girl sits down on the bench next to Buddy and says, "Look," and points to a tree stripped of leaves and says, "that tree's wearing a wig!"

Buddy follows the line of her arm. Looking up, he finds the bare twigs and branches have collected white plastic bags from the wind.

"Yes," Buddy nods, "yes, it is. A white wig. Do you think it's pretty?" he asks, but the little girl is running to catch up with her brother, who is running so she can't. He makes a note to tell Rose of Sharon about the wig-wearing tree, about the little girl, that she had red hair, that it was braided, about her brother who wouldn't let her catch up.

A breeze higher up shifts the plastic bag tresses; in shreds, they play out like seaweed caught in a current. It's time he should be getting up, moving again, getting his "daily" in before the breeze drops down where he is and the wool top coat he wears is no longer enough. He likes it though, the chill. Nothing quite beats a good shiver to make a man know he's alive, and maybe that's part of it, the way he hit it off with Lincoln's girl—that he was still here, still shivering and feeding green pigeons in the same park where he used to push Lincoln in his pram, lord, how many years ago? Close on to eighty, Buddy guesses. And here was Lincoln's girl, talking to him on the phone from Philly! "My, my," he says, rising.

There is no frost on the ground or glazed icy patches today and Buddy moves along from the bench with a confident step, thinking about the bags turned to ribbons in the trees and wondering how they're removed and that they must be removed by park maintenance people from time to time because he's not noticed them before, and he does look up. He's often followed the path of pigeons when a cyclist cranks through their midst and the birds explode with iridescent pinks and purples and greens winging into the air. He is happy for the cyclists — able to peddle, able to move at such speed, feel the air slip past them — and imagines it must be like sailing, the gentle swells in the bike path like ocean swells, the wake of swirling leaves and birds like the wake his cutter once left on Sheepshead Bay.

Buddy takes the park route that will carry him back past the Brooklyn Botanical Garden and home. Home is the brownstone on St. Terence in Park Slope. He's been urging Lincoln's girl to come visit the place where her father grew up. He's baited a hook with talk of Grandmother Olive's old hand-painted trunk. He wants Rose of Sharon to see the old place, the place where he grew up, the only home he has ever known. *The boy, the one who had run just fast enough so his little red-headed sister couldn't catch up, how old was that little boy? Eight? Perhaps eight,* Buddy thinks, and wonders where the nanny or parent might have been, that person responsible for such youngsters out for a day in the park. Had they been waiting ahead? Or farther along? Perhaps somewhere behind? There'd been the tree with the wig and the pigeons and the wind dropping down, or threatening to drop down, and he hadn't noticed. But now, as the good tread on his tennis shoes grabs the path with each sure step—now the whereabouts of a mother, a father, or both seems important.

Eight was awfully young to be left on one's own. He'd been eight when someone, a nurse from the tubercular clinic, put him on a train from Arizona to New York. He'd been in Arizona with his mother, his mother's sister Aunt Ethel, and Aunt Ethel's two girls, the twins, Buddy's cousins—all of them not doing well despite the dry climate and medical care.

"Mother Olive will take care of you," Buddy's mother had said before he left her at the clinic. "Be a good boy," his mother had said.

At the station, he'd been given into the care of a towering black conductor who safeguarded his journey home. He wants to look up into the trees to see if there are wigs in this neck of the woods, too, but keeps his attention on the path, on the pulverized granite underfoot. You can't change the slip-ups God's made, or the miracles, the fate of a long and, for the most part, happy life—a hole might open up—take the birds, take the little girl running after her brother with two long red braids dancing across her back.

To keep her alive, the little girl who sat for a second next to him on a bench, he will tell Rosie (he's decided he'll call her this from now on) about the wig-wearing trees and how the little girl pointed. How trash wasn't trash at all but adornment. He won't mention the absence of parents. Rosie's no little girl, but if he'd got to thinking on his long-dead mother, Rosie might get to thinking on hers, or her father. *No use in that*, Buddy thinks.

She always calls back, that Rosie. He can almost predict the hour. Nearing the botanical gardens, he slows. He will pass the time of day with the docent who sometimes stops by the brownstone with a casserole she's made and often accepts a glass of chardonnay (she's not much for reds, that one) and tells him about her day. Yes, he will talk with Barbara for a while, and then be home in plenty of time for Rosie's call.

He finds Barbara in a foul mood, rooty-looking clods tumbled across her workspace, and a scowl on her face. "You'd think," she says, "these would've been planted in the fall, before the first hard frost. I've just found them. Peony tubers. Not a bluebird's chance in hell if they're planted now."

"Spring maybe?" Buddy offers.

"Not the best. Two, three months ago—that was the best." She holds a specimen up, wags it for emphasis. "You know these were the national flower of China until a while back? Plum flower now. Big mistake. Nothing beats a peony for beauty and longevity."

Buddy eyes the tuber with doubt. Not one to cross swords with a woman making a point, he says, "Beauty and longevity. Sounds a bit like me, eh?"

"Really. They sometimes live to a hundred and more." She glances up from the workbench, smirks, and offers, "Beauty? You?"

Buddy smiles, a sheepish grin. "Stop by later, if time allows."

"Never mind that. I'll walk with you now." Her hands are grubby as she threads one beneath his elbow, grabs her coat with the other. "No use crying over spilt milk, right?"

"Right," Buddy says, the sheepishness absent from his smile.

"Besides, I have news. And a favor to ask. You know that trip—"

"To Italy? Yes. Have you bought your ticket? About time—"

"Yes. Will you—"

"Of course I will. Don't worry about a thing."

Going Home

t Poseidon Park, Irene is goose-bumped all over. She's rewrapped her ribs with a dry Ace bandage and now layers on undergarments, overgarments, and a long, double-breasted wool coat the color of pine needles. She sort of regrets the blow-up with Wil. Would he really have slugged her if Buddy hadn't been there?

Poor little Buddy. She shakes her head. *Not so little. Already taller than Wil. Hell's bells, almost as tall as me,* Irene thinks. He's got a birthday coming, she remembers, and makes a note to find him another dog. Olive wouldn't make her grandson turn down a gift just because times were a little hard. Besides, the brownstone could use a real pet. She doesn't count the black squirrel Wilbur feeds peanuts to in the back yard. A squirrel isn't something a kid can play with. "You can't teach a squirrel to fetch, Wilbur," she says, although Wil is not there, nor is Buddy. "Ah, Wil." He wouldn't have slugged her. Maybe upended a table, made a mess of this place. He'd done that before. Of course, the fault was always Irene's, if Olive had anything to say about it.

54

Such a burden you place on him. That's what Olive said every time. Not so much in words as by gesture—a stiff turn, a shrug as if bee-stung on the neck.

The knots in Irene's slipper ribbons are tedious to untie. If she kept manicured nails like Flo, she might have an easier go. She stays at it, slowly working the wet satin loose. She knows well enough from the two times when the knots got the best of her and she used a pocketknife to cut the damned ribbons. Both times she'd ended up taking the slippers and new lengths of ribbon to Olive so they could be sewn back on.

She shakes her head—not over the knots. There are no easy answers about Wil. Olive knows why Irene signed on with Poseidon Park. You take what you can get. The Madame Alexie M. act keeps her brother and Buddy on the payroll. Irene *knows* Olive knows this job keeps them employed, makes it so Honey and Olive and Mae and Buddy—the ragtag leftovers of a large family—can continue on at the brownstone, take on respectable boarders, keep Jane Smith employed for Mae.

There's a pan of steaming water Foster's had somebody heat and bring in for her comfort. As far as Foster's concerned, Irene's third act waits for the clock to tick around to three, maybe later, depending on how long it'll take him to drum up enough ticket sales to offset the payroll; the hot water's to keep his Madame Alexie M. from screeching like a banshee between shows, lest her cold feet carry her home. She's managed the knots. Sinking her feet (twin wrinkled icebergs) into the warmth, she mutters, "Ah, the sweet benefits of being a star."

Being the star is part of Wil's problem. He's not. She is.

Youngest, not to mention the sickliest (all that gasping and wheezing through nights until the whole farm house was awake), Wilbur has been the center of Olive's attentions and worries for as far back as Irene can remember; she'd been five when he was born and she remembers a lot. Point of fact, he'd been the big reason Olive packed up their life on the farm. Olive might say otherwise, might claim her decision was so each of them would have a better go at life.

Irene sighs. The water is good; her feet are thawing and, if not rosy with color, they're at least less blue. She pulls her long coat around to capture warm air coming up from the pan and leans back in the chair. She would like to be in Cuba; it's never cold in Cuba, but the days of touring that far south with Dottie's mermaids and nymphs are gone. Her wanderlust is faded. She has no need of its return. Whenever or wherever that lust had begun, she'd let it go. *The truth is,* Irene thinks, and not for the first time, *if the choice had been mine to make, I would've never left the farm.*

What a crowd they'd made in that big yellow car. The 1907 Winton with a boot in the back (Edison called the boot a *tonneau*) bounced over a lot of miles with Mae on one side of Irene and Flo on the other, Budd and Edison driving by turns, navigating by turns, alternating with Olive to navigate from the passenger seat up front or to hold Wil in the back.

Irene dries one foot then the next, remembering the ruckus she'd put up to stay on the farm. These same feet, smaller then at age ten, braced against that mahogany wardrobe Olive steadfastly emptied item by item. She remembers how her back had pressed into the wall. Her willfulness should've brought a strap to hand, but Olive hadn't whipped her, hadn't, in fact, hardly offered a look in Irene's direction as she straightened sleeves or pleats or collars, folded arms or sides in and doubled the whole into halves, the halves doubled again, and gentled each garment into the stars and moon trunk at the foot of the bed. Olive could've packed 'til Yostel's Pond froze—as far as Irene was concerned; she'd promised herself not to budge or be budged from that corner niche. Then Budd, Irene's oldest brother and best hero, had given a nod to Olive and said, "C'mon, Stick."

"Not without Father," Irene had answered.

At Poseidon Park, Irene pulls on her stockings. Hosiery is expensive and she's careful not to run this final pair she owns. The trunk Olive packed is still around, in one of the rooms at the brownstone. Olive moves it according to need. Last time Irene was welcomed in at St. Terence Street, the trunk occupied the parlor. Painted with moons and stars and square-looking flowers with funny rectangular leaves, "Clymenia Tabor" stenciled in black over a blue stripe around the lid—it was big enough to hide inside.

Yeah, Irene thinks, *if it weren't for old Clymenia dying . . .*

She pauses, one shoe on, the small buckle on the strap giving her a hard time. *If it weren't for that—what?* She might still be on the farm, for one thing. She wouldn't have Bucky's baby swimming around in her belly, for another. If there's not a single other thing she's glad of, it's this little fish inside. *There's meaning in that. A future in that.*

Suddenly, Irene wishes Clymenia Tabor had been more to her than a foreign grandmother who spoke Norwegian or Danish or whatever it was with a sprinkle of English slipped in that Irene never understood. She'd been Olive's grandmother, a great grandmother to Irene, a booming big woman who'd smelled like old apples and horse liniments. Irene shakes her head. Granny Cly lived for a long, long time. Then she died. Then the stars and moon trunk came into the Williamsport farmhouse, and Irene, in the niche between wall and wardrobe, threw a hissy fit.

"I was a hellcat," Irene tells the second shoe strap. She'd kicked at that trunk as Budd swung her out of the room where Olive calmly, almost as if she were somehow the deacon at church passing the basket from one row of pews to the next up the aisle, had moved what belonged in the room into the trunk, into Clymenia's stars and moon trunk, a trunk that had not belonged there.

WHILE FOSTER WOULD quite naturally suppose Irene rests between acts, she opens the door a crack, finds no one about, and leaves. She carries a sack with the wet jumpsuit, satin slippers, halo of blue stars, and a handful of dirt she's kept on the dressing table of every venue she's ever booked.

The dirt is inside a length of bamboo with a cork. It's farm dirt, a fistful she took with her from the farm and kept in a shoe in her closet for the longest time—her years between ten and fourteen. When her mother said she could tour with Dottie Clay's show, she'd put the dirt in a penny-candy bag. In Cuba, she'd picked up the bamboo holder. Why she keeps it is a question she's asked herself more than once because it's not about going back.

Outside Poseidon Park's gate, she decides against taking a taxi; she'd be crazy to spend the dough with the subway so cheap at a nickel, especially crazy now she's walked off her job—again. That first time anger directed her as much as anything else. This time it's fear. Or is it just caution? No. It's fear. There's a life she wants and she believes she can have it. And the fear is she'll throw what she can have away by putting her baby inside that cannon. She's done being careless. *Let some other fool, if there's another one out there, climb in. Not me. Not anymore.*

She boards the subway train, sits with her bag full of a past life in her lap, and thinks she would stop by the brownstone, if Olive weren't out in Hollywood visiting Flo. When Olive's home, Irene will try to make things right. She makes a promise she will.

The train moves underground; lights in the tunnel flash on and off, patterning everyone in the car. One minute she's thinking, *Cuba would be so good right now,* and the next minute the tropical leaves of the warm place she will probably never see again are not green and lush, but yellow and papering the walls of her mother's bedroom on the farm.

When that paper went up, her father had passed Irene a look that said he thought Olive was as crazy as she did. It was the same hopeless expression he offered when a calf got the scours and no amount of stroking the silk hide of its fine, still neck altered the course of events to take place. While Joseph sang *Sleep, my child, and peace attend thee, all through the night*—the poor sick calf died. On the train from Coney to Manhattan, Irene hums the melody; she can't remember all the words, none of the second verse. If Joseph were still alive, she'd ask him. He often hummed or sang the same lullaby beside the bed she had shared with Flo.

Would Olive know? She might. "You'd like it," she whispers, promising her child she will learn all the words, all the verses, when Olive returns.

The train rocks along, lulling Irene. She closes her eyes to the flickering shadows and lights, imagines the room on the farm with yellow morning pouring in through an east-facing window. Empty nails slant up through the yellow fronds of jungle wallpaper from where the framed watercolors have been removed. There'd been eleven in all—portraits of Joseph and Olive Johns's family. Among them were two coffin drawings with Edith Annie in one and Ella in another—the sisters who came and went before Irene was born. They were pink in their pale washes of swaddling, with tiny closed eyes, almost as invisible as fingernail clippings. They could've been twins, except for the dates penciled on the bottom of each: 1889 and 1896. The dead babies had fascinated Irene, not in a haunting way, but that they'd been there and gone—two sisters she'd never met.

Irene wonders where the portraits are now. Olive's never hung them in the brownstone, not that Irene's seen. None were very good—flat, round faces of herself and her siblings, her mother, her father; red hair, brown hair, blond hair, short or long or braided hair; the shape of a mouth, the dominance of a nose, blue or greenish-blue or grayish-blue eyes, a dimple, a curl, a shirt collar or brooch pinned to a wide bosom identified who was who. Even the great-grandmother Irene barely knew, the one who had smelled as if she were trying to mend herself the few times Irene was in her company—even Granny Cly had been removed from her nail on the wall. The only one left on the wall was the self-portrait of her father, Joseph.

Joseph's portrait was the worst, his countenance obsessive and grim, the line of his mouth stern. Not that Joseph Johns's paintings of any of his family were good. *It was just wrong,* Irene thinks, *for the most forgiving man I've ever known to appear so unforgiving.* She's forgotten all the words to the lullaby Joseph once sang but not his flat face on that wall with those yellow leaves and the long row of empty nails.

THE TRAIN SLOWS. Irene's body shifts forward. A boy about seven or eight says, "This is our stop." He's moving toward the door as Irene opens her eyes. The lace on one of his boots is untied and she thinks she should say something to let him know.

"No, son. We're for the next one," a man still seated says. "We don't get off here. We get off at Forty-fourth."

The boy turns, slouches back down on the bench next to his father, obviously disappointed not to be getting off. With his hand on the boy's knee, the father says something Irene cannot hear as he nods at the untied lace.

There is nothing about the man that should make Irene think of her father, not by his old country accent, an accent Irene thinks may be Polish, or by physical appearance. Her father was taller, broader, and had had no foreign trace in his speech, other than Pennsylvanian. Yet she does think of Joseph, of how he had not been there to stop the wagon loaded with the stars and moon trunk and crate after crate of what Olive had packed and directed Budd and Edison to load into the hired wagon.

The wagon had belonged to the man who gave Edison the Winton touring car, an old farmer who preferred draft horses to automobiles. He was, Irene recalls, Mr. M. Rathke's father-in-law. The father of the boy with the untied shoelace looks a little like Mr. M. Rathke, her Williamsport teacher, had looked the last time Irene saw him — short and rosy and a little puffed up, like a pastry.

The train brakes again and the boy and his father rise before a full a stop is achieved. The two sway in the aisle, the father's hand on his son's shoulder, the shoe lace tied — all things in order for their exit. If she stares, she is unaware. The screeching brakes of the train have reminded Irene of the stone wheel in that barn of her childhood. How the wheel had made a similar noise when the blade of whatever

her father was sharpening touched its steel to the stone. She'd
wondered then how many implements there could've been in
their barn for him to sharpen? Would her father never come
out? Call back the farmer and his wagon full of every practical thing she'd ever known? He could have saved her. He
could have held her back from . . .

From what?

The boy and his father are gone. Light and dark ripples
of tunnel lights shutter across Irene, but it seems as if she's
not really moving, not really on a train but in Williamsport.
The farmer with his wagon is gone. She's seated between
Budd and Mae at dinner. Edison, Flo and Wil sit on the
other side. They are eating cold chicken. They will climb
the stairs and sleep their last sleeps in Pennsylvania beds.
Tomorrow they will all be gone from the farm—everyone
except Joseph.

This time when the train brakes, Irene rises with her sack
of costumes, her handful of farm dirt corked in a bamboo
bottle, and exits. She watches the car she's just vacated take
on passengers heading further uptown, watches the doors
close. As the train pulls away from the station, Irene imagines she is at the table in Williamsport where she sat facing
Edison. She'd hated him then for taking the Winton from
the farmer. She'd hated Wilbur for being sickly and small and
causing their abandonment of the farm. She'd been ten and
passions ran on a love-or-hate level she could not seem to
master. She'd never hated Budd, even though he'd betrayed
her in the worst possible way by hauling her from Olive's
room the last morning at the farm.

"I loved you all," Irene says to no one. There is only the
tunnel, the empty tracks, the diminishing rumble of metal
on metal.

She takes the stairs up to street level less swiftly than normal. Her legs are strong but the rib still grieves if she moves with too much exertion. Has she acted in her normal, headlong and foolish way? Has she left an income she and Bucky will have a difficult time surviving without? Will the pittance she gives Olive to help with the brownstone mortgage make a difference when it's no longer there? Olive will understand, won't she? Her mother will surely understand, once Irene explains.

And Bucky? Has she overestimated what they share? Up top in Hell's Kitchen, the day is as broken with gloomy clouds as it had been at Poseidon, but Irene's step picks up. The stubborn buckles on her shoe straps are holding. She will make amends with Olive when Olive returns from the west coast; she will ask about Joseph's lullaby and tell her mother why she needs to know the words. She will hang the wet spangled jumpsuit to dry the minute she gets home and, while it's hanging off the corded line Bucky put up for her from one side of their one room to the other, she will make a sign for the suit and pin the sign from shoulder to shoulder. The sign will read: Retired.

Sing Cheung's Bones

oses Cheung of
Williamsport, Pennsylvania, sits
on a crate within the alcove of an
abandoned building, massaging
the base of his skull where scar
tissue ends and his hairline begins, looking beyond pedestrians and traffic to the far side of Grant Street in Chinatown,
New York City. This view is not as it was in 1909, the year of
his departure, and yet somehow seems unchanged despite
boarded windows and heavily chained double doors. Moses
sighs to find himself face-to-face with a dead building from a
dead time. It's remarkable, the games a mind can play. For
twenty-one years, he's been seeing the bustle and sweat of
Heung Fat's Noodle House as it had been: steam rising to
the rafters, patrons filling the chairs, plate after plate of food
filling the tables, and lines of high-pitched conversationalists
lined out the doors.

A smile bends the good side of Moses's face. Yun Li, the for-
mer cook at the Noodle House, had done everything within
his power to procure Moses's well-being after the death of
Sing Cheung — Moses's father and beneficent friend of Yun Li.

Two years before Moses departed fromChinatown, his venerable father had died on a return voyage from England. Why he died was unknown. Bad joss was reason enough for Sing Cheung's Chinatown community.

It was good joss, the community agreed, Sing did not die far out at sea, that his body was not slipped into the bound-less ocean. Instead it was brought to shore where his bones could be recovered and returned to Celestial China.

It was bad joss, they nodded, that the identity papers Sing carried were unreadable by the white ghosts who mistook the successful businessman Sing was (an unsurpassed mas-ter of the tonsorial trade with numerous employees and two shops, plus a traveling barber) and had, instead, deemed Moses's father an indigent immigrant chink.

It was further bad joss that Sing's body was interred on Hart Island, where there was a prison and prisoners dug long trenches and settled the coffins end-to-end, three-high for adults, five-high for children. Aiyee! Such bad joss, the com-munity agreed, to be buried in such a place. Brokers, who could prepare Sing's bones for return to China, and Moses were denied access to Hart Island's Potter's Field. Two years passed. No amount of bribery cut through New York City's bureaucratic red tape. Petitions to procure permissions to access the venerable bones of Sing Cheung were denied.

From the shadowed alcove on Grant Street, Moses sees through the passers-by as if they are ghosts from earlier decades; traffic noise blurs, becomes the mutterings and cluckings of his old community. Back then, every man who had felt the razor of Sing Cheung's artistry feared ravings of his bedeviled spirit. Every man who had undergone ear cleanings in the parlors of Sing Cheung, and the grand-mothers of such men and their wives and the concubines of such men (if they were thus fortunate), all feared the lunatic unrest of Sing Cheung's unsettled spirit. Aiyee! All but Sing's most respected son, Moses.

Born in the year of the Tiger, Moses, nineteen in that year of 1909, did not fear for himself. He feared for his father's unrest. He was tortured, no, he was plagued by this unrest. Whispers emerged between the many shops, "Aiyee! The son and the father—both are dishonored!"

Across the street, an old man pauses, stares into the dark recess where Moses sits, shields his eyes from the sun, palm flattened like a visor. Acclimated to the stares of strangers— scarring such as his doesn't go unnoticed—Moses is unrecognizable as the young man who left the place of his birth in 1909. Dark-hatted, dark-coated, a dark spot within a dim alcove on the dying end of a once busy street, Moses stands when the old man loses interest and continues on his way. It is time he continues as well. Moses fingers the lump against his thigh where Phoebe has caused him to bury a glove and some ribboned hair deep inside his coat pocket. He should not be where he is. He should rise and walk, find his way to the place Phoebe has told him he must go. They will meet there. He's certain she will come. He steps into the sun.

Old Dogs and Their Stories

January 2008

**rom the first** phone call he'd answered from Rose of Sharon, Buddy felt he knew her the way he knew little girls who ran up to him in the park to point at trees with wigs. He needed no more than someone approaching him in a friendly or needful manner to be drawn to them.

Rosie had tentatively asked, "Budgy?" when he'd answered. He'd said, "Buddy. Buddy Johns," and she'd said, "Buddy. Hello. Thank you for the condolence card," and he'd said, "Who is this?" and she'd said, "Lincoln's daughter. Rose of Sharon. I think we're cousins."

People are like pigeons or friendly dogs, Buddy thinks, *the ones running free or the ones at the end of a leash. You can make lifelong friends out of pigeons and strangers—even if you never meet the same one twice.*

What nags Buddy, not greatly but still enough to give him pause, is that he'd brought up Irene. Ah, but she'd been a pip. He'd love her forever. She'd always be his best and favorite— more than aunt—friend. She'd brought him Pal, hadn't she?

How, Buddy had asked himself, *could he not mention Irene?*
"When I was eight Irene gave me a dog," Buddy had begun.

He could come up with some reason to break off the
phone conversation with Rose of Sharon, but he hopes a
story about a dog will move Rosie's interest from what his
aunt Irene had looked like when he last saw her, her discol-
ored and swollen face . . . her ginger curls.

The past cannot be altered and the best Buddy can do for
his own peace of mind is to try to avoid the darkest memories. He's already conjured the little girl with red braids to fill
his mind's eye. He's already shared with Rosie his day in the
park—its pigeons, how the trees wore white wigs, and his
surmise that maintenance crews must come with extension
ladders from time to time and remove the tattered shopping
bags. Unfortunately, Rosie has locked her pit-bull attention
onto Irene's untimely death.

He can't undo what's been done. Now—distracted by
what he wants to forget and confused by what he wants to
remember—he wonders what to say next. He's lost his train
of thought; seconds tick by as he waits for some slipped cog
in his thinking to click into place.

Rosie says, "A dog? What kind?"

"What?" Buddy says. He has his phone on speaker and
sometimes the clarity's not there, but most often the sacrifice
is worth having his hands free to work on a model as he talks
(he does like to talk) or listens.

"What kind of dog did Aunt Irene give you?" Rosie says.

Yes, Buddy thinks. *Irene at the station with Pal hidden
under her coat.*

"A Chesapeake. She had friends up around Saranac who
bred Chesapeakes." Buddy's last view of Irene interferes
with the one of her at the train station to meet him with

Pal. On his table in the brownstone there's an unopened box with a sweet Concordia yawl pictured under the cellophane wrapping. In his bedroom there's a shelf that runs wall-to-wall holding replicas of cutters and sloops he once handled, maneuvered along the coast — sometimes as far down as Cuba — although he never quite made Barbados. "He wasn't, though. Not really. Irene just said he was."

"Oh?" Rosie says and Buddy has the impression she is as far away from the topic of dogs as he is.

"I was a kid. I didn't know one breed from the next."

"And?"

"And she did have friends who raised Chesapeakes who lived in Saranac. She had friends everywhere. What I mean is, I know what a Chesapeake Bay Retriever looks like now. Pal was no more a Chesapeake than I am."

Buddy hadn't believed the dead woman in his aunt's apartment was truly his aunt. He'd stood in the hall at the age of twelve, hands jammed in his pants pockets, a wad of upholstery batting he'd dug out of the armrest of the detectives' sedan gripped in his fist. A mistake had been made, or a lie had been told. He'd leaned into the hall wall; he'd listened to the radio playing inside Irene's place; her favorite program was on. Wherever she was, she'd hate missing Fibber McGee and Molly. The radio audience was laughing at Fibber's antics and Molly's retorts. He'd wanted to hear the stairs creak behind him; he'd wanted to turn and find Irene's gingery hair rising into view, her face, her step onto the third floor landing, her smile as she saw him standing there, hands jammed in his pockets, waiting for her to get home.

But what he'd wanted wasn't the way it was.

"Buddy?" Rosie's voice comes over the speakerphone.

"What?"

"The dog?"

"There wasn't a dog."

"I thought you said—"

"Right. Yeah. Pal." Buddy nods at the speakerphone and picks up the box with the boat model inside. "She had him inside her coat." Buddy slides his pocketknife under the cellophane folds on one end of the model box and peels open the closure. "Just a pup, like me." The model parts slide out of the box. "No more Chesapeake than me." He chuckles. "Black, with a spot of white on his chin like a goatee, and another spot of white on the end of his tail. Irene said he must've had white puppies on both sides of him, when he was still growing inside his mama, and some of their white rubbed off on him."

Buddy aligns the model pieces end-to-end then rearranges them into a mosaic of balsa boat parts in the shape of a geometrically squared dog. "When she'd come around, you know, in the off-season, she'd call up the stairs from the foyer, 'Where's my Buddy? Where's my Pal?' and we'd both come at a gallop."

There's a buzzer that sounds three times and Rosie says, "Budgy, I have to get that. Someone's at the door. We'll talk again soon?"

The model parts wait to be pieced together or restored to their package, the package, with all its bright possibilities of what might someday be built, captured right there on the front.

SHARON FELT SOME remorse, not a lot, but some, when she rang the door buzzer at Bet's Philly apartment to excuse herself from the conversation with Buddy. He likes to talk

and has proved this point time and again, sharing the minu-
tia of his day: the finest pigeon in the flock; its wingspan;
details of color, depending on how bright the sun or how dim
the day; a small girl wearing a wig (either red braids or some
sort of shaggy white that made no sense whatsoever to Rose
of Sharon).

Their first call went something like: "Hi, Budgy?"

"Yes, hello?"

"I wanted to thank you for sending condolences after my
father died."

A pause. "Which one was he?" A longer pause. "So many
dead, know what I mean?"

A quick response from Sharon: "Lincoln Johns. California.
Your cousin, I think? Or maybe your uncle?"

"LINCOLN!"

She'd pulled the phone away from her ear.

"What a fine boy. I used to babysit him. Fine, fine little boy.
Lincoln. Yes. I was sorry to hear."

Now they talk as often as twice a day and he has invited
her to visit.

She has wished Buddy had been her grandfather instead
of Wilbur. But Buddy belongs to the same generation as her
father, and she's not so certain she would trade in her father
for Buddy — Buddy, with his poet's heart versus her father
with something of an 'Onward Christian Soldiers' slant on
mankind. There's something to be said about a wrapped-up,
all-neat-and-tidy aspect to having the answers and knowing
them irrefutably like Sharon's father had, whereas deep con-
siderations on the shape of a leaf or attributes of a pigeon —
well, they seemed without boundaries. And boundaries were
a little bit like skin, weren't they? They held all the stuff
inside . . . in.

She shakes off a laugh. *Budgy.* She'd told Buddy she would continue calling him "Budgy" as long as he called her "Rose of Sharon." Stepping outside Bet's apartment and ringing the bell wasn't the kindest act, nor the first time she'd come up with sound effects to end a call, but her ear had grown numb and she'd switched hands so many times they tingled with prickles of going to sleep, or waking up (she can never tell which). Besides, dust had accumulated on Bet's mini-blinds over the sink, a light fur of dander, and Sharon, needing both hands and a step stool to clean them, had given in, really, without much consideration, to the bell trick. "Let's talk again, soon," she'd said.

"OK, Rose of Shar —"

"Bye, Budgy."

"Bye . . . Rosie."

She'd wanted to say something, she's not sure what, to Buddy about calling her Rosie, but the dial tone was there and the dust on Bet's blinds needed her attention.

SHARON NEEDS BOUNDARIES. The promiscuity of her first year without Teddy, despite "reconnection" theories the grief therapist conveyed, proved as much. Her aging parents, she realizes now, had been a godsend then. Their continual transportation needs to and from hospitals and office visits, grocery shopping, salon visits for Appleonia's ever-and-constant weekly coiffures into up-dos from the sixties and a shade of tree bark hair — tints no respectable redwood tree would ever wear (a shade which Lincoln insisted upon for his bride of sixty years), and keeping their Carpinteria cottage shipshape — had kept Sharon's boundaries in place.

How dare they leave her to her own maintenance and

care? She snaps the blinds out of their casing and begins cleaning the slats. They are not as dusty as she'd imagined, and when she is done the lemon-scented ammonia suds are as clear as when she began. She is adrift since Lincoln's passing. Somehow or other she, Rose of Sharon, is the one moving off, while he, ever firm and substantial, watches her go, his head tilted, a curious smile without any real concern shows faint wonder as to how she'll fare.

On the chrome sink faucet Sharon's reflection is an abstract of pastel shapes rounding and bending in unlikely ways. She removes her fingertips from the sink edge, shrugs off a beginning shiver, and takes a cup down from the cupboard. It is a museum mug from the Tate in London. Bet collects mugs from museums, and a shelf in her cupboard is dedicated to great houses of art she's visited since leaving home for Brown. Sharon is glad for her, this daughter who has seen so much, been so many places, who touches—very possibly at this precise moment *is* touching—some page or cover of a book containing the most remarkable images and histories of works of art and the great minds who made them.

Bet's growing weary of Sharon's visit. There is, Sharon's noticed, the least little rise of Bet's eyebrows when she comes in evenings, as if slightly surprised to find her mother, her ever-present mother, still, in fact, waiting just inside the door, or seated on Bet's sofa where there are never any rising hills of wanna-be wrinkles; there is an all but unnoticeable hesitation before Bet's lips find Sharon's cheek, offer a quick peck, and the inevitable question—*How was your day?* The same phrase often spoken by mother and daughter simultaneously.

The forearm braces she'd left Dr. Pena's office wearing haven't been worn for nearly two weeks, not even when she vacuums or mops. She is, alas, healed.

When the microwave beeps an end to heating water in the Tate mug for tea, Sharon moves to the hard little chair at the dining table. She cannot keep cleaning what does not need to be cleaned. What if she went into business? A housecleaning service? This time Sharon lets the shiver run from shoulder to shoulder and down her spine. *Clean up after strangers? Not on your life. Not on my life, anyway.*

Then Buddy comes to mind. An old bachelor, an old brownstone — the dust alone would probably be endless. Besides, her curiosity has been aroused about an aunt whose death had been labeled a "cold case" in 1930. A touchy subject with Buddy by phone, but if she were there, face-to-face, perhaps she could draw him out. Maybe not. Her interest in a long-dead aunt is not keen — merely a passing interest, a puzzle to think about, a way to remove her interests from losses, from emotional breakdowns she'd just as soon not go through again.

The phone is there. Her options, quite suddenly, seem clear: a) arrange for a flight back to Cottonwood, where, she is certain, the green-tined iron garden rake lurks to nail her again with its tines, where the garden hose is coiled and ready to strike, where her imagination will bring a coyote into her courtyard to torment dark evenings; or b) call Buddy and take him up on his invitation. He has bribed her with talk of antiques Olive brought from the farm, in particular an old trunk that belonged to his great-grandmother, or was it great-great? Clymenia Talbot. Sharon takes a sip of green tea, eyes a niche in Bet's apartment where an antique trunk, depending on size, might fit perfectly.

"Budgy . . . ?" she says when he answers.

"Rose of Sharon! Glad you could call back. Who was at the door? You got a gentleman friend there in Philly?"

"Nobody." Sharon quickly moves on. "Is your invitation still open? About a visit?"

"Rosie! It's okay to call you Rosie?" he asks, but doesn't wait for her to respond. "Of course! When can you come?"

"Is tomorrow too soon?"

WHEN ROSE OF Sharon showed up at Buddy's door on a Monday in late February, he clapped his hands like a boy who's just seen a brand-new Ivers Johnson bicycle with solid teak rims under the Christmas tree.

He'd offered her a choice between the basement bedroom or the one she occupies. General living space separates his ground-floor bedroom from hers and contains a small maple dining table with a sailboat model underway, four mismatched chairs, an overstuffed sofa—the sort of nondescript brown no one but an old bachelor could possibly find any merit in owning—a single beige occasional chair, a low cherry-wood coffee table, a television too big for the corner it occupies, a scarf-covered trunk, a narrow desk with just enough space for a computer monitor and keyboard, and an iron floor lamp Sharon thought might be an original Art Deco piece. The lamp's shade is not, Sharon thinks, original to the base. Old, yes, and yellowed with time, but not glass. The cord to the lamp seems original with its multi-colored, fabric-covered round plug on the end.

For Sharon, the plug poses a threat, and she has taken to unplugging the lamp when she goes to bed, plugging it back in when she gets up. Unplugging it again when she and Buddy go out. He's adamant about not fixing what's not broken but allows Sharon to plug and unplug at will. There is not the dust she'd imagined there might be (he has a housekeeper who comes in weekly), but there are *things* she can *put her hands to.*

The basement bedroom, the one Sharon decided against, is also a storage room. It houses his washer, dryer, hot-water heater, a fat-tired red Schwinn bicycle with a bell, boxes, lop-sided stacks of blankets and quilts, plus a half bathroom. A narrow path allows access to an exit out to a backyard with a black-barked tree and a black squirrel who visits to feed on a peanut Buddy leaves in the tree where the low branches fork. There's a clear plastic bag of peanuts-in-the-shell on the ledge where the hot-water heater sits near the door.

Buddy rents out the brownstone's upstairs flats—the third floor to two women Sharon thinks are probably sisters, probably in their forties and probably done with men by the lack of effort either one shows for style in clothing, hair, or common courtesies like a nodded greeting in the foyer; the second floor to a young Korean man Sharon has seen in his dark business suits mornings when she goes to the foyer to retrieve the paper. He is friendly enough, nods, offers a crisp white smile as he exits out the front door.

She's been at Buddy's for three days. From the guestroom she hears his even snores. There's a comfort in knowing she's not entirely alone. She doesn't admit it to anyone, never to Bet and seldom to herself, but the complete absence of human sounds in her house in the desert *is* bothersome. It's as if the sun, as it drops below the horizon, drags what there is of life with it and leaves a vacuum behind.

Her move from Carpinteria to Cottonwood had been to make a new start but also, perhaps more importantly, to escape the closeness of neighbors, the density of life, a density that seemed to want to suck the breath from her chest, and she feared, not persistently but enough to aggravate her restful hours, she might become agoraphobic. Or another sort of "phobic" she hadn't yet discovered.

The weather since her arrival in Brooklyn has been achingly cold. Even so, Sharon turns off the radiator in Buddy's guestroom and levers the window up to wedge a slim paperback romance between the sill and the frame, insuring the gap stays gapped. She has dreamt of natural gas asphyxiation and the room where she dies, almost dies, in her dreams becomes a tomb no one discovers until she's turned into mummy leather. Buddy's guestroom could be the undiscovered tomb of her dreams. It's an unreasonable fear. She knows, absolutely, how unreasonable it is; nonetheless, she wedges the gap every night.

Tonight, big-band music drifts in from down the street—Harry James, maybe. Her father liked Harry James; his collection of 78s had filled several shelves.

Why had her father never mentioned Irene? She was his aunt as well as Buddy's. And murdered. Well, maybe murdered. A cold case. A mystery in the family. And not a word from Lincoln Johns about her. He'd told her about Aunt Flo and her modeling career, the fight-promoter husband and the husbands that came before him—a used car dealership second husband and the no-account first one that Flo had had to support. He'd told her about his Aunt Mae, the one who must've had a stroke or something similar when she was young because she never, or hardly ever, left her room. He'd told her about Flo, Mae, and Wil's brothers, Budd and Edison—Edison with his one green eye and one brown. He'd told her about another aunt—Sharon can't recall her name—who'd married a farmer and stayed in PA. But not a word about the aunt named Irene.

When Sharon asked Buddy why he thought Aunt Irene

had been kept a secret from her, he'd said, "They didn't hit it off all that well. I guess I can see it."

"See what?" Sharon said.

"How you might not have known of Irene."

"I can't. Why didn't my dad say anything? He must've known her."

"Mm, not by much. I was twelve when she, when she," he paused and shook his head, "and Lincoln was still wearing diapers. I used to change him up from time to time."

"Did you? You don't strike me as the diaper-changing type." She was seated on the opposite end of the sofa from Buddy, a seat closer to the trunk from the farm, the one Olive had shipped to Brooklyn ahead of the family, the one Sharon could already picture perfectly situated in Bet's Philadelphia apartment commanding attention with its hand-painted moons and stars.

"You were so young," Sharon said, "but you remember her as your favorite?" This last part she'd offered as more question than statement. She had grown remarkably fond of Buddy in a very few days and it seemed to Sharon that anyone Buddy had admired would be someone she, too, would've admired.

In Buddy's guestroom Sharon tells herself *Breathe, breathe* . . . and is glad for the muffled rhythm of Buddy's snores and how they intersect with musical notes from the outside. She tries very hard not to think about Irene's death.

Staring at the book wedged under the window, her eyes adjusted to the dark, she thinks what light there is must come from a half-moon she cannot see from her bed; Glenn Miller's "String of Pearls" now serenades the neighborhood and she studies the plumbing fixtures in the room. The pipes are painted white like the walls and run up the corner nearest the head of the bed. They run along the top of the wall on her left, make a corner, stretch to the next corner, then run straight down to the radiator. The bathroom on the ground level floor is on the other side of the wall behind her head.

Sharon will track the pipes and how they run the room back and forth and up and down and back again in the way insomniacs count sheep until exhaustion takes hold. As she has done each night of her stay, she realizes what she already knows: water, not gas, goes to the radiator. Water, not gas. And yet, she cannot will herself to turn the heat back on.

The music stops. Buddy's snores are now *a cappella*. The paperback romance is in place. Eyes closed, she imagines the photos and tintypes from much earlier days Buddy has shared with her and sees the one of Irene as a girl, maybe ten, a studio-sitting, a three-quarter stance capturing waist-length hair and a sideways glare at the photographer—pouty, full of resentment for the time required to pose. *It's the look of a petulant girl, impatient to be somewhere,* Sharon thinks, drifting into sleep.

Lynn Doiron

Part II

Changes

HELL'S KITCHEN, NEW YORK CITY
AND HOLLYWOOD, CALIFORNIA

1930

The radio in Irene's Hell's Kitchen apartment looks like a walnut cathedral. Originally, both knobs were Bakelite and the color of day-old cream, but now the tuner is black and Irene turns the dial until The Ipana Troubadours come into the room with a zesty samba. The tuner is black because Bucky removed the original one so that she would stop changing the station from his favorite. It was New Year's Eve, 1929—he'd wanted "romance" and she'd wanted a Lindy Hop. Romance it was. Then, lunkhead that he is—she wags her head, smiles at the shiny black replacement—he forgot where he'd hidden the original and she had to find another.

She turns the remaining cream knob to lower the sound—a little something to buffer street noise is all she requires. Vehicles in the street below, their horns and brakes, an occasional backfire, become secondary to the samba, to the foxtrot that follows. A taxicab pulls up below, someone gets out (too tall to be Bucky or Foster) and the cab pulls away, makes a turn at the first corner. How different cars are these days, she thinks, as the rounded and bulbous yellow teardrop shape disappears from view. Nothing like the long, boxy Winton, all angles and straight lines, that she'd climbed into back in 1909. It was yellow, too, like the taxicabs nowadays.

She'd been upstairs in her parents' bedroom on the farm, unwilling to leave, watching Mae and Flo take their seats in the back of that great yellow contraption. Edison had climbed in after them. Budd had stood next to the front passenger side, waiting and ready to help Olive up.

Where had Olive been? She'd been hiding behind the big lilac bush down below the upstairs window; she'd been looking up, watching Irene count her brothers and sisters as they filed into the car. When Irene saw her mother lurking there, Olive stepped out into clear view from behind the heart-shaped foliage. "Bring that girl on down," she said to Budd.

"Ma'am?" Irene heard Budd question.

"Haul your sister out of the house. Now will serve better as not."

Irene mouths the words into the window just as she heard Olive speak them twenty years past. *Now will serve better as not.*

She fingers a circle around the moisture pattern her breath leaves on the all-but-opaque window. *How different it is,* she thinks, *to see things from here, from an opposite edge of time, like hitting your mark on the land-side of the dock at Yostel's Pond and pacing how you'll run it, and when the last step will be, the spring step to get you off as high as you can get so you can ball up for the best splash. And then, surfacing, how you'd mark the number of strokes it'd take to get back to that dock.* Irene couldn't see her mother back then as a woman moving along a current of change, a woman not so many years older than Irene is now, at thirty, who was making a run, the best way she knew, and making a leap from what she had into something, or into somewhere, she, Olive, hoped would be better.

Two decades is a long time for understanding to come, but Irene knows now, in ways she's never understood—Olive could no more let Irene's momentary heartbreak about leaving the farm put the whole family off schedule than Irene can allow Wilbur's carelessness to change the course of her about-to-be family.

Irene's drawn an ordinary circle in the moisture vapor; she gives the circle a tail and a fin near where a gill is transformed into a brief curve that might be gill or smile. She draws a second small fish, and a third. They are all there, waiting. She will try to be the best mom she can. She will learn right along with her babies how to be a good mother.

In 1909 Olive's fish, small and large, were pooled in the Winton where she had conquered the front passenger seat as Budd's co-pilot. She wore a wide-brimmed straw tied off with a scarf thin enough to see through. The scarf veiled her face; an ankle-length dustcoat veiled any trace of her traveling suit. Touring goggles, the same as Budd's, hid Olive's gray-blue eyes; and an expression that was neither eager (like his) nor forlorn (like Irene's) dominated her countenance. Olive's material world was eastbound on a train headed for Brooklyn; her real-world, flesh-and-blood hopes were wedged into the back of the Winton: Mae, Irene, Flo, and Edison with five-year-old Wil in his lap.

Budd steered the Winton, moved slowly from the house and the barn where the stone wheel screamed as it sharpened tools. A bend in the road and what was behind them was truly behind them and gone.

Irene frowns at the fish she has drawn on the window. Before today, she hadn't thought of her father in months, possibly years. He'd been left behind to stare into the wardrobe hung with his shirts, his pants, his suit coat, hung with nothing of her mother's, no evidence of her or her siblings other than their empty beds. She taps the fish. "Will I be so easily forgotten by you as my father has been by me?"

She has the stoppered bamboo container, her fistful of dirt from the farm, but the dirt was of the farm, not her father. The farm had stayed big in her mind while Joseph Johns, in stature and everyday ease and humor, faded. He had, after all, done nothing to prevent them from leaving. Whoever he had been to Irene—he wasn't anymore.

She looks beyond the drawings made on the glass in the direction of a persistently honking horn. As her focus comes back to where she has doodled she sees the movement of her reflection, but not the reflection itself. More like an idea of having been. Like that self-portrait left on the wall—her father's grim likeness on that god-awful yellow-leafed wallpaper.

Still wearing her coat, Irene removes the container from the pocket where she'd stashed it, shakes the dirt back and forth. The road the Winton travelled had seemed endless, always there, moving under the car, going on out in front, coming from out of a hill or around a bend to be there for the wheels to roll over.

The Ipana Troubadours are replaced by the A&P Gypsies; the street below is quiet or seems so. She is sleepy and curls on the bed for a nap, pulls the covers from Bucky's side up and over the bulky green coat. The groans of seat springs and leather seem with her more than the A&P Gypsies with their guitar and violin strings, their horns, the horns from the street and their blaring. She allows *what is* to punch holes in *what was* and remembers how ardently she'd prayed for a breakdown from the backseat of the Winton; she had prayed in the way Nessie had prayed for a husband. Nessie got her wish. And Irene got her breakdown but too late to make any difference.

Near sleep that first day on the road, she'd heard Mae say to Edison, "I will run away and go back when she's not expecting it—wait and see if I don't." She'd heard Olive shout to Buddy above the road noise, "If I make it there with all of you, I will have the only things worth saving out of that union. You are the only reason I stayed. Come to think of it, you're the only reason I left. I had to give you all a chance."

In the back seat of the Winton, Irene had opened her eyes; she opens them now, understanding in 1930 what she did not comprehend in 1909, recalling, verbatim, what Olive said next: "It's a new world."

Irene's pillow accepts her whisper as if the words are orig-inal, a new-born idea springing only from her.

She naps, half in the now and half in the drowsy sleep of back then, her head bobbing against the chest of Mae, Flo's head doing the same against Irene's lower arm. There are fields of late-summer corn she does not see but walks through; there are clouds of time when Edison drives and Budd is the co-pilot. They seem so real, Irene doubts she is dreaming—hopes she is not.

NOW HER CHEEK rests in her mother's lap, her mother's dust coat opened and moved aside to allow for the less dusty pillow of Olive's travel costume.

"Remember Granny Cly?" Olive asks. She could be talk-ing to anyone—the boys in the front, Irene's sisters leaned into each other beside them in the back. On the open road, with the wind in their ears, Olive's words catch like sledders let loose on the rise above Yostel's Pond in the winter, words swiftly gone, out of reach, to all but Irene.

Irene lets her mouth droop the way she's seen Edison's droop between snores. The last person on earth Irene wants to remember is Granny Cly.

"Granny Cly was my father's mother and they, my father and Granny, wanted me married. I had no interest. I was dead against it," she says, her words dropping down to Irene's ear before whooshing to join what they'd passed. "I was . . . I wanted to run my own life, have my way, like you want to have your way now. I was grown, not a girl anymore," she says and Irene feels Olive's fingers smoothing tangles from her hair.

"I lived in my father's house with my mother and Granny Cly. But," Olive tugs her fingers through a tress and Irene flinches as if a fly has landed, but she doesn't open her eyes.

"Sorry," Olive says, and the roll of the Winton in and out of wagon wheel ruts in the road is like a carousel ride for Irene. There is water nearby; she can smell the damp green of river willows, the dusky pungency of stinging nettles. "But, I believed," Olive says, "I believed I was like you believe you are now—independent, able to decide what was best for me."

"I can," Irene mumbles into the pleats of her mother's skirt. She lifts her head and leans an ear into Olive's bosom. "Why'd you do it then? Why'd you marry?"

"Coincidence," Olive says. "A pamphlet arrived the morning after your father proposed. I'd told him No, of course. He was, well, a good-enough sort, but I was having none of it." Olive's cheek rests against Irene's head and her words arrive like a bedtime story.

"There is no one I respect more than my father," Olive says, "but my mother, so far as both he and Granny Cly were concerned, was their workhorse. I wanted no part of that. Then the pamphlet came. It was from Denmark . . . *to secure the happiness and security of Danish maidens.* It was Celibacy Insurance."

The word is strange to Irene and Olive explains about how a choice to remain unmarried, to remain single, might be made—if you had an income. Granny Cly's old neighbor in Bristol, Massachusetts, Marta Olsen, had drawn an annuity from her Celibacy policy for years. Marta was a spinster, not only in the physical sense of being unmarried and older, but as she purchased turnips or a new parasol—anywhere, everywhere, on paper, in a contract between herself and the Celibacy Insurance Company in a country on the other side of the world—Marta Olsen was a spinster.

"What's a spinster?" Irene asks.

"I suppose a spinster is, at least in some ways, an Independent Woman." There is a long exhalation from Olive and Irene senses her mother is more than tired of the subject, but she goes on as if it is washday and all of the laundry is not yet on the line and what is on the line is yet to be taken inside and pressed with the sadiron and put away in the tall, mahogany wardrobe.

"I couldn't see that then," Olive says. "We had the most awful quarrel."

"You and Grandfather?"

"No. Me and Granny Cly. Over the pamphlet."

"Marta Olsen's pamphlet?"

"The pamphlet ordered for me. I thought Granny was meddling with my life by ordering such an insult."

"Was she?"

"Yes. But I misunderstood. She meant for me to have

options. I saw it as just the opposite and said yes to your father's proposal. I said yes out of anger, Irene. I said yes out of headstrong willfulness."

The veil draping Olive's wide straw softens her usual hard lines. "Be careful," she says, staring beyond Budd and Edison to some distant point down the road. "Willfulness is a dangerous thing. You get yours from me and I am sorely sorry for that."

WHILE IRENE NAPS in a cold Hell's Kitchen apartment, Olive paces the length of an in-ground pool in the backyard of Flo's latest husband's home in Hollywood, California. She is gripping her upper arms where a cardigan sweater hides them from a relentless noon sun. It is near three on the east coast, and Irene, her wayward child, now a wayward woman, will be preparing for the third act of the day at Poseidon Park. Olive is never easy about Irene's show times. She has worn herself out with worry and thrown in the towel where Irene's safety's concerned. Yet she paces.

"Good morning," Flo says, first cup of coffee in hand. Her dimples are just as deep, perhaps more deeply embedded than ever, in her heart-shaped face, and her hair, even for Florence, is a brighter shade of blond than any natural shade the girl has ever known, made brighter yet, somehow or other, by the geraniums spread wildly over the white satin folds of her dressing gown. So much red and green on a field of such white is unseemly, Olive thinks. "Good morning," she says in return.

"Is Michael about?" Flo asks.

"He was," Olive says, "but left at the crack of dawn." These modern girls! These pretenders at married life! But not a hint of Olive's dismay shows. "I fed him," she says. "He has a boxer's appetite, that one."

"But such a fine unbroken nose," Flo says. "Trust me, if he'd been in the ring, I'd never had said yes. How *can* you wear that sweater? Honestly, Mom."

"Leave us be," Olive says. "It's the one you gave me for Christmas a few years ago. I'm happy to have it — cold or warm."

"How I do hate the cold. I'd live in Brooklyn again if I could take this sunshine back with me. And these palms."

"You've forgotten to mention the ocean," Olive adds. "Or have you had a change of heart?"

"No; I'd forgotten. *And the ocean*," Flo adds. "Shall we go there today? And Mom . . . would you fill me up?" Her hand is out with an empty cup tilting back and forth.

From Flo's kitchen Olive can hear the day woman who comes in to make beds and pick up after her daughter and her daughter's husband. She imagines the woman is put out by the spotless kitchen that met her upon arrival, the spotless ashtrays found throughout the house on every possible side table and mantle, newspapers and magazines all tidied up to fit inside the gilded rack for such things. She hears what sounds like a shotgun blast. It's just a car backfiring, echoing along the canyon behind Flo and Michael's home in the Hollywood Hills, but a shiver runs Olive's whole length, creeps under her scalp and seems to wait there for some heartbeats to pass. She shakes herself like a dog coming out of water as the shiver passes and then turns with Flo's refilled cup just as Flo passes her and says, "Never mind. I'm up for a swim."

With the exception of Mae, they all loved to swim. She corrects her thinking: All who survived long enough to learn loved to swim. It was a Joseph Johns's trait. Not Olive's. Some things a body can master, despite what goes on inside. Some things a body cannot. Olive had never mastered an abiding fear of water, but she'd put passion, physical passion in its right and proper place. Mae had failed to master either one.

Dumping the fresh cup of coffee into the sink, she rinses the brown that might leave a stain down the drain. "Good-bye, Joseph." Sometimes Olive still hears herself saying good-bye to a man who's been dead for a good while now. She was saying it even before they loaded into that damned car and left the farm; she was saying it on the journey; she says it when she watches coffee disappear down a sink drain. She'd never worried about Nessie, her oldest; there'd never been a need. With Budd and Edison, she should have. With Wilbur, of course she'd worried. His lungs were such an asthmatic mess back then; he'd required her mothering attentions— still did—but for different reasons. But Mae and Flo and Irene . . . look where her worries had taken them.

Olive, ever sure of what she is sure of, and unsure of what she is not, hugs herself at Flo's kitchen sink. Spilt milk is spilt milk; no way on God's green earth to get beyond that.

She pulls the Bon Ami out and powders the sink. She powders the counters, pushes the sweater sleeves above her elbows. Joseph Johns was an impractical man. He was, and ever had been, better at dreaming than making dreams happen. He'd been a man with prospects who made nothing of them; and what Joseph Johns made nothing of, made nothing for the futures of his children; if Joe couldn't or wouldn't, then she would and could and did.

"Mom!" Flo exclaims, passing the kitchen on her way back out to the pool, "what has my sink done to you?"

"What?"

"It's down for the count, Mom. Let up, OK?"

Olive stops. She nods. Flo is out the door and into the pool in one effortless motion. She watches for Flo to break the surface after her dive; she does. Olive wipes up the residual Bon Ami film.

Five years before she left Joseph, she'd said, "There will be an end to this, Joseph." Her pulse had been thin as string as another blood-covered baby howled outside her womb.

"Just look at the love bestowed upon us, Mrs. Johns!" he had answered.

"Swaddle him, Joseph! What are you thinking? Wagging him around in the air like that! Do you think he can fly?"

"Like Irene?" he had winked at the then five-year old Irene standing in the doorway to their room. "We will teach him, won't we?"

Watching Flo from the kitchen window as she makes even strokes down the pool and back, Olive recognizes the clean style taught by Joseph. And yes, they, he and Irene, had taught Wilbur to swim. You taught them all, Joseph, except me. And, of course, Mae. With some things, we, she and I, were un-teachable.

ON THE EAST coast, Irene stirs. Her room is dimmer and the afternoon is hardly half done. Foster, by now, will be livid, refunding patrons who've paid to see what is not going to happen, not again, ever. There will be no Irene soaring over their heads.

She hurts—the rib is that sore yet—but grins under the blankets, and pulls the raggedy quilt, the one coming apart at more seams than those still holding, up and over her head. There is a faint knock at the door. Too comfortably warm, she ignores it. If it's Foster come after her, let him break the door down; he'll have Billy Hell to pay. If he's brought the cops, let them break it down. If it's neither, then whoever it is will come back. She is, she believes, on a right track and no one, not in this moment or the next, is going to budge her from this snug sleeping car of a bed.

n Buddy's guestroom on St. Terence Street, Sharon is having a dream she can't quite shake. She knows it's a dream and that it may even be one of her telescoping dreams in which she is dreaming herself dreaming, in which she is watching herself move from room to room and sometimes the rooms are familiar and remembered, and sometimes they are not: the room with the blue-green table with the three pendulum lights, strangely set in motion to sway back and forth, sending the circles of light over one way and then back; a room full of white light and an unmade bed with impressions, indentations in the bedding where someone has recently been; a long hallway that she can't seem to get to the end of and, sometimes, when she opens a door off the hall, she finds another unmade bed with fresh linens stacked on the end. There's a thumping she must attend to and when she goes into the rooms to change the sheets, she finds herself back out in the hall. In the hall there are stairs she must climb and other doors she must enter. Sometimes people occupy the rooms. The people look up at her. She doesn't know them. What she knows is that the thumping has something to do with the pendulum lights set to sway. She believes the double French doors are open and wind is playing them open and closed to thump at the doorjambs over and over again.

"Am I upstairs from myself?" she asks three men playing cards. They are college-aged young men, fresh-faced and smart-mouthed, although they don't say anything to Sharon, not verbally. They smirk. They dip their heads as if sharing some derisive remark about her. They shrug. There are fresh linens in stacks on the corners of the card table and they seem to be betting pillowcases and elasticized fitted sheets on their poker hands.

"Do you know how hard it is to fold those sheets into tidy squares?" she asks. But the thumping is there and she leaves them to their games.

She thinks there must be a way from this corridor to Arizona. She just needs to find the right door.

"No," she tells the self standing outside the card room who is faced with two sets of stairs, a set on the left and a set on the right, both sets leading up. The thumping seems to be coming from somewhere down and she can see another self below. A long way below, like five stories down, but all the stairways go up.

"Wake up," she tells the self in the bed in the room below all the floors. The floors are clear; she can see straight through to lower levels where all the rooms appear empty. She pushes her foot against the flooring, some sort of plastic—solid and thick enough to hold apartments up—but not real glass. She stomps. "Close those damned doors, will you?" She stomps again.

Sharon's leg jerks, jerks again. Pulling a pillow over her head, she tries to block the noise of doors banging against the

doorjamb. She blinks. Blinks again. Stares at the pipes running up the corner of Buddy's guestroom and turns on her
side to face the closet wall. The stiff, flaking costume she'd
retrieved from the stars and moon trunk hangs there. It's a
jumpsuit. The once white fabric now yellowed in squares
where the fabric had been exposed. She'd hung the costume
on an upper closet door pull; a small pool of flaked spangles
litter Buddy's guestroom floor where the costume has continued to shed through the night.

The thumping starts again. *What is that!* Exasperated
by fitful and much-interrupted sleep, she turns on her back,
turns again toward the pipes. Her hand goes out and she
touches the pipes running up the corner closest to the bed.
They vibrate with each measured thump.

She is suddenly out of the room, the floor underfoot varnished wood and not plastic or plexi or breakable glass, and
at the bathroom door she yells, "Buddy! Are you in there?
Buddy! Can you hear me?"

"Help."

"What? Buddy, I'm here. Unlock the door."

"Call nine-one-one. I've broken . . . something."

"Are you okay? Buddy? I'm calling nine-one-one."

"It's cold."

"What? Should I break the door in?" Sharon puts her back
to the opposite wall and runs against the door. Her right
shoulder bounces off the door panels and she feels the vibra-
tion through her bones, a sharp ache in her right forearm
where the ulna has mended. The door doesn't offer a quiver.

She remembers plugging her cell phone into the charger,
but where did she plug the charger in? There are so few out-
lets in Buddy's place. It's gray dark outside as if the sun wants
to be up but hasn't quite made the rise. She turns the knob

on the floor lamp. No light. She crawls under the table to plug the old cord in. In the bathroom! She plugged the charger into the bathroom outlet. She uses the landline, a red *princess* phone Buddy has joked about as the one he reserves for incoming calls from the White House. "I'm calling . . . Buddy? It's ringing!"

To the operator, she says, "Hurry. Please hurry. I can hear water running. He thinks he's broken something." There's a Con Ed bill on Buddy's table and she reads the address off too quickly, reads it again more slowly. She pauses, says, "No. I don't know the nearest cross street. Don't you people have maps? There's water coming under the door." This is a lie, but Sharon imagines there might be water coming under the door any moment.

She leaves the phone off the hook and tells Buddy, "They're coming," and thinks about throwing her body weight into the door again but says, "Buddy? I'm going out front. I'll find somebody to get this door open. Buddy?"

"It's so cold," Buddy says. "I can't turn it off. I can't get there." But she's gone.

She braces the street door wide open with a garbage bin hauled up from the sidewalk alcove, then takes the stairs to the Korean's door on the second floor. "Help!" she shouts. "Is anyone there? Buddy's fallen in the bathroom. Anyone there!" She's halfway up the next flight to the rooms of the unfriendly women when the young man opens his door. His face is lathered for shaving and one stroke has been made with the razor as he hands off the razor and disappears downstairs. She hears the door splinter open below and quite unexpectedly sits, heart racing in ways she didn't know it could.

A half hour passes before the paramedics arrive. This is

not their fault. The Con Ed bill on the table is not Buddy's but a friend's — someone who is travelling; Rose of Sharon cannot remember who, but she vaguely remembers a detail in an earlier long-distance phone conversation with Buddy that so and so had booked a winter walking tour of Umbria, Italy. The Con Ed bill belonged to so and so. Buddy would be paying it for her. She remembers "Umbria, Italy" because she has always wanted to go there. And Tuscany.

When her heart returns to normal, she leaves her seat on the stairs, catches a glimpse of the Korean tenant bent over a naked Buddy — primarily hidden inside his bathtub. The bathtub is draining. "Blankets," the young man requests, and she brings all the blankets from the guest bed where she'd slept, dragging them from the room and around the corner to where they are needed.

She's unnecessary in the chaos, can't comfort Buddy, is unable to sit on the unmade bed in the room with the wedged open window and flaking costume, and feels invisibly in the way in the living area or kitchen. The stairs offer anonymity — she can't explain why — and she resumes her seat there.

When they remove Buddy from the brownstone he is wearing an oxygen mask and looks like a great cocoon strapped onto a narrow gurney. She signs something. They leave without informing her where he will be.

"Yes," a paramedic said in response to her panicked questions, "he will be fine. Possible hip replacement in his future, but it'll all work out OK, won't it, buddy?"

Sharon didn't believe the medic knew Buddy from Adam, or any man since Adam. "Buddy" was just his way of saying "Dearie" to an elderly person in need. Then the medic offered Sharon a nod, the sort of nod that said, "We've got him now — no worries."

Above the oxygen mask, Buddy's eyes squinched as he studied the medic's features, trying, Sharon thought, to place his rescuer's face, as if he were one out of many who had come—must have come—into and out of Buddy's long years. Yet, to her knowledge, his life has been one of good health, accident-free.

THE STAIRS, ORIGINAL to the brownstone, are armored with brass—a diamond-pattern imposed on the hard rigidity for traction; the diamond-pattern grooves are no longer grooved so much as indicators of grooves because they hold accumulated soil from foot traffic. Decades of cinders and trace motor oil picked up when crossing a street fill the patterns; perhaps the infinitesimal crushed pieces of leaves, grains from beaches at the end of subway lines: Coney Island or Long Island or beaches Sharon has not heard the names of, to date.

On these steps, perhaps even on these armored treads, Buddy toddled, Olive carried fresh linens up to the rooms of her boarders, the rooms where she slept, the room where Sharon's grandfather Wilbur and grandmother Honey made love and fathered her father, Lincoln. Lincoln had perhaps crawled up and down these steps, with Buddy watching, checking for wet diapers. Now Buddy is swaddled and on his way to an Emergency Room in a city she knows next to nothing about negotiating, while Kevin (the Korean has introduced himself as Kevin Song) is upstairs completing his morning toiletries so that he can leave for work in a somewhat timely manner. Now the day has a sun filtered through layers of damp atmosphere and the bathroom has no door.

She's sat for some minutes, letting people, the living and

dead, take the stairs in leaps and on their hands and knees. *What have I done? What have I done?* she asks no one in particular.

When Kevin Song moved the trash bin back into its curbside alcove and closed the street door, he said, "What happened?"

Sharon, shaking her head, answered, "He slipped?" But her answer was more question than statement.

"The tub is pretty slick on the bottom. Oily." Kevin responded, his smile lost on her.

What in the wide world was there to be smiling about?

Then Kevin Song had excused himself to get ready for work.

Sharon stands. The banister is thick, a big man's hand-span thick, and she uses it on the way down, one thought-out step at a time, her hand coming up slightly, briefly from the brown painted wood, lowering to take her weight, lifting again. The coats of paint to the railings came without interim sanding, but she doesn't notice the paint-filled scars where someone . . . a mover? a resident? has let something hard-edged fall, leave its lasting impression of having once traveled these steps. She has thought about these scars before, when standing in the foyer in the morning . . . yes, only yesterday . . . about how gorgeous this sturdy staircase could be—stripped to bare wood and stained, perhaps with a cedar, some stain with the warmth of natural wood, something amber, or honey-favored.

What Sharon thinks about now is the bathroom door. Who to call? Who to fix what is broken? A broken hip? A new hip to replace Buddy's old one? *Oily. What have I done?* she thinks, ashamed of her shiny, sleek hair.

Stepping over pieces of the shattered door facing, she puts her head inside the doorway to take a look. There is her cell phone in its charger on the bathroom counter and there is her toiletries case—a satiny fabric inlaid with shiny and less shiny stripes on the outside, pale blue as so many of her personal things are.

On the inside of the pale blue—compartmentalized with clear plastic pockets to hold everything a girl can possibly need while far from home—are her maintenance products: salves and creams, toothpaste and brush, make-up, fragrance, shampoo, spray. She has no need of opening the case. The *oily* is there, inside, a conditioner she uses to keep all the wiry ways her hair has a tendency toward from not showing their "wilder" side. It would be better to close the door to the bathroom now, but the door is hanging from one hinge. It will not close.

Sharon's feet are the color of her toiletries case and, for a moment, she wonders if she has put on her ice-blue tennis shoes. She must get dressed, find a way to the hospital where they've taken Buddy. The Con Ed bill is on the table. The name on the bill is Barbara Riordan.

"I'm off now. For work," Kevin says, standing over the doorframe's splintered wood.

She has not closed the door from the foyer into Buddy's apartment. He offers a smile. His teeth are too white, too perfectly aligned.

"He'll be fine. Buddy."

"Yes."

"Are you OK?" he asks.

"Yes."

He hesitates, turns, and a few strides later Sharon hears the street door open and close. Was there something she was supposed to say? Something she should have elaborated upon? Of course she wasn't fine. Of course Buddy would never be the same. Did she look like an eight-year-old? Like someone who *could* be all right after all of what's just taken place? Someone who picks up her dropped Barbie and begins to dress and undress her in ball gowns or tropical bathing suits? Someone who can't wait to condition her white shiny hair?

She fills a pot with water and puts the pot on the stove. In the bedroom she moves the flaking costume from the closet pull and drags out her suitcase. She'd meant to do laundry today. Nothing is clean. Few things were when she left Bet's place in Philly, but there is always time.

Right.

When the kettle whistles she's dressed in what she'd worn yesterday, blue feet now inside white ankle socks and blue shoes. She's called the hospital and received an update on Buddy who is "resting" and scheduled for surgery "any time now" and not "feeling any pain."

The floor lamp is still lit and the light through the shade offers a spiced mustard glow replete with flecks of what are most likely signs left by generations of houseflies who've briefly rested and flown. The computer is there and she flips on the surge protector switch. She will email Bet and let her know of this latest disaster. The floor lamp goes off and the surge-protector's red ON light doesn't appear. *A-mazing,* she thinks, knowing a fuse has blown, not knowing where the breaker panel might be, knowing the laundry she hoped to at least get washed before calling for a ride to the hospital is conceivably not going to get done, knowing she is, very possibly, going to be in need of a paper bag. She crawls under the table and unplugs the lamp cord and looks at the two prongs for a few moments — both the same length, both the same width. From hands and knees she lowers herself to Buddy's varnished floor, rests her cheek on the wood and takes in the landscape as an ant or a daddy-long-legs spider might see the world.

There are the doorframe remains like a diminished range of icebergs on the smooth sea of wood in the short hall outside the bathroom. There is the computer tower under the child-sized work desk with its non-glowing ON button standing up like a submarine's entrance and exit hatch thingy. There is the nondescript brown skirting on the overstuffed nondescript couch, the leg of the low cherry-wood table, the corner of the stars and moon trunk with a blank patch of sky-blue the only painted surface showing. *The demon trunk,* she thinks, *with its omens and signs that lured me here.*

She gets up, no longer feeling the need for a bag to breathe into, and, with tea in hand, she sits at the far end of the couch and sips until the cup is empty.

It is barely 8:30. She would like to be helpful but doesn't know how. Oh, she will clean up the mess in the hall—but then what? She will be at the hospital when Buddy comes around. She will. She has made a promise to herself that she will be there when he comes around. But . . . oh, how she hates hospitals. *Hates them.*

"Demon trunk," she says, looking at it as if it could answer, or smirk. But as she glares at its hardware, she realizes there is something intriguing about the way the hasp only half comes down and makes a branch-like fork, of sorts, against the eye that a padlock would loop through.

The stairs to the basement are dark; the basement is dark. She makes her way with some caution, hand palming the wall as she goes. The door to the small backyard is double-locked and she turns the tumbler to soft-click the dead bolts

open. Light, shallow as it is, enters the dim interior. The peanuts in their shells are there in the bag. Outside, she places
one peanut in the lowest fork of the tree. *The black squirrel
Buddy feeds is nowhere in sight, but that's* OK, Sharon thinks.
That's OK.

Breakdown on Neversink Mountain

 **n a mountain** named Neversink in June 1909 Irene is watching a bird soar. The mountain overlooks Reading, Pennsylvania. The great yellow automobile has finally broken. The detour Olive *thought* would be good has been their undoing. "There are things I can show you," she had said.

The bird Irene watches came from nowhere, fighting its way against drafts off the mountain. When it wings overhead, Irene rolls back from sitting on Granny Cly's quilt to stretch with her back to the ground, but the bird is too fast — she's lost him.

Mae had *stood up to Mama. She had.*

Behind Irene, Budd and Edison work on the Winton. They've been at it for what seems like hours. Irene itches to get on with the journey. No. Not get on with it. To go back. Pulling her arms from behind her head where they've been a pillow while she studied the treetops and looked for the bird, she turns, props her chin in her hand and looks up at Mae. "Mae, we could run off. We could go back."

Mae frowns, slashes a stick she has picked up from

somewhere as if she were skipping a heavy flat stone meant to reach the Schuykill River, as if Olive stands someplace along the silver snake of it. But Olive, down by the boys near the creek where it crossed the road and the Winton broke down, has her hands full (Irene has checked), one holding Flo's hand, and the other holding Wil's, to keep them out of harm's way, and the way of the boys as they work.

The wind on Neversink slides past Irene and Mae with Olive's questions to Edison: "How long will it take?" "Are you sure that goes there?" "Oh. What *was I thinking*, to suggest we take such a road?"

Irene says, "We could, Mae; we could."

Mae slashes the air. "Nah."

Irene grunts. This is not the same Mae who stood up after that last meal with their father. How odd he had been, talking about chores over cold chicken and yesterday's bread as if suppers would always have his family in their same chairs and at the same table.

"You know, Budd," he'd said, "I think we might just need Edison to give us a hand with that stump below the barn. It's been pure hard on the horses and hasn't given over." He'd said this with no sign of wishful thinking and asked, "What do you think?"

When Budd made no answer, Joseph turned to Edison and said, "Are you up for it, son? I think the three of us, and the horses, could pop her out in no time."

Irene had studied the newsprint they'd been eating cold chicken off of because all but two of the plates had been put on a train in boxes marked PLATES. She would pretend, too, that this last supper was not THE last supper.

Mae, not one to speak unless spoken to, had said, "You know, Daddy, I'm a big girl now. Not like Budd, naturally, or Edison, naturally, but I am grown." She'd paused, let her eyes move over the newsprint under her chicken bones. The hiss of the gas-lights was all there was and the loud way Edison had of eating.

"And, naturally," Mae had continued, "a woman's not made to work with a strength equal to that of a man, and I couldn't work equal to Edison, or Budd, I mean, if Edison should feel up for it. But there are the horses, you understand, and I could encourage them. I could be good. With the horses. They know me."

Mae did spend a lot of time with Jake and Pearly, Irene thought. She nodded her head and opened her mouth to agree— *They do know her. And me.* But Budd said, "We're leaving, sir. In the morning. For Brooklyn. Aunt Florence's." Then the sound of Edison as he chiseled the last meat from a chicken breast was the only sound.

Florence and Wil had watched Olive. At five and seven they'd chosen sides.

Irene kept her eyes on Joseph, who rolled the bones of his leftover meal in the paper, pushed back from the table and stood. "Fine chicken, Mrs. Johns," he said. "Very fine. Thank you, boys. Thank you, Mae." He'd left the table then, walked out of the house with the newsprint parcel of bones.

On Neversink, Irene says, "C'mon, Mae. Why not? We could hide out. We could go mostly at night. We could be like Huck Finn and Jim."

"No, Irene. We could not."

Irene, on her stomach now, releases a great sigh. "I hate this smelly old quilt." She studies the stitches joining each odd scrap of cloth, a worked row of grass green like iron rake tines set at an angle, a worked row of blue, of yellow. "How come you don't call me Stick, like the boys do?"

Mae slashes the air. If a gnat had been there, it'd be a home run. "Because," she says.

"Because why?" Irene asks.

WHY DO SISTERS *ask so many questions?* Mae asks herself. She can't answer Irene because she doesn't know *why*. She can't even look at Irene. And she can't begin to figure out where to slice the air next.

In another world Mae would mind Jake and Pearly, brush them, feed them. "I think I can handle the horses," she had restated that night at supper. A calm had taken her. Every day she was a storm, inside and out, a turbulence without a place to let loose. But staring down at the newsprint that evening, with its greasy chicken skins and wing bones, her eyes had settled on a word. She can't remember what word. It might've been *the* or *this* or equally inconsequential. All she knew about what took hold of her was that she felt centered, like the eye of a tornado.

"Dearest, you're going to be handling hats," Olive had answered.

"Hats," Mae said.

"Hats," Olive said.

It took a moment, Mae remembers, for "hats" to sink in and replace Jake and Pearly. She would be working with hats, in Brooklyn, at Aunt Florence's. Even Aunt Florence's namesake, Flo, would be handling hats.

"I don't see how hats are going to help Daddy," Mae said.

"Mae, dearest, hats are going to help us," Olive had answered. Everyone had been excused from the table by nods from Olive, each with their small newspaper-wrapped parcel of bones to be taken out back and placed in the post-sized hole for such leavings.

"Daddy *is* us," Mae said.

"Daddy may be us, child—but we are not him."

Olive's eyes were not angry or impatient, and when Mae remembers that calm force in her mother, she wonders if that same force is what becalmed her when she replied, "Dearest Mama, I will always be him."

MAE HAS WORN a sore spot on her hand from swatting the air on Neversink. Two days on this journey and she would sooner be dead than where she is.

"Well," Irene says, "You can if you want."

"Can what?" Mae answers.

"Call me Stick."

"No," Mae says, and this time, when she slashes the air with the stick, the stick sails out to about where the bird Irene had watched work against drafts had been. "No," she repeats, "Irene, I cannot."

How, Mae wonders, can a girl as pretty as Irene—oh, Flo has her blond curls and blue-eyed ways, but they are shiny dimes to the gold dollars that make up this sister—come to favor such a name? What possesses the girl?

Mae's own name is a bad fit. She doesn't dislike her name; she dislikes herself for being all things other than the things May, the month, holds and harbors. And she cannot change. Mae does not believe a change in a name solves anything. She scowls at the valley.

"Want me to find you another one?" Irene says.

"Leave it," Mae answers.

"THE SCHUYLKILL DRAWS rain and snowmelt from two thousand square miles." Olive's voice comes up from behind Irene and Mae as she leads Wil and Flo to the quilt. "By late summer, Tundra Swans, migrating from the central arctic to Chesapeake Bay, will pass above here." Her arm sweeps to include the entire valley. "And Connecticut Warblers from southern Canada will darken the skies on their way to winter in South America." She names the creeks—the Wissahickon, the Maiden, the Manatawny, the French, the Perkiomen.

Below them, Reading's sprawl of factories, smokestacks, and houses—all closely hugged to one another—creep out into the countryside dragging a network of fencelines and hedgerows to crisscross open spaces. *Such a world, such a world at our feet!* Olive thinks. They are a drop in the current of migrating families drawn by cities, towns swelling beyond natural boundaries, beyond rivers, as surely as southern climes draw northern birds.

This detour had been pure idiocy on her part. It is hot, even with the breeze, and sweat dampens her high-collared blouse at the back. She nudges Wil, whose head rests in her lap as he blows on a blade of grass pressed between thumbs. He doesn't complain when she stands to find easier air. She shakes two days of travel wrinkles, rearranging but not erasing them from the folds of her skirt. "Well."

"What?" Mae says, while Wil continues tormenting the grass, Flo sleeps, and Irene stares down a horizon line that is not going to change.

"Nothing. Stay put. Don't let Irene out of your sight."

A little downhill from the Winton, Olive wets her handkerchief in a stream. Her handkerchiefs are edged with tatting she worked herself during long confinements with child after child making itself presentable on her insides for eventual entries into this outside world. She imagines letting the square of cloth float away, wonders, if she let go, how far it might travel before hanging up on a root? She straightens. Budd and Edison will succeed with the Winton. They will continue. If not on to Brooklyn today, then at least off this damnable mountain; they will make their way off Neversink.

Placing the handkerchief over her face, she tilts her head back and breathes through the wet. When she lowers the handkerchief, the sky is all blue above with no trace of clouds, not a thing like the day she'd decided, with certainty, to leave Joseph. To leave the farm. She'd looked up from the chicken-scratch yard, past the turned gate set in a line of picot-edged picket fencing, fencing in sore need of paint, to the shaggy field beyond and its raggedy black and white Holsteins—every last head of them bent to the pasture or grinding away at their cud—and fixated on their pink udders. Pink udders manufacturing more milk. Milk that Joseph and her older sons, Budd (who could be anything in this wide world he wanted to be, given half a chance), and Edison (who might lack some charm but could fix anything set before him with fingers that, Olive figures, will never meet a part they don't already know on some level, in that way some folks will never meet a stranger)—fine boys, who will, with their father, pull all that fine, white warmth in long streams into pails. When she'd looked into that sky on that day she'd seen the whole of it as a place churning endless spilt buckets of milk—a sky capable of drowning her boys, three in all, and her four girls.

There's a clarity in this sky above Neversink, she thinks, rewetting her kerchief. She will go back to the quilt with her children. She will cool their faces, their hot and hungry young faces, the best she can.

SUN GLANCES OFF the Schuylkill like lamplight off a mirror and it runs with a gleam so bright that a train running parallel goes unseen by all but Flo who shouts, "Look!"

When Irene follows where Flo is pointing, she sees the train like a dark caterpillar inching along right next to the bright ribbon of water.

"I bet it's the one with the circus!" Wil says.

"What circus?" Irene asks. "What circus? There's a circus? Can we go? Can we go please?"

IN HELL'S KITCHEN, Irene is dreaming a long snake of a silver river and a caterpillar train; there's a calliope full of sound and gongs. She pulls the quilt close, has a half-waking moment wherein she knows the hour is changing and the gongs are part of CBS programming. The quilt smells of Ivory detergent flakes, clean and good—99% pure.

Bet's Visit

BROOKLYN

February 2008

ose of Sharon enters Buddy's brownstone on St. Terence Street with the key she has been given to keep while the hospital keeps him. The brownstone is toasty warm, but she remains bundled in her ski jacket. There is something about the confines of the quilted-blue coat zippered shut she finds comforting; in the midst of strangers wherever she goes, and in the middle of strangely furnished surroundings, she is somehow not quite so strange to herself—more whole inside the jacket than out.

Clutched between her body and left arm, a vase of stargazer lilies and larkspur angles enough to spill water on Buddy's wood floors despite the fact she'd emptied the water to almost nil before taking them from his room. Keys in her right hand, she passes the dislocated bathroom door, sets the keys on the table, and takes the vase into the kitchen. There are other flowers from friends on his table, flowers she brought home the previous day to make room on the sill in room 618 for newer arrivals. The length of his hospital window sill is shorter than the length of his flower-sending friends and relations. Only two days since his accident! Word does travel fast, Sharon thinks, removing a card with Get Well Soon wishes, signed, *Your Barbados Cousins, Freida and JD.*

It is midday and the door to Buddy's bedroom is open. His bed is made with fresh linens Sharon has laundered in the downstairs basement after Kevin located the breaker box and brought power back into play. The near wall of Buddy's room has a shelf filled with dust-catching models of sailboats; the far wall is mostly windows, mostly shuttered with venetian blinds Buddy left opened. Light from those windows falls across his bed in narrow bars and filters out through his door and into the living area where it meets with light from a single, uncurtained window in the kitchen's end wall. The result is an indirect mix of natural light in the living room. It is a dim light casting no shadows from the half dozen bouquets in their various floral shop vases.

The "demon" trunk with its moons and stars and the stenciled, half-missing name of someone around the top, is no longer a curiosity; it now seems to Sharon nothing more than an odd piece of leftover space-hogging furniture. She's begun to have doubts about the niche she'd imagined it filling in Bet's Philly apartment; not doubts about the niche — the niche is adorable — but about the trunk's ability to do the niche justice.

She will be the best distant cousin she knows how to be. Water pours from the tap. She will keep his flowers as lively as she is able and finds aspirin to grind into powder and add to the filled vases. When the foyer buzzer sounds, she is at the counter, riffling through cards she's plucked from clear pitchfork holders, knowing none of the names of Buddy's well-wishers. *Barbados?*

As far as she knows, there is no one who could possibly want to see her, but Sharon opens the door anyway. Cooler air from the foyer is a pleasurable thing; the foyer itself is empty; the staircase up to the flats on the second and third floors is empty. *Good.* She has not been eager to run into Buddy's tenants, especially not the young Korean. She walks to the street door and shouts through the waffled glass, "Yes? Who is it?" She wants to add, *No one is here!* but stops herself from being quite so foolish.

"It's me!" Bet shouts back.

"Bet?" Rose of Sharon says. "Really? Bet!"

"*Really!* It's freezing out here."

Sharon, still wearing her blue coat and blue-knit scarf, opens the door. She'd been on the verge of unwrapping, hadn't she, when the buzzer rang? Her eyes go instantly hot—*Bet! Here!* On the porch to Buddy's brownstone in Brooklyn! Bet, smiling her crooked smile of surprise, waiting to be hugged and brought inside from the cold. Her Bet! Rose of Sharon is suddenly not so much the mother of this young woman as she is the child—needy in every sense of the word. She is guilty of being lost, of overwhelming loneliness, of overwhelming guilt for having caused Buddy's accident, his placement in a hospital bed some few miles away, and, finally, she is supremely guilty of feeling monumentally sorry for herself.

"Did I catch you on your way out?" Bet says, looking over Sharon's Snow Day bundling.

A few moments later they are in Buddy's living room, settling on his sofa, still coated, mufflered, holding each other's hands. Sharon puts her hand to Bet's wool ski hat and Bet's hand goes there as well and the hat is off. Bet's hair, like a shorn lion's mane, is spiked with some sort of gel that has given up on its task of standing in points. Sharon's hand runs over the flattened spikes, pulls some few back to point, her knuckles smoothing down the silk of Bet's cheek. Tears that threatened to spill on the front stoop are streaming.

"Sh-shh," Bet says.

"I am such a mess," Sharon says.

"Yes. But we will be better now, won't we."

Rose of Sharon nods like a very small girl would nod when she can no longer speak, too embarrassed to look up, too shy to let her daughter see her in such a pitiful state.

"Mom, you look great," Bet says.

"Your lying has not improved."

"It will. Let me get warmed up."

Bet takes the room in, its smallness, the largeness of the television against one wall, the round dining table behind the sofa and to one side, with barely enough room to pass behind and access a room on the right, two bad paintings on the back wall, one of red flowers, poinsettias, perhaps, but knifed to the canvas with such a heavy hand they could be gore spilling from a green human stem. "Nice place, this."

"Nicer, with you in it," Sharon says.

"Did Buddy paint that?"

"Paint what?" Sharon says, turning on the sofa to take in the art on the wall. "Oh, that. No. Tony Curtis. Imagine."

"I've not heard of him. But, then, you can't hear about all of the talent out there."

"Acting was his talent . . . but you! Here! How did you get the time off? I'm, I'm . . . here, let me have your coat."

Bet's mother looks overheated, her complexion a shade of strawberry ice cream, her hair not the smooth shimmer of perfect white coming down to point gently at her cleft chin. It was the perfect size cleft for a woman's chin, hardly more than a dimple, not overbearingly deep like that actor's from earlier years, the one who played Spartacus. Tony Curtis? No. Kirk Douglas? Bet gives the flower-gore still life another look and says, "Tony Curtis, of course."

"What?" Sharon says from the coat closet just inside the door to the foyer, then adds, "My god, this coat is longer than you are tall." It is black, wool, maxi-length, big buttoned, tall-collared. It is a man's coat, bought from a man's shop, and a purchase—after she had it tailored—Bet is pleased to have made.

"If you like it, I could have one tailored for you. If you'll be spending more winters back here—it's just the thing." How her mother goes out in this cold in a jacket that barely falls to her waist is a puzzle. And *no hat!* At least none that Bet has seen. Rose of Sharon is too young to be slipping in mental acuity. She is the sharpest woman, in many ways, Bet has ever known—never mind the bias of an only child. But she's keenly aware of her mother's flaws—her oft-times near-panic in regard to microbes strange hands have left on strange doors; her newer claustrophobic element; her insistence on keeping a window ajar even when it means cool, air-conditioned air escapes out into the desert, or winter heat flows out to join winter cold in Philly. Here, Bet is certain that upon looking, she will find a window wedged open *somewhere.*

"No, thank you," Sharon says. "I'll stick with my little blue number."

"Is this the trunk?" Bet asks.

"What do you think?" Sharon says with a voice full of expectations and enthusiasm—and the least little bit of misgiving.

Bet runs her ungloved hands over the trunk's surface

where grains have popped splinters up to buckle just on the verge of making themselves wholly known, of splintering completely away. She runs her hand back along the side. Much of the surface is held in place by paint and cracking varnish. At some point in the trunk's past, moisture, extreme moisture, has done its damage. "Who's this?" she asks.

"Who?" Sharon says, coming back around from the closet.

"Here, on this band of black. It looks like an odd name. Clym . . . n . . . a . . . Ta . . . or. The paint's chipped. Clymon? Talor?"

"Tabor. Clymenia Tabor."

"A family name?"

Sharon runs her fingers over the slight ridges. "Yes. My grandmother's grandmother's name."

Bet turns from the trunk to take in her mother's appearance. She's half a head taller than Sharon; the difference would be less if her mother stood up straight, the way her mother used to stand up straight, the way Bet still stands up straight, having been too long badgered by Rose of Sharon to do so.

"Let me fire up Buddy's kettle for some tea?" Her mother's head tips to the side with the question.

"You wouldn't have a cold one in there, would you?"

Sharon is at the refrigerator within a few steps, obediently in search of a cold beer. Her righteous indignation and usual debate on the merits of a cold beer when the weather is frigid versus hot tea are absent.

"No arguments, eh?" Bet finds this pale rendering of the mother she's known — the one who brimmed with excellent intentions and unending advice, the one she'd grown to adolescence with — is even less of this world than when she was in Philly. She moves into the kitchen, where there is barely enough room for both of them and the open door to the refrigerator, blaming her father's death — at too young an age — for her mother's fading presence. Ted and Rose of Sharon had made one person; he, the outgoing, nothing-is-too-distant-to-shoot-for type, and she, she . . .

"When did I ever argue the merits of a beer?" Sharon's words circle the pint of cottage cheese on the wire shelving in Buddy's fridge.

Always, Bet thinks, but the response has some perkiness. She puts her hand on her mother's shoulder and says, "Atta girl, Mom." Sharon's shoulder is all bone, barely cushioned by flesh, in fact, more cushioned by the blue ski jacket than any fat the jacket protects.

Sharon turns with two bottles of Miller Genuine Draft. "This is it," she says. "Will they do?"

Bet's heart sinks. Her mother is still, after eight years, stocking beer her father drank — in an era of beer varieties seldom witnessed in history! Her heart sinks over not just the beer, but so much of life yet to be sampled. Restaurants, men. Romance, dance steps beyond an Arizona two-step, fashion in colors beyond ashen pinks and freezer blues, travel — the whole world, or if not the whole world much of it — was there for her mother to sample. She'd been pleased, pleasantly surprised when Sharon agreed to take Buddy up on his invitation to visit. It was a brave step — out of the norm — for her mother.

"They'll do," Bet says.

"I know that look, and just so you know, I haven't bought any beer; blame the Miller on Buddy, not me." Sharon's eyes are full of defensive amusement; a good sign to Bet, even with the thin clouds of remembrance or some other emotion present, like small, white birds of worry or regret.

"Glass?" Sharon asks.

"I'm good."

"Just what your dad would've said."

"Just what most people would say, Mom."

"Well. Yes."

The bottle, already popped out with sweat in the heated room, is wet in Bet's hand. She takes a short draw and follows her mother the few steps back to the table crowded with half-spent floral arrangements.

"I can stay through the weekend, if you want," Bet says. "I have a few days saved up. If you need me, I can stay." Behind her and to the left is the door into Buddy's vacated room; to the right and just past the kitchen is the door to the spare room where Sharon sleeps. "If you have room," Bet adds. "If you don't think Buddy would mind."

"Buddy? He'd be head over heels for it!"

"And you?"

Sharon stands abruptly, chair legs scraping the floor. "Let me grab a couple saucers. I'm certain Buddy doesn't own any coasters and your hand must be cold, not to mention the beer will be going warm."

"I figured you might like the company," Bet says. Cupboards open and close; Bet listens for some response and takes another short draw on her beer. "Mom?"

"Yes."

"Yes, what?"

"Yes, I have found actual coasters. He is just full of small surprises, our Buddy."

"And so are you."

"How do you mean?" Sharon bends to place the coasters.

"Well . . ." Bet waits for her mother to stop fingering the coasters, pushing them incrementally to where exactly each should sit in relation to where each of them are seated; she waits for eye contact her mother seems loath to offer.

Rose of Sharon is a woman in crisis, Elizabeth "Bet" Appleonia Johns decides, and the crisis is more or less about where to position cardboard coasters with brown circular stains marring a Yacht Club logo.

When Bet stops the movement of the coaster by putting her bottle squarely down and rests her wet palm on her mother's hand, Sharon gives a little jerk away.

"Mom?"

"My jacket is ridiculous, isn't it?"

"A little. Yes. But the blue suits you." This is not the moment, Bet decides, to mention how much the color does *not* suit her mother. *The blue suits you?* Bet knows she can do better than this. "Great fit," she adds. "It sets off your hair."

Sharon's eyes roll back in her head. "I'm ridiculous," she says. "Have I always been? I haven't always been, have I, this way?"

"No—"

"When did it happen . . ."

"What?"

"When did this ridiculous mess of me get to be—me?"

"You are not *ridiculous*, Mom."

"But you said—"

"I did not."

"Did, too."

"Not."

Bet offers her mother a half grin, a grin that dares another comeback. There is a playfulness about to open between them right in the middle of tragic floundering and self-doubt. Sharon sits. Her forehead lowers to rest on the top of Bet's hand, the hand Bet has placed over her mother's to still Sharon's continual pushing and pulling at the coaster.

When Sharon's shoulders begin to convulse, Bet says, "Mom? Are you laughing or crying?"

"Both," Sharon says. She is honest, always, and in ways Ted was sometimes a wee bit remiss, a wee bit willing to bend a true fact to work with a situation to the satisfaction of most concerned. A little white liar, Bet's father could be—when required. Not her mother. She might fail to answer, say nothing at all, but she was not a truth bender. Bet finds this attribute slightly ridiculous, but admirable in its way, because she always knew whatever came out, came out of a black and white space in her mother's thinking. Not that her mother couldn't or wouldn't change an opinion: she would, in a heartbeat, if facts worked themselves around, or presented themselves in such a way that new facets came to light.

"I am such a mess," Sharon says. "And I just seem to scatter it wherever I go. Look. Look at poor Buddy."

"Shit happens," Bet says.

"Your dad used to say that."

"Everybody says that. Besides, *wherever you go* doesn't involve a whole lot of scattering—you don't *go* anywhere much."

Bet's right hand, the one she uses to lift a drink, remains between her mother's hand and forehead. She pulls it away and takes up the beer; the coaster, soggy with sweat, comes up with the bottle.

"Exactly right," Sharon says, "and here you are, smack in the middle of my current scattering."

"Mom, I can go. My backpack's still packed. Say the word." *How did things go so caddywampus?* Bet wonders. *One second, I'm her savior and the next, a part of her mess?*

Sharon says, "You must stay. I can't tell you how much it meant, means, to find you here, with me."

"And yet . . ."

"Did you know I'll turn sixty on my next birthday? I'm nearly twice the age Irene ever knew, and I don't know how to take a step without somebody holding my hand."

"Who?"

"You at the moment."

"I meant who are you twice the age of."

"Irene. A dead aunt, great aunt, I just found out about. I told you about her. Didn't I tell you about her?"

"No. Well. You've talked about a lot of cousins and family. Olive someone-or-other who crossed the prairies with eight kids—"

"Six. And not *the prairies*. For a history major, you're not much on history."

"Family. It's different."

"Yes." Sharon's beer is untouched; Bet's is touched to within a half inch of empty. She drains the bottle and walks around to the kitchen. "Recycle?" she asks.

"Bag on the hook next to the stove," Sharon says, listening for the bottle to slide down the walls of the plastic bag, for the refrigerator door to open, for Bet to say, *What? You mean those two you brought out were the only brews in the house?* Instead, after the bottle clunks the side of the stove as it finds the recycle bag's bottom, Sharon hears the stove's pilot click and the low flush of flames take hold.

These sounds are good, Sharon thinks, as the tea kettle rattles across the burners. She has not heard Bet slosh the water around inside the kettle to check for quantity, but, then, she would've felt the weight of the thing, the fullness of what was contained.

Sharon says, "I'd like to have known them, the family I missed."

"You would? Granddad was enough for me," Bet says.

"My father? You make him sound . . . didn't you like your granddad?" Sharon can't imagine her own daughter hadn't loved Lincoln Johns. Then, quite suddenly, she can. He'd been so unlike Bet's father. Exactly opposite in demeanor to Teddy, Lincoln had been quiet, shy unless prodded to speak when there were more than just the two of them, father and daughter.

"I didn't know him," Bet says.

"He was a little shy, I guess."

"Shy?" Bet almost snorts. "Hm. If you say so."

Sharon runs her finger down the bottle, leaving a path through the sweat. "Standoffish, then."

"Mom. Granddad was pompous. I'm sorry, but he was."

It seems to Sharon they knew two different men who went by the name Lincoln Johns. The father she knew and cared for was more than a father, he was her companion, closer to her than her mother; he was her friend, after Ted's death. *Pompous?* Just because Ted had been all charm did not make Lincoln Johns "pompous." But then, what had he shared with Rose of Sharon? What had Lincoln Johns given in exchange for her time and care? A partner to watch Animal Planet, a program she would have preferred *not* to watch?

Bet brings two steaming cups in, sets them down on the round table and takes up the beer Rose of Sharon has barely touched.

"He was a little czar, Mom," she says. "I barely remember Granny Apple, but what I do remember is how all the chatter stopped in a kitchen when Granddad entered."

"No. It wasn't like that," Sharon says, but even as she says, *It wasn't like that* she remembers it was exactly so.

"He glowered," Bet says. "He was a glowerer."

Sharon nods her head to one side, studies the cup of tea centered on a saucer that does not match. Nothing in Buddy's home matches, whereas everything in the home of her parents had always matched, was never chipped, never wanting for symmetry or balance. If something tilted, it was set aright.

"He may have been a little stern," Sharon says. "He had sound principles." The plastic vases of flowers past their prime would not have been on a table in Lincoln Johns's home, or in Rose of Sharon's home during those months after Appelonia's death when Lincoln Johns lived there. "He wasn't a drunk. Or abusive. He was nothing like his father, Wilbur." Bet can't understand, or know, what Sharon knows about meanness in family relations. Lincoln Johns was not mean. "He wasn't mean," Sharon adds.

"Nor was he kind," Bet says.

To her surprise, Rose of Sharon says, "No; he wasn't kind."

These small discoveries are not new; Sharon has made them before. She has, in the past, been made suddenly aware of how cold her father could be—not *could be, was*. But they hid themselves away, these brief epiphanies, like a wristwatch that works, continues ticking (if wound) even after it's put inside a keepsake box or a drawer because the style does not fit the fashion or tastes of the would-be wearer. So it's put somewhere safe, somewhere special, somewhere that, in a little time, will be forgotten and allowed to run down.

There is no happy *Ah ha!* in finding that watch stuck down inside the toe of a sock.

Sharon blows steam across the top of the cup. Bet does the same. There is a question Sharon can't quite ask. It has something to do with knowing and not knowing her own flesh and blood. Who is this child, really? Certainly more Ted than Rose of Sharon. And who am I? Am I more

Lincoln than Appleonia? She shakes her head, a dismissive shake, and Bet says, "What?"

"Well. All that's true."

"About Granddad? True for me. Yes. True for you? Maybe. I was my daddy's girl and you were yours." A little drawer opens on a brocaded jewel box full of special keepsakes as Sharon realizes, not for the first time, what a gift this child is in her life.

"So," Bet says, looking from teacup to flowers to trunk to art on the walls and back to teacup.

"Of course I want you to stay. You must meet Buddy. He loves pretty girls. I doubt he'd forgive me if I let you leave without meeting him."

"And then?"

"And then I don't know," Sharon says.

Bet moves from her chair, teacup in hand, to the trunk. "Can we get inside this?"

"Yes. It's ours. Buddy's lure, remember, to get me here." Then the lid is open and Bet is on her knees in front of the moon and stars, pulling out the contents: a green felt cloche with a flattened feather; flat programs and posters advertising vaudeville shows; roughly framed caricatures of strange look-alike people touched with slight blushes of pink at the cheeks, blue rounds for eyes, two among them that seemed infants with oddly adult features; costumes so stiff they threatened to crack with unfolding.

Sharon kneels, too. "These things were all Irene's."

"Is this a kaleidoscope?" Bet's holding a length of bamboo with a cork in one end and no lens on the other. "Never mind. It's not. Tell me again — Irene was . . . ?"

"My father's aunt. And Buddy's. He used to fish her out of the ocean after she was shot from a —"

A knock at the door interrupts Sharon and Bet says, "Let me get it."

"Who knocks on the door? I mean, why didn't we hear the buzzer at the street door?" Sharon says, but Bet is already up and opening the door to the foyer and the young Korean man is there saying "Hello" and "I live upstairs. How is Buddy?"

"Hello!" Bet says, and "Come in, come in."

Oh no. Not him. Sharon uses the trunk to leverage herself up from the floor and moves to stand next to Bet who has already moved aside to usher the tenant from upstairs inside. She thinks about exposure, about Buddy, naked in a puddle of cold water, in the bathtub for hours, about the young Korean coming to his rescue, about how badly she had handled every moment of that awful morning.

Bet's strong hand is out, shaking his. "Bet Johns," she says, "another of Buddy's cousins."

"Kevin," he offers. "I live upstairs. Hello," he says, nodding toward Sharon. "How is my landlord doing?"

"Better, much better," Sharon says, returning his nod.

"Good. Very good." His glance around the room is brief and he says, "Will you tell Buddy I stopped by? I didn't mean to intrude."

Bet turns to Sharon and says, "You aren't intruding. Please, come in. Sit. Would you like some tea?"

She is thirty and in command, unexpectedly as in command of Rose of Sharon as ever Lincoln Johns had been, as ever Teddy Brown had been. Half the age of Sharon and solidly grounded about what will be and what will not. She is not terse, not stern, but charming. She has acquired Ted's handsome ways. She is disarming. She is looking for an out to her mother's boring company by inviting this unknown Asian inside a home she has laid claim to simply by being there.

"Kevin," Sharon says with a sudden crispness that brings both their attentions around. "I will tell Buddy you stopped in. He will be glad. And thank you . . . for the flowers, for this visit." Then Kevin is on the foyer side of the threshold, the door is closing, and Sharon, with her hands behind her on the doorknob, is leaning her back into it.

The expression on Bet's face is both perplexed and oddly amused, eyebrows lifted to wrinkle creases along her forehead, and the play of a smile at her mouth. She is Ted's child so totally and completely, amused by the silliest things, this sudden comeuppance—this countermanding of events. Bet says, "Hello? Mom? What was that all about?"

"What? Allowing our neighbor to go on about his business?"

"Is that what you call it?"

"More or less. Allowing us to get on with our business, too, I suspect."

"He's cute. He might've become 'my business' if you'd given me half a chance."

"He's on the second floor. Go on up. I'll clean up this mess." They both survey the trunk's contents spread over the floor, the sofa arm, leaned against the front of the sofa's skirt, hung off the top edge of the open door into Buddy's bedroom. The opaque sequins that had flown from the green hat and all else they'd taken from the trunk were everywhere—on everything—like fairy dust, but big and opalesque. Examining one stuck on the point of her finger, Bet says, "What are these from? I don't see any—"

"A costume. I hung it in my room. Those damned things just keep shedding; they're everywhere!"

"Is this her? Irene? She looks like a child." Bet holds a program taken from the trunk.

"What's the date? If it has one . . ."

"Nineteen-thirteen. But it's just penciled in."

"If the date's good, she was fourteen. She *was* a child."

"But this is a program for *An Aquatic Extravaganza!* You mean to say she headlined at the Hippodrome when she was fourteen?"

Sharon nods, unaware of the hole Bet is staring right through her because she is caught, totally captured by the face in the photo. Not the hippodrome program photo, but a studio photo she holds of a girl with a familiar face — almost painfully familiar. She could be looking at herself, not her near-sixty-year-old self, but her young self, at twelve or fourteen if, when that age, she had not always photographed as if stunned by the presence of the camera, if she had not frowned, if she had not glowered.

Stomachs are strange bodily organs. And hearts. And heads, or the brains, the gray matter within heads — all those neurons and synapses and whatever else transmitting what the eyes take in — directing a game of leap frog. Sharon's stomach seems to sit between her ears; her heart's settled into her womb; brain — *brain?* Sharon can't locate her thoughts, where they originate. The hands of Irene in the photo are plump with youth, but they move, squeeze the circa 1913 studio prop (a dark wooden chair back) with almost subtle impatience as Sharon grips the trunk's front open edge. Sharon, her lips closed, draws a deep intake of air through her nose. "Ivory," she says. "Ninety-nine percent pure. Bet?" Sharon asks, "Can you smell that? The soap?"

"Soap? No. Old gym socks, maybe." Bet is smiling at Rose of Sharon. A smile full of patience and charm and good humor. Sharon has looked away from Irene's portrait to her living daughter to find a remembrance of Teddy's smile, and when she looks back, at Irene, she and Irene are separate again. The Ivory Soap scent is ninety-eight percent gone.

Sharon will ask Bet to leave tomorrow after she visits Buddy. It may be awkward, but she will nudge her daughter back to Philly. The moon and stars trunk is open, its contents strewn about the room. She will fold them away, one by one—but she will do so at her own leisure, in her own time.

Rose of Sharon is, she's decided, like the Tony Curtis still life—a badly managed rendering of what the artist set to the canvas with a palette knife and awkward perspectives. Those who love and had loved her had done the best they could, but the self she'd become was, like Curtis's canvas, an abstract of the real thing.

She smiles at Bet and winks. "Yes. Fourteen. Hard to imagine." She doesn't say "I think she's my hero" or anything remotely as foolish at that.

"She reminds me of someone," Bet says, looking over Sharon's shoulder at Irene's studio photo.

"Yes," Sharon says, offering no opinion beyond her response and a nod. She does not say she sees herself there, or the self she might have become. She says nothing about finding an otherworldly twin to herself, one who possessed all the attributes Rose of Sharon so wants to own, one who, right or wrong, made her own broad strokes to the canvas.

BUDDY HAS A knot on his forehead and a new hip. The knot is the size of a strawberry and has tiny scabs patterned over it like strawberry seeds but black. When he fell in the tub he must have hit his head on the hard-bristled brush Sharon uses to massage her scalp. She can say nothing of his new hip, but the scabs on his forehead are so perfectly spaced, Sharon thinks her massage brush must be the cause. She leaves a light kiss just to one side of the scabs.

He says, "Go on, get outta here," but his gruffness is all show. When he adds, "If you don't stop blaming yourself, don't come back," he is grinning.

You, Sharon thinks, *don't know the half of it.* He'd been on a stretcher and carried out the front door when the tenant from upstairs ran a finger across the floor of the tub and said, "Slippery stuff." The tenant (what is his name?) had a buttery complexion with a face like a cub scout, and dark, dark eyes — black as motor oil with glints of rainbow green.

"And who is this standing in the doorway?" Buddy asks.

"Bet Brown," Bet says as she enters his room. She's wearing her black maxi coat with the tall collar and takes long strides to his bedside, extending her hand, offering one of her manly handshakes. "What a great thing to meet you."

"I might say the same," Buddy says. "What's that?"

He is looking at Bet's hands and a scrolled paper she holds rather gently as if to prevent creases.

"I'd hoped you might tell me," Bet answers.

"Questions already," Buddy says. "You *are* your mother's daughter."

Sharon touches the leaves on a houseplant someone has sent to cheer Buddy's hospital stay. "Speaking of that," Sharon says, "I was thinking about going out to Coney. I heard there's a little museum."

Buddy's forehead wrinkles below the knot as he looks from daughter to mother to the scroll in Bet's hands. "Speaking of what?" he says.

"Of questions," Sharon answers. "I thought I'd check out the Parks, what's left of what used to be there."

"Ah." Buddy nods. Some emotion flickers across his face,

an emotion she can't quite read, as if he wants to offer a caution but then reconsiders. Or he's thought of something but before he can put the thought to words it has vanished. She follows his glance away from her to the scroll. "Did you want me to check out whatever it is you've got there?" he asks.

"Oh. Yes," Bet says, not quite as in control as normal. "I'm headed home," she checks the wall clock across from Buddy's bed, "very, very shortly. In thirty-six minutes, to be exact, and I wondered if you knew anything about this — about who this might be?"

Buddy unfurls the scroll. It is slightly larger than a page from a paperback but many times thicker. "Ah," Buddy says. "The man himself."

"The man?" Bet says.

"Old Joseph Johns. My grandfather. I never met him, not that I recall. But I remember asking Grandmother and she said it was him, the one she left back at the farm." He stares at the faded watercolor and frowns as if trying to picture the grandmother he knew with this man that he'd never met.

"Strange-looking," Bet says.

"He is that." Buddy nods and hands back the scroll which had snapped into its tubular shape as if being unfurled was a physical pain to the paper.

For a moment Bet looks at the scroll in her hand. "Mom," she says, "will you put this back for me?"

Sharon accepts the portrait of Joseph Johns. She is not going back to the brownstone before she heads out to Coney, but she accepts what Bet has given her without question. It is what she does best. "M-m," she says with a nod.

Bet says, "I've got to leave or I'll miss my connection. Buddy, a pleasure to meet you. Take care of Mom."

"Mom can take care of herself," Sharon says. "Listen. I hate to do this, but I'm not headed back to the brownstone and this will get creased in my purse, so . . ." She holds the scroll out for Bet to take.

"Mom, I —"

Sharon lifts her brows as if to say, *Yes?*

"Here," Buddy says, "leave it with me. We'll put the man in the drawer here with my cell phone."

And then Bet is gone. Buddy is left with Rose of Sharon. This is the sense Sharon has of how Buddy feels: Left with Rose of Sharon. He says, "She's a fine girl. Must favor her dad."

Sharon nods, hesitates, says, "Yes, quite a lot. You know, don't you, I'm not going down to that museum out of morbid curiosity."

"Could you hand me that?" he asks, and Sharon picks up a pudding cup from his hospital table that's been pushed out of his reach.

"This?"

"Yes. Thanks. Never thought for a minute it was."

"It's that she, Irene" — Buddy has put his finger in the pudding cup and is scraping the remains off the side of the cup — "that she," Sharon continues, "lived *big,* and I" — He is sucking his finger, going back to scrape the cup one more time — "and I," she clears her throat, "and I feel like I need to know her."

"Need? What I need," he says, "is another one of these." Buddy offers an exaggerated sigh. His new hip is nothing but the empty pudding cup, *ah, well*—he may not survive an empty pudding cup!

She will not badger him with questions about Irene, not today. She will not ask *how* Irene's body had looked when he identified her for detectives. He talks easily of the good times but not the bad. When Sharon has asked him the names of the detectives, Buddy draws a blank. If she knew their names, and if, on the off chance they left behind records, notebooks scribbled with findings, well, that *would be something*. But Buddy can't or won't recall their names. The most he has offered is that one was jowly, the other one thin and Chinese, and that when he got out of their car (he remembers they drove a Packard), he left a hole, knuckle-deep, in the backseat's armrest upholstery.

"Listen," she says to Buddy, "I'm going there to look for the living Irene, not the dead one."

Buddy says, "Sure. Look, have a good time. Who was it said you needed to go in the first place? Me. So gid outta here, kid."

Olive's Heritage & The Heifer

PENNSYLVANIA

1909

rene Johns had paid little attention to the direction they headed in 1909. Before their departure from Williamsport, her mother and Budd had debated the advantages of heading north toward Elmira, New York, or south to Harrisburg and then west into Reading.

To Irene, ten at the time, all destinations were foreign. None were *home*. The end destination of Brooklyn held the appeal of its name. It must, she believed, have a *brook*. Flo's monotonous chanting of "Brook-brook-brook-lyn, brook-brook-brook-lyn," had caused Irene to consider this and caused Mae to reach across Irene's lap and pinch Flo's leg as a warning to stop. At seventeen Mae had an uneasy nervous condition that could not bear redundancies; even the repetitive nature of a meadowlark's call from the fence line put Mae on edge, caused an open window with a lovely breeze flowing through to be closed with such emphasis the framed glass shuddered. Flo, whose given name was "Florence" (after Aunt Florence, their mother Olive's sister), had stopped chanting, but the *brook-brook-brook* of Flo's tinny voice had, by then, taken hold of Irene's imagination.

Wedged between Mae (who, by the nature of her name and the nervous edge to her personality, had never been given a nickname or called anything other than Mae) on her right, and a now-quiet Flo on her left in the back of the Winton, Irene was *not* happy. She was miffed. And righteously so. She was not prone to scowls. Her broad grin was as natural to her countenance as moonrise was to the night. Not at ten, nor at thirty, would Irene conceal a smile to hide some physical imperfection. At thirty, that imperfection would be a chipped tooth; at ten it was the gaps between permanent teeth still growing in. Not of a dissembling nature, when she was miffed, she was *miffed* and her pout was full-on.

If Irene had any presumptions about her own appearance, pouting or otherwise, *pretty* would not be among them. That her little-girl lips were full was, if she made such comparisons (which she did not), *not* a thing of *beauty*, not in the fashionable sense, and especially not when compared to the perfect confection of little Flo's tiny mouth. "Like a rosebud, a perfect pink rosebud," was the consensus among the senior Johns, and Joseph Johns had rendered the same in his portraiture of little Florence, diluting rose madder in his tin of watercolors to match the fragility of Flo's bud-like lips. Indeed, in the decades to follow, Flo's prettiness of features and golden curls would carry her down a road to not one husband but three.

But in June 1909, the Winton's engine roaring along like wooden spoons beating a drum, the road to Brooklyn (by way of Harrisburg and Reading) was the course they followed. And if Irene's full-on pout of full lips was described as a sulky scowl, whereas Flo's expression, even at the tender age of seven (in response to Mae's pinch) was thought of as *simpering*, well, so be it.

Members of Irene's family, her immediate family—
although *most* would never consciously admit to it—were
handsome. The exception was Mae who, even in sleep,
seemed unable to relax. Her features did so want to jump
about inside her skin. It may have been Mae's unease, cou-
pled with the physical angularity of her jaw line and an odd
shift in the line of her nose (just where that little bump from
an early fracture remained, fourteen years later), that kept
her on the shy side of *handsome*. It was impossible to say.
Not that Mae was studied by other family members as she
slept. But there had been that one time when Flo had wet the
bed and Irene was forced to move into bed with Mae.

Irene, who could sleep through anything—*anything*,
would have slept right through the spread of warm urine over
the sheets, incorporating the warmth into a current of Loyalsock Creek where it fed from a sunny pool into the shadows
of whatever she dreamed. She would have, if allowed. But
no. Olive awakened her, yanked the sheets from the mattress,
and that had been that. Irene found herself plucked from
dreamland and the currents of Loyalsock and plunked down
alongside Mae—Mae, who whispered in broken ways the
almost-words of an unpleasant place. Not continually. If this
had been the case, Irene could've slipped back into dream-
time as if to the ticking of a familiar clock. Instead, it was
as if she'd been placed next to a dog with a flea. Some peace
would come—as if the dog of Mae's sleeping self had circled then settled to nap—then the flea would bite and Mae
would scratch with a flinch of her leg or small broken gasps,
little snorts that weren't quite yips, and Irene's eyes would
flutter open, yet again, with wonder about why she should be
punished in such a way—not Flo, but herself, Irene. She had
not been the one to wet the bed.

Irene learned from these small injustices of girlhood. Not in any way that she would recollect as particular "learning experiences" or look back upon in later life to view as tiny steps toward understanding the nature of Justice versus Injustice—but, subconsciously, they would stick. "Life" and its accumulated actions (and inactions) would rarely be considered by Irene with any great depth, even more rarely in metaphorical terms. Irene was not that kind of thinker.

The truth, as evidenced by her hasty jump from the sycamore platform and very nearly suiciding at the end of her cape, was that she was preternaturally propelled *forward*. To her credit, she never jumped, made a dive, or exited an amusement park cannon wearing any item of costume that might jeopardize her safety again—but in the waters of *life* not yet tested, she remained, perhaps, overzealous.

This enthusiasm for adventure, especially in all areas athletic—more precisely in all things water-related, caused her mother no small amount of concern. Olive Johns's stubbornly ungovernable girl confounded Olive almost daily—always had done. To say Olive prided herself on a certain ability to cut through nonsense and get straight to the heart of any matter under consideration would be an overstatement. That she did just that was true, but there was no pride involved—merely fact. In the same way she could ferret out all the ingredients of an above-average casserole at a church potluck without asking the contributor of that casserole about its preparation, Olive knew the exact measurements of her offspring. And she knew these within the first six months (one year on the outside) of their births. Excepting Irene.

Olive Talbot Johns had grown up with the sure knowledge that she was more a product of her father, Millard Talbot, than she was of her mother, Margaret Louise Hillard.

If considered in a quirky, round-about way (not natural to Olive's manner of thought), Margaret Louise Hillard had already delivered five children (to a previous husband) by the time Olive was born, whereas her second husband, Millard, had fathered only one. It could follow, from a child's perspective, that there was *more* of Millard to be added to the mix that would eventually become Olive than Margaret Louise Hillard could allow. After all, Margaret Louise would bear four more children after Olive—some features of physical appearance, not to mention personality, would, in those mysterious ways of God and Nature, have been held back, in reserve so to speak.

Olive Talbot Johns's pinky fingers angled in toward the ring fingers on each of her hands. It was an angle that could not be straightened and the only feature inherited from Margaret Louise; the rest was pure Millard. Where Millard made a handsome boy and, as a young man, had a no-nonsense way of getting at things—whether that "getting at" was physically, with a steady and purposeful stride, or mentally, through uncluttered thought processes, Olive made a handsome woman who, equally, "got at" things. She was not one, nor would she ever be, to be likened to a fine wine with all its complexities; rather—if such comparisons were required—Olive was a stout brew.

If an element of pride existed within Olive, it was in the man her father was. Her admiration of Millard Talbot was boundless.

At the same time, Olive Johns had considerable affection, if not respect, for each of her own children. To think in terms of "respect" applied to a child was one of those nonsensical ways of thinking, a trait neither she, nor her father, Millard, would have indulged in. Respect was a factor to be earned;

Olive believed her younger offspring would build and grow, eventually earning her respect, just as had happened with her eldest children. Oneska, the oldest ("Nessie" as she was known in the family), was already a wife and mother with a hardworking, Methodist husband, and excellent prospects for a sound future. Budd (Olive's right arm) had proved himself to be someone she could rely upon, when the need arose, in ways his father, Joseph Johns, had revealed himself as incapable of mastering. Budd, in Olive's estimation, was darn near the man Millard Talbot was — and that was no small amount of *respect* to place at a young man's feet.

True, Mae was of an age that Olive could wish for better results. But, there had been a stunted old peach tree on the farm that had, eventually, produced a sweeter fruit than all the others. (Olive put the thought out of her mind that Mae might have more Margaret Louise Hillard root stock about her than a mother would wish for in her child.)

As for little Wilbur and pretty Flo — time would tell, but if physical beauty were to sculpt its way around to include the kind of internal character necessary to earn respect, they would be more than fine. Edison? Well, Edison *was* fifteen in the summer of 1909; all eventualities, Olive had to admit, were possible with that boy.

It was Irene that vexed Olive beyond a point that she felt comfortable being vexed — had done so since a few days of her birth. At her mother's breast, Irene had nursed with, not a vengeance, but such wild abandon that she could not contain all of her mother's milk, and there it would come back, cascading in warm milky-blue to cover Olive's bosom. Pulling away from the infant when Olive's motherly instinct told her it was time, brought on a writhing and wailing not easily borne. But Olive had borne it, for nourishment's sake. It was not gluttony; a child is not capable of gluttony. Nor was this a Joseph Johns feature; Olive could not ascribe *wild abandon* to any facet of Joseph Johns's actions or character; in fact, a little *wild abandon* might have made a difference in their jungle-papered bedroom. Nor was this an Olive Talbot Johns trait; if seasoned with a generous amount of good common sense, it might have been—but, to date, what sense Irene *chose* to exhibit was seldom *common* and often put one among them in jeopardy; generally, Irene herself.

IT HAPPENED AFTER repairs had been made to the Winton on Neversink Mountain—just after the sky went the color of lavender when the June sun dropped behind the hills. The fault was not Irene's—her pout had long since relaxed into the open slackness of sleep. Mae, Irene and Flo were a tumble of dominoes in the Winton's back seat, all leaned and slouched toward Wilbur (once again in Edison's lap). All but Edison dozed. Olive, who had thought to relieve Budd and give his hands a break from clutching the Winton's steering wheel, had commandeered the driver's seat once they made flatter ground. But driving was not her forte.

Budd, having regained the position of chauffeur after Olive's brief foray, felt a calm exuberance. His mother's timidity with the power of the big touring car had never lessened. *Acceleration* was his, when the road allowed. Often a series of switchbacks, the road now ran before him like a curled ribbon gently stretched and pressed to relatively level, serpentine curves. He was in his element. Trees rushed by at a pretty fast rate on either side, and a thread of hope remained that he might get the family to a boarding house his mother had arranged for them to stay at that evening. Then the road,

often little more than wagon ruts cut through the countryside and never far from the banks of the Susquehanna,
offered up a loose heifer.

Budd tried to steer clear, while "Cow! Cow!" rang with
alarm above the wooden-spoon drum-roar of the car. Olive's
shouts were two broken legs on a brown-eyed Jersey too late.
There was not enough road for both.

When the cow stopped the car, Flo and Irene rolled to the
floor in the back. Edison clutched little Wilbur more closely.
He remained asleep, as did Mae, in her twitchy way. Of
course, the car stopped the cow, but not dead.

"Mama!" Budd groaned in exasperation.

Olive looked hard at her oldest son through the streaked
dirt on her goggles.

"What!"

He could not see her eyes through the dirt on the driving
glasses, but she could see him. He thought, *If we'd just driven
north to Elmira, New York, we'd be there by now. But no . . .*

"What?" Budd echoed back; he hadn't moved, and he didn't
remember he'd called out her name.

From the back floorboard, Irene asked, "What's that noise?"

"It's nothing, Stick," Budd said.

"It's *something*," Irene responded.

"Stay down back there, Stick. You okay? Flo okay?" Budd
asked. "Mama? Are you all right?"

There was a fine trickle of red from a scratch on Olive's
forehead; Budd saw it and pulled out his handkerchief just
as Olive said, "I'm fine."

"You're not fine," he said, and leaned across to daub at the
cut, while Irene, insisting, said, "Can't you *hear that*, Budd?
Mama?"

"Irene, be still and shush *now*," Olive told her, but Irene was up and over the side of the Winton and out on the road next to the bellowing cow before "now" passed Olive's lips.

The young cow was smaller than Joseph Johns's Holsteins and dusty-colored, the same pale shade as the road. Yellow bones splintered through the hide of both her back legs and Irene had never, for all her ten years of life on the farm, heard anything so pitiful. Its great dark eyes rolled back to expose more white than brown, but Irene threw herself at the cow's head with the need of a frantic mother to calm a child she loved.

"There, there, there," she soothed then began to hum Joseph's lullaby.

Budd was up and over his side of the car in a heartbeat. "Irene! You wanna be killed or somethin'? Back off from out of there, Stick. C'mon. Back off."

Olive stood in the car, tall behind the windshield, shouting, "I *will* tan your hide! Do you hear me? Irene!"

Then Edison was there with no Wilbur and Irene was snatched as the panicked cow swung her broad head up in a wild arc, trying to rise but unable with her mangled legs. The cow's head slammed Irene (her face would stay bruised for some weeks). She went out, without a wince, in Edison's arms. The Winton's front bumper and grillwork held up; the Winton was built of strong stuff.

Twilight was gone when Irene came back to her senses. The cow was gone, too — she didn't know where. She knew she was on a wide quilt that smelled like old apples and liniments, that her head was in Olive's lap, that Flo was holding one hand and Wilbur the other. Mae sat with her back to the rest of them, watching the road. There wasn't much to see of the road — a fuzzy plum-colored rust against a backdrop of black forest.

There was blood in Irene's mouth and, shoving her tongue against the bottom molars on the left side, a couple teeth felt loose. "Where's Budd? And Edison — Mama, where are our boys?"

When Budd and Edison returned, long links of towing chain spiraled back into the Winton's storage area for future use.

Sing Cheung's Potential Peace

CHINA TOWN, NEW YORK CITY

1909

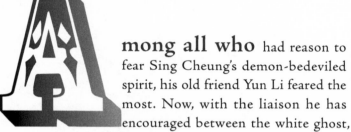 **mong all who** had reason to fear Sing Cheung's demon-bedeviled spirit, his old friend Yun Li feared the most. Now, with the liaison he has encouraged between the white ghost, Ellie Bowles, and Sing's most honorable son, Moses, Yun Li often smiles and claps the backs of the waiters in Heung Fat's Noodle House. Frequently, his heavy-handed gladness causes Deshi, the oldest among them, to falter. Laden with heavy trays, Deshi has thus far recovered, continued to service Hueng Fat's ravenous patrons. But it is perilous, this joy of Yun Li's over the good joss befallen Moses. Perilous for frail Deshi.

Yun Li's joy began the previous fall with the initial pleasuring union of Moses with the white ghost. Aiyee! Yun Li has shared with Deshi, and all who would listen, "That she is white is a misfortune. But the potential for Sing Cheung's peace is worth this small sacrifice." The community agrees. It is good joss, this liaison. And to have found her so soon after the Mission House Quaker, Benjamin Smith, had departed, leaving Moses without a tutor—further good joss!

There is a red trunk pushed against the wall and a paper picture of Jesus thumb-tacked to the doorframe of a room two floors above Heung Fat's Noodle House. This room is where Moses lives. This room, Moses has told Ellie when she complains about the malodorous air, was procured for him by Yun Li.

The cot creaks. Air from the window lifts the paper picture of Jesus again and again. She will buy a frame for the print; there is, Ellie believes, something unseemly about air blowing in through a cracked window to trifle with Jesus in such an off-handed manner. The eyes of Ellie Bowles are more hazel than the brown eyes an illustrator has given Jesus in the print; Ellie's skin is a paler shade of white, but would be, she has decided on more than one occasion, as she has never lived in the Holy Land or even seen an olive tree except at the botanical gardens. She has not the longish face, nor the wide shoulders of this Jesus; her hair is not brown but an almost white-blond. It was white, but yellowed to a honey-gold in her teens and is perhaps three times the length of her Savior's as depicted. She glides her hands down the back of Moses, stays them at his hips, as narrow as hers and she is, by all accounts, small-statured as womenfolk go. Her hands follow his hips' movements; her eyes follow the movements of Jesus.

She believes herself overtly spoiled, the consequence of a fine pedigree and the boring sameness of wealth. Yet, wealth has its limits. Nearly ten years into the twentieth century, restrictions placed upon young socialites forbade activities deemed "too excitable for a young lady's well-being." Ellie Bowles is not easily *forbade* her least desire, much less what has become a minor obsession. The print of Jesus rolls upward and back.

On the other hand, she is no fool. She knows of young women who have been put into asylums in order to save them from themselves. She does not know these young women personally, but through stories via a well-intentioned aunt.

Ellie's mother died young. There are, Ellie has noted, few rumors and little said about that. Aside from an old-fashioned portrait on a porcelain oval the size of a gentleman's monocle, Ellie knows next to nothing of Belinda Bowles. It has been a very long time since she has asked any questions of her aunt. To ask her father or grandfather is out of the question. Such questions put her father off to such a degree he finds himself in need of a trip to somewhere beyond New York City. Her grandfather was quite deaf, and her aunt, when queried, seems always to find a way around any direct response—alluding, within a day or a week of Ellie's girlhood curiosity, to the perils of too much passion.

Ellie Bowles is cleverer by half than to continue to cause discomfort of any kind to those who would bring her sugared cookies and make certain that flowers cut from the garden by household staff stayed free of browning petals.

Ellie knows herself to be no great beauty, not even pretty, not in the way her dead mother may have been, but neither is she a dullard. She has long understood the power of reputation, the threat she might pose to her grandfather and aunt by appearing less than she has been trained to be. She had reactivated her interest in church life with a vigor soon touted as half angel, half saint. Her work with poor immigrants at the Mission House, while such work teetered on the edge of acceptable for a young woman of her social status, has been allowed. Ellie has been lauded for her charitable heart, her tendencies to do good works and, until very recently, excruciatingly bored. At present, she is a good deal less bored.

The next time the wind riffles the print on the doorframe, her body tremors its own release and she bites into Moses's shoulder with her small teeth.

"Ellie," he says.

"Aerie," she corrects. She has never desired Moses to change in any physical way. He is exotic. He is smooth as ivory and exquisite. He is beautiful, whereas she is not.

"Ellie," he persists, "forgive this humble question, but has your honorable grandfather been able to procure my permissions to honor my father's tomb?"

"Permission," Ellie corrects. He has rolled from her body and she begins to dress.

"Has he?" Moses asks.

"There is no justification for such a visit, Moses."

"No justification?" He seems to be digesting her answer, quietly pulling on his cotton pants.

She stands, plucks at the edges of a silk flower on her waistband. The flower is nearly the size of the face of Jesus in the picture by the door. These continual queries from Moses regarding his father's remains reduce her pleasures, considerably.

"No justification," he says again.

She answers by moving her head from side to side, slowly but decisively. She is working the lower part of her braid back into presentable shape. When she is finished braiding, she will wind it into an "S" configuration and hairpin the rope she has made into place. She will not ask Moses to apply the hairpins as she has asked in the past.

He responds with his own side-to-side headshake. His hands hang loose, almost as if unconnected to the ends of his arms; his arms rest like levers across the fulcrums of his knees. "*No justification,*" he repeats a third time, barely audible, almost a hiss, and Ellie raises her brows at this sibilance. If she didn't know Moses better, after all these months of what he calls "pleasuring," she would consider his tone insolent.

"My father's," he pauses, seems to be crafting what he will say, or fighting off anger he hardly knows how to contain. "My father's beloved soul is troubled. Does this not trouble you? He has no peace. He is tormented and without rest and persecuted by every form of malevolent devil. Is this not *justification?*"

She holds the hairpins between her lips, removes them one by one and sets the S-shaped braid of hair in place at the nape of her neck. Air in the alley has calmed; the picture is still. She wonders, briefly, why she brought Him into this room. For her own spiritual protection? As a potential guide for Moses? A moral reminder that she sinned, and sins often?

She picks up a gray glove and begins the arduous task of fitting her hand through the opening. "Your father is beloved," she says, "just as Jesus is beloved by Our Father in heaven. There are no torments, Moses. There are no devils besieging him." Ellie knows Sing Cheung had not, to anyone's knowledge, accepted Christ as his savior before his untimely death. Moses has told her that "the knock" had come more than once upon the door to his father's soul and Sing had not answered. But this does not mean, Ellie reasons, that he didn't harbor, in his innermost heart, the desire to answer and be saved.

She has managed the closure of all the fabric-covered buttons at the wrist of one glove. She is petite, with the exception of her hands and feet, and the gloves, dove-gray, are specific to her needs, special-ordered from a glove factory in Philadelphia. She picks up the second glove, settles her skirts as she sits on the trunk, a trunk the color of dead roses, a trunk that is an eyesore. She says, "This is difficult to explain, but I will try, again. The mysteries of God are not for us to understand. We must leave these matters to Him. I believe your father knows peace. And you—"

"My father is driven about, beaten by demons as if in the hell of your Jesus, and I am not allowed to honor him? To ease him by showing that I am a dutiful son?"

"Rubbish," she says.

The door slams and riffles the picture, briefly, as Moses leaves.

Lynn Doiron

Part III

Poseidon's Museum

haron avoids men holding signs. "Will work for food" at unexpected intersections is off-putting. She doesn't make eye contact, rolls the car window up when she's driving. *Why is that?* On foot, she shrugs off an uncomfortable coldness, her pace as brisk leaving the museum as it had been getting there. She's made her way past the groaned roar of guy wires, stabilizers of some sort for a stories-high telescoping column with no visual reason for being—not that she can determine—other than providing the wires *something* to stabilize. The groaned roar is fearsome, a sound she could hear through her feet. Tragic. Hollow. Aching. Before realizing the source, she imagined tar-pit dinosaurs roaring their last anguished breaths, the vibrations of eons of past pain quivering the air she breathed.

A stabilized pole? Signifying nothing? She turns, walks backward, lets her eyes thaw from the flash-freeze of frigid air, blinks at what she leaves behind.

What would possess a woman to climb inside a cannon? Did she not understand? Like the dinosaurs didn't get what the trap was until they were in too deep?

She has walked a mile, maybe three, facing forward until her eyes feel like frozen grapes, walking backwards and then forward again. She needs to find Atlantic Avenue, the street Lorraine, Poseidon Museum's volunteer, has written instructions to locate.

Because Sharon's feet are numb, she imagines Irene inside the cannon, feet braced and numb with cold, waiting for Wilbur to give her the signal, knowing he sometimes failed in that quarter, that she must stay rigid and ready to flex with the spring of the lever. Were her feet as numb as Sharon's?

Taking in the Atlantic, she notes again how lumpy it seems, like cottage cheese of a wrong color, like oatmeal—not at all like the Pacific. The museum had not been what she'd expected. Neither old nor imposing, the single-story structure was plain as a shoebox, a simple sign hung from chains: Poseidon Park Museum.

Artifacts inside had been as sparse as Buddy's hair, cases holding them smudged with handprints, enough smudges that—if placed end to end—could circumnavigate the globe.

"Do you have anything here about Irene Johns?" Sharon had asked.

"Irene Who?"

"Johns."

"Never heard of her."

"Sometimes she used a stage name. Madame Alexie M.?" Sharon said.

Lorraine shook her head. She was watching a soap opera on a small TV tucked into a bookcase behind the counter. Sharon had the impression Lorraine would've liked to say, Shh! but the music rose to new heights and someone selling toothpaste caused her to turn down the volume.

"Madame Alexie M.," Lorraine said.

"Yes. Or Irene Johns." A pair of bright clown shoes—yellow, green, blue, red—every piece of stitched leather another primary color—sat under the smudged glass countertop. "Or," Sharon adds, "anything about cannons. The cannons people were shot from? Human cannon balls?"

Lorraine stood, rubbed the small of her back. "This sitting does me in."

Sharon nodded.

"You might take a look at the video."

She followed Lorraine's nod toward a back corner. Another television, slightly larger than the tiny one Lorraine watched, was there. Two rows of folding chairs were arranged in a quarter-circle out from the set.

Lorraine said, "I've got time to set it up for you, if you're interested."

"Yes. Please." If Sharon was curt, so be it. Friendly warmth was no longer a commodity. Her freezing jaunt had frozen what manners she'd had, made her brittle, as patient as melting ice.

Seated in the nearest chair, the farthest away from the end wall, Sharon watched Lorraine start the video, move behind the TV and draw a window shade down.

"There. All set?" It wasn't a question; Lorraine's soap opera had resumed and she'd resumed her seat behind the counter in less time than Sharon imagined possible for a woman her age.

The video started. No sound. No knob. No remote to bring the sound up. When Sharon turned to call Lorraine back, she noticed the end wall wasn't wall but floor-to-ceiling glass. Light through the side window behind the TV had glared off the glass in such a way it had only seemed a wall. Rising to investigate, Sharon found the display full of photos and mementos from Poseidon's heydays. A poster caught her attention. Then a pennant. And another. A chipped sign with hand-painted names. A red megaphone with a huge number 5 and the cents sign in black on the side.

While the silent video ran its course, Sharon examined the case contents: a stuffed dog (real, not a plush toy) wearing a clown's red-trimmed white ruff; an ebony walking stick with a tarnished silver knob worked in the shape of an overblown rose; a long, panoramic photograph of the tiered seating that rose up from Poseidon's ocean-side stage. Sharon's ungloved hands pressed the smudged glass, her forehead leaned against it.

The tiered stands in the photo were packed. White straw boaters the men wore stood out crisp and stark amid an abundance of darker hats. Black and white and shades of gray, the photo had a diver, in the foreground, toward the right. The diver, a woman, wore a white bathing suit and white bathing cap. Poised to dive from a tower platform, she seemed the photographer's primary target. On the diver's right, a ramp angled up to a higher tower and a horse, not much bigger than a pony, also white, neared the top of the ramp. "I bet she's a horse diver," Sharon said to no one but herself.

"What's that?" Lorraine said.

Sharon pointed at the glass, pointed at the wide-angle shot of the stands and the crowds that once paid to take seats in those high-stacking tiers and the horse-diving woman, the horse. Whatever she intended to say to Lorraine stuck in her throat.

Irene was staring out from the middle ground of the long photo.

Sharon knew that face! Knew it from tintypes and newsprint photos she and Bet had turned in their hands. *Was it just yesterday? Now, Irene, a big-as-life smile, right here, behind the glass!*

And behind Irene, in all its glory, the Texaco cannon!

Irene and the cannon were hardly more than variations of a vast array of gray tones. The white-suited diver and white pony running up the ramp took the eye of ordinary beholders. Then Sharon spotted the glimmer of white from Irene's full-blown smile, tiny in the photo, but unmistakable. Sharon had known it as well as she knew her own face.

Lorraine didn't have access to the display case. Knowing who provided the contents, she made a call, scribbled notes, and handed them to Sharon. "This man, Theo, owns everything in the case, including that photo. It's a print. He says the original's in color. Take it from me, you can't always trust everything that man says. For a price, he says he can make you a copy."

"Where is this?" Sharon asked.

"Not too far. A couple, three miles. You'll wanna cut through to the street that runs parallel. Here," Lorraine had said, suddenly a true-blue, dyed-in-the-wool volunteer, "let me draw you a map. I'm always happy to send the ex a little business." She smiled.

The smile seemed genuine enough, but Sharon suddenly felt a little gullible, a little wary of east-coast ways, a little suspect.

SHARON STUDIES THE scrap of paper in hand, turns right. Buildings on either side of the street block the onslaught of freezing wind as she continues.

The photo—mischievous guile "writ large," as Bet would say, on the face of the woman before the cannon—is foremost in her thoughts. She's certain Irene knew the camera was there, certain Irene had grinned it down, along with the cameraman, as if they were Davy Crockett's bears. Would Sharon have found that lens and pinned it with her smile? She shakes her head. All photos of Sharon are essentially the same: she blinks; she turns aside; she attends to anything other than facing head-on whatever was, or is, before her.

Her blue woolen scarf is slack around her shoulders. She is cold but a cold not as bothersome as it had been when Irene was all ghost, when the cannon seemed myth or bad fiction.

Ahead of her an old man walks his short, fat bulldog. Short and fat also, the man and dog seem a match—both khaki brown and white in what they wear. As she passes, the man says, "Selma, heel," and the dog sits, tongue lolling. Bulldogs can't smile, but Sharon could swear this one is. Beyond them on the sidewalk, she grins, struck by a sudden awareness of Buddy as a boy, of Pal, of them galloping down stairs to meet Irene in the brownstone's foyer. She turns to wave at the man and Selma, but they are not looking her way.

Resuming forward motion, she picks up her pace to find the store with the owner of the original photo. Then it hits her: the photo behind the screen of glared-over glass was not, *not* what she'd thought at all. Irene hadn't focused on the photographer. She'd been peering into a future, looking across years into a time she was eager to meet. *She was looking at me!* Sharon thinks. *At me. This generation, us, here, in the now. At the children she knew would come, as Buddy had come to Budd. And Lincoln to Wilbur. And Rose of Sharon to Lincoln.*

Irene had grinned down—not bears but time, to find the face of her grand niece. And she had.

AT THE CORNER, Sharon waits as a car passes. The store, Mister Junque's Atlantic Avenue Collectibles Emporium, is across the way. She's giddy, feels Irene walking next to her, in tandem, step for step. There's a determination, a happy determination in their strides. Irene is as happy as Rose of Sharon for this, this epiphany of kinship. Here, then, is Rose of Sharon, alive on a street parallel with the ocean, separated from the bumpy, oatmeal sameness of it all by the presence of a long-dead aunt, and eagerly intent upon borrowing (how else to think about it?) from that aunt's, Irene's, bigger-than-life *life*.

Sharon stops.

If there'd been people coming behind her, they'd have had no time to dodge where she stood, side-by-side with the ghost of Irene.

This is about you. Not me. This is about your life, not mine. You're asking me 'What happened? How is it I am dead so long?'

Tutors and Advisors

*ubbish!*
Moses leans his forehead into the hall wall. *Rubbish,* she has said in answer to his pleas. It seems what is most necessary of understanding is not understood, by either of them. They are occupants of different worlds; they do not speak the same language; they will not survive this chasm in understanding.

He lifts his head, stares at the filthy wall. How has he come to this place? He has escaped from her presence, escaped from his room one floor down where slop jars wait outside closed doors to be emptied. The stench on this level is less—but the foul odor pervading his spirit is stronger. He needs Benjamin. What would his friend, his first tutor in the new ways, say to him? He would not say *Rubbish.* Gone from Mission House, Benjamin is not absent from Moses's heart— nor his mind.

Remembering the drawing, Moses is back in the Mission House on Grant Street with its large blue cross painted above the door where immigrants and missionaries enter. They come to help and be helped. But it is the Quaker

Benjamin Smith who comes to share and to be shared with. It is Benjamin, his desires to understand himself within the family of man, who expands his Quaker beliefs to encompass what others believe. Moses is the student, the son of the old ways of Sing Cheung, in need of understanding the new, in need of learning the language of English. Yet Benjamin is, equally, student, in need of knowing the old, the wisdom of great Asia.

Moses sees the drawing Benjamin made as they studied English. He had asked about China—how people there lived, how they were employed. His way was round about.

"In Pennsylvania," Benjamin said, "there are many trees and rivers. We use the trees to build houses and wagons and make axe handles to cut down more trees." The small smile on Benjamin's face as he looked up from his drawing of an axe, of a felled tree, of a house built of straight lines with a chimney is present in Moses's mind. He had returned the smile, understanding the word "axe" and how, through the machinations of others, a tree became a weapon to be used upon itself.

In the hallway one level up from his room, Moses whispers to the filthy wall: "Is Ellie a weapon carved out of beliefs to cut down the beliefs of my father?" He has not been able to leave the building. His mind is in need of calm.

Benjamin, nineteen when Moses was seventeen, had continued, "The rivers are full of fish we catch." A student at Pennington Seminary, he was Sing Cheung's tutorial choice out of all the possible tutors at Pennington. Moses lowers his head. This choice had been made before his father's departure for England. His father would not have chosen Ellie; his father possessed wisdom that Moses did not.

Benjamin had said, "Boats and barges move on the rivers

from town to town. Are there rivers in your China, Moses? Are there trees?"

"This is my China," Moses had told him. "I am born here."

"We are both Americans, then!" Ben had exclaimed.

Looking up and down the shabby third-floor hall, Moses slumps, weary of his father's beliefs and his own. Below, in the room where he angrily left Ellie, there is a letter his father left. It is dated May 23, 1907. It advises *Moses, son of Sing Cheung: Use time wisely. Mission House Quaker Smith is good. He educate for America. Yun Li is good. He guidance for old ways. He guidance from mischief. I return before Tsing Ming. We educate old father in way of new bliss.*

Is it proper, Moses wonders, *to ache for a river to move me from here, to want for the fellowship of Benjamin?* "If you had returned, as promised, Venerable Father, all would be as fate would allow." The walls and stairwell absorb Moses's words. At street level, there is Yun Li. Fate has allowed this guide for old ways to remain. *Aiyee,* Moses sighs.

IN THE ALLEY behind Heung Fat's, Yun Li exhales. Sing Cheung is dead for two years and his bones are yet unclaimed. He counts his forty-third knee bend, rising from where he squatted. He draws a great breath. His rhino chest expands. His clean-shaven head shines with sweat. Without the auspices of Sing Cheung as his benefactor, Yun Li might have remained a beggar in Shanxi Province, a mongrel cur who could only find scraps to eat when he bit the hand that held them. Good joss had placed Yun Li in the path of Sing Cheung on a day when Sing Cheung stumbled on a busy road. Good joss Yun Li had no money for dice in the alley that day; good joss Yun Li could pull Sing Cheung and the trunk containing all the tools of his tonsorial trade from the path of horses and wagon.

He counts his forty-sixth knee bend. He has guided Moses in Sing's absence. Aiyee! He has given attentions to Moses with better care than he offers his first infant son from the womb of his concubine. If only his wife could produce sons and not more worthless girls! But she is fat now, with a third, and, if good joss prevails, perhaps this one will be male. A strong boy — not dainty like Moses.

His count falters. Any male child will be honored. He will light incense at the Joss House and ask if his misleading thoughts may do harm to the unborn and what, if any, remedies may be procured to undo the harm.

Aiyee! And the ghost with yellow hair.

Yun Li grunts. He completes forty-nine, fifty knee bends and sits on a broad stump used to hack off the heads of chickens. Old blood has turned the wood as black as his cooking pots inside Heung Fat's. Settled, he considers his efforts, the advice he has given young Moses in Sing Cheung's absence.

He shakes his head. Moses was wrong to take up an apprenticeship with Sing Cheung's barbers. Yun Li nods. Sing Cheung had made the community aware with an announcement when Moses was small as a swan that his son would attend university. That Moses would be a man learned in the ways of America, in the ways of law.

Yun Li shakes his head. *Aiyee!* What choice did the boy have? He needed money to bribe the greedy officials to release Sing Cheung's revered bones from that place.

Yun Li nods, flexes his beefy hands. *I do what is best by making a place for Moses here to earn wage. Bad joss for Deshi is good joss for Moses.*

Yun Li shrugs. Sometimes he misses the small ancient

waiter he had worked with since coming to America; sometimes he does not. Joss is joss. He shrugs again.

His head bobbles from left to right and back again. The yellow-haired ghost offered such promise, he thinks. Now it is summer. Now it is 1909, the year of the rooster. The ghost has been pleasured well and often by Moses. Why does she withhold her influence? Why does she fail to intercede on behalf of Sing Cheung's spirit?

Yun Li wipes his forearm across his forehead; his forearm is as big as Moses's thigh and speckled with flour run through with dampening sweat. He fears the unhappy spirit of Sing Cheung, wild and roaming, lost without peace as his bones remain interred in devil-ground. He nods. By appeasing Sing's spirit with the educational successes of Moses, Yun Li could be safe. But, Yun Li shakes his head, this white ghost has been a mistake. Very bad joss she found Moses.

Finding fault with the actions he has undertaken in Sing Cheung's behalf is difficult. He had not consulted the Joss House crescents when Moses first mentioned her name. In this alley he had listened to Moses and nodded with solemnity as the young woman's family connections were revealed; with each revelation, prospects for the recovery of Yun Li's mentor, Sing, improved. And, Yun Li lifts his meaty forearms up from his knees, when Moses related the closeness with which the young woman leaned into his arm, sitting, as Moses reported she so often did, next to him rather than across from him at the table in the Mission House, or how she placed her hand near Moses's, the gloved thumb of hers touching the small finger of his—*Aiyee!* Yun Li, his gold tooth shining with pleasure, had known exactly what to say!

Yun Li's arms lower. In Cantonese he berates himself, hisses "Aiyee!" to the empty alley. "I was wrong. Bad joss I did not consult joss that day." He wags his head, scratches his non-existent nails through the fretwork of speckled flour. His gold tooth is hidden, a sign of his thoughtful ruminations.

"Aiyee," he had said to Moses in the beginning. "That she is white is a pity. But, Moses, this you will put aside."

Perhaps, Yun Li thinks, Moses could not hide his disgust. Perhaps Moses had not been so good at pleasuring the white ghost.

Good joss for Yun Li that such a requirement had not been desired of him; bad joss for the yellow-haired woman. Yun Li's gold tooth shows when he considers the great wealth of his manhood. Yes, he nods. *Bad joss for her.*

Seated in the alley, he is waiting for Moses to show for work because today he has advised the son of Sing Cheung to remember his father. He has advised Moses to be firm in his petitions for help from the yellow-haired ghost. And clear in his English.

MOSES HAS PROMISED Yun Li a report. He moves along the filthy wall. His step is light on the floorboards. What Moses had learned from Yun Li in the alley about pleasuring—Yun Li's oak trunk of a body using the alley wall like a springboard to move into and away, Moses and Ellie Bowles had refined into softer unions. The requirement to pleasure had been a duty. He had found no dishonor in this coupling between himself and Ellie Bowles. He had not been obsessed with the woman. Her mastery of giving pleasure had grown in their year of afternoons, so much so he sometimes forgot the reason they explored each other's bodies. But when Sing Cheung's restless spirit swam inside the perfumes Ellie left behind in the room, Moses, vexed for his father's peace, always found his focus returned. Today he feels dirty, no longer clean; he has lost honor. He does not wish to be heard or seen.

Descending the stairs, he holds his breath. Full slop jars line the hall on the floor with his room. He continues down, recounting his efforts.

He had fought against his impatience with Ellie.

He had made daily visits to the Joss House.

He had offered up Christian prayers—

Yet his revered father's troubled spirit robs Moses of sleep. Ellie will never understand what Benjamin Smith had embraced. Benjamin, who delighted in finding The Golden Rule included in all number of faiths and philosophies, who now taught at a small school in Pennsylvania, had never held Ellie's view: *The Golden Rule, regardless of what ancient text might hold the maxim, is only so written there by the ultimate power of Almighty God.*

The Latterby Brothers' Circus

PENNSYLVANIA

1909

---

*June 15. 1909 * The Crier * Cartersmile, Pennsylvania*

CLEAN PERFORMANCES

Latterby Brothers' Circus Shows Good Times at Hawksdale.

at Reading Today.

Baby Galore Has Been With Latterby shows for Nine Years—Tons of Gossip Regarding the People Who Live Under the Canvasses.

Hawksdale, June 15 – The Latterby Brothers' Circus Amusements & Shows gave two supreme performances here yesterday afternoon and night with whipping wind and occasional hail which scattered the parade riders and drivers but not for long. The Queen of the Show, Equestrian rider and Mistress of Eliza the Elephant, Queen LaTina, wore a cape to protect her costume and found it difficult to keep her headdress of ostrich plumes from flying off as the boaters of men gathered to watch her pass had done. Cages of wild animals were displayed. A pair of

Strongmen played toss with a miniature clown, entertaining people greatly, while the Snake Charmer, Baby Galore, wandered through the crowds in attendance despite Mother Nature.

The Latterby Brothers' Circus owner and manager, John Latterby, is pleased to return to Hawksdale where his grandparents resided for many years and he spent pleasant summers as a boy, and he prides himself for the family atmosphere The Latterby Bros.' Circus has maintained over the past dozen years.

Dirt and sawdust rings are replaced with "curb rings" for the Latterby shows, the enclosures made by heavy circle planks bolted together. A colored spokesman said of the rings, They's easy to handle and fast as a jack to put up and stays put where we puts them.

In the rings some fine acts were offered, notably among them being Eliza the Elephant's handstands followed by her novel dance act with a rhythmic samba, Queen LaTina's leap to a quartet of moon-white horses seemed a leap of pure faith. Other feats of interest were a troupe of trained dogs, the Gypsy aerialists, and a menagerie of clowns.

Burgess Herrington Ellis's orders in regard to games of chance appeared unnecessary, as Big John Latterby disallows any such shenanigans with his shows. Not one catch-penny device was discovered on the premises and the deportment of performers and crew were exceedingly within the boundaries of propriety. The Latterby Circus family numbers in excess of 100 employees and a lot of horses and llamas, some the

property of the performers. The citizens of
Hawksdale may congratulate themselves for
being orderly. Not one fracas occurred. I
should further like to report that during the
sixteen years of reporting news of the circus,
recent times have found not one in ten of
the circus-employed is addicted to drink,
and they are frugal with their earnings.

Among the visitors were County detective
George McMare and Z.R. Lindel, of
the West Penn Railway Company.

The side show features, always interesting,
included David "Davey" Edwards, who,
while legless due to a train mishap in
his youth, manages an Irish jig the
audience always attends with applause.

From here the show went to Harrisburg,
where wind and hail did not assault the
ostrich plumes of Queen LaTina. The
next jump for the Latterby Brothers'
Circus is Reading, Penn where excellent
weather and attendance is expected.

———

Mr. Junque's Atlantic Avenue
Emporium of Collectibles

CONEY ISLAND

2008

 haron takes a card from a holder on the counter. *Theo Ricci, Proprietor, Mister Junque's Emporium.* Ricci wears a mop of white hair pulled into a band in the back, a shirt so sharply white it could cut. She knows Theo and Lorraine, no doubt once a hot item, danced at more than one of the Coney venues when the parks, Poseidon among them, still dazzled crowds with strung lights and night rides and broad plank-floored expanses where couples could dance. "Lorraine sent me your way," she says.

"My third ex, that one," he says and she wonders how a man can manage to make information like that seem a come on. Not with the words. *Third ex* spells a lot of failures. Not with the smile he didn't offer. And yet —

"I know. She drew me a map." She doesn't say, *Lorraine mentioned you are quite the Lothario. I should be careful of your charms. And not too eager about the photo, or anything else.*

"A map?"

"How to get here. Very helpful. Who let who go?" This is

out of her mouth, the familiarity strange. "I'm sorry. What I mean is, from outward appearances, you both seem like keepers to me." She is uncomfortable with what she's said, but decides against another apology.

Theo grunts, straightens.

Perhaps she is, after all, on the right course. Camaraderie. A small exchange to break the ice of stranger-to-stranger negotiations.

"It was mutual."

Sharon fingers her way through a box of postcards on the counter from Coney Island's heydays. There's nothing of Poseidon Park and her neck prickles with heat under the multiple wrappings of her scarf. For a moment, everything feels too close and she swivels, faces the storefront, believes she must escape, find some breathable air.

"You OK?" he asks.

"Fine. What can you tell me about that trunk, the red one, in the display window?" She's out the door and inhaling deeply, her sudden giddiness on the wane. Then he's too close, his white shirtfront actually touching the shoulder of her powder blue jacket.

Clouds of Theo's breath float past her ear as he tells her about his janitor son who works in a warehouse, sweeping up and organizing. The red trunk came from there. It was a rented warehouse the cops used after the perps had been fried or freed or whatever. His kid said the stuff kept piling up. He was just "making room."

"There was nothing worth anything, nothing like drugs or weapons—no guns or knives, no heroin or cocaine, no crack. My kid said the cops sent that stuff some other place. No. There was nothing worth much—an old dress from the turn of the century, some fancy hair combs with ivory roses, a bad-faded picture of Jesus with a tear in the paper like someone had tried to cut out his tongue. Stuff like that. Now I think about it, I made a few bucks on what was inside. The hair combs, they were antique, and the dress, it was ruined, but collectors always think they can restore the worst awful messes, the worst shattered silk." Theo nods.

Sharon shivers. Where he stands is too close, trespasses upon her space. Sky the color of frozen rocks reflects off the window, and she takes a step closer, leans her forehead near the glass to peer inside. His display windows, two stretches on either side of the door, four tall panes to a stretch—hold a lot of merchandise. The red trunk she had mentioned is filled with red-collared, black-scuffed, white bowling pins; there's an antique wire chicken meant for holding eggs propped against the trunk; picture frames with no pictures, stringy wire where a painting of something ought to be; a line of old mugs with anchors and Navy insignia make a porcelain border at the base of the sill.

Sharon says, "Looks like a good trunk for bowling pins. Makes a good window display. You should hire somebody to clean this window."

Theo takes a step away. The prickles subside from her neck.

Back inside the dim junk store, a florescent light blinks and the contents on the back shelves—high-top button-style shoes, oxfords, and cowboy boots with bright-colored leathers in the shapes of cacti and stars on the uppers—dance in place as Sharon pauses, wondering when she should mention the panoramic photo with Irene and the Texaco cannon.

"How old are you?" Ricci asks.

Sharon has the distinct feeling he is about to ask her out for dinner or lunch. The prickles return. If he lifted the folds of her scarf, he would see them. How long since any man, young or old (other than Buddy), has given her the least thought at all?

"I ask because some elderly customers remember wearing shoes like those. I've got buttonhooks, too, if you're interested."

"Sixty. And, no," Sharon says, "I'm not quite old enough to have struggled with buttonhooks."

"Lorraine mentioned you're interested in the Poseidon Park panoramic, the one in the case at the museum."

Now there's a surprise. He knew all along why I came, she thinks then answers, "Yes." Her pocketbook is about to be cooked.

Outside, one-hundred-and-forty dollars lighter than when she went in, she carries a print of the hand-tinted original panoramic rolled and rubber-banded under her arm. She pauses in front of his store window, wraps the blue wool in closer coils around her neck, and pulls the edges up to cover her ears. Beyond the displayed assortment of junk, Theo Ricci is watching her. He waves. She looks from him to her reflection.

The ghost she entered the store with is no longer there—only her own ice-blue mummy-wrap mirrored self. Going, she doesn't look back—one wave from Theo Ricci, Proprietor, is one wave too many.

Leaving China Town
EN ROUTE

1909

ll Aboard! But this train is not the train to Williamsport, Penn. Moses continues in his patience. His time to board has not come.

Carts stacked with crates and portmanteaus roll along the platform. He watches from his bench. He will miss the red trunk he has left to Yun Li's care. A fixture in his life, he often hid inside the trunk as a boy. Knots and burls patterned the interior lid like Cyclops demons, but Moses had been able to imagine the shapes as herons. Herons are a sign of good fortune and long life. Herons and peonies gilded the trunk's red-lacquered surface; his youthful imagination flew them inside the trunk. They served him better than one-eyed monsters; herons might carry him to reunite with a mother he could not remember.

But Sing, waiting for his son to return to his studies, had chided, "Moses, come out of hiding. This is not the basket that will carry you into the arms of America. Come out, Moses. It is time."

Yes, Moses thinks. *It is time.* Soon the train will arrive to carry him away from New York City. He could not bring the trunk. The trunk is of the old ways. He wonders if, in 1907, his venerable father left the red trunk behind for the same reasons; if Sing Cheung had wished to hide this emblem of his origin? If his father had taken the red trunk on his journey to London, perhaps he would not have died on board the steamer the day it returned to New York. Perhaps the good-fortune-and-long-life talismans of heron and peony would have brought him home safely.

This is not the basket that will carry you, Moses. Moses takes a deep breath. If education is meant to be "his basket" then he is where he should be. Benjamin is in Williamsport and the new mentor, Mr. M. Rathke, is also there. But it is Ben, Moses believes, who will pull him from this river of ghosts.

Yun Li understands the red trunk's importance: it arrived in America with Sing Cheung, and so it should be returned to Shanxi—with his father's bones.

The bench where Moses sits has iron arms painted black. His traveling case is on his knees and holds two changes of clothes, his shaving mug, brush, and lathering cake, a Bible, the teachings of Confucius and Lao Tzu. There will be more books in Williamsport; Benjamin Smith and Mr. M. Rathke have assured Moses of this in their correspondence.

What Moses has not shared with either Mr. Rathke or Ben are the many ghosts, some actual and others unseen, tormenting his days. The unseen ghosts slide under the floorboards or the tables Moses waits upon at Heung Fat's. In his rented room, they work their way under his cot. How could he explain to them what he cannot see?

He has expressed to Ben the shift of attitudes in his China Town community. *You will remember,* Moses has written, *my father's sister, Auntie Lu? She can no longer procure the best prices on cuts of pig at market. Unhappily, too, Heung Fat has been seen to berate my dutiful friend Yun Li in front of the dishwashers and waiters! I cannot help but think these misfortunes will vanish and they will regain their honor when I am absent. I hope, dear Benjamin, my ill fortune will not follow with me and bring bad tidings to you.*

Moses brushes lint and a pale hair from the new suit Yun Li has purchased for this journey. In his breast pocket he carries two letters. One is from Ben, advising Moses to leave New York as soon as he may, that arrangements have been made for him to board with Mr. M. Rathke, and, if Moses should arrive in Williamsport during Ben's regular teaching hours, Mr. Rathke will gather Moses from the station. *You will know him at once,* Ben has written, *by his round happiness of features and stature. Do not let his eagerness to embrace you put you on guard. He is all goodness, my friend, as well as a scholar of Latin and Greek. Embrace him in return, as you have so often embraced me, for he is truly a friend and will prove so.*

The second letter is never far from Moses. It contains the last written words from his father. As instructed, Moses has continued to consult Yun Li, his mentor of the old ways, when problems arise.

"What am I to do?" Moses had asked.

Yun Li had listened, never rising from the stump where he had waited for Moses to appear in the alley. He had listened to Moses pour out his great frustrations with the white tutor Ellie Bowles. He had alternately pecked at his yellow tooth with the pad of his finger or studied the pad, seeming to look for evidence of some omen left by the gold from this tapping. When Moses paused, Yun Li said, "She is a white devil. You will find another, not a devil, to teach you."

"I will leave this place," Moses answered.

Yun Li clamped his great hands on Moses's shoulders. "Aiyee! Then you *have* obtained the papers to allow you access to Sing Cheung's tomb? May I accompany you on this journey?"

"I do not have the papers," Moses said.

Yun Li's gold tooth, which had glittered in the dim alley, disappeared behind closed lips.

ON THE PLATFORM the announcement is made for the train Moses must board. He stands, uncomfortable in the high stiff collar, adjusts his bowler, and waits for people pressing toward the car to pass. He wears the four-in-hand knotted tie like an elegant stroke down his shirtfront. At Yun Li's insistence, the tie is red—the color of dragons. His queue is braided with dark ribbons and coiled to hide under his hat.

He takes a bench seat on the train, straightens the tie, touches the bowler. The bench seats face each other across the aisle and run the length of the car. They are wood and slick from many travelers. Passengers seated across from Moses take turns staring at him.

Why did he agree to this suit? To impress his new tutor? The tie is too brash; the hat too tight; his perspiration too salty. He blinks, blinks again. If he takes off the hat to wipe his brow, they will see his shaved head, his ribboned queue. He will be more Chinese, less American.

There is a "middle quiet" Moses knows from the teachings of Sing. His father has described this calm as "a bright cloud of great beauty housing the heart," and Moses, as he waits for his journey to begin, closes his eyes to access this "middle quiet." But the teachings of Sing have abandoned Moses. *Aiyee*, Moses thinks. *As I have abandoned you, my father, this seems only fair.*

The train jerks forward. Moses opens his eyes, sees a stern matron across the aisle. The matron wears a hat with a bird attached to the crown. Both the woman's and the glass-eyed bird's attentions seem fixed upon Moses as if he is a worm not worthy of plucking. He closes his eyes, meditates.

When he reopens his eyes some minutes later, the matron is looking elsewhere. She is very wide. A boy—her son or perhaps grandson—leans into her side. The bird on her hat is very fixed, a pigeon with a frozen amber eye. The boy stares at Moses. The pigeon stares at Moses. Moses stares beyond the windows.

"Nein, nein, nein!" the matron says to the boy.

Until she spoke, she was American. So was the boy.

Moses keeps his gaze fixed on the middle distance where trees become trees rather than green blurred splotches, where cows become cows, and horses, horses. They always were, of course. The matron was always German. How could anyone know she was other than American-born behind the facade of pale skin and hair and eyes as pale as a dusty bronze statue? How could anyone know Moses is other than Chinese? He is American-born, but who could know? Who could know he is as much, if not more, a citizen of the United States than the woman and boy?

The dead bird reminds Moses of hats Ellie wore. He does not like thinking of Ellie.

The matron's pale eyes—full of perpetual suspicion, a certain wariness of some impending surprise—remind him of Ellie. Her summer-wheat shade of hair, although shot with gray, also reminds Moses of Ellie. Will Ellie become such a woman with age? A bulwark of sorts? A matronly wall of bosom and spreading hipwork?

The train moves through high morning toward noon; warmth in the car intensifies. Moses blinks; his eyes burn with sweat. People look, and look away. His blinking is offensive; he offends himself. He puts his hand into his breast pocket and retrieves a handkerchief. His long fingernails are exposed. He sees an old farmer's neck pull to the side, the grimace of disapproval on the matron's face, the furtive curiosity of the little boy. "Nein!" the matron says.

He stuffs the handkerchief away. "The only way to begin a new life is to erase part of the old," Yun Li had said to Moses while the tailor made chalk marks for alterations on the suit Yun Li purchased for him. Moses will erase more than his abandoned Chinese dress. He will cut his curving nails. He will cut his queue. He will stop shaving the temples and crown of his head. He will erase every part of his old Chinese ways that he can.

The train rocks along over the tracks. He watches his hands and the place where he has tucked them between his knees. On Grant Street, Moses fit in with those who did not know him, but not among those who knew him — which is an odd way to exist. To those who did not know him, he was of the same culture, shared the same broad family kinship. To those who did know him, he had become more than the orphan of Sing Cheung. He had begun the burial of his ethnic heritage, his Chinese family, even as the loud, steaming, boisterousness of it yet thrived.

A little girl sings. Her voice startles Moses from a meditation in which the burning sweat no longer burned his eyes, and the heat in the car went unnoticed. He jerks his head up to locate the voice. He will work on acceptance. He will acclimate himself to the scrape and scratch of their vocals.

The German matron and small boy have been replaced by a woman whose face has forgotten how to smile; she holds a baby; the singing girl is bent over the woman's knee as if bent over a saloon bar. She is short as a pygmy and probably less than four. Her hair is as red as used bricks and matches her freckles. She is singing *Old Sue-zanna, don't you cry for me,* and looking at Moses. Her gaze is direct. She does not look away, but sings as if on stage with a voice to carry to the balcony tiers instead of a narrow train aisle.

He forces a smile toward her.

She stops singing. "Why don't you take off your hat?" she asks.

"Thank you," Moses answers. His English is perfect. "But today I must wear my hat."

"Oh. But why? It's so hot! The other men aren't." She is small and she has pushed her eyebrows up until her small forehead is all wrinkles. She is a child, Moses thinks, who wants to smile but is worried.

She smiles anyway.

"It would not be good for my head to be without its hat today," Moses says and smiles in return. "I hope you will forgive me."

"But you look silly. It's too hot to wear a hat."

Moses felt silly wearing a hat on any day, but especially here on such a warm day. He inclines his head slightly, offers a half-nod acknowledgment of the little girl's wisdom.

"Mary, shush now. Leave him be," the tired woman holding the baby says.

"Yes, Mama."

Mary wears a ribbon as yellow as canaries in her brick red

hair. She does not bother him again about his hat, but she does not stop watching for him to remove it. When Moses takes his hat from his head and places the bowler in his lap, she smiles; all of her baby teeth show. Without looking up from the baby she rocks at her breast, Mary's mother smiles, too.

At the next small town, they leave. Mary waves as she follows her mother to the exit. New passengers board. Moses allows the hat to remain on his lap until Mary waves from the platform. Not many strangers are as accepting as Mary and her mother had been.

As the train pulls out of the station, Moses re-dons his bowler; his braided queue trails down his back.

With relative ease he regains the meditative calm he had found before Mary sang. Her concerns for his comfort have eased him somehow and he dozes, head dropping forward.

Suddenly his bowler is off. The forearm of someone is next to his cheek. Wrapped around this forearm is Moses's long braid of hair. The face that belongs to the forearm is recklessly marked. At first Moses thinks they are freckles, fiercer than Mary's, but American freckles all the same. But the mouth of his attacker—so unlike Mary's—is missing teeth; there are gaps. The forearm drags Moses up chin-to-chin with his attacker and he sees the freckles are not freckles but sores, or the scars from where sores have been.

A voice too young and too crackling between high and low to be a man's says, "Look-ee here, Ned, I got me a monkey by the tail!"

Moses is swung around. Two women, old mothers who sit on the far end of the car, are statue-still. Everything seems frozen as the boy, certainly younger than Moses although double in Moses's size, drags him toward the old mothers.

The landscape beyond the train window is still. Moses and the boy are the only moving things.

"What have I done to offend?" Moses asks. He would bow, he would offer politeness, but he is falling down the train's steps, crashing into the side of the boy who drags him along by his queue. There are two others. All three set upon him. They are unwhiskered. They are unclean. Moses is embarrassed for them.

They are skips and skids away from the train when the boy releases Moses and the kicking begins.

When the kicking ends, Moses does not lift his face from the gravel alongside the tracks. His mouth is full of blood but he asks, more of the pebbles than of the boys, "What have I done to offend?"

"Well, now," the boy says, "this hair here, it offends. We're gonna get riddah that chink tail, Monkey Man. Oughta light up like a fuse."

All for the Sake of a Clown

**oming off Neversink** Mountain Budd and Edison exchange a look—the Winton's driveline has held.

"Don't take her out of first gear," Budd reminds Edison for the umpteenth time. Edison understands the Winton better than Budd; he knows the grade going down and the touring car's limitations. "I know you know that," Budd adds.

Edison does not mention the Jersey cow. The side of Irene's face is the color of prune juice. Nobody mentions the cow.

As the Winton rolls into Reading, Penn's outskirts, a circus parade is lining up to begin. Edison parks in a field where handlers are tying off camels to a long rope staked at either end.

Irene is over the side of the Winton as fast as she'd gone over to rescue the cow. Her feet are all over the place, dancing around Olive's skirts and then out of view, so much so that her name is much shouted out—first by Olive then by Budd and right on down to Flo's shrill, "Irene! Come back. Mama says! Irene!" Asthma keeps Wilbur quiet. Not that it matters who shouts.

In answer, Irene stops, eyes following a clown shorter than Wil, with a pointed hat and a white dog with a hat just like his and that thing they wear around their necks that stands out. When Mae and Edison almost catch up, she inches farther ahead.

Another shout comes. Another stop on her part. She is not bored with where they all are—there is just so much where they aren't! There's a woman with a snake curling up from her waist; the woman's waist is as big as a tractor and the pocket the snake is rising out of is as big as an apron. There's a man nearly as tall as the water tower on the farm walking stiff-legged among them.

"You would think," Olive says, standing next to her, "you'd never been to a circus. Take hold of your sister's hand." She nods toward Mae. "And Mae, you hold on as hard to her as you need—the last thing I want is one of you gone missing." Her eyes fasten on Irene—clearly the "one of you" in mind.

Mae's hand is better than Olive's. Mae had stood up to Mama—that one time—she had. And standing up to Olive went a long way in Irene's little book. She seems taller, Mae does, and wider than normal today. Mae's face is as familiar to Irene as her own face in the mirror but pimpled. Today Mae seems bosomed out in the front in ways Irene hadn't measured before. She hopes seventeen won't do that to her; who would want such a lot of extra to carry around? Where did her bosoms flop when she swam? Mae doesn't swim, but if she did, Irene thinks, she'd need to be extra strong to pull herself through water and win any race with a chest like that.

"C'mon, Mae!" Irene urges. "We can go faster than this."

The small clown with his dog has disappeared and Irene, eager to find both clown and dog, reaches her free hand around to grab Mae's hand holding hers. She chugs along backwards, lugging Mae forward with "Hurry, we're missing them. I bet that dog's doing tricks. C'mon, Mae. You can do it. C'mon." She's remembering that last supper, thinking of Mae's left-behind bones — she has spirit, her sister does — if only Irene can get her to let go.

Lucky Flo! She has the advantage of Budd's tall shoulders to watch the parade pass by; and Wil has likewise been lifted to Edison's back, although not all the way up to his shoulders. At fifteen, Edison's shoulders can handle Wil up top, but Wilbur, at five, cannot handle the height at the top of Edison's shoulders. He is fearful of going that high and so hugs Edison's back like the shell on a turtle's back.

"C'mon, Mae, please! I'll only go between there," Irene says, pointing to a slight gap between two young women. "I can't see a thing from here. *Please, please,* Mae . . . before the whole parade's done and gone."

She has tugged and pulled Mae to a point a few bodies deep from the road. Mae loosens her grip; Irene is gone. *Good old Mae!* she thinks, rustling the skirts of two young mothers as she squeezes past them to the curb.

The red circus wagon has passed out of sight; she can just see the tail of the last elephant — but when you are ten, everything seems just beginning, and, as far as Irene is concerned, she *is* at the very start, the beginning.

Wil and Flo join Irene. Flo stands next to Irene and when the strong men pass — there are two of them — Flo says, "I bet Edison's muscles will be that big pretty soon."

"Budd's muscles already are," Irene counters.

"Yes, but Edison's got a book and he's going to catch up with Budd really soon. He's going to be the next Sandoval, don't you know?" Flo says, and Irene says, "We'll see." Everyone knew Edison did pull-ups on a beam in the barn back in

---

Williamsport. Flo, Wilbur, and sometimes even Irene sat on Edison's back while he did push-ups. Mae never would, not even when Edison said, *C'mon, I can handle you.* Irene can't argue what's plain — Edison's muscles were growing.

"I'm going to ride a horse in a circus someday," Flo says. "I'm going to wear shiny clothes and stand on my head in a saddle just like that — only pink."

Irene has no response for Flo; her attentions are on the small clown she'd pursued while still held back by Mae. He has a big head, the clown, with a little tufted patch of hair that reminds Irene, oddly, of old Mr. Rathke. But the little tuft of hair on this little clown's big head is bright, bright red to match his clown mouth. When the clown smiles his teeth are yellow and chunky big and he has small blue triangles under his eyes. Irene waves with wide, side-to-side arcs of her arm and the clown, who also wears very long shoes, shuffles to the sideline and, tucking one arm behind his short body and holding the other one across his chest like a pledge, makes a deep bow. Then, like a jack-in-the-box, he springs off the ground and makes a backward flip in the air.

With the clown's stunning back flip, Wilbur churns straight up from where he'd sat on the curb. His target is Irene because she is his nearest big sibling, but he comes with such a force — arms churning, head down like a battering ram, his impact on her middle sends her down, elbows skidding sidewalk planks.

"Why'd you do that?" Irene winces at about the same time she hears Olive call out, "Irene!"

"Yes, ma'am! I'm still right here," she shouts back. She will not cry. Budd and Edison are somewhere, not far. She will not cry over a couple scrapes with some wood poking out. Irene did not cry over splinters and scrapes.

"Why'd you do that, Wil?" she grumbles again.

Flo says, "Leave him alone. He's just a fraidy cat. That's all — a kitty-cat-fraidy-cat."

Wilbur wheezes, catches his breath, and glares at Irene, not Flo, when he says, "Am not."

OLIVE RETIRES WITH Irene and Wilbur to the grassy field beyond the train tracks where Edison parked the Winton. Wil has worked himself into a spell of bad breathing, and, if the splinters in Irene's elbows fester, there'll be Billy Hell to pay.

The field had been more or less vacant — a few carriages and wagons, the handler and a few camels, but mostly empty when they found it. Not the handiest spot in relation to the parade route but handiest for Edison's parking skills: Pull up and set the hand brake. He's a no-nonsense boy, that one, and had worn a look of pleasure — Olive might almost say pride — at having maneuvered down the mountain without further mishap, despite Budd's continual warnings. And then to have found such a wide-open space to stop. He had (it showed in his cocky bearing) *rescued them.* He was, Olive ventured to think, a hero in his own mind. He would not like it one bit that the vacant spaces surrounding the Winton had been filled with a series of portable zoo enclosures, the Latterby Brothers' circus menagerie tethered within kicking distance of the grand yellow car. For a lad of fifteen, Edison is a possessive sort. No. He wouldn't like this at all.

Olive picks her way along the backsides of camels and horses as the handlers replace plumes and fancy jeweled devices with plain halters made out of rope. Better these than the elephants — tall as the farmhouse she's deserted, on the far side of the Winton, she thinks. She's slow as she goes, sheltering Irene with her left arm while her right hugs Wil against her skirt.

"Ma'am?" A handler gets Olive's attention, then says, "Y'all be fine. These is gentle as ol' milk cows, so long's y'all don't spook 'em."

She nods, a disbelieving nod, and the handler comes around from where he's been depositing pitchforks of hay at intervals and says, "If y'all don't mind, I jes walk along here between the hind ends of these friends a mine and you and yore chill'ren."

Olive gives a more believing nod. "Thank you," she says. "We're just going there." She tilts her head toward the Winton, three elephants away.

"That's a fine automobile, ma'am. We wuz eye-ballin' her earlier, me and Red, and we both say how's we thought she wuz fine. I bet you look mighty fine, too," the handler says, looking at Wil, "behind the wheel of that automobile." He offers a wink in Irene's direction.

At the Winton, Olive says, "Thank you—"

"Earl. My name's Earl, ma'am. And y'all close that pocketbook back up now. Mighty fine automobile. Yes-sir-ree. Mighty fine." His chin rests on his hands which rest on the top end of the pitchfork handle. Round-shouldered and as loose-limbed physically as he is loose-tongued with women and children, he asks, "Y'all fixin' to leave?"

"No-sir-ree," Irene says. "We only just got here!"

"That's a fine bunch of berries and stickers you got pokin' outta yo arm there," Earl says. "I sure hope it ain't on accounta us folks."

"No, sir!" Irene answers.

Olive sees clearly both her children are smitten with this

dark man. She says, "Shush now, Irene." To Earl, she says, "We hadn't thought to leave for a while yet, although . . ."— she pauses and turns to look down the lines of tethered circus stock—"although I fear we may have parked in an area where we oughtn't have . . ."

"When y'all'r ready, you jes ask any ol' rowdy for Earl and Earl'll help y'all out."

(Later, it will be difficult to say whose wink came first, Irene's or Earl's. Irene offers hers because this thin, stooped, colored man, not much older than Budd but bent about the shoulders all the same, reminds her of her father—who is neither thin nor stooped nor colored but soothing. Earl is soothing. Earl offers his wink because that one eye closes on him from time to time; and when it closes, it has not one blessed thing to do with intent.)

In the back of the Winton Olive works on extricating splinters from Irene's elbows. Wilbur watches Irene's face contort with reactions to the sewing needle Olive pries against each sliver of sidewalk planking. He is waiting for Irene's face to go all streaky with tears; he will wait a long time. It's not in her nature; he knows this, even at five.

From the moment Earl said how fine Wilbur looked behind the wheel of the Winton, the boy's breathing has been easier.

"What's wrong?" Irene asks Olive.

"Eye strain," Olive says. "Some of these splinters are tiny. Hard to get at."

"You can dig harder, Mama. I can take it."

"I know you can, Stick. But digging harder won't help. These things take patience."

Wilbur watches Irene watch her elbow while Olive works the splinters, and Olive watches the tiny splinter she struggles with niggle its way free. She doesn't notice Irene's double blink of surprise when referred to as "Stick." Olive never calls Irene "Stick." Truth be told, Wilbur doesn't think his mother realizes she's even said it.

After the better part of an hour, Wilbur wakes up when a woman—the fat woman, the one with the trick pocket on her dress and the big snake draped about her body—shows up at the car. The snake is absent. Wilbur is disappointed about that; he may be a fraidy cat about clowns, but he's not at all scared of snakes. The dress she wears now doesn't have a trick pocket.

Irene wrinkles her nose at the liniment odor that arrives with the woman, an odor Irene associates with old apples and Granny Cly's quilt, not to mention the old painted trunk, by now, no doubt, somewhere in Brooklyn. Before anyone can do much about it, the odor is strong on Irene's elbows from the salve the fat lady rubs over the rash of divots left behind where the splinters had been. Olive shakes her head, sputtering objections as the woman applies the salve—but it's too late.

The fat woman takes a hard look, squinting her eyes at the prune-dark side of Irene's face, nods and turns away.

How a woman of such size, barely able to waddle from one point to the next, managed to appear, without any warning, at Irene's elbows—which, by way of proximity, is to say at Olive's side—is pure mystery. But here she is, a great hulk of a woman, here and then gone, leaving Irene's elbows polished with some home-brew remedy that reeks to high heaven, and with hardly more than a *Howdy do*. What remains, beyond the rank smell of the salve, is the scowl on Olive's face.

"Well." She says nothing more. Wilbur nods, agreeing; Irene rubs at her smelly elbows, which hurt.

"Socialite Found Strangled!"

n 1909, Jerry Mahoney "the younger" is twenty-one; a well-groomed handlebar moustache helps to hide his youth. His father, Jerry Mahoney "the elder," grooms the curves of his handlebar moustache to hide the jowl line of his jaw. Neither father nor son is vain—not a bit of it. They are Irish. They are in law enforcement. Employed by the finest city in the world, they will leave a bump on the head of anyone inclined to debate the question.

Jerry "the younger" was born the year pickpockets and cutpurses found themselves facing more than "shadows" on the lookout for petty thieves in parade crowds. The New York City Detective Bureau was born that same year— 1882. In a letter from Jerry "the elder's" grandmother, Fiona Mahoney in Ireland, she deemed the birth of the Bureau and the boy in one and the same year "an omen." And so it was. Young Jerry was fated to become a detective. There was never a doubt.

A great oaf of a lad, he made detective grade by age twenty-seven and was assigned a Chinese partner slim as a billy club to interpret for him on a China Town murder.

Xiang Liu is a boy by all appearances, except for a hardness in his eyes. A handlebar moustache might hide some of his youth, Jerry "the younger" has thought, but anyone faced with Liu's lifeless eyes would be foolish not to worry.

First partner, first case. There is no ambiguity about the cause of death in China Town. The victim had been strangled and stuffed in a trunk, her body undiscovered until complaints came from another occupant of the building about the smell "from upstairs." The victim's family includes a retired Union Army doctor, a man of reputation and social status. Consequently, the press is all over the details. Headlines read: "Socialite Found in China Man's Trunk," "Beware! The Yellow Peril," and "Yellow Menace Still Among Us!"

A week into the investigation, this appears in small print: "Youthful detectives, one yellow as clay and the other one Irish, have failed to apprehend—" The New York City Detective Bureau replaces Mahoney and Liu.

"Officially," Mahoney the elder says, "you're done with it, son. Unofficially?" His voice leaves a question parked where the blade of his carving knife slices the ham at their supper table.

Jerry the younger nods. He has copied the notes made at the scene, when the corpse was removed, details about the trunk and the victim he could not forget, even if he tried. He holds forth his dinner plate. A slab of pink ham slips from the tip of his father's knife to weigh it down. The victim's long hair had been cut at the nape of her neck and taken, as if a souvenir. The trunk she'd been stuffed inside was red; the latch was brass. Her hair combs, fancy and carved out of ivory—along with her dress, petticoats, button-top white kid boots, one glove, the kind that reaches up to an elbow with pearl buttons to open at the wrist—are stored in the trunk as if the thing were an evidence locker.

He fingers his moustache, draws back the plate with his portion of meat, says, "Yes, Da," and nods. Mahoneys don't quit a case because some high mucky-muck says they must.

Buddy's Room 618

uddy is waiting for Rose of
Sharon. It is late, nearly dark, but she
said she would stop in after her trip to
Coney. He has not been bored. Bet had
stopped back with Kevin. She'd missed
her train. "What the hell," she'd told him. "I'm here anyway.
I've decided to stay."

"Your mom know?"

"Nope."

"There's an extra bed downstairs. Or use mine," he'd
offered but she declined, said she had a place, and Kevin had
nodded. He'd looked, Buddy thought, a little surprised—but
in a good way. *Nothing beats a good surprise every now and
again*, Buddy thinks.

Now it's late. He's tired. He's a little bored. Not like the
old days. Not like when he used to wait in a dinghy off-
shore for Irene to fall from the sky. He was twelve, had a
head full of sandy hair, a full round face, and arms strong
enough to keep the boat oared beyond Poseidon Park's cannon range. When the concussion of the cannon blast came
muffled across the water and Irene became a momentary blur

in the air, he'd begin rowing in earnest. There was always the chance she might exit the cannon less than perfectly; the cannon might misfire, fail to eject her with the force needed to send her high-flying; she could enter the water somehow broken, dazed, or even unconscious.

But Irene never did.

At least not unconscious or broken. If she was dazed in those moments of blur across the Coney Island skyline, or as her body shattered the salt-water surface, she didn't share her confusion with Buddy, not that he can recall.

Has he shared this with Rose of Sharon? He has a hard time remembering what he has told her and what he has not. A sea of years flows out behind him; sometimes his memories are like a freshly cut wake on the water—sharp at the onset, wide at the horizon, vanishing into that thin flat line where ocean meets sky. He is old. The hair on his head as missing as the day he was born. The skin on his arms loose, all but empty of muscle, nothing like his longshoreman days. He is old and Irene is dead.

His eyes close. Mornings are better for memories. Tomorrow he will ask Rosie if he's mentioned the dinghy, the oars, the waiting off shore.

ROSE OF SHARON'S tennis shoes make sucking noises as she makes her way to room 618. The corridor is wide. Light reflects off everything. The floor shines like a glossy sun, many glossy suns, one following the next as her steps grab and let go, grab and let go down the hall.

Why do hospitals smell the way hospitals smell?

She hopes the Korean's not there. What *was* his name? Nothing against him. It's just that when he's present, guilt wells up again about Buddy's fall, his hip . . . *her fault*. Absolutely her fault. Undeniably her fault.

She would like one of those nosegays people carried in Shakespeare's day to ward off unpleasant smells, the stench of disinfectants. Sharon's stomach spasms, goes knotty with organized fear. She enjoys cleanliness in ways that make her appear obsessive compulsive — to some. But the wiping down and out of accidents, of urine spills and blood, infections and vomit — these genuine proofs of life expunged with a swipe of Lysol or Pinesol or some Sol or other triggers an internal mechanism Sharon can't quite locate. She would have it removed, this thing that equates disinfectant-clean with the absence of people. If she could, she would have it removed. This smell of *erasure*. Of things gone, and going, amiss. It's Ted's room, Ted's corridor, Ted's death.

Grab and let go. Grab and let go.

She has no nosegay; the knots will pass. What she does have is the panoramic photo of Irene in front of the cannon.

She is at Buddy's door. She is inside. *Is he sleeping?* No! He is smiling. She is a girl, pure girl in his eyes, she feels it, the transfer of his affections, as if his eyes are paint brushes and her near-sixty body the canvas he reworks into a Rose, his *Rose of Sharon*, not wearing blue, but magically ruffled in pink.

PART IV

The Latterby Brothers'
Circus Crew

READING, PENNSYLVANIA

1909

here there," a voice offers, "there now."

Moses is everywhere lit with heat and ice. His skin is stuck through with sharp feelings his hands can't hold. His hands won't close, refuse his every command, and above him there is a shadow wider than gloom pushing his frame to the edge of sense and sanity. A drop of water moistens his lips. Another drop comes. "There now," the voice offers, "there now."

Behind his closed eyes, all is brilliant. He remembers blinding white.

THE RUSTLE OF cloth comes and with it is the same voice, the one he heard sometime before, the voice of someone who has perhaps screamed all day and now there is only this rasp of leftover sound. "There now. There now." The words are tenderly given; fabric moving against fabric accompanies the words. He slithers his tongue out for the drops of moisture and believes a woman delivers them.

"Hold on, son. Hold on," the voice says. He spasms with the light touch she offers his lips, the touch of a pale spirit who means no harm but harms all the same.

"There. There now," she repeats. "I can't stay. Earl and Red are about to remove my ramp. I'll be back. You rest." He feels a loose coolness on his neck, as if his queue and the black ribbons have been unbraided and wet and placed over his throat like a sheet of light feathers. He moans; the sound is a baby's whimper to his ears.

THE BOXCAR DOOR rattles toward closing in response to Alice's pull. She won't shove it home. "He'd die in there. Wouldn't do it to Bobby, anyway."

Bobby is Alice's boa constrictor and right now Bobby is in his cage at one end of the boxcar and there's a poor burnt-up mess of a China man on a straw bed covered with canvas at the other. "Sad," she says, shaking her head as she turns to steady herself before starting down the ramp.

"Who's you talkin' to, Sis?" Earl asks.

"Well, who do you see?" she says.

"Jes' yo'self," Red answers for Earl.

Alice lumbers down the ramp, her great haunches swapping sides to carry her weight. "Spoken true, Red. Spoken true. I am one to talk to myself. What surprises me, Earl," she says, a little winded for her efforts, "is you'd ask."

Earl holds up his hand, fingers splayed. "Sis, y'all back off'n me now."

Red says, "How come you messin' with old Sis, Earl, anyways?"

"I'm not messin' with nobody," Earl answers. "Y'all want that door left that-a-way?"

"Don't I always?" She fixes Red with a narrow squint and says, "Just who are you calling old, son?"

Earl says, "Yes'm. Jes' . . . if the boss sees—"

She keeps Red pinned down with a mean glare and a fake frown as she answers Earl. "And when's the last time you saw him checking our doors?"

"Yes'm," he says. They slide the ramp up on Bobby's car and continue on.

She's been nine years with this outfit and if her path did not cross with such hearts as these, she'd be the worse for it. They restored her faith the way singing gospel as the saved walked into a baptismal river did during her early-girl years. Not her own walking in and dunking—Alice Towne didn't need saving, didn't trust preachers. Not like she trusted Red and Earl. She's found circus crews mostly genuine. If sometimes dishonest, they were always real.

"Red," she calls after them, her voice a thready rumble, "you leave Earl alone now."

"Yes'm, Sis," Red calls back. Some of the crew are inclined on occasion to call her Ma, but she sets them straight. "Sis" is the closest to family ties she allows.

The frown she'd held for a minute toward Red and Earl slips into a grimace. She's more than tired, would've laid herself down right next to that poor boy if she'd thought nobody would miss her—but she's too big not to be missed. This isn't the time, and she knows it, to have folks checking on her whereabouts. John Latterby's not the most charitable sort about hobos and less fortunate folks, plus he's none too happy about Phoebe and Sis's interference there. No, whatever the outcome, she decides she'll do better by all to go on with her business as if there's not a dying Chinese boy sharing Bobby's car. She'll look in on Phoebe, take her some dinner, continue to rub John Latterby the wrong way in that arena, avoid bringing on suspicions in another. Raffe went to the trouble of saving that boy; Alice won't undo what he's done.

WHY ALICE "SIS" Towne got fat, why she keeps getting fatter is a mystery. Her current stage name is Baby Galore but nobody who knows her calls Alice "Baby" unless they want to end up slapped sideways and sprawled across the mess tent floor. She'd been slim as the main act's "Queen LaTina" is now—but that was a long time gone.

Unlike Phoebe, the Queen LaTina of broadsides and posters, Alice never straddled a horse or wrapped her legs around the neck of an elephant with her toes tucked behind its ears. She has made dives from considerable heights to splash in a bucket of water. She's been a juggler, a target for knife-throwers, and, while she was pretty (she had been pretty enough to make an evangelical minister sin), a snake-charming magician's assistant, and a tightrope walker. She gave up the tightrope routine once the fat got her, turned in her spangled tights for a clown suit with blue circles bigger than dinner plates and took on the name "Bubbles" until the magician died and the snake he had charmed, Bobby, became hers. By then she had chins and a face with the wide appeal of a giant orangutan. She's not orange or hairy, but her eyes slope in long crescents and her cheeks seem to have grown an extra set to hang behind the first. John Latterby came up with the name "Baby Galore." He thought the repeat of all the "B" words—Baby Galore and Bobby the Boa Constrictor—made a good name for the act.

Raffe doesn't call her anything. He's the animal handler and good with all aspects of husbandry, whether two-humped, one-humped, or no-humped (as with llamas). There's an old camel heifer straining to give birth and Raffe's arm goes inside her and he says, "I've the hooves."

Alice has stopped on her way to the mess tent to see if she can bring him back a bite. She nods in response to his words. He smiles, glad to have a foot. He has a gap between his front teeth nearly as wide as a finger and his skin has grown a gray frost overall, like the age dusting his wiry hair is a contagion not stopped at his hairline. He is from somewhere like Persia and, while Raffe has other responsibilities beyond shepherding the Latterby camels, it is with the camels he sleeps every night.

"Good," Alice says. She does not interfere. If it looks as if Raffe might jump the gun with his knife and kill the calf to save the mama, she might interfere. If allowed. Her "allowance" when given came with a nod from Raffe; she wouldn't trespass otherwise. Raffe knew by feel when a calf was dead inside. Alice knew by a dead sigh that came out of Raffe, settling the matter. "Tricky business, this getting born," she says.

The calf pops free. "Good," Raffe says. "Now we peel you free with mama's tongue and my palms. Now we peel you free."

In the boxcar where Alice kept Bobby and Raffe kept hay and such for his herd, the burned boy, or young man (it's so difficult to tell), may not be fine. He is their secret. They will make him right—if they can. His survival so far is a foothold. Raffe shrugs at what Alice does not say. Alice agrees: one life at a time.

AFTER SUPPER AND seeing to Phoebe's needs and taking a paper-wrapped sandwich around to Raffe, not because he asked for one but because she figured he ought have one, Alice makes her way back to the boxcar.

Earl and Red have re-lowered the ramps. Such a nuisance this extra work of putting them up and down, but there'd been trouble in more than one town when the crew went mostly absent and curious local kids went snooping. There'd been one boy near-strangled and crushed by Bobby several years back. And some parrots loosed from another car had never returned. John Latterby had had watchmen keep an eye on the train cars. Times weren't the best for a colored man shouting at white boys—which is what Red did one night. He still owns a limp from the beating he took back when.

"Said I'd be back, and here I am," she says. A low June sun shoots a wide shaft of twilit yellow across the hay-covered floor. The dark corner is silent where this newest stray, this unique somebody from somewhere, rests. The calf Raffe pulled from the camel's womb is just as unique. All life is unique to Alice "Sis" Towne. Then again, she's a realist. What can't be fixed, can't.

She lifts the cloth from his neck, lowers it into a pail. Bubbles rise in the water as the cloth loses air and she lifts it, slowly, lets the song of its trickle plink on the surface and wrings out the excess. She is torn between dribbling to his lips or draping the coolness back over his neck's raw musculature, his jaw, where the broken bone has been set by Raffe. The arm, too, set like a prancing dog's broken leg. She wants to see into his eyes, past the dark glaze of pain. She moistens his lips.

"I am sorry," she tells him, "about this damned heat." She

rolls him toward her wide bosom. "How you do shake," she tells him, "while I'm sweatin' lip to fanny." The tarpaulin Raffe's rigged over loose hay has wrinkles. She pushes them out, lets the boy-man roll back flat. "Sun's leaving. It'll be down soon."

She lowers her ear to his mouth, squints, as if such an effort to open her pores will allow something from him to catch on her skin. "Are you still with us, son?" she whispers.

His chest is burned; she cannot put her ear there to listen. "Breathe for me, son," she says. "The least you can do is breathe." When the tickle of his breath finds her cheek, she whispers, "Yes. Good."

All For The Sake Of The
Same Little Clown

READING, PENNSYLVANIA

1909

hile Olive tends to
Irene in the Winton, Budd looks
at his pocket watch, not the
time but the case. It is plain gold.
The dent in the cover was there
when Millard Talbot, Olive's father, dropped the timepiece
into Budd's palm, not on Budd's nineteenth birthday (most
recently) but on the occasion of Millard's sixty-fifth.

"Every man needs a good timepiece," Millard had said, adding, "Go ahead, boy. Hook it to your belt loop."

"Yes, sir," Budd answered, hooking the chain to his belt
loop.

"Shouldn't go missing, if you hook it on right," Millard said.
"But if it *does* go missing, and an *honest* man finds it, he'll
know where it ought be returned. See here?" He flipped open
the cover. "Property of Millard J. Talbot, Williamsport."

"Yes, sir. An honest man will know. Thank you, Granddad.
I will try not to let it go missing."

Without checking the time, Budd knows it must be sup-
pertime or close to it. The crowds have thinned; several
attractions have posted signs as to when they'll return. Mae

and Flo wait in line at a hot dog stand. At three pennies each, it's the cheapest and easiest way to get them all fed.

The pocket watch chain hooks through a buttonhole in Budd's blue surge vest. His suit coat is in the Winton; June's too warm for such, and the stiff, detachable shirt collar is in the auto as well. There's a fine blue stripe in the stuff of his shirt, and his cuffs are unbuttoned and rolled back. Edison wears the same shirt stuff, his cuffs rolled up in a like manner, plus a brown tweed cap. But Edison's pants are knickers, not long pants like Budd's blue serge. The knickers are brown, lightweight wool. Budd shakes his head—*Wool, in this gall-danged heat.*

"You worried about time?" Edison asks, nodding toward the watch.

"Nah," Budd says. "We've got time for a bite. Supper hour, I'm thinking."

"You could say that," Edison says.

Mae and Flo make the front of the hot dog vendor's line and Budd says to Edison, "You mind going on and giving the girls a hand?"

"Sure," Edison says. "What should we do about Mama?"

Budd slips the unopened watch back in its pocket, steps aside to allow a family—four stair-step boys and their parents—to pass. There seems, Budd notes, a general migration of the folks toward the west end of town. "I believe she'd want us to go on ahead. You know how she is," he says, stepping forward again, "common sense and all that. No one was hurt beyond walking and there's bread and apples and pears—"

"Yep," Edison says. "She'd want us to take care of us and see what we can while we can."

Budd's favorite exhibit, so far, is the two-headed chicken; he wants to talk with the owner, who, Budd supposes, is the person who bred such a strange bird. It's a hen, a Rhode Island Red, with two herky-jerky, bobbing heads and two sets of amber eyes—but Edison moves them along, hot dogs already consumed. They're passing right by the two-headed chicken set-up.

Edison's all about *strength*—human strength—and the strongmen (there are two) were making their way down the trampled grass that served as a walkway of sorts between rows of small canvas structures. "C'mon, Budd," Edison urges, "or else catch me up later."

Budd's practical side tells him it would be folly to allow the family to separate; he figures the two heads on the one chicken is, more likely as not, nature's fluke. *Still*, he thinks, *it would be interesting to talk with the owner.*

Edison is moving off, the back of his head and brown tweed cap melting into a sea of tweed caps moving up and down the grass corridor. Budd boosts Flo onto his shoulders, offers Mae his arm, and leaves the two-headed chicken behind. He'll allow Edison his "Strongmen." Edison is, after all, four years younger, a kid, only fifteen, still in knickers.

The strongmen wear tight shirts and leggings with wide, bronze-looking belts cinched around their waists. Their boots are lace-up and conform to their calves. Every bicep bulges and expands inside the long sleeves of the shirts as the men pose and flex, drawing spectators away from whatever attentions had held them to attend their imminent act. Their costumes, Budd thinks, are the color of dusk—like a purplish summer twilight on the farm—and their poses, synchronized to mirror, *exactly*, what the other one does, are phenomenally grand, even to a two-headed chicken enthusiast.

Because Edison set off immediately after the strongmen passed the chicken exhibit, they all have a front row view.

When four clowns tumble into the arena, Budd and Mae exchange a look of pleasant delight, but Edison says, "Hey! What gives?" It's obvious he finds the clowns an intrusion on this spectacle of rippling manhood.

"That's the one made Wil knock over Irene," Flo says and points at the small clown with the red tufts of hair and chunky yellow teeth.

The strongmen strike their identical poses: heads at a tilt to watch the two small clowns race around like misbehaving children; each folds one muscular arm across his bulging chest to hold the elbow of the remaining muscular arm; the chins of each strong man rest on the knuckles of a clenched fist. To the crowd, they present two studies (in exact imitation of one another) of puzzled impatience.

"They're part of the act, don't you think, Budd?" Mae says, referring to the clowns.

"Not a very good part," Edison says. "You see me laughing?"

Mae shakes her head, but Edison has already turned back.

There *is* laughter—from all sides—as the troublesome clowns run between the legs of the strongmen and climb atop their biceps while the strongmen strike one pose of consternation after another. Then, simultaneously and quite suddenly, each man swoops up a clown and raises each over their heads like barbells. The little clowns squeal. The crowd roars with laughter. The strongmen give the little ones back to their "parents"—one dressed as a dumpy woman and another dressed as the dumpy woman's husband. The little ones run back in, play peek-a-boo between the muscled legs of the men.

Then they are up, held in the air by one strongman, one little clown to a palm, as if they are plates on the ends of sticks about to be spun in some juggling act. The crowd gasps. Mae shakes and turns her face into Budd's shirtsleeve, unable to watch what might happen.

"They know what they're doing," Budd offers. He's lowered his head, spoken into her ear, has tried to sound confident, reassuring—but the murmurs and small gasps of awe mingle into an ongoing moan. His sister's head is not the only one turned away.

"I can't bear it," Mae says.

When the clown with the red tuft of hair sails through the air to be caught by the other strongman—released as he has been with the power and rotation of a discus thrower—Mae breaks the circular barrier, jumps the bolted curb of ring, rushing to save him.

For a split second there is absolute silence; if a pin drops, Budd will hear it. He stares at Mae sprawled under clowns and one strongman.

Then, chaos.

Her leg is broken. It's clear.

Women. With the exception of his mother and, occasionally, Stick, Budd cannot figure them.

MAE'S LEG IS splinted by the circus doctor. She can't climb into the Winton, much less fit in the tonneau with Edison, Wilbur, Irene and Flo. She will, Olive knows, flatly refuse to ride in the front, even if her splinted leg *should* fit.

If nonplussed by this latest mishap, Olive doesn't miss a step. Of course, her first concern is for Mae, who had flung herself through the loitering crowds along the exhibitor's concourse with all the pomp of a crazed mother hen.

What has gotten into the girl? The stand she'd made at the dinner table about that stump and those horses, Pearly and

Lynn Doiron

Jake, was a warning; a turn in the girl's character was there, in that stand-off. Olive knew it then. Now this?

Olive turns her attention to the Latterby Brothers' brother in attendance to Mae's needs. "Big John" (by name if not stature) has been efficient about Mae's "accident," summoning a doctor to his boxcar office to care for Mae's hysterics and leg. He'd been there, straw boater in hand, when Olive arrived at Mae's side. There'd been no exchange of recriminations between Big John and Olive, nothing beyond her withering glare. He may not be directly responsible for Mae's injury, but he is, in Olive's estimation, certainly responsible for the presence of the circus in Reading, Penn.

Any circus owner worth his salt knows a good reputation opens doors for future engagements; a bad reputation does the reverse. A truly *bad* reputation for any length of time puts a lock on those doors and hangs a bankruptcy sign.

It's Big John's practice to fire any employee known to indulge in the habit of drink. (He would have fired his brother long ago, if his brother were merely employed!) Coarse language is prohibited. Games of chance are prohibited. Accidents, on the other hand, are difficult to govern.

Big John sees a headline for the following day's local paper: *Young Woman Maimed by Strong Men and Family of Clowns at The Latterby Brothers' Circus!* He recollects the dwindling receipts for upwards of a year after a team of horses pulling the circus wagon were startled by an automobile's backfire and ran, headlong, through a dry goods store window. Although none but the horses had been injured (one had been cut so badly the circus doctor put a bullet in its head), the mayhem caused and the stir in the papers put a dent in attendance for more than one season.

Without verbal recriminations, and despite Big John's

general distrust and dislike of all things motorized, he offers to purchase the automobile — as an act of goodwill. He nods toward the reporter from *The Reading Daily*. The journalist scribbles. The headline the following day will read: *Big John Latterby of The Latterby Brothers' Circus, in an act of goodwill and generosity, assists mother and her six children from Williamsport, Penn. on their journey to the great state of New York. The magnanimous entrepreneur stated, "Allow me, on behalf of the circus, to purchase your train fares."*

"I know nothing of automobiles," Big John says. The reporter is absent and Big John's acknowledgement is closer to a private confession than public announcement.

"I do," Edison says.

Olive frowns.

"I'm soon sixteen," Edison says. It takes no coaxing, on anyone's part, to get Edison to stay with the auto. He will train one of Big John's rowdies in all matters pertaining to the operation of the Winton, its upkeep and repairs.

Before shaking hands on the deal, Budd says, "Mama?"

Olive will not meet his eye with an answer. The two men's hands are met.

Demon Dreams In The Boxcar

Reading, Pennsylvania

1909

lice watches Bobby consume a rat she's kept on ice for three days. The rat is a lump in the curve of the boa's body. Phoebe had had a lump in the curve of her body, but it's gone now. Alice takes a bite of biscuit. Her first patient of the day had been Phoebe, the show's Queen LaTina. Her last patient of the day had been the girl with the torn-up arms and crabby mama. No, it was the young woman under Johann, Gus, Bucky, Zed and Miranda. "Maybe," Alice tells Bobby, "I ought not count her. You scared whatever sense she still had clean away. Earl and Red tried to carry her into John's tent, but two young men, her brothers, they said, wrestled her from them. It's a wonder her leg didn't get broke again.

"These crazy folks, Bobby," she says, stroking her throat to help the biscuit, more like hardtack than biscuit, go down. She's got a goiter coming up; it'll be round as an orange soon enough and she's not at all sure what she'll do about that. Meanwhile, there's the true last patient behind her.

Reaching into the cage to stroke Bobby's lump, she asks,

"What am I going to feed him?" The stroke is not so much to help Bobby move his food along as a need to touch a living thing other than herself. A body needs touching. Nothing beats being held. The red-headed boy in his mama's lap — he might've, she thinks, been held a might too much. She couldn't quite figure the girl; not a thing like the boy and his mama. Not a bit put out, except by the cure, and who wouldn't turn up their nose to that? But she was, the girl, full of something that showed in her face. It wasn't fear or amazement or a judgment about size, about fat, or prettiness. It wasn't about the right or wrong of things.

It's not often Alice is stumped by a look.

She says, "Why didn't I think of that sooner?"

She's finished the biscuit. The rat is a lump inside Bobby — unmoved by Alice's strokes. That feisty girl and the way she wore the damage to her arms and purpling down the side of her face — like a reward for having fallen, skin freckled the same kind of ginger as her hair, same gingery brown as the new camel calf. "Milk," she says to Bobby. "Camel milk. We've figured it out, son; that we have."

"I KNOW THIS maybe don't sit well with you," she says, "as you've probably never had camel's milk, but Raffe tells me he grew up on it, back over where he came from, and Raffe, he's a fine old, *old* man now."

Moses keeps the tip of his tongue exposed, waiting for drops of anything. He comes back from darkness more often, is gaining a sense of hours, the motions and commotions outside, the quiet thick heat pouring from a sky he can't see, the voices of hungry stock, the voices of those who silence them, strains of urgency, patience, impatience.

He tastes the cool dribble of sustenance, swallows, knows something other than pain in exchange for remaining alive.

"He comes from Persia, Raffe does. Have you ever been to Persia? It's got a fine sound," she says. "Purrs-zhah. Isn't that fine?"

There is a Persia and a Sumer. They are swimming with Gilgamesh under a river in a place far away, Moses thinks, his focus tilting with shivers and this woman, steadily wetting his tongue, feeding him images from a time, a table, a place.

He swallows. For a while they are infant and mother: the cooing of tales like hymns or spoken carols; the camel calf's coming; the baby Phoebe won't bear; John Latterby's diddling with a girl half his age, she, Phoebe, no innocent, *but still*. The milk (has he had a teaspoonful yet?). tepid and surprisingly rich. Benjamin Smith and Sing Cheung hover behind the woman who is steady of hand. She moves aside, lumbering up, standing, blocking the ghosts of living and dead.

"There's a line to see Bobby," someone shouts from outside.

"Bobby's just had a rat," she answers. "He won't move much—it'll be a sorry act."

A rat? Moses listens for the rustle of skirts. His hearing is less precise than before. He waits.

With the woman present, he remains wakeful, on the periphery; there are shadows of ghosts—but only shadows. Alone, unbound to reality, he slips into the madness of a split face—half his father, half himself—and Sing Cheung is half Moses. A woman with a breast in the shape of a weasel is there who sits, composed as a Brahman Queen, naked from the waist up, who wants what she wants with a greed so slavish, Moses cries out *Aiyee!* In half wakefulness, he pleads with Sing Cheung, *Please don't, please don't hurt her.*

No matter which face Moses turns to the woman, her weasel breast sways. He knows neither he, nor Sing, can escape, but that his father, perhaps, has the answer. Sing Cheung has fought demons longer than Moses, knows the rules better than Moses; more to the point, Sing is accomplished with cutting tools, with tonsorial razors, and could remove, if Moses turns his face away, the offending weasel breast. Sing could do this with little effort, but Moses shrinks from so much blood, the thought of what would come. He does not show his other face to the woman.

The door to the boxcar rumbles shut. *Has she gone? Come back?* His darkness is absolute; he takes a shallow breath and knows the air is yellow-green, plumed as incense seeking a high, red ceiling. He begins, breath by breath, rebuilding Mesopotamian myth, the great wall of Uruk in the kingdoms of Gilgamesh replaces the weasel breast.

The Roster

orry, lady. This isn't the number we need."

Sharon is not fond of being called "lady." It rankles. What rankles even more is being told the number she's brought is useless — but still . . . a little courtesy goes a long way and her driver's license is in his hand. "Lady" was no part of her name. "What number do you need? This *is* from her death certificate. Irene Parilee Johns. Nineteen-thirty." The desk sergeant, or whatever grade his insignia stands for, remains stone-faced and uninterested. Is that a yawn he suppresses as he flips through papers on a clipboard? Or a facial tic, a working of muscles he can't control?

A commotion sets in behind Sharon. A string of epithets and curses and private bodily parts used as modifiers spew out in a female voice. She's heard them before, but never so *vibrantly* strung together.

The desk sergeant can't be more than forty, she thinks. *If I had begun the grand adventure of motherhood at a younger age, I could've had a son his age. But not like him — not jaded. How do they, how can they harden to such a degree?* She tilts her

face up toward him, studying him, his jawline rigidly working to show no change, no emotion whatsoever.

"The cold case number," he says.

"Can't you cross-match this number with that number?"
Sharon asks.

"Nope."

"Seriously? Nope? Really?" Her response is peppered with
prick, cunt, cock-sucker, and other charming notes from the
unhappy woman also visiting the precinct. It seems, insofar
as Sharon can figure, the woman's been told she can't smoke
inside; a city ordinance. *Thank God,* Sharon thinks.

"Seriously," the desk sergeant says.

"But you do have her on file—Irene Johns, right?"

"If you say so."

"Don't be fresh." She is surprised by her reaction, or, not
her reaction in and of itself, but that she has actually voiced it.

"Ma'am?" He produces a smile, a small one his overworked
jaw allows. She has struck a chord. He had a mother who'd
taught him some manners after all. She removes the tintype
of Irene from the folder she's brought along. It's the one of
Irene as a girl, no more than ten or eleven, the one with a
smile to soften the heart of even a hard-nosed desk sergeant.

He takes the tintype in hand. His features soften—Sharon is witness.

"She was a child, then—when she died?" His face has that
four o'clock shadow men with heavy facial hair must contend
with day after day, even though it's barely nine.

And here is Sharon's nemesis: the lie. To tell it? Or not?
If she shrugs, or even if she remains as stolid as he has been
throughout her inquiry, Sharon knows he will read her body
language as a "Yes."

Deceit is as bad as a lie.

When, she asks herself, *is a lie, or deceit, a good thing?*
"Not ever," she hears Lincoln respond from the grave.

She shrugs, gives a little bow of the head as if acquiescing to the desk officer's question. It wasn't a real question, was it? No. Surely what he said was more statement than question. She feels better; her shrug is his misunderstanding. This is not her lie.

"What I can do," he says, "is locate a roster of NYPD's finest for that year, what was it, nineteen-thirty?"

Sharon nods.

"Hey, you never know. A name might pop out of it that, who was it . . . your uncle?"

"My cousin. My dad's cousin."

"Right. Your dad's cousin might remember. You never know."

"You never know what?" Sharon asks.

"There might be some files kept by the investigating officers, that sort of thing. Might be a case number scribbled somewhere we could use to help you out."

She thinks about Buddy, the flightiness of his recollections. Could he pick the name of an investigating detective out of a roster seventy-eight years old? There had been two of them. Two detectives. Could he, perhaps, remember just one?

When her hand goes out for the tintype to be returned, the sergeant is slow to respond, as easily charmed by Irene's eager face as she had been.

"You're going *where?*" Buddy's face is ruddy and bright despite three days of confinement.

"The cemetery." Sharon folds a dead leaf from the hospital sill into the palm of her hand. "The one you told me about. You know, for show people."

"What on earth for? There's no marker. You'll never find her."

"I might find something." She plucks a yellowing leaf from a stem. "These need water." Buddy, wonderful as he most often is, has developed a case of something akin to jealousy when she talks about places she's been, or intends to go. "Be right back."

He had flicked his hand back with dismissal at the archival roster she'd brought him to study—not at all the reaction she'd hoped for, preemptively closing a door, at least for the moment, on an avenue of inquiry.

Returning with a pitcher of water, she says, "Sometimes, and I know this sounds nutty, but sometimes I can stand in a place and get a feel for what it *really is,* or was. Like a sense of history or time . . ."

Voice trailing off, she won't mention Teddy behind her at the kitchen sink in a house where he never lived, or how she once felt the presence of Indian ponies, a whole herd of them, moving past her as she watched a sunset in Arizona. She could smell their lathered sweat as the dust seemed to rise up around her. It hadn't, of course—but she *felt* that it had.

Buddy won't look at her. He says, "Is that so. History. So you're a time traveler now." There's an edge, sarcasm Sharon hasn't heard before.

"Well?" Sharon waits.

"There's no point, Rosie. It's just grass where she is. Grass they dig up and plant another crate in. Sometimes more than one. Then they replant the sod. There's just no point, that's all I'm saying."

"How can it hurt—me going?"

Buddy's hands are like pale, fat crabs turned on their backs as he studies his fingers, moving them like legs with feet that can't get a tread. He can't look at her. His eyes are hot; if he looks straight at her, he might actually cry. Johns men don't cry.

He collects himself. Irene deserved better than what she got. She made mistakes, sure—who doesn't? She made some wrong choices, sure. But she deserved better than what she got. No headstone, no marker. No mention of her—all these years.

"Go on then," he says.

"Not without your blessing," Sharon says.

"My blessing?" He forgets not to look at her. But she is feeling the loam in a potted plant on the sill, checking out what needs water.

"Yes," she says, turning. "If you're that unhappy, I won't go."

Briefly, while she faced away, so tall and thin, Buddy wondered how he ever thought he could see any part of Irene in her. Then, with her turn comes that smile where her lips fail to part but the corners rise and the eyes, the eyes focus—so directly at him. He looks away.

Oh, Buddy, Sharon thinks. *You're losing her all over again, aren't you? Why do I keep doing this? Why do I upset the living to connect with the dead? I do it with Bet, bringing up Ted. I do it here.*

He's turned, but too late. She says, "All right. *Forgidaboudit.*"

Buddy says, "No. Go. You should go. You need to. That's all. You need to go, so go."

"Buddy . . . " She pauses then says, "Well," for the umpteenth time with no follow-up.

She is between the dried potting soil and a hard place. The fondness they share is real—a living thing.

"You got that roster with you?" he asks. He's mustered up some enthusiasm, whether real or for show, Sharon can't tell.

"Right here." Sharon moves to her handbag on the foot of his bed.

He says, "You go *feel* the cemetery, OK? I'll give this a look-see while you're gone. When you get back, we'll exchange findings — OK wid you, Rosie?"

He says "Rosie" the way Humphrey Bogart says "Rosie" when he addresses Katherine Hepburn in *The African Queen*. He is OK with this. He is really OK with her going upstate.

"You know," he says, "there just might be some Johns Family cousins in that neck of the woods. That's where it all started, the show gigs, you know, with Dottie."

"How do you mean?"

"Those girl cousins of mine, the two swimmers. What were their names? They died. At that clinic where my mother died. I don't think either one of them was much over twenty." He wags his head. "TB took a lot of lives. A wonder I never got it. I guess the point is, they did. Anyway, they used to tour with Dottie and that's how Olive felt safe about letting Irene go, you know, so young and all, at fourteen. If her sister could let her own girls, one of them was a year or two younger even than Irene, then Olive must've thought Irene would be in good hands."

"Oh," Sharon says. "Cousins. I'd wondered what kind of mother . . ." Her voice trails off, newly amazed by Buddy and all he hasn't said.

A New Kind of Religion

e listens. Someone is moaning. A woman says, "There, there" and "Hold on, son" many times. His mouth doesn't work. One eye will not open. The other eye does. A frightful wide face lowers close to his own. It has a small nose. Its thin mouth seems not to move with each *there, there*. When her head turns he sees hair the color of a bird's nest, browns and silvers, the twigs of it skewed out like a halo, a large burl at the back held in place by combs.

That she is watching him watching her interests Moses. How she looks to where her hand moves with the salve she applies, the line of her mouth thinner, harder. What she finds registered in his eyes, registering in hers.

He cannot reconcile the moaning as his own. Yet the dull drone of a swarm from someplace distant fades to quiet when she touches a finger to his lips, returning as she commences with her applications.

She is bigger than many trees; she could house a hive.

"So, you can see me. Alice Towne. And you are?"

Her eyes have silver in them.

"There now. Easy," she says. "I know you can't say. Sh-sh."

She holds a thin square of white up between her face and his; water rains from the bottom edge. When she lowers the cloth, he imagines a slice of paper-thin cloud, soaked with rain, arranges itself on his throat, the lower-right side of his face.

It is a handkerchief, her handkerchief, she tells him.

For Moses, it is a piece of heaven. It is relief. He opens himself to the sensation of pleasure, a lightness of existence where he is carried on many wings, the drone of another body, his but not his, is no longer plaintive, as if this Alice Towne is no human being at all but a sheltering tree of great width and height, and he is weightless, carried by her or to her. Or, that he, Moses, is capable of flight.

HE SCRATCHES THE mouth of Jesus off the printed picture. There are still words coming from this Savior in blue robes with his faith shining out like rays of sun from his head. *Come to me, lamb of God, lamb of my Father,* he says.

It is easy to move, as easy as ever it has been in Moses's life. The heart is a simple thing and the heart of Jesus approaches Moses and the heart of Moses is turned toward the honey-blond hair of Christ.

As he takes a first step, he is air moving on air, the picture riffles, lifts to show its flat edge.

He pulls at the silver tack holding the print in place; the tack will not come free of the doorframe. From the scratched hole comes a swarm of hornets; their wings are deafening. He goes into the hall, where Ellie is waiting, but Ellie is not Ellie. She is other; she is a monster; she is a stinging fly; she is the mythological cow he has read about with Benjamin — Ios, the cow cursed by Hera. She cannot be both; she cannot be both fly and cow.

"Sh-shh," she says.

How can you be fly and cow, he asks, more curious, less frightened, from inside his dream.

Moses hears, "Better. That's better."

"M-mm-mm." His eye opens, pulls away from the paper dreams, finds the woman near his bed, a black-splotched, copper-green snake wound about her neck and shoulders.

"That's good," she says. "You're awake."

"M-mm," Moses says.

"You had me worried, son."

He might, if he could speak, tell her about the cow, the fly, the steps almost taken, the silver tack, but he cannot speak, only murmur, only shiver with the thought of those ghosts he's abandoned, how close he had come to abandoning this space. It's a space full of odors, of stale hay and something greener, of body sweats and perfumes, of rustling skirts and invisible sounds as the snake moves his great head out to observe Moses more closely.

"So," Alice says, "Bobby, meet our friend."

"M-mm," Moses says.

From her shoulder to his unharmed cheek, Bobby drops a cool nose, touches the unscarred part of Moses. He has survived. He will grow a new skin; he will let Jesus entertain cows and demons with wild-goose chases.

WHAT IS TRULY real and what is possibly illusion, Moses cannot answer; the strain of staring elongates light into streams and a figure backlit by sun at the threshold could be an angel.

The streams go out of focus. The blur is a yellow flower as big as a dinner plate. Ellie, the sin of all he has done and not done, accompanied by a great rumbling.

"Better closed," Alice says, "the hard light bothers his sight."

Brilliance gone, cracks of light remain where the angel had been. A new odor permeates; it is sandalwood.

"Son," Alice says, "this is Phoebe. Phoebe, this is Raffe's latest stray."

Moses is burnt, broken, pathetic, but he is not a stray. Nor can he respond or see the faces of these women: Alice, who anoints him with salves and brings consolation to mind and body, who pulls him from nightmares, who brings an angel scented with sandalwood to move through the yellow flower; the angel and Alice—they are his saviors.

"He's had it rough," Alice says.

"So I see." There's a pause, a rustling of skirts, a rattling of the door rolling back. "Sis," Phoebe adds, "you're not gonna leave!"

"I am," Alice answers.

"I'm no nurse. I don't know what you expect."

"I expect you to make this poor creature easier. Sit back down. You owe it."

Phoebe sits where Alice has been seated near Moses's head. "Can he talk?" she asks.

"Won't know 'til Raffe unwires his jaw."

The door rattles shut.

"I've gotta tell you," Phoebe says, "I ain't no nurse."

He hears water plink into the bucket as she rewets the rag; he imagines the droplets on his lips and they are there.

"Oh, you like that, do you?"

Perhaps his contentment is evident. His savior has moved; her skirts have rustled up and away from the floor pallet to some other place in the car. No floorboards creak, not as when Alice moves in the car; he can't locate her sandalwood scent. He works his jaw. The pain comes sharp. He wants to say her name.

"Aw, look," she says, "I'm only just here. These legs. They go all crampy sittin' on that damned floor."

Ah. She is not far. Only out of view.

"That's them puttin' the ramps up. Did you know you'd be sharing this ride with a queen? Queen LaTina—that's me. No, you don't need to bow or nothin'," she says.

He blinks his good eye, but where she is, he does not know for certain, and if she sees, he does not know. She has lit a woodbine and the smell joins the odors of ointment, stale hay, rotting herbs, incense and sandalwood.

"These are somethin' else. I see you blinkin' off the stink, but I won't catch nothin' on fire. We've had enough of that already, wouldn't you say? I mean, if you could say."

She moves back into his view. He can tell little about her features except she is slight, almost transparent. She leans over him, seems to be taking in the various places of his face, says, "You don't get what I say, do you?" The train lurches into movement and her hand on his chest stops her from falling. Chance places her hand in contact with an unharmed part of his body. Moses does not wince. He is happy for the touch. He will not be riding alone. In a moment, she will bring drops of water to his lips and he will taste her goodness, her kindness, her companionship again.

"I mean," she continues, smoke curling as if from an altar, "I can call you a dirty chink and you won't know the difference, seeing's how you probably don't know American, English, and all. But I won't. I might," she pauses and Moses hears the hiss of the woodbine extinguished in the water. "I might, if I

knew what that meant, you know, 'chink,' what that means . . .
I might, but you don't look no more dirty than the rest of us.
Lord knows we could all do with a wash. And some kindness.
Don't you dare ever, and I mean never ever, say to Sis I said
such a thing. Got that?"

Moses is still. His thoughts are still. His good eye is closed.
His heart is open. She is the salve; she is the hurt. *She needs
my reassurances,* he thinks, and blinks. Blinks again until she
sees.

"Good," she says. "I'm taking that as a promise."

He blinks again; the deal is made. He will not say a word
about mentioned kindness to anyone.

On the floor of the boxcar, skirts bunched near his head,
high-buttoned boots not far from his right hand, Phoebe sits.
Light comes through cracks in the door like bright lengths
of straw sparsely scattered to hang up and down, shift inside
the car like stretched fireflies. Moses is hourly more aware of
his whereabouts, his particular whereabouts within a particular structure. Where he is in the greater world of physical
train tracks is a matter he does not concern himself with —
there would be no point.

"I lost a baby yesterday," Phoebe says.

Her voice is not strong. The noise of the tracks — the
creaking boxcar as it holds to the rails with every bend and
bump, is an ongoing roar, but he hears and moves his hand to
the edge of the pallet. He does not touch her boot, does not
lay his hand over it as if it were a soft leather house holding
the pulse of the world.

She draws her legs close against her chest, rests her forearms across them and her head on her forearms. "Didn't look
like no baby," she says. "'Course, you don't look much like
no man in your current way of lookin' either, and that don't

make you less one, does it?" Her breath comes sharp. Her foot is not where Moses can touch it.

"*Do not look at Moses, do not, do NOT!*" is what Moses intends, but he fails.

Her ear to his lips, she asks, "What?"

If she would stay so close, he thinks, where her throat is so near my cheek, where her hurt is my hurt and my fears are closed into boxes and locked up with chains, where even my father sleeps—if she would stay so close—there are no demons.

Phoebe says, "I don't understand how you talk, what you mean, what kinda word that is, or if it's talkin' at all or maybe just pain comin' out, like bawlin' from some kid who can't help but bawl."

Moses keeps his good eye closed, hears her resettle. The train rocks sharply. She winces, as if she is the wounded one. *What happened? How are you injured? What has hurt you?* he wants to ask, but she has covered her hurt with humming a small song. The tune does not go very far before starting again—a few memorized notes like a chant. Small gasps punctuate each repeat. She is catching herself. She is trying to breathe. It is not about shock, about seeing his melted self. *It's all right,* he wants to comfort, but cannot.

Track miles click away under them. Fireflies come and go, come and go, through the cracked door. He is sorry for her hurt.

Phoebe says, "What a thing, cryin' over a wad of soft blood. I mean, if that don't beat all I don't know what does."

Moses is vaguely aware of the iron smell of blood; he'd thought it the tracks, the train, the cage metal at the far end of the car, the shovel blade or iron rake.

She says, "Just 'cause I stick a fan of pink feathers on don't make me no queen. I guess I know that."

She says, "I had a name picked out for him and all."

She says, "Bobby," and a half-laugh escapes. "Sis was fit to spit nails 'cause that's the name of her snake and she thought I was disrespectin' the baby by namin' him so. Lord knows, she does love that snake, but no matter about that."

She says, "It wasn't her blame snake I was naming him after but my brother. I didn't tell Sis that. Nobody knows I even *had* a brother."

Phoebe lowers her head to the edge of the pallet and says, "Bobby." Doubled over, drawn up like an infant—she offers long, keening wails.

His hand moves to her hair. He has heard such keening at graves during Tsing Ming when mourners cried out to the spirit world to chase demons far from their loved ones. He holds his hand there, on her hair, over her ear, where all the firefly moments of hurt and regret click and click. He is willing her wounds to leave her and come into him through his fingers. His hand is as light upon her as he can make it, all but absent, willing a middle calm to enter her thoughts, give her rest, as she has given him the most peace he has known since waking from his long nightmare.

When she stills, he withdraws his hand. She places hers on the cheek where Alice's snake left a wet touch earlier. Her thumb runs along under his eye and she says, "I like this good eye."

He has not seen himself except as he imagines, except as he's interpreted reactions from Alice, Raffe, Alice's snake, and now Phoebe—whose eyes he cannot determine the color of in this half light. When she takes in the closed side of his face, she does not grimace. Her attentions are brief. Returning to view his good side, she says, "Yes. I like this good eye just fine."

MOSES WAKES. HER hand is on his chest, on the night-shirt Raffe has given that Moses might not be naked. When she stirs, her eyes are full of rest and the firefly lights the door allows show Moses her eyes are brown, but unlike her dress, flecked with amber and gold. When she moves, her scent gathers up to combine with dry straw, the pungent odors of salves Alice applies, saddle soap, sandalwood. She lifts his head, gently, moves her arm under to pillow his neck while humming the tune she chanted earlier—the same few notes coming again and again. Moses tilts into her, wanting his good eye against her breast where the sandalwood is strongest. His pain whistles out. She says, "Sh-shh. Shh, my Bobby." Incense curls from her bosom and into his dreams where he is all light; all the strings of light from the day that shone in through the boxcar door like straw and fireflies are streaming out from him now, finding her, streaming back into him. His winces are the fireworks of pain and unutterable bliss.

IN CHINA TOWN Yun Li chops celery. *Aiyee! What to do, what to do?*

Two detectives, the same two that hounded him about Moses Cheung's whereabouts the week after Moses departed—are back, across the street from Heung Fat's, one on the step and one in a chair where the proprietor usually sits when his pharmacy is empty. *Aiyee,* Yun Li thinks. *May the fat one's chair leg break.*

The fat one looks as well-fed as Yun Li, but younger by half in age, and the other, a thin China youth, has a nose like a chop knife.

Yun Li is safe stirring his noodles. But youth is youth.

Youth is impetuous. Youth is eager. And hungry for success. They had been removed from the murder in the headlines: they were too young, too Irish, too Chinese.

If they trick Yun Li, they will take him to a cold place. No warm concubine to soothe him. No wife. No small son to bounce on his knee. He uses his sharpest knife on the celery. A gift from Sing Cheung celebrating Yun Li's promotion to head cook, the knife's hilt bears his name and Sing Cheung's.

What to do? So much stink over the death of one ghost.

What if another one died?

Who knew the stinks in the rooms upstairs could be told one from the next? Or that June would be so warm? Or that on the day he planned to remove the trunk, the police would come? The youthful detectives? Yun Li had spent as much time at the police station as he usually spent in the kitchen the second week after Moses boarded the train.

What to do?

His thoughts collide and separate, reckless. He had made offerings of incense and begged for another murder, one the detectives *could* solve. And, *Aiyee! over on Pell Street another body found.*

But now these upstarts are back. Small crescents of celery slide from his board into a broth; a second stalk goes under his knife. His motions are sure. He will ask for guidance at the Joss House.

His workday ends. He leaves through the front, not the alley. He is prepared. It will be good to face these devils and be done with them. The one who sits with his newspaper doesn't look up. He makes no gesture by hand or a nod of his head that Yun Li should cross the road for further interrogation, but Yun Li crosses.

"You heard from your friend?" the pale oaf with his curving

moustache asks without honor, without lifting his eyes from the page.

The Chinese youth translates. His eyes are hard as black glass. He studies Yun Li from his black-slippered feet and cuffed baggy pants to the various stains on Yun Li's long apron. He watches the clean width of Yun Li's large hands. He translates what Yun Li says in a menacing way, and Yun Li smiles, in spite of himself, at this piss-ant boy daring to threaten his immense body.

"No, sir," Yun Li says, and it is the truth. Sweat bursts like wellsprings to run salty into his eyes. He blinks.

The young oaf in the pharmacist's chair turns a page of the newspaper. "Tomorrow, you come down to the station-house. I expect you to bring the truth. If you don't, plan on a stay. Got me?"

AT THE JOSS House, Yun Li pays fifty cents and lights two red candles. He aligns incense sticks in a bowl of sand and uses the candles to light them. He wipes his hands across his apron, tosses the marked pieces of wood. They fall with one head-side up and one tail-side up.

This is excellent counsel! He pats his belly. *These meddle-some boys who think they are men will not miss a humble cook tomorrow.* He will be there, but they will not.

live Johns and five of her six children who left the farm in Williamsport are on an eastbound train. Edison, as jaunty as ever a fifteen-year-old farm boy could be, is on his way back to the Latterby Brothers' Circus in the Winton, the sole occupant and pilot of the yellow touring car, a young king of the road possessed of such buoyancy he cannot help but whistle into the oncoming wind—at least for the mile and a half along the tracks to reach the circus grounds. Olive imagines her son's exuberance, his freedom just so; wouldn't she feel much the same? Wilbur's head rests in her lap; Flo's blond curls lean into her left arm; Budd, Mae and Irene occupy the bench seat across the aisle from where Olive sits board-straight watching over what remains, as if they are hours that might vanish as Edison has done.

It is not yet 7 AM. With a great deal of luck, they will change trains in West Philly and disembark at Jersey City to board the Fulton Street Ferry for Brooklyn, where they'll be welcomed by Olive's sister Florence (will she still recognize

Florence after nearly twenty years?) by 10:34—still morning, still the better part of the day to settle in.

Edison's absence weighs against Olive's optimism. Is it Budd, checking the time on his pocket watch—is it this action causing a malaise Olive would sooner not feel? She likens herself to the watch's fob ring, a hard circle without a center, responsible for the tether of these children, these hours of her life. If not the fob, the stem—the winding apparatus which sets all in motion. She glances across the aisle. Budd, Mae and Irene. Wilbur is on Olive's right, Flo on her left. Edison, were he present, would sit on Wilbur's right. "It won't be forever. Just for the summer," Budd said. "Think what I'll learn," Edison said. *What choices did I have?* Olive asks herself.

Budd slides a large wicker basket from under the bench seat to support Mae's splinted leg. *Thoughtful boy.* She corrects herself—*man.* She says, "Irene!" and Irene turns on her knees from her view out the window, straightens her middy, tugs at her collar, folds her hands into her lap in a gesture of pouting impatience. It's as much as Olive may expect as she turns from Irene's unhappy sulk.

Olive feels Mae's discomfort, and not on account of Mae's splinted leg. The leg will heal. It's the recollection of having come upon Mae, the girl's impropriety, privately, of course, but indecent all the same—of having interrupted Mae breaching those normal curiosities a child might have in regard to his or her own body. Olive flinches, remembering. It was just the one time. Yet, Mae's mind, to Olive, seems unset. There are edges, precipices inside Mae's thinking; there is danger in the moans Olive has heard in the night as she stood on the stairwell, listening to Mae struggle through sleep. *When,* Olive wonders, *will the girl become herself? The*

young lady she is required to be? Life for Mae on the farm has
been one thing; life in New York will be another.

Leaving Mae with Joseph had not been a consideration.
Joseph Johns, crooner of lullabies, comforter of the sick
calf—although survivors were rare—would've ruined Mae,
made her a farmhand, allowed the girl too much time with
the stock. Irene, if she didn't fling herself off some real preci-
pice or drown, might've survived Joseph. Already both of the
world and in the world, Irene is Olive's invincible child, the
one vested with Viking blood (if the rumors be true) from
the Talbot side. But Mae?

"Irene!" Olive hisses and Irene, again on her knees facing
out, turns from the window, avoids Olive's stern stare, rolls
her forehead into Mae's shoulder.

Mae, in the private domain of her own inner thoughts,
does not open her eyes or budge from a near uncanny still-
ness, other than the visible cast of her thoughts behind closed
eyes. It seems to Olive that Mae has a running battle going
on inside, angels and demons wrangling with each other until
little is left for Mae but chaos. If Olive knew what to say, she
couldn't, or wouldn't. Such topics are not spoken of, at least
not between any mothers and daughters of whom Olive is
aware. To speak of such would be fundamentally wrong. Mae,
Olive believes, is coming to terms with these fundamentals;
not easily observed by a mother, but necessary, yes, necessary
that one find one's own way—as Olive had done. It will be,
in the end, more satisfactory for Mae to have grappled the
devils of torment and temptation and to have won.

Budd says, "I think Mae and I should take it easy about
changing trains in West Philly."

"We have to change trains?" Mae says and repeats, "We
have to change trains?"

Olive says, "Yes. We must change trains. And with very little time."

"Where?" Wilbur asks.

"We'll ask the porter," Budd says. "And if it's very far, Mae and I will catch the next train headed for Jersey."

Olive hesitates. A few decades or so down the line, Olive thinks, when Budd is a middle-aged man, his edicts will not be questioned anymore than he will question Olive's now. But now is not the future and she says, "Not possible, son."

She gives no explanation for discounting his suggestion. She has resolved, with certainty, her family will not be further sundered. Olive is not, however, in the habit of exposing her *softer* side. What possible practicality can there be in *that?* No. A strong front is the answer. A straight back and a strong front.

The vanguard her family will create to protect Mae's splinted leg as Budd carries her to make their connection is fully plotted in Olive's thoughts. She will take center front, Wil and Flo on one side, hands held as tightly as they might in a game of Red Rover; Irene on Olive's other side, clenched and in hand; and, like the prow of a ship, they will plow a path through the platform crowds, sufficiently protecting Mae's leg from the bustle. So be it, if they miss their connection. Ferries run on the half-hour to Fulton Street.

EARLIER, WHEN THE train left the Reading station, Mae watched Edison wave from the platform. Waving his cap in long arcs, Mae had thought him the perfect illusion of happiness. Departure—from farm, from Edison, from any sort of privacy—is true panic, though she shows little, closing her eyes, keeping them closed, sheltered against any views to an internal misery her mother might perceive, were they open.

Hadn't Irene sensed Mae's troubled self? Tried to reassure Mae in regard to feelings she, Irene, could know nothing of? Little stick of a girl, this sister, who'd offered to sacrifice her small wondrous being to drive that despicable automobile, join the circus, if only she might be allowed; Irene, who — if she knew how close Mae had come to agreeing to running away when they were stranded on Neversink Mountain — would've suffered, and suffered cruelly, from such a liaison. Mae nods. She will not speak. She is torn in two. One of them — either Edison, the perfect illusion of happiness, or Mae, restless and tainted by thoughts unbecoming the person she ought to be — is wrong. Mae nods. They are, she and Edison, a curiosity as strange as any two-headed chicken. Every edict of society, of family, makes it so.

WHEN IRENE OFFERED to trade places with Edison, Budd said, "If you were big enough for your feet to reach the pedals, Stick, you'd probably be the driver."

"No she wouldn't, Budd," Flo said. "*Girls* aren't allowed!"

"Girls are too allowed — it's *natural* as anything," Irene said, adding, "What about Queen LaTina . . ."

Fact was, Irene had never, not actually, *seen* Queen LaTina — only the wild-eyed stallion, or what she thought was the wild-eyed stallion, tied off in the field near the Winton.

Flo said, "Queen LaTina wasn't even there! But the snake lady was. That fat one, with the trick pocket. She was helping Mae and that snake was, ooh, creepy to see, wasn't it, Mae?"

Mae had nodded a nod the others might take as a response or simply another of many nods she made for no apparent reason.

"Shush now, both of you." Olive took Irene's arm. "That awful woman. I hope that ointment hasn't caused an infection." Pushing back the sleeve of Irene's middy, she inspects the damage, turning Irene's arm from side to side. "Not this one. Let me see the other."

"It was both," Irene said, but Olive unbuttoned Irene's other cuff and pushed the sleeve up as far as the wool would go.

Running her gloved hand over Irene's elbow, she offered "Well. You were ever a fast healer, child."

IRENE'S WHOLE WORLD at the moment is inside this train car. Edison, already part of a world bristling with queens and camels, wild-eyed stallions, a gargantuan snake and a gargantuan woman who, according to Flo, wore the snake like a winter scarf around her throat, is gone from them. That *he* should remain with a circus train, while she, Irene of the sycamore platform and dare-devil dives, is stuck on an everyday-go-anywhere train is vastly more puzzling than healed elbows. When Olive's attentions are elsewhere, Irene turns the trimmed square of her sailor collar toward the aisle, takes to her knees, watches the outer world slip past, and exhales damp patches onto the window glass.

The passing lands look like Pennsylvania: green hillocks and barns, houses and fence lines and broad shade trees at the ends of straight, long roads that disappear almost as they come into view. Will she know when they cross into a foreign state?

"I-rene?" Olive says, and Irene re-smoothes her middy and dangles her high-buttoned, booted feet again. Then, as if it had a higher importance than Edison (as no mention has been made of Irene's brother), Olive says, "The quilt! We've left Granny Cly's quilt in the Winton!"

As Irene absorbs news of the quilt's loss, compares it (smelly, awful thing that it is) with the loss of Edison—he is suddenly not the brother at the outset of a grand adventure, but abandoned, left behind. Envy (which had replaced her sorrow) transforms into pity. *Poor Edison. Nothing but that raggedy quilt to remind him of family, the farm, them.* He will, she believes, survive; he has all those muscles he's worked into being a hard ball near the size of a baseball inside his arms. *Feel that, Stick!* Irene remembers him asking time and again.

Irene scuffs her rounded boot against the wicker basket supporting Mae's leg, thoughtfully, knowing she won't miss the quilt, or its crazy stitch-work in loud blues and greens and reds over odd shapes of black. Nor will she miss the grandmother she barely knew, her mother's grandmother—the oldest woman Irene ever saw, or probably ever would. How can she miss a stranger? Not like Edison; not a thing like a brother with hard balls inside his arms he asked you to touch every day, who smiled over breakfast and chiseled away at chicken on a bone until a girl had to wonder if there would be any bone left when he was done. She misses Edison already. And Joseph.

"Budd?" Irene says.

"Yes?"

"Are you going to go somewhere, too?"

"I am going somewhere, Stick," he says.

"Are you going to go somewhere away from me?"

"Come here." He opens a gate to his lap so she can climb in.

She's waiting for Budd to answer her question: Is he going to leave them, too? *I am meant*, Irene thinks as she climbs into Budd's lap and rests her head against his shoulder, *to be a boy*. If Budd goes, how will I know how to be the best kind of boy I can be, without actually being one? She can't think of Wilbur as any sort of person to be like. He cries at the drop of a hat, is more girl than she is—only with different parts—and why a dangly bit of nothing between his legs should give him the rights to be all she, Irene, so wishes to be, is an unfairness she can't understand, an unfair turn of fate, an unlucky event.

"That quilt's an heirloom," Olive says and asks Budd to send a telegram for delivery to the Latterby Brothers' Circus before it leaves Reading. "I'm afraid what Edison might do with it," she says, adding, "Or not do."

Budd says, "Next stop is West Philly, right?"

"Are you, Budd?" Irene asks.

"Oh, right," Olive says.

"I can't see us making that connection; there's hardly five minutes," Budd says and nods toward Mae, who seems to be sleeping, although rigidly upright and angled on the bench seat. "If we miss there, I'll have time to get a message off to Edison before the next one. Our porter thought we'd have about an hour."

Olive says, "Of course, son."

The train rocks along through countryside Irene doesn't see, and because Budd doesn't answer her question, she is pretty sure he has plans to head out of Brooklyn just as soon as he can manage an escape. She closes her eyes so as not to watch her mother's fingers curl and uncurl Wilbur's red locks as he sleeps, or pretends sleep, in her lap.

After a time, Budd wakes Irene. "I'd carry you, Stick, if I could. But this trip is Mae's on account of her leg. You understand?"

Mae is watching Irene as Irene nods and says, "Sure. I understand."

Where The Sod Ends

NEW YORK

2008

here are, even in charity plots, headstones and markers for the lost stars of other eras. Rose of Sharon is reading the names and dates on such markers. *Curly, May his A-Paws in Heaven be as Loud as it was Here on Earth.*

What she can't understand is why there is no sign, no plaque, no coarsely carved stone for Irene. Other Vaudeville veterans have been so honored, so remembered, from comics and jugglers, clowns and vocalists, bell-ringers and accordi-onists, contortionists, ventriloquists, and dog trainers to their show-stopping-A-Paws-getting dogs. She shoves the thin sprinkling of snow again and again with the toe of her shoe. Hay-colored grass, then red dirt. Hay-colored grass, then red dirt. *What kind of mother, what kind of family, would do this? Abandon you so absolutely?* Sharon's left dozens of red-dirt divots like these; has stood in depressions where someone's been set in the ground and the ground, over years, has caved to fill gaps decay left in its wake.

Nothing.

There is no sense of presence, no scent of *otherness*, no

whiff of brine from a skin too often drenched in the ocean. Nothing. She leaves another patch of toe-turned earth, moves on.

The air is uncannily still. Her breaths hang where she stands, even as she moves away from them. She sees them when she turns back, little clouds of herself left to dissipate into the crystal clarity of nothing.

There'd been nothing from the cousins Buddy mentioned—the second and third generations related to the tubercular victims, those twin dead swimmers. One very old woman with advanced Alzheimer Disease. No family resemblance; no connection whatever. Nothing.

She's been foolish. Again. No broken bones. No headlong plunge to end up on the steel tines of a green rake—but a misstep, nonetheless. Behind her, some distance away, the hired car waits, engine running, meter running. It's bulbous, black and long, a Chrysler, she thinks, hovering in its own breath. Giving the hay-colored grass a last kick, she faces it squarely—the shining black certainty of it. She's failed.

PART V

Yun Li and Job Security
China Town, New York City
1909

un Li has a lie for his concubine: he has been throwing dice behind the pharmacy with the off-duty waiters and cooks from other noodle houses. He has a lie for his wife: he has been with his concubine who gives him healthy sons, not the barren one, although his second concubine's skin is silk and she is so young. He is later than he had meant to be but not so late that a good lie won't work.

They are good women, all of them. He will not need to beat them for questioning. They will not question. But it is good foresight to have the lies ready. *No wonder women are worthless*, he thinks, *they are so changeable.*

The one in the alley will not change again. He sees her ghost face just before it closed. Very bad teeth, very bad, Yun Li recalls. Her mouth so open, yet all that came out was a croak. He is better now. Now he will not have to take time off from Heung Fat's, his position as top cook is secured, he is safe and can bounce his sons on his knees; he can work; he can bring home good money; he can breathe without feeling giddy, without watching the front window for the partnered detectives who would be busy, very busy now, with solving other crimes in other parts of China Town.

He sweeps his wide hands down the front of his black cotton shirt and comes to the stiffness that is a part of himself. He will go to the young, barren concubine first. *Aiyee, her skin so pale and smooth, without wrinkles or puckers or the rounding belly of another expected birth.*

Tired from so many hours at work and then hunting, he takes the steps up. They are outside stairs, made of wood. They groan as if they will give way and break with his weight, but they won't. They have not broken before, and with so much good joss, why would they think about breaking now? He is full of his achievements, and somehow, as he ascends, he is both at the first step and at the last, monstrous in his shape-shifting, long as a dragon, beneficent, glowing on the dark stairs as if lit from the inside.

With no rail on his right, he uses the wall on his left to steady himself, his hand a five-fingered glowing world lifting up from one place, leaving a phosphorescent glow of his handprint behind, settling onto the next pattern of bricks as he continues. At the third floor, he enters, feels his way down the narrow hall, finds the third door, keys it open.

His young concubine sleeps. She is curled on her side like the least of his sons, dimly lit by a narrow slot of moon through the long row of shallow windows running just below the roof. Yun Li's breathing comes hard. He will find her a ground-floor room. Yes. His job is secure. Yun Li can afford a room closer to earth. He will have the scribe advertise for him. Oh. And he mustn't forget to have the scribe send a letter to Mr. M. Rathke in Williamsport, Penn. Young Moses must never come back.

Edison in Love

PENNSYLVANIA

1909

 dison walks to the field where the Winton is parked. He knows he'll find Bucky there behind the wheel: the little clown Mae broke a leg trying to save; the little clown he has thanked for almost a week now for this peach of a job; the clown who has ridden with him in the Winton from Reading, Penn. to Franklin; the boy clown, barely eight, who pretends he's in control of the parked car, even though his feet can't reach the pedals.

It's early. Earl and Red move slowly among the camels and other stock, shoveling manure to carry away. He hasn't seen Phoebe today, or Big John — but there's nothing unusual in that. He wonders aloud where Sis might be. Alice Towne, in her floral wrapper, big as old Pearly and nearly as slow, is usually more places than Edison expects to find her.

"What's that you said, Ed?" Bucky's voice is like a branch snapping. The camels turn their heads toward the Winton.

"I was wondering where Sis is this morning. You seen her?"

"You need her for something?"

"Nah. Just wondering."

Bucky, a circus tumbler, tumbled from his mother's womb

eight years earlier (with the aid of Sis) on a train en route to Montana out of Rapid City, South Dakota. He's out of costume, clown shoes gone and feet bare, scalp wig with tufted patches of red hair in a box in the sleeping car his folks call "Home." His chunky false teeth they make him wear for the show are in the box, too. Bucky hates the teeth; they make him gag. He worries, he's told Edison, someday he'll swallow them and then his mother will beat him, but not as hard as his father.

Behind the wheel of the Winton, he's wearing Edison's brown tweed coat and cap; the sleeves are rolled back more than ten inches. The coat's lining is coffee brown and shines in the early sun. Ed's cap is nearly a fit; Bucky has a big head for his age. Some folks have called him a "dwarf" but he's not. Ed's assured him he's not.

Bucky can't see over the steering wheel. He's short for his age, especially his legs, but in knickers and regular shirting, he's a regular boy—just not very tall, not yet. He plans to *be* tall. And to go places a circus train can't. He told Edison as much the first time they met—a different field, a different town, but pretty much the same as today.

"CAREFUL WITH THAT steering wheel, son. It came off on us once, up near Harrisburg," Edison had cautioned. He was just back from the Reading depot where a different sort of car moved off with the crowd of folks he'd never admit to missing. Family gone, he hadn't known what to put his hands to, or where to direct himself, except to the Winton. For half a second, he thought the short stranger he spotted in the Winton's driver's seat was Wil or Flo or Irene. Somehow or other one of them had stowed away, been left behind—and not missed by Olive until after the train had departed. He'd been wrong.

"I'm careful enough," Bucky answered. "You the mechanic?"

"I'm the mechanic. Name's Edison Johns." It was an odd flip-flop of the heart—relief to find he wasn't going to be strapped with family anymore and disappointment in the same breath. "You?"

"Bucky."

"So, Bucky," Edison said, dropping into the passenger seat, "where we headed?"

"I don't know. Someplace without tracks'd be OK by me.

"How about we're in Egypt and there's a pyramid out over yonder we need to reach before sundown," Edison said.

Bucky looked where Edison pointed. "That mountain?"

"Pyramid." Edison nodded toward the horizon. He pulled a quilt from the tonneau and folded it down until it would fold down no further. Tucked beneath Bucky, it gave the boy another half foot of height and Edison, though he wouldn't know how to phrase it, a sense of comfort. There was the automobile—new to the Johns family—and there was the quilt.

"This is *fine!*" Bucky said. "She's a beaut, ain't she?"

"She is that." Edison stroked the steering wheel Bucky's small hands pretended to guide. "Even better when she's cleaned up." He was grateful beyond measure for Mae's unfortunate display of motherly protection. "Say, Bucky, there's a little guy, maybe a dwarf or a midget, I need to find and thank."

"Zed's our littlest guy," Bucky said.

"Well. I owe him—Zed is it?"

"What do you owe Zed for?"

"For breaking my sister's leg."

"You gonna hurt him?" Bucky's smile faded as he leaned into a pretend turn long enough to have gone around Neversink Mountain.

"Nah. I need to thank him, someway or other. If Mae hadn't tried to save him, I'd be driving this fine car east, toward Brooklyn." Edison pushed his cap back, pulled it forward. Here he was, younger than Budd, on his own *independent* adventure. Something Budd hadn't done. Something Budd mightn't ever do.

"It was me," Bucky said.

"Not Zed?"

Bucky shook his head and Edison said, "I think you and me are gonna be pals."

EDISON'S JOB PAYS a dollar a week, all the food he can eat, a bedroll and a place to unroll it. Every next town is a new town to unfold the spectacle for the crowds, work with the roustabouts, set up and take down tents and enclosures. Gus and Johann offer pointers on improving muscle flexes and poses during his off-hours. He's got a driver's uniform and visor cap for chauffeuring Big John to neighboring small towns. During parades, he's not on the sidelines — he's at the wheel of the Winton, Big John in the passenger seat, leading the whole shebang!

In a pasture on the outskirts of Franklin, with Bucky, half Edison's age, at the wheel, Edison Johns is the king of all he surveys. Earl and Red have moved on; he may not see them again until evening, after all things circus have calmed and the penny-card games begin. Edison's participation in the games is infrequent, what with his knowledge of cards next to nil and his pennies few. In spite of a three-penny limit, his weekly salary is picked off in a matter of two, sometimes three nights' play. Paid on Sundays, he's generally busted by Tuesday.

Women play, too. If he had half Sis's luck, if he could win the way she does, he'd never miss a hand. And, if he never missed a hand, he'd never miss seeing the queen when she showed up.

The first time he saw her, close-up, in the same tent set up for eating as where they played cards, she stood just behind Sis, smoking a woodbine. He'd never seen a woman smoke—same as him. She wore a plain brown dress, not a plume or spangle in sight. Unlikely he'd be dazzled, but he was. Couldn't take his eyes off her dress, off the bosom of that dress with its silly, puffed-pigeon look. Her heart was somewhere under all that. No telling what all else rose and fell with every breath she took. And it wasn't her red hair that rolled his knickers up—he came from a family of heads one shade of red or another. But roll his knickers did. Edison was in love.

He makes every effort not to miss a game. Often as not, when he locates Sis, Phoebe, the queen's given name, is not far away. "It's an odd thing," he says to Bucky, "Sis not around yet."

"Phoebe's exercising horses with—"

"Gall dang it, Bucky. Why didn't you say?"

PHOEBE WALES IS a celebrity, technically proficient with jumpers and possessed of a toned musculature Edison admires. Pennsylvania farm boys do not, as a rule, attend ballets, but he has curled the edges of an advertisement with an illustrator's rendering of Isadora Duncan garbed in flowing Grecian white tunics, flowers set in her ringlets.

Isadora captured Edison's imagination—not with her graces (although "her graces" played a major role) but with her biceps, Phoebe now captures his dreams. She is *The Queen*, Empress of his privately sinful actions before sleep. Her perfect symmetry haunts him and her hands, how she places them on the bulky shoulder of the fat woman as she watches the penny-ante gaming, the comfort and ease as those hands settle upon Sis, haunt him. He wants those hands to settle on him.

When he fights his infatuation—not often, but when he does, he thinks it's just that he misses his womenfolk, his family. Or it's the overwhelming bulk of Sis creating an *illusion* of perfection in Phoebe. Then again, he is fifteen. Strong tremors are about. He does not puzzle himself with the slightest worry about how a young man, such as he, who has grown up with a fair share of females, finds himself tongue-tied and dumbstruck by more of the same.

If he's tried to filch a peek at Mae during their growing years, or touched her where he oughtn't have—he won't say as much. He'd never give away Mae, any more than she'd ever give away him.

ALICE FIGURES EDISON for a fool; a young one but a fool all the same. Phoebe is, as nearly as Alice can figure, twenty-two to his fifteen. She's not the innocent the boy is, but then, more than likely, the girl's seeming-experience is a big chunk of his cow-eyed infatuation. No cure for that but what a few stings won't fix, Alice figures.

She heals where she can, the best she can. She expects no pay for her bother—she makes pocket money gaming. She knows how to handle snakes, isn't easily bluffed, and fears nothing except what she doesn't know. What she doesn't know at the moment is what's ailing her. She's all but stopped eating and keeps getting bigger. It's more than a little troublesome, that.

With Phoebe, she knew the girl had done herself harm, had broken the life growing inside, was a broken thing herself by the time Alice found her bleeding. And the young man sharing Bobby's boxcar, he'd been done much harm — although not self-inflicted like Phoebe's. They were a pair, Sis's patients: one, outwardly a thing of great beauty and inwardly scarred; the other, outwardly scarred and, by what Sis witnessed gradually coming to light, inwardly a gentle sort.

His name is Moses; he's written it down.

"You are making me better," he's written. Such a surprise when they came, these words. How he talks is yet to be heard; Raffe says the jaw's still mending.

"Don't thank me, thank Raffe's little camel," Alice answered. "He's the one sharing his mama's milk."

"A generous little brother," Moses wrote and nodded his thanks to her.

He can walk, but not very well and not without help. There is, Alice believes, *magic* in the salve she uses. His right ear will never be normal; the salve could not resurrect soft lobe tissue the flames ate. He has regained partial use of his right eye (the left had been untouched), but the scarring will ever be with him.

Lowering herself to the milking stool borrowed from Raffe, she sits next to Moses. The stool is built of stout stuff. The wrapper she wears is muslin, as lightweight and fine a dress as the one with the trick pocket. Cut from the same pattern, this one is white, a bit of lace on the turndown collar.

He writes, "Are you an angel?"

Alice salves the back of his head, feels the tremble his nerves involuntarily give. "Clothes, these costumes we wear, can be hurtful things. Deceitful," she says. "Tell a lie without saying a word."

"As did mine," Moses writes.

"You weren't wearin' much when Raffe brought you in, but what I could see was a gentleman's suit, a businessman. And any man of a mind to wear a suit and trousers and can afford the price oughta be able to. Turn on around here and let me take a look at that eye. If we're not careful," she says, "you may just get the use of this one back. Might even get back some eye lashes." She looks to his good left eye. "Not so serious, Moses—not so serious."

When Phoebe knocks on the boxcar siding, she's at the top of the ramp. "May I come in?"

Moses turns away from the light and the door.

"Yes. Make yourself useful and come give me a hand up off this stool."

SHE IS QUEEN LaTina, the star of the show, a favorite of John Latterby, for the time being. She moves by Moses's pallet, his face turned from her, and uses her body as a counterweight to Alice's white-veiled bulk.

Phoebe's been here before, many times, to assist with Moses's care. She's been with him before he could remember a presence, when he's been unconscious with pain, when he's confused her with some horror he finds in his dreams and carries into his waking hours. He's been a victim to meanness. She touches her hair, an absent movement, wonders what it might feel like to be kerosene-soaked and set afire.

"Thanks," Alice says. "Gettin' down's one thing; gettin' back up's another. What brings you here?"

"Escape."

"That puppy still nipping at your heels?"

Phoebe nods. "I thought I might hide out in here. He found me with the horses. He might not look for me here, with the snake."

"Snake's got a name," Alice says.

"Yes," Phoebe answers. "Bobby."

Tea with Mrs. Ubreski

HELL'S KITCHEN, NEW YORK CITY

1930

**rene is rested,** clear-headed, less sure she's done the right thing walking off her job. The "Retired!" sign she's pinned over white sequins on her jumpsuit is blurry on the damp costume—blue ink washed beyond the block letters she'd printed. Nobody came after her. When Bucky came in and saw the sign, he'd hugged her so hard the sore rib pinched.

He's sure she's done the right thing and says, "Let's celebrate! I'll take the night off. We'll—"

She pauses from rewrapping her ribcage. "Fine with me." She winces. "Take the rest of the year off. The rent will pay itself."

"Why you have to talk back with so much sass?" There's too much hurt in his voice for it to be real. "You know I say I'm takin' the night off every night and I always go on and go, don't I?"

Irene unwinds the roll with one hand and smoothes with the other, keeps the tension in the elasticized cotton as tight as she can bear. "And you'd know I wasn't right if I didn't sass back." She draws a sharp breath, not so sharp Bucky hears, not when he's facing away, his hand holding the door-knob.

"Come here," she says, "I've got something for you." When he turns, her hands are free from the bandage, the end tucked inside the top edge where cleavage is recently more than it has been. She wants him to leave without worry. She wants to inspire within him a sense of wellness about her. As he nears, she grabs his ears, pulls his head to the point where the bandage end tucks away, and says, "See that?"

He nods, chin nuzzling the bandage edges.

"Mind where that end begins, Bucky my lad, 'cause you're the one's gonna unwind all this binding at dawn." Her fingers splay through his hair as she kisses the top of his head, pulls his head back, rubs his nose with hers.

His arms circle under her shoulders, rolling them both to the side. "Come here . . ."

"Unh uh . . . dawn."

IRENE LEANS INTO the door. Bucky's gone—in good humor. She's not well, but the show, as they say, must go on. If she'd let him in on what was going on under the bandage he would've stayed, lost his tightrope-walking gig at the car-nival—been fired sure as anything. Or, convinced he couldn't miss work by her arguments toward that purpose, would've gone, lost his balance with worry about what couldn't be helped with her, fallen, maybe broken his neck. His neck was thick as a bull's, his hands like two great hams. A smile makes it way to her lips: *It would take more than a fall to break my Bucky's neck.*

The round knob of the door is at her back, the smile altered and moved to hang off her heart. In so many ways

Bucky is her farm, her Susquehanna, her Loyalsock Creek. He is where she most wants to drown.

Hands cushioning the hardness of the painted black knob from her low back, where the knobs of her spine duck out of sight into meatier buttocks and thighs, Irene squints, whispers, "Bucky," as if to do so will bring him physically into the room, "what a lark you'd be the one."

She moves from the door to the window, opens her palms and places them on her abdomen, the stretch of her fingers almost meeting. *They will have their opinions about you,* she thinks; *they always have their opinions. But I have mine, and you, little fish, are a keeper.*

"Forgive me, Mama," Irene says to the small space she and Bucky call home.

Olive is, of course, in California, but Irene will ask her forgiveness, will make amends, when she returns. She will fix the rift between them. "I'll even make peace with Wil."

"A cup of tea, Irene?" she inquires of herself. "Yes," she answers, "the Viking is in need of a cup of strong tea." She disengages the gas hose from the gas lamp and reattaches it to the burner spout. Tea requires a trip down the hall with the teapot to fill with potable water. She would take water from the tap for tea—boiling would surely take care of any ills the water might carry—but the plumbing has gone to the circus. That's what Bucky says when a store, meant to be open, is closed. Or a car meant to run, doesn't—*Gone to the circus.*

THE KETTLE WHISTLES. There's a knock at the door. She decides, with a bravado the earlier nap has allowed (she is always braver when rested), she will face Foster or the police or whoever has come to berate or arrest her for jumping ship at Poseidon. She's made the right choice. She's thinking beyond her immediate self. The "Retired" sign might be watered down, but her resolve is stronger.

Opening the door with a flourish, she finds Mrs. Ubreski. Mrs. Ubreski is many things besides Irene's landlady. She is several sacks of potatoes lumped into one great flowered bag of a dress. She is two long creases that used to be dimples sagged now in a face of many folds and wrinkles. She is a midwife who has ended the lives of unborn babies while still in the womb. Irene has never partaken of Mrs. Ubreski's feminine surgical talents—not for herself—but she has brought other young women to Mrs. U. She has held the red hands of small women with too many children to find sleeping space in cramped quarters for all of them, much less the new starts caused by loving husbands too eager to wait for preventions to be set in place. Mrs. U. is a facilitator for improving the futures of those already taking breath, as a rule.

"Jak sie masz?" Mrs. Ubreski asks.

"Fine, fine," Irene answers. "And nack shee a mosh, you?" she asks in return.

"Gud, gud. The baby is gud, too?" Mrs. U. points her chin toward the little fish.

"What?"

"It's alive, yes?" Mrs. U. makes a singular nod as if one large potato toppled forward, then toppled back into a fixed place at the top of the many sacks hidden inside her dress.

Irene squeezes Mrs. U.'s hand for perhaps longer than she should, wondering while she grips all that hardened tenderness how the woman knows . . . she has not said a word, Irene hasn't, to another living soul.

"We can—"

"NO!" Irene grabs at her side, doubling forward. "No, Mrs. U.—we cannot do that."

"Nie? OK, OK." Mrs. U. turns with Irene's hand clutching hers and leads Irene to the small dark table with two straight-backed chairs on either side. "Sit," she commands. Irene sits.

"You will marry this man?" There is a dismissive tone in the question Mrs. U. asks, as if a doctor has informed his patient she has cancer and then adds, most casually, in a statement that might be a question but isn't — *You will die from this, you know.*

Irene shrugs and the lift of her shoulders reaches down to her dumb rib. She does not wince.

"I don't think you will," Mrs. U. says.

Irene does not know this, does not know how she thinks about marriage, about contractual love, about contractual anything.

"We shall have some tea, tak?" Mrs. U. says, and Irene says, "Yes. Let me –" but Mrs. Ubreski is already at the whistling kettle, turning the burner off, bringing two mismatched cups from the shelf over the sink with the faucet that *has gone to the circus* for now.

Bucky? saying "I do"? What a thought! She's known Bucky, not continuously, but since the first backward flip he made for her at that circus where Edison was dropped off. Wilbur had brought her down with one headlong dive (has he always had it in for her?) and she'd seen no more of Bucky — not for years. Not until Bucky heard about Edison and came to offer condolences to Olive. What year was that? 1918? No. The year before. Bucky had been too young to enlist, but Edison and Budd had gone.

Could she, Irene, marry that same little clown?

She watches Mrs. U. fuss with the teabags, look through the small ice box for milk, in the curtained cupboard for sugar, then hold the sugar bowl out.

"No?" Mrs. U. says. "Then I shall have two."

Irene nods. In her short span of thirty years, she's known a great many clowns, had even loved a few — the way a sister loves a brother — or, as with Maximo, the way a child loves a father. Clowns, comedians, songbirds, tenors, jugglers, fat ladies, snake charmers, tightrope walkers, tumblers, equestrians, the horses and ponies the equestrians rode — these were her family, and had been for a dozen years. Longer. Since she'd left Dottie Clay's Mermaids and struck out on her own, more or less.

Irene rises from the stiff chair and in one step is behind Mrs. U. who has her great potato-like head tipped over the teacups. Leaning her forehead to meet the sparse strands of white Mrs. U. has pulled into a bun, she says, "What would I do without you. I'd be an orphan without you coming round."

"Tak; it is so?"

"Yes. Except for my nephew, Buddy, they've all washed their hands of me, Mrs. U."

"They would do better to have you inside them, tak." Mrs. Ubreski takes Irene's hand and holds it inside her own as if she held a small, fledgling bird.

Irene hesitates. "I'm not so sure. I make them crazy with worry."

"When we worry," Mrs. U. says, "it is gud . . . it is gud we have some ting, some *one* to be in this place. This almost ready. You sit, tak?"

"All right, I sit, tak." Irene fingers the edge of a robe that is Bucky's. The wool is patterned with Navajo Indian triangles and stripes in red, white, black and brown. The material's too thin to have ever been a rug, but it's rug-like in design, in the look of it.

Mrs. U. places the cups. "Shall baby have no papa, then?"

Irene is still, thoughtful. They have an understanding, Mrs. U. and Irene, of all matters feminine. No judgments. If their eyes meet, it is with trust that whatever passes is real, even if unfocused, even if seemingly indifferent. Irene does not know what Mrs. Ubreski's life was like during the Great War, when she still lived in Poland. She does not know if Mrs. U. lost a brother or father or even a sweetheart, husband or son over there. Mrs. U. does not talk of those times. Even when Irene shares stories about the loss of her brothers, Mrs. U. nods but does not tell tales of her own time in Europe. She does not, not to Irene's knowledge, have family in the States.

When Mrs. U. leaves, Irene can see the crows on the wash line down below the fire escape. The alley is filled with lines and crows. There are potholes; rain has filled them and the puddles look like pewter, harder than water should be allowed to look, and darker by many shades and gradations than the hard fist of the Atlantic. Staring at the puddles below the crows, the dance the crows make trading places back and forth from one line to the next, she notes the light is going. Soon it will be dark. She twists the wire clamp free from the gas-line hose, slides the one-burner spout away and brings the gas lamp over with its spout to attach, clamping the wire ends snugly in place. Hearing the hiss at the turn of the lever, she strikes a match. Instantaneously, warmth diffuses from the lit lamp.

Irene sits again in the straight-backed chair. Her bare feet are cold and the bed she shares with Bucky is there, no more than four steps away. She has meant to write a letter to Wilbur's wife, Honey. She has meant to tell Honey in her own words how difficult it was to fire Wilbur today, to tell him to pack it up and hit the road. She wants Honey to understand that her life, Irene's life, was virtually in her brother's hands and that, where Irene was concerned, Wilbur was careless with those hands and what they held. She wanted, Irene did, for Honey to know the lives Wilbur handled so foolishly were two now, not one. If Honey knows this, she will forgive Irene.

Her feet are cold as ice. Her hand shakes with cold. She will do better to write the letter from bed, feet snuggled under the old quilt, the one from the farm all those years ago; the one Edison brought back after his jaunt with the circus.

When had it stopped smelling like apples gone bad? *My God, how I hated this quilt.* But she's done with hating now. She is. Forgive and forget—that's Irene's motto. All her ill feelings *have gone to the circus* and, with any luck, they'll never come back.

October 30 1918 * The Crier *
Cartersmile, Pennsylvania

HEALTH CONDITIONS

Few Fatal Cases Reported
During The Week

Situation Clearing In All Sections
Where Epidemic was First Alarming

*Hawksdale and Pennyloaf Now Suffering From
Epidemic: Over Sixty New Cases Reported!*

Hawksdale, Oct. 30 – The board of health
reports that despite the fact that 61 new
cases of Spanish influenza erupted the week
ending two days past, the conditions are
regarded as improved this week. Cases in
Hawksdale with pneumonia complications
are few and the malady has resulted in no
deaths at the county seat in forty-eight hours.

At Pennyloaf, a neighboring coal town
in Hickock township, which appeared
free of the malady a week ago, forty
cases were reported yesterday and the
town is under strict quarantine.

Clymer holds the best record in the
county with not a single case as of
yesterday reported due to quarantine
measures established several weeks ago.

Pneumonia, resulting from influenza, has
taken a heavy toll in the home of Private
Thomas Cobb, of town, who is serving with
the American forces in France. His only
two children, both girls, have succumbed to
the malady. Mary, his oldest daughter, died
on Wednesday and Jane, aged six months,
died on Sunday. The wife and mother,
prostrated with grief, has also been struck
down with the malady and her condition is
critical. It is unknown if she will recover.

Belinda, the 13-year-old daughter of Mr. and
Mrs. T. B. Raymond of West Trenton Street,
died from the malady on Tuesday. The family
located in Cartersmile only a few months
ago, having moved here from Williamsport.

MOSES ACCEPTS A mask from a Red Cross sister at the
Williamsport train station. In this day in 1918 he is one
among dozens of white-masked travelers as he boards for
New York City. He feels as if the direction he's embarking
upon is more than physical, as if H. G. Wells has written a
new *Time Machine* with a Pullman car that will carry Moses
back in time.

Inside, bench seats facing a center aisle have been replaced
by seats facing forward in two steady rows down either side.
Moses moves with a barely perceptible sway to the natural
stride he once owned. He takes the first available seat one

row from the forward wall, glad for the cotton mask and curious stares he will avoid.

On his left is the Williamsport platform. Phoebe is there, her arm raised in a slow arc of both *Hello* and *Goodbye*. He watches the station move away. For himself, he is unafraid. But Phoebe is reckless about such things. She may have already removed the mask she promised him she would wear. Should he stand and stop the train? Would he be foolish, or wise? Foolish, he breathes into the mask—and would rather be foolish than here. The Williamsport platform has floated off like a raft on a river's current, with her, Phoebe, its only occupant waving *Bon Voyage, Hurry Home!*

Under his coat, under his crisp white shirt ironed by Phoebe, under his skin, he has the sense space is opening around his organs (a lung? his heart?) until the pieces packed inside seem untethered. He lowers the green baize shade on his left, takes his unpunched ticket in hand, and waits for the conductor to enter.

"Morning," the conductor says. He wears his cotton mask, strings tied off in the back, mask itself pulled under his chin, clean-shaven, dark-skinned as Earl and Red from the old days, but dusted overall with age like Raffe had been.

Moses answers, "Good morning," his punched ticket already back in hand as if it had never left. Bound for Grand Central Station, he is a solitary man of yellow complexion wearing a soft felt hat and a mask that fails to hide the fold of one eyelid pulled in a scar. These masks—do they stop death from entering when death comes?

Had Yun Li worn a mask at his work in Heung Fat's kitchen? If so, had he worn it in a manner much the same as the conductor, pulled down under his chin, so that now Moses is summoned to China Town's Grant Street to attend

Yun Li's bones? Moses—who has found a middle calm between beliefs and is no longer bedeviled by dreams of spirit-chasing demons—knows Yun Li as faithful and generous. It is Yun Li who has attended Tsing Ming to appease Sing Cheung's restless spirit these nine years of Moses's absence. The scribe who forwarded Yun Li's desires that Moses attend his bones is an honorable man. He is the same scribe Sing Cheung had used and now intervenes on behalf of Moses as well as Yun Li.

"Yun Li," Phoebe has counseled, "cannot be disregarded because this influenza has claimed his life." And so, Moses returns.

She will be home by now, Phoebe, removing her hat with the brave little quail feathers and too-small brim for the times, placing it on the bureau near the door in the bedroom they share. He might buy her a new hat in the city, a hat with a curve like the beginning roundness to a bell. This hat will say what Moses seems unable to convey: that he loves his wife in a ripening way, as if they are one fruit grown around a single warm pit of beginnings. He is still a boy whose feet cannot find the ground when she moves through a room he is in or he moves alongside her to rhythms of seasons, the days beginning, the days at an end. Yes, he will look for a hat to please her.

He recalls, like so many past faces and forms that enter unbidden, the young chauffeur John Latterby kept for as long as he kept the yellow automobile. Moses, in the absence of Phoebe, feels as crazed as that boy had been over her. Moses himself had seen little of him, the lad Sis referred to as *the puppy.*

"There is no escaping him," Phoebe had said. "I would ask John to keep him on a shorter leash. Damned kid doesn't hear a word I say, but John is"—her hair had been a cascade of red Moses guided a brush down as she talked—"so unpredictable."

"The puppy is becoming who he will be," Moses said. Raffe had loosed the mending to his jaw and Moses, who brushed Queen LaTina's hair every evening, often talked with her and she with him. "He will understand in time."

"I wish he'd become who he'll be elsewhere. But I won't cost him his job."

"How soon the summer will end. Then he will leave, return to his family. Is this not the case, Sis?"

"As far as I know," Sis had answered. "Thick-skulled, that one. Understanding, like you said, might be a long time coming."

Understanding had not come before the auto and its driver left the Latterby Brothers' parade; drink, not Phoebe, had informed Big John. Summer, wearing the amber skirts of fall, had come to an end, and with it the youth departed. Where he went is not a thought familiar to Moses, who is where he is by various turns of fate and chance, who nightly brushes Phoebe's flame hair with a tenderness she returns in all the small ways a woman can offer.

Unexpectedly, he does wonder what became of the chauffeur, what chances befell him, or he them. The world is not ordinary. Yun Li is dead and with him the presence of the white ghost. Undefeatable Yun Li, whose gold tooth would beam over small delights in his kitchen and who twice a year paid money to a scribe to remind Moses of his duties, duties he, Yun Li, shared the burden of and would attend as he could—so long as Moses prevailed with education—student or teacher. To Yun Li, both satisfied Sing Cheung's afterlife world.

But Yun Li would write, or have the scribe write, of the white ghost, Ellie. When he did, her face came before Moses, her figure, this woman of learning, of manners, of small white collars pinned with filigreed brooches or angelic cameos, this woman with alabaster skin, of pinch-waisted calling coats, of dove-soft gloves, of petulance and psalms, this woman who had taken his virginity and, he supposed, had given her soul to him—a soul Moses had not wanted or known how to handle.

Moses grimaces. All he could offer the woman was sorrow—and the unending guilt of a son. He had locked the room with the red trunk and the picture of Jesus hung by the door and not returned.

A soldier has taken the seat in front of Moses. His tunic is rough; the insignia patch on his shoulder is one Moses has not seen before: a circular horn and leafy branch. President Wilson has been in Versailles for three months; peace is at hand or, if not at hand, very much hoped for. Moses hopes this soldier is on his way home for good—this man who wears the uniform of what he does.

Moses wears the suit of a country schoolteacher; he is invisible to others in what he does. He is comfortable in his suit of invisibility, comfortable in his cotton mask hiding the scars that cause people to turn away.

All but Phoebe. Phoebe turned toward him. Phoebe let her gentle breaths as she fell into sleep warm the bad side of his face.

The close landscape beyond the train window blurs below the half-closed shade. There is a horizon hidden beyond what Moses has lowered. Knowing the horizon exists is enough. Even a night without moon or stars has its horizon, he thinks.

He turns from the window to the back of the soldier's head again. A woman sits next to the soldier, a woman as old as any Moses has seen. She is short, and from directly behind her all Moses can see is the pointy tip of a pheasant feather. It is a way to pass the hours of travel, reconstructing her features with a wide nose, small eyes, no chin to speak of—features only glimpsed for a moment. When he involves his thinking in such ways, he avoids memories he would as soon forget.

He is grateful the letters from Yun Li will no longer arrive. The soldier is gone; the pheasant feather is gone. Moses touches his breast pocket, feels the stiff envelope of the last letter from Yun Li's scribe. A photograph of Yun Li, his first wife, two daughters, one son, Yun Li's concubine, four younger sons by her—all together they made a prosperous grouping. Unlike the other letters, elegantly composed in English, this last is in Chinese. To Moses, the brushed strokes on the pages are pleasant constructions he once put away from himself, just as he had put away (by removal) curving, manicured nails. He had never re-grown the queue lost to fire. The Chinese self he had tried unsuccessfully to erase occupied Moses like an unborn twin—a twin Phoebe nurtured and often called out of hiding.

The photo of Yun Li and family is a good omen; Moses will put away the Yun Li of old days—advising, advising, advising.

He will put away the tailor Yun Li had paid to construct Moses's new suit for his original departure, the advice to wear the red tie, the bowler; he will put away the advice from Yun Li to depart at all; he will put away the beating and the fire.

Were Moses without his scars, so would he be without his Phoebe. He draws a clipping from his wallet, an illustration of Queen LaTina cut from *The Crier* in 1911. She is there, in the thin yellowed paper, his Phoebe, his Queen, her arm stilled in a wide arc of waving to the crowds, just as she'd waved to him as the Williamsport depot moved away, leaving the long wake of tracks Moses yet travels upon.

Moses goes to the scribe's tiny office on Grant Street two times.

The first time is to attend to the matter of the bone broker and seeing Yun Li's remains off to Celestial China's Shanxi Province.

The second time is to receive Yun Li's bequest. There, in a black-lacquered box with inlaid ivory and jade, is a braid, thick as a whip end, of gold-blond hair.

Moses wears his cotton mask; the scribe wears his cotton mask—they are bandits exchanging ill-gotten goods. No. They are intermediaries between the dead and the living.

Moses pays the scribe. He puts the box under his arm and leaves. The box contains more than the hair. Ellie Bowles's tremulous love letters to him are there, bundled and tied with greasy string. Ellie Bowles's dove-gray glove with a thousand buttons is there.

Buddy and the Archival Roster
BROOKLYN

2008

uddy flips back to page one of the archival roster provided by Rose of Sharon. He's found one name and hopes to come up with another. Barring interruptions from physical therapists with wheeled walkers for him to push down hospital corridors and volunteers with wheeled carts full of books he has no interest in opening, he might succeed.

The pages, copied by someone Rosie has cajoled at the precinct into providing, contain information regarding employees of New York City's finest in 1930. Each entry includes Name, Height, Complexion, Nationality, Occupation (before joining the Department), Marital Status, Grade (within the Department), Date Appointed and Assigned, Date(s) of Transfer(s), Date(s) of Promotion or Reduction, Date(s) of death, resignation, or dismissal, and Cause. Somewhat surprised when a name struck home, he'd circled the name "Jerry Mahoney" with the pencil he used for checking boxes on the hospital menu. Mahoney's birth date (he'd have been 42 in 1930 when Buddy rode in his Packard to Irene's place), his height (6' 3"), his weight

(249 pounds) — all of that fit smoothly with Buddy's recollections of those days.

"OK, Rosie. Found one." Other than Buddy, the only life
present is the piggyback plant from Barbara and a leafy column that looks like a stalk of corn from Kevin. He doesn't
count cut flowers as "living." The arrangements are pretty to
look at but already goners — the remains of one life caught in
the world of another. Like those tattered bags caught in the
tree at Prospect Park. *A wig,* the little girl said.

Unopened roses hang from bent stems in an arrangement
on Buddy's sill. *No wig there.* His eyes blur. *Such a waste. Cut
to die. Suffocate in a stifling room.*

Jerry Mahoney. Buddy remembers a handlebar moustache,
iron gray like his hair where it showed from under the brim
of a felt hat, a dark hat (was it brown? blue?). Mahoney had
looked determined and bored, in the moment, and distant,
as if answers had already been determined, the criminal, if
there was one, brought to trial. As if justice had already been
served.

His height and width had been equal to a lesser giant's, a
great oaf with a handsome moustache, a man in a dark suit
which, for his size, fit with yet some room to grow. "I guess
this kid ain't on the right side of the law," Mahoney had said.
"What do you think, Lou?"

Lou, that's what Mahoney called him.

Buddy finds the "L" listings: Learner, Leed, Lewis. "Lou"
could be "Lew." Description indicators don't fit. He skips to
"Lo" beginnings, finds no last names listed as "Louis."

In room 618 a reading lamp lights Buddy's hospital table,
the stapled pages, the details of faceless men, save one: the
inscrutable Lou.

Did Lou answer Mahoney? Buddy can't remember an

answer anymore than he can forget the man—an Asian, not a line on his face.

"Of course," Buddy says to the surrounding dark, realizing the Asian hadn't answered Mahoney. He'd asked a question instead, using a pig sticker as he asked, scraping the undersides of nails: "How we make him on right side?"

He was small, immaculately clean, very smooth, very cool, skin like marble.

Buddy takes a deep breath. He is beyond ninety, no longer a boy of twelve or fourteen or whatever age he had been when fear ran like ice water over and under his skin. He'd already been big as most men, as tall as his father had been, and nearly the height of Detective Mahoney when the detectives arrived.

Buddy rubs the slant of his thumb, examines the angle caused when he cut off the tip with an axe at age ten. He smiles at the scar, remembers the blood, had thought he might die—but did not wet his pants. It wasn't until that day in the foyer of the brownstone, the Asian detective's remarks—knife in hand—that Buddy felt the humiliation of warmth running down his leg.

Years have erased the terror once felt. He frowns, picks up the pages. Was "Lou" a first name or last? He will start again. *Petersen, Planck, Pope, Putnam.*

"'It takes less than a heartbeat ...'" Buddy says to the blank column under the "Q" alphabet heading. "'... a single flick of the wrist.'" Those were the words Lou used as he turned the small blade under his manicured nails. Buddy's young ribs had felt the blade's scrape—imagined, yes, but somehow real. Heat had risen, filled his ears, as it does now, eight decades later. He's thankful no nurses, no nieces, no neighbors are present to see.

He can't find a name to attach to "Lou" but Lou is there, hiding, marble-faced within the lists, small and venomous, a poison-dipped whip Mahoney could set into motion with a particular glance or word. Shrugging off a chill, Buddy considers the menace. Even if Lou lived a long life, he'd be dead now. *He'd have to be, wouldn't he?*

Addressing the stapled pages, he says, "I have done what I told her I'd do," and removes the "M" page with Mahoney. "Nothing I can do about Lou."

Roster set aside, he takes up a sailing magazine with a sleek, white craft tilted into the wind on the cover. Lavender washes the sails, feverish pinks and varying blues stripe the sky behind the vessel — the middle blue the color of patterns in Grandmother Olive's china. He has sailed into and away from such skies. He has leaned into the wind and controlled where his sloop or cutter would cut. "Ah, to be there again," he says, eying the cover.

Crabbed hands holding the magazine like a framed picture, he closes his eyes. The image is not what he wants. Jerry Mahoney's moustache curves like the horns of a water buffalo — a moustache very much out of date in 1930; a moustache like the one Buddy's seen in tintypes of Grandmother Olive's father, Millard Talbot. There is a watch, somewhere, engraved with *Millard Talbot,* a gold pocket watch Millard gave to Buddy's father, a watch that was returned to the Talbot farm while Buddy's and Edison's remains stayed in France.

How simple it is, Buddy thinks, to remain in the world when you're metal, particularly gold, even if dented. Or, if your name's on a list.

He glances again at the magazine's cover, sees Mahoney's waxed moustache in the rigging, again in the bend of the sail, the hint of a marble cheekbone struck pink with sunset in that southern sky. A slit of the darkest blue near the magazine's border could be, when Buddy looks askance at the setting, the Chinaman's eye, suddenly fixed in time on the pig-sticker knife which, Buddy thinks, must be somewhere beyond the surface of the magazine cover's bright sea.

They are all dead. Buddy's not senile. Yet—if he could physically rise from the bed and move to the window, look through the arrangements of cut flowers on the sill to the parking lot six floors below—he thinks he might see their Packard, Mahoney behind the wheel, Lou leaned into the chrome circling the left-front headlight.

He draws a breath. The smell of soured water, the unopened roses, their bent necks . . . "I'm too old for this," he says, turning the reading lamp off. "Too old to be obsessed with the dead. And she's too young."

His life's altered considerably since Rosie's arrival. What she needs, he believes, is someone to get her interested in her own life instead of his. Like the innocent bystander when drive-by shootings take place, he understands he's not Rosie's target—just the last man standing from Irene's era. She doesn't mean him harm—yet he's harmed, laid up in a hospital bed with a new steel ball joint in his hip and recollections of times he wished hadn't surfaced.

How did she put it? If she could just get a handle on the detectives who abandoned Irene's case, she might find an answer as to why. If they were deadbeats, lazy, eager about the first beer at the pub after work, that said one thing. If they'd investigated all facets of Irene's untimely death, that was another. If they held show people in low esteem, viewed them as flim-flam artists on a level with prostitutes and pimps—just how much effort would the investigating officers have spent?

Buddy works his fingers, angry with himself for not realizing more, for not asking more, for not questioning Mahoney and Lou at the time about the show they were running. He laughs, the image of the stain darkening the front of his khaki pants warm and vivid behind his closed eyes — the humiliating directional nod toward his crotch Lou had made.

Buddy clicks on the light. He will go through the roster names again. If those bastards screwed up, their screw-up needed airing, needed made right.

"Did you miss me?" Sharon says.

"Were you gone?"

"You're not angry with me anymore, are you?" She fingers the fringes of his hair, plants a kiss on his forehead. "You look . . . rested. Happier than when I left."

Buddy gives her the smile that says she is the queen of this moment. He is grabbing papers up as if caught in the middle of a porn magazine — not one he wants to hide. This is the Buddy she met at the door on her first day of arrival. The uninjured Buddy, the unharassed Buddy.

"Do I?" he says. "I've found a name. Jerry Mahoney. I think it's him, the lead detective. And another name that might've been his partner, maybe not. Sounds the same, a big 'maybe' is all."

"Excellent!"

Shedding her coat, gloves, and scarf, she sits in a chair she's shoved close to his bed. The overwhelming sense of failure she'd carried back with her from upstate New York is as removed from her as her wonderfully blue short coat. She'd dreaded telling him what she hadn't found, dreaded mentioning the old cousin. If Buddy remembered her at all, news of her failing mind wouldn't be welcome. With the least little bit of luck, he won't ask.

She says, "I love that you're getting behind me on this, Buddy." She doesn't say, *You started it, mentioning an aunt I'd never heard of, letting me sort through that damned trunk.*

"I owe 'em," he says.

"Irene? Bucky?"

"Yeah. Them, too."

"Owe who, then? Who'd you mean by 'them'?"

"Those jerks, Lou and Mahoney." He jams the papers her way, no longer a stapled unit.

"Whoa! You did tear through these, didn't you?"

"Yeah. That one," Buddy says, jabbing a circled name. "How would you say that name?"

The circled name is "Xiang Liu."

"Not a clue. Do I look Asian?"

"Don't you think it might be 'Lou'?"

She can tell Buddy wants her to say yes, and she does. "Yes. I can see that. Or Lee-ooo."

"Exactly!" Buddy exclaims. "Damn near didn't find it. I kept skipping the X's, figured I'd remember an X name, you know, but then I guess I lost my temper. Or, just got stubborn, you know, about finding Mahoney's partner, so I went straight on through the Z's. Missed Liu the first time through. But I got him. I got him now."

"You know what this means?"

"Tell me," he says. "I got my own ideas, but you tell me yours."

"We can maybe access their records and come up with whatever number it is that guy at the precinct needed. Maybe we can get our hands on evidence, you know, from the crime scene."

Buddy shakes his head.

"What?"

"Why can't you accept it was an accident, Rosie?"

"Because they, what's their names—Mahoney and Liu—*they* didn't. If they had, there'd be no mystery two generations later about why she died. What killed her . . ."

"Gas killed her, Rosie."

"You know what I mean." She tugs at his pajama sleeve with a small pinch of impatience before setting up a triage for wounded and dying floral arrangements. Commandeering his hospital table, she commences, dispatching the roses and other losers while keeping the best—larkspur, star lilies, mums, carnations, woody corkscrew willow and green fillers. Blocks of green Styrofoam are filled with previous holes; they no longer hold the stems upright. She should trash them all, but the good ones hold so much hope, especially two star lily blooms barely opened.

She positions the vase on the sill so the backside is against the window. "No one will see from down there," she says, tilting her head toward the parking lot.

"You don't see a Packard down there, do you?" Buddy says.

"A what?"

"Never mind." He is smiling and Sharon smiles back.

"Hey, what about you?" she says. "You said you had your own thoughts—about these names you've uncovered."

"They shouldn't get away with it, that's what I figure."

"They? The killer, you mean?"

"Mahoney and Liu. Those detectives. Especially that mean little prick. I didn't mean that. My language has gotten awful."

"*Forgidaboudit*," Sharon says. "I've heard worse. Hell, I've said worse. Besides, a prick is a prick by any other name. Smells better now, don't you think?" Inhaling disinfectant scents and zombie-clean odors, she welcomes the improvement. "Way better than the stink of slime water."

"What if she suicided?" Buddy says. "I know she didn't. But, what if everything points that way? It did—back then. But I knew her, you know? She wouldn't." He's very still, hands quiet; the animation he'd shown minutes earlier—gone.

"I didn't know her, still don't—just what you've told me. That and the photos. And I don't believe she'd kill herself, either. Doesn't fit with the Johns family character."

Buddy offers an unconvinced nod and says, "Yeah."

She would've liked a bit more conviction.

Buddy rolls the hem of his sheet in and out. "It's just how she looked on that floor, all loose and scattered out. She was always so—together. Swimmer's body. Great shape. She could do anything. Nothing scared her. Nothing." He pauses, surveys the new sill arrangement. "She didn't look that way dead. She looked—"

"What, Buddy?" She watches the fat roll of the hem grow to the size of a cigar while he searches for words he can't seem to locate or—having found them—is unwilling to speak.

Finally he offers: "Afraid. She looked afraid. *Of everything.*"

Fred Astaire and the Snake

rene's feet must be warm. They are not, when she tries to pinpoint their location, at the ends of her legs anymore. *They have gone to the circus,* she decides and thinks they'll return when her head clears of sleep, of half dreams, of this black water snake with its horrible breath.

She has written her note to Honey. She has written more than one. Did she finish? Is the pencil still in her hand? Is the floor near the bed white-capped with crumpled false starts: "Honey, he will kill me," "Honey, I've had enough," "Honey, I know you will understand, now you have Lincoln, I had no choice—"

She wishes the snake would go to the circus. She wishes someone would band his mouth shut.

... Lincoln. Honey big with Lincoln.

She was stirring a pot at the stove. She was big enough to bust, springy curls plastered by steam to her forehead. She was stirring, Honey was, at the stove. Honey with the spoon. Wilbur with the signal whistle. Wilbur dropping the whistle and chain into Honey's broth. He'd hated that whistle. *Not me,* Irene thinks. *Not me he hates. The whistle.* How will we get out of this?

Wil?

She hears the spit of Honey's broth, the light rattle of the whistle's chain as Honey fished it against the side of the pot with her wooden spoon. She hears the quiet hiss of the snake. The hiss becoming song. *Such a happy snake. He sings like Fred Astaire! And why shouldn't a snake sing "Heaven...I'm in heaven"?* She's never known a snake with such bliss; even his breath comes sweeter, easier to take.

The black snake in Irene's dreams is birthing babies out of its mouth, one after another. They come fully formed, beautiful, glistening with newness like sun on a still morning lake. She chooses one, swallows it down.

A girl, good.

She chooses another.

A boy.

And another.

The room fills with glimmering life as the snake lets each pass from his mouth, pale whispers, fine, extraordinary.

Irene pirouettes, taking them in. She is dizzy. They are strangers, a paying crowd, a crowd that wouldn't be, except for the off-chance she might come from the cannon in pieces. *It's you thugs again; you, in your straw boater, and you, in your frock, waiting for me to rain down an arm there, a finger, a toe . . . ooh, ooh, look! it's raining hair! No other reason for you to be here, your two bits tidied away in the ticket taker's till, the day's take tallied. Your eyes follow me—a gnat, a slow bullet, a train, a chasm, no trestle; plush Pullman with its bed of blood where my daughter is trying to sleep.*

Irene Parilee "Madame Alexie M." Johns, a woman of Nordic ancestry, a woman in spangled white tights, is coming apart, piece by piece; dying—and she's doing it just for you.

There is a deep scratch in Irene's dreams, a needle of time hopping back, offering bits, but not the whole, of what's happened and yet to happen. Babies coo across the floor. Irene is floating above them; she delights in their gurgles. She is pleased she will have more than one. Their coos become gasps. She must gather them up. Already some are blue. They are boys. She will have sons, if she can save them. This one is Edison. This one, Budd. Born again. Out of her reach. The blue baby boys scramble across the floor, choking. Choking, not on her floor, but in the same trench. Blinded by the same gas. Killed by the same blast. Her brothers are dead. She remembers them, sees them, but not as they were reported to be—pieced, as best they could be, into two separate graves in France. She sees them as they were—strapping and handsome and big. And now they are gone. And now the dreamed babies are still. The boys of her womb are blue and cold.

Wilbur, in his know-it-all boasting, had told Olive how Budd and Edison died. What the Great War had done. A drunk, up at the Clover & Jug, had told Wilbur. A blind drunk who stayed drunk, according to Wil, so he could forget what it was like over there—but he didn't forget; he talked of it night after night.

Irene churns in her sleep, struggles to wake herself out of this place she does not want to be. *I should've been there. I coulda stopped him doin' that, coulda flattened his dumb face in before he told Mama all that. But I was . . . I was someplace else. Where was I then? Not home.*

THE FLOOR IS as cool as a white cotton sheet. It seems not like wood at all. She draws her knees up. She is empty. Then she is full. Her daughter, the first little fish she'd picked from the stream of babies, will swim with her in the Loyalsock, is slipping through currents and watching Irene, even now, from a shoreline in Pennsylvania.

And Irene is watching her strong, practiced strokes. She has direction; she will win against the current. Olive paces the shoreline, shouts from the bank, calls her to come back, on the instant. She is thunder and fury, Olive is.

Heaven, I'm in heaven. Fred Astaire and all the babies from the snake's throat hold hands around the room, paper-doll cutouts, one attaching to the next and the next and the next. *What about me?* they say.

Sh-sh.

PART VI

The First Day of School

September 1930

oses Cheung is forty in 1930 and waiting inside a one-room schoolhouse where the light slants parallelograms of yellow onto the plank flooring. He stares down at his desk: a scarred wooden affair used by Mr. M. Rathke for years, through generations of snowy, round-eyed children with cowlicks and pigtail braids, sky-colored eyes, each child the teacher's for the daylight hours, except during harvest, the Sabbath, holidays, weekends. And after Mr. M. Rathke—Marion, as Moses had come to call him—the desk was used by Benjamin Smith, then Moses himself, the Williamsport teacher of this small school beyond the reach of town, of larger schools with smaller rooms.

"Goodbye, Marion," Moses says aloud.

The room listens. Corners soften with rosier shadows, warmed by their old caretaker's name.

Moses sighs. His benevolent father, Sing Cheung, so bedeviled for years, will be glad of Marion's company. The loss Moses mourns, his father will relish. For a flicker, the two occupy seats at the back of the room. They are whole, sharing notes. Each becomes more. The back row blooms, briefly, with knowledge. Moses wants to join them, become a solid part of an ethereal ever after—an impossibility for the living, yet to be woven of shared wisdom, at one with what surrounds and is contained, free . . .

"No," he says. The phantoms are gone.

The desk has many scars in the wood, and his fingers, always delicate, sensitive to textures and temperature variations, find a particular arcing scratch in the walnut. It was made by a pebble wedged between the desk surface and stacked boxes of books; when the boxes were rotated off the desktop, the pebble left its track. They were Benjamin's books in Benjamin's boxes. The flow of the scar is warm.

Benjamin's gone to reservations in the deserts of Arizona to teach brown children the ways of his Lord and the English alphabet. A tender man with tender ways, Ben, the last teacher to occupy this geometry of space and time, has left this desk to Moses. Ben did not attend Marion's funeral on Sunday. Not physically; however, Moses had felt his spiritual presence.

Moses positions his chair. He will see the first foot as it steps inside. Suddenly, it seems possible: he will teach a child, many children, even in the absence of mentors. The first foot through the door on this first day of a new school year is a little time off from entering; shadows from a low branch on a beloved sycamore outside the door make pattern movements on the floor where that first foot will fall.

He's grown fond of Pennsylvania Septembers since his arrival in 1909 nearly half his lifetime ago—nineteen years and three months. He's never wished to leave. He's always been glad of arriving. The sycamore's shadows bobble across the school's plank flooring. He is reminded of Alice, the shadow she was, how her movements brought comfort in a time of near-blindness. It does not seem possible, the hurt he knew then.

His fingers move from the scarred desk to his face.

A small, plain bird zips through the shadows the sycamore's thrown, turns at the slate board and finds the hole to the outside again—the same way she entered. Moses watches her flit like a bat at dusk, eager for night, but this lost traveler sought pure sun, and found it.

His lunch is in a shoebox on the edge of his desk. His smile would be wry, right across the whole of his face, but only the left side lifts and turns down. Thick, angled skin holds the right side in a frown. Inside the box he will find cheese and two rolls, an odd scrap of paper with Phoebe's signature kiss, the hurried lipstick impressions of her continued affection.

Life is no more fair than unfair. Moses hears Alice as if she leans above his burnt body. The sycamore shadows bobble; Moses almost feels the train moving him over the long miles between county lines and borders.

"Safe journey!" Moses tells the bird that has vanished, or the phantoms who sometimes reappear. "Safe journey," he says again as the first foot of a new school year steps over the threshold.

The Mahoneys of Elm Street
PEEKSKILL, QUEENS
2008

"

**Are you waiting** for me," Sharon asks, peeling her scarf in rounds from her neck, "for Sharon Brown? The niece of Irene Johns who died—"

"Everyone does," he says. "Early or late, everyone does."

Indeed, folded into his motorized chair like a pile of disarranged laundry, he might have already done so, except for the remark. Sharon senses he's not particularly thrilled with her presence, yet can't slow her forward progress. Here, not three ping pong tables away, is a Mahoney. Not just any Mahoney, but *the* son of *the* Detective Mahoney who investigated Irene's death. As a boy, he may have heard his father speak of Irene. After all, she was the first woman to be shot from a cannon on *this side of the pond*, as Buddy called it. If there were case files, personal journals Mahoney's father had kept, wouldn't this Mahoney be the keeper? Or know who the keeper is?

"You're wrong there," Sharon says. "I don't think everyone waits for me. I'm glad you did though. You are Mr. Mahoney, right?"

"Dies," he says, powering his chair slightly forward.

Since meeting Buddy, she can't say why, but strangers, especially the over-eighty variety, throw her off balance—usually in a good way, but off all the same. Actually, to her surprise, it feels good more often than not, as if whatever it is maintaining the fire or spark inside them is pretty much inexhaustible, despite how life proceeds.

She hadn't known what to expect when she came face-to-face with Mahoney. Someone who knew a fork from a hairbrush and could manage these tools on his own, someone with language skills, who could hear her, who could speak, answer questions when asked. After all, his career had been doing much the same as she did now—investigations of crimes. When Buddy successfully recognized the Mahoney name, she felt as if she'd just won the Lotto. The downside (and she seemed always able to find one) was Buddy's anxieties regarding what she might find. He'd known, he shared with her, too many friends who had vanished, right before his eyes, while remaining on earth in body, their minds shredded by age and confusion. Sharon resisted this notion—not without worry, but resisted all the same.

Now, her momentum does slow. She feels wrong, or in the wrong place and lifted out of time. It may be the motorized chair; her grandfather Wil spent the last years of his life in a chair, though not motorized. Or the twisted man in it, his twisted and knotted fingers—so like Wilbur's. Or the colorless eyes that seem able to see, yet Wilbur's could not, not in the end. Those eyes had been useless. For a moment, this moment, the man she is meeting is Granddad Wil, gnarled with a cruel meanness that took her breath away every time they came into contact.

All this in a split second, the way a ground squirrel will

dart from the side of the road and there's no way to dodge its path and all you can do is hope there's no thump as you pass. They were like that, recollections. Though reflections upon Wilbur Johns were more armadillo-like—armored and lumbering—than rodent. When she ran up against a memory of him, whatever lightness of being she may have felt vanished. Perhaps the weight of DNA, of genetic inheritance, knowing she wouldn't be exactly who she turned out to be if not for him, became too dense in those moments.

Mahoney is watching her. She feels it though she hasn't moved, is no closer to his chair than before, is still yards away, in fact, at the precise place where the ping pong table's green net stretches. Fingering the wing nut, the one used to tighten or loosen tension, she feels his blind eyes gauging her movements and wonders how he can do that. But then Wilbur used to track where she hid, find her tucked behind Grandma Honey's dresses in their closet. A shudder climbs Sharon's neck as she remembers being yanked by her hair from the dark recess into the light.

"I used to have a car that same color of blue," Mahoney says, startling Sharon, bringing her back into his presence. Mahoney isn't Wilbur. Isn't blinded by diabetes. Isn't dead. Judging from the nostalgic lilt to his voice, he has, like Buddy, a fondness for pale, icy blue, and she believes she may just be able to regain her balance.

"Did you?" she says. "You are who I think you are, aren't you?" She pauses. "I'm Sharon Brown. We talked, about case files, my aunt. You said—"

"I said, 'The Mahoneys of Elm Street, that's us. Been in the business since time began. Granddad with the Royal Irish Constabulatory. It's in the blood.' That's pretty much what I said, if I remember right."

The rec room is empty of other residents. Mahoney had wanted their meeting here, in the midst of craft and game tables, and at this specific time. Sharon is five minutes early, or had been, when she arrived at the receptionist's desk.

The ping pong table's net is stretched and ready for play; the paddles are absent. To the right, there's an opened Scrabble board, four wooden holders placed on each side. She glances around, half-expecting to find a purple Crown Royal velvet bag (Appleonia had always kept Scrabble tiles in one), but doesn't. Nor does she find the Scrabble box. There's an octagonal Chinese Checkers board on another table, but no marbles. Easy chairs and a sofa face a wall-mounted television; the TV's remote sits on the sofa arm, a quiet surprise for Sharon who has begun thinking this isn't a rec room so much as it is a tease. All manner of interaction might take place—if not for the missing parts. A cruel thing, to put toys out one can't play with. Except, perhaps, the TV. *Zombie makers*, in Sharon's opinion. Thankfully, Mahoney seems to have no interest; the set's not turned on.

"You remember pretty much right on the money," Sharon says. "Where is everybody?"

"Asleep. Or a wedding. Take your pick."

She's taken some steps toward him, propelled once again by the nearness of potential answers.

"They called it an *American* Rambler, you know, the one came out after the Nash Ramblers. The wife said I was nuts, wanting a station wagon, and where did I think I was going to park it, and how we couldn't afford a garage."

Sharon figures the car's color matching her ski jacket's blue is probably a good thing, promoting his friendliness towards her, but comparisons of volume—her size to that of a station wagon—gives reason for pause. If there were a mirror present, she'd be checking the width of her thighs, and, come to think of it, begins to wonder if old Mahoney isn't doing precisely that. She asks if they can sit.

He does an odd thing with his mouth—the suppressed smile thing—wherein what would be upturned corners and apple-swelled cheeks is instead an arch over a protruding bottom lip, then his gnarled hands try to spread, an action a magician might make to pull attention to an empty top hat on the table. However, Mahoney's empty top hat isn't a hat at all but two empty pant legs folded and pinned just above where knees had once been. Then he winks. He has, Sharon knows, taken no offence.

"Anywhere you like," he says. The sofa, near the TV, seems her best bet and she steps around his chair, glancing behind, finding him at her heels, close enough to crash into her ankles if she should suddenly stop.

"I wondered," she says, "about really old case files. From the '30s. Like I mentioned."

"I was just a pup," he says.

The pale blue legs of her scarf hang to her knees and she removes it before sitting. "We all were once," she says. "Even your father. He was young once. I guess I hoped he'd left some records behind. Diaries? Personal journals? Something like that. My aunt didn't." If she could take the oh-please-feel-so-so-sorry-for-me whine out of what she'd just said, she would.

He says, "I'd rather talk about cars. You got one? The wife was right. Should never have bought one. Got it so when we wanted to take off, as a family, go places, you know, lakes in the summer, mountains for skiing in winter, we could just do it. You know, learn how."

"To ski?" Sharon asks.

"Maybe," he says, "and swim. Maybe learn how to be close, closer than my old man ever was with me."

"Sounds like the right thing to me. Family. Closeness."

"So, you got one?"

"Family? Mostly dead now. But, yes, a daughter — she's a librarian in Philly — and a few cousins scattered about."

"Miss Brown," he says, "you got a car?"

"I do. And it's Mrs. or just plain Sharon." He may know the difference between a fork and hair brush, but how on God's green earth can she bring him around to the reason she'd come all this way to see him? Warmth wells up behind her eyes. "It's in Arizona."

"Guess we're not going for a ride then."

"Guess not." The scarf is a ball of blue folds in her lap and she brings it to her face, buries her nose, hides in it.

He says, "I'm a bastard, that's what the boy says. Wife said the same. Not true. I'm the middle son of five. A dead ringer for my da, or was, when I had legs."

She nods, a silent agreement that he is, indeed, a bastard for not staying on target with why she has made this trip to upstate New York. She had felt the presence of Wilbur when she first came upon him, the weight of old meanness, old times. These feelings had gone, been replaced by something good, something akin to Buddy's spark for life.

"How about if we talk about why you came," he says.

By the time she's leaving, she likes old Mahoney well enough. His gruff is friendly-gruff, an old watchdog who can't help but wag his tail. And his constant motion, navigating the spaces between furnishings as if cruising neighborhood blocks, checking between chair legs for vagrant game pieces or items amiss — has caused Sharon to believe what he'd said earlier about police work being *in the blood*. At eighty-three, he's still patrolling.

In 1930, when this Jerry was five, his father, Detective Jerry Mahoney, investigated Irene's death. He'd said, "My sainted mother, God rest her soul, could not keep Dad quiet. Job talk. She'd leave the table. My wife, too. You'd think I might've learned. Didn't."

Sharon said, "Nothing about a human cannonball? Seems like something a young boy might remember, if his dad mentioned."

"Sorry."

"I'm curious," Sharon said. "Why'd they leave the remote within reach, you know, for the TV?"

He tilted his head, studied her, and without an audible *Why do you ask*, seemed, nonetheless, to ask.

"I mean," she glanced from game table to game table and back where he sat, "they don't seem too keen on actual play here, do they? No tiles for Scrabble, no marbles — "

"No batteries in the remote," he said, lifting the device from the sofa arm and flipping open the battery box to expose an empty hole.

"I don't get it," Sharon said, interrupted by wide double doors buzzing open. Hall chatter entered ahead of a man pushing a walker. Within moments two other walker-assisted residents had joined Mahoney and Sharon. Then an identical motorized chair, driven by a woman, parked next to Mahoney's and he said, "How'd it go?"

The woman shrugged.

The operator of walker #1 said, "What you'd expect. Who's this?"

The woman said, "She's his appointment, his excuse for ducking the service."

Sharon said, "I could have come at another time. Are they friends, the ones who married?"

"You might say," Mahoney answered.

"What wedding?" the woman asked.

Walker #1 said, "Jerry's been having her on. You know how he is. Every wedding's a funeral, every funeral's a wedding."

Pushing a cart with paperback books and an assortment of boxes, a much younger woman in a hoodie and sweats appeared and said, "Anyone missing their marbles? I've got batteries here, and no, Miss Jo Anne, not for your private tools. Paddles? Anybody up for ping pong?" A few dozen slow-moving people began to settle here and there in the room. The TV came on.

Mahoney said, "My partner's back," as he nodded toward the woman occupying the other cruiser.

Sharon said, "OK. I'm going. Keep me company to the reception area? I get lost in these big hotels."

He laughed at *hotels* and she smiled.

At the reception desk, she said, "You know how nothing could play out, back there, until that cart arrived, Jerry? That's pretty much where I am with my aunt. I need a number. And the person who maybe wrote that number down was your dad."

"Could be my no-account son has it."

"No account?"

"Worthless," he clarified. "How do you think I came to be here? And a boy who won't tolerate his dear old da hanging about probably let go of all his dear old da had held onto. Boxes and boxes. But don't be surprised if they're cleared."

On Elm Street in Queens the hired car driver says, "This the one?"

"Yes," she answers, only a little hesitant to pay, exit, and watch the Lincoln Town Car disappear. *The one*, Rose of Sharon thinks, would be overstatement, if not for the address. In either direction, narrow two-stories begin and end with little space to walk between. She doesn't like the closeness and has bitten the inside of her mouth, anxiety over the top—yet she's here, still breathing, and without the aid of a paper bag.

There's a tiny yard of brown grass in front of this house and every house within view. There's a fence, chain-link, the same as most others. Remnants of shoveled snow mark the base of the fence. There's a gate. There's a bell and the clapper makes dull thudding sounds when she clangs it. No one parts the closed drapes to peek outside. She shouts "Hello!" and rechecks the address.

Unlit Christmas lights sag off the gable ridgeline, eaves, and frame the front windows. The siding is white clapboard.

She edges between Mahoney's house and his neighbor's to discover a yard in the back with an outbuilding at the far end. "Hello? Mr. Mahoney!"

At the outbuilding, Sharon steps onto an approach to a single-car garage. One wide door is swung open; inside, a man kneeling on the floor tinkers with engine parts. "You lookin' for me?" he says.

"Jerry Mahoney?" she asks. He has heard her, probably from the first shouted "hellos."

"One of 'em," he says without looking up from an expanse of cardboard (a dismantled box from a freezer? a large screen TV?), his attention riveted somewhere between oil-stains on his cardboard rug, a lawn chair holding a wrench, and parts to god-only-knows-what scattered before him.

He settles back on his heels. Long-limbed, stooped about the shoulders, he gives Sharon a fleeting sense of an older Ichabod Crane. A dark moustache frames his mouth like a tuning fork.

"I'm Sharon Johns." She offers the name with force, as if—if properly equipped with a motorcycle—she might do a wheelie. She hasn't come this far, boarded various trains, stepped off in unknown terminals where people spoke Russian, Hebrew, Chinese, and languages she could not identify, to turn away. If she is put off by his total lack of hospitality, she is more than delighted with finding him and repeats his name.

He cocks his head. "So I've said."

"I'm Sharon Brown."

"Brown? I thought you said Johns?"

"Did I? Johns? I meant Brown. Sharon."

"If you're *real estate*, I'm not selling. If you're Avon, the lady of the house is out—"

"I'm not here to buy, or sell. Your dad sent me." It's plain as plain, he's never heard her name mentioned; the appointment the other Jerry said would be made—that hadn't happened. It was a fluke, pure chance, she'd found this Mahoney at home.

His stare—at her or through her—goes back to the puzzle of parts in a semi-circle where he kneels. He is not interested in the history of *how* she arrived or why his dad might have sent her. He is not interested—period.

"Interesting, your dad," she says.

"What's he done now?"

"Done?"

"I only hear from you people when he's flashed some—"

Sharon says, "Nothing. I mean, I'm not a case worker."

Mahoney grunts.

"I found him," Sharon says, "to ask about old cases, notes his dad might have kept. He sent me to you."

"Should've called," he says.

"I thought," she pauses. "I thought I'd take a chance on finding you in." This is, she thinks, not so much a lie as an omission. Faulting the elder Mahoney is not going to make points with the younger.

"Old guy said he'd set it up, right?"

Sharon nods.

"Should've said. Old bastard shouldn't get away with this shit. Does it all the time. Says he'll do something, and doesn't." He shakes his head. "How you think he lost that foot? Then the other one?"

"Saying he did things he wasn't doing . . ." she guesses.

"Old records," he says, "you want old records? I'll give you old records." What tools Mahoney holds clank to the floor and he's past Sharon and heading out of the building, half-way to the house, shouting, "Old records? You just wait."

Sharon stops at the house, at the ripped screen door, warped beyond closing. From inside he shouts, "You comin' or what?"

"You said I should wait."

"Lady, I'm not haulin' them out there to you."

In Mahoney's house, slimy shrimp — the little pink ones used for cocktails — plug the sink; Chinese take-out car-tons litter the counter; clabbered milk hardens in unwashed glasses; red sauce in frozen runnels adorns the stove top and front. It's a narrow, long room and she's through it quickly, now wearing, she's certain, the same whiff of decay — but not minding. She will find, she knows she will find, the case num-ber she needs here — or something, some entry made in 1930, that will inform Rose of Sharon Brown (had she really given her name as Johns earlier?) and the world, at least those who care, of the true facts of what occurred. She hopes for a floor plan, a layout of Irene's Hell's Kitchen apartment, a physical sense of the place. She hopes for physical evidence.

Mahoney stands at the end of the hall, makes traffic cop gestures indicating she should enter the room on his left, then sweeps back up the hall, past where she hesitates and out. The screen door thuds, bounces its warped wood off the doorframe a few times, quiets.

It's daylight outside and a rectangle of light has crossed the room she's meant to enter and fallen across the spot where Mahoney had stood. The fact she's not already inside that room, not already kneeling beside boxes she imagines stored on shelves lining a far wall is a wonder — or should be. Why isn't she moving forward? She's stuck in the middle, no thought of retreat, one hand splayed on a damp wall, staring at a place where a nasty-tempered son of a son of a son of a cop stood a second ago.

A cricket moves over the toe of her shoe and then along the baseboard as if scouting the way. The hall is dim, a downstairs interior passage in a two- or three-bedroom house, maybe four-, depending on the upstairs. When the cricket moves through the rectangle of light, it's the strangest-looking cricket she's ever seen, not a cricket at all but a cockroach, and she moves. In two strides it's a dead thing, crushed underfoot, and she's inside the day-lit room.

If there's a bed in this room, she can't see it. If there's a rhyme or reason to the storage — chronological, geographic, alphabetic or otherwise, it's in an unknown code. There are trunks on end and horizontally stacked; there are boxes to the ceiling, suitcases with beige/tweed patterning and tarnished brass latches, canvas mail bags and hundred-pound flour bags spilling papers. Behind all this, there's a curtainless window where wintry light slants through to brighten the threshold where Sharon stands, her shadow thrown into the hall at her heels.

Buddy and Mrs. U.

HELL'S KITCHEN, NEW YORK CITY

1930

uddy Johns is almost thirteen and seated on the edge of Irene's bed. Detective Mahoney sits in a kitchen chair he has tipped to rest against the wall—the sort of action for which Buddy's grandmother Olive would've boxed the officer's ears, but Olive is gone to Hollywood, California to visit Irene's sister Flo. Mahoney's partner, Xiang Liu, is lifting an edge of Bucky's old Navajo robe with the tip of his pocketknife blade, and Irene, wearing the robe, can't stop him. Buddy readjusts his left heel so that neither foot rests on the lines where the floor planks meet. What Liu touches, Buddy feels, as if the blade has a breath and breathes upon him.

Daylight comes through a window frosted with charcoal soot, frozen grime that has, on warmer days, melted to run in almost straight paths down the pane, refrozen again and re-melted again, until an accumulation of brine and cinders seem thick as Coca Cola glass. Buddy's feet are a safe place to keep his gaze fixed—not on the lines dividing the floorboards; and definitely not on where the lines lead: the loose-flung body of Irene, all her parts bent in directions they

305

ought not to be, her face oddly blue or the color something blue might cast in its shadow (like the heart of an iceberg). *Why doesn't somebody cover her?* Buddy thinks. *It's not decent.* He studies the way his shoelace disappears up under the hem of his pants, but the contents of his stomach bolt. He is at the sink, yellow bile stringing from his lips, retching, when all there was to bring up is already gone.

His arms on the sink tremble; he braces them more stiffly. The last thing he wants is the breath of Liu's knife, or the stare of Liu's eye, cast his way. Mahoney has told him to wire his grandmother, inform her about Irene. The problem is, Buddy can't remember the last name of Aunt Flo's third husband. His first name is Mike; he is the second Mike she has married; he is a fight promoter—but what fights or what fighter, Buddy hasn't a clue.

Liu is beside Buddy; the thin evilness of him leans an elbow down on the lip of the sink. He holds the limp gas supply hose, points the flattened end toward Buddy. It is an empty weapon, the clear poison clamped off at the wall where the hose is attached to the pipe. The door to the hall stands open.

Buddy will not faint; his hands clench the sink's edge— cold white steel. He is nearly thirteen; he is a man; he knows it even with the stain marking the crotch of his khaki pants.

Outside, three levels down, a car backfires. Buddy flinches. A car—he has jumped to the sound of a car. He will try not to jump again. With the back of his wrist he swipes at the trail of spittle on his chin, turns toward the door and sees a woman filling the entrance. It is Mrs. U.

Irene often speaks of Mrs. U.

Buddy knows her the way he knows Flo's third husband— from stories—although they've never officially met. She is big, if not tall. She is lumpy, in a soft way. Maybe it's the dress she wears that makes Buddy think of Olive. Nothing else reminds him of Olive, yet he is moving toward her, burying his head (he is much taller than she) into her thick neck. She is armored in odors of cabbage and tobacco. He hears Liu make a noise, a choked laugh, a derisive smile brought to sound but lopped off, probably on account of some sign offered by Mahoney.

Her protective arm is closed around his shoulders, and when she turns with him, when they face Mahoney and Liu, neither detective says a word. To Mahoney she says, "You will break," but he does not lower the chair's raised front legs, he does not adjust his tilted lean against the wall, nor does he stop them as she shelters Buddy down the stairs.

Mrs. Ubreski (she has introduced herself to him now) occupies the room below Irene's.

Buddy watches her move to a one-burner, light the flame and settle a teapot over the heat. In this room winter sunlight pours through the bubbled glass; the bubbles are flaws in the glass. There is no build up, no thickening between what is outside and what is inside.

What is inside is sparse. There's no radio built in the shape of a rosewood church; no small circular table but a long one, the kind Buddy imagines monks might sit around dipping broken chunks of bread into some awful broth. There are no hand-embroidered scarves with smiling teapots chased by happily running forks and spoons on the deal dresser bureau, no scalloped valances capping the singular window. *Has she lived here long*, Buddy wonders, *or recently arrived?* Oddly, the absence of clutter—Bucky's juggling pins, unicycle, long bulbous clown shoes, and Irene's souvenir ostrich-plume headdress once worn by a pony she rode down from the heights and into a bucket of water (not a bucket, a tank, but so small in proportion to Irene and her horse that a bucket seemed the best way to think on it)—oddly, the absence of clutter in Mrs. Ubreski's apartment makes the space seem smaller than Irene's.

Buddy remains on the threshold, heels planted on nickel-sized octagonal tiles in the hall. The tiles are yellow, the grout is black, although it may have been white, blackened now by years of coming in and leaving—the soil ground in until every piece of tarnished yellow appears to be set into black.

She motions him in, nods toward a chair at the table (there are only two chairs). The table is larger, even, than the narrow bed. He doesn't move as she tends to the cups, to the tea, to the water, then moves a chair closer to the door. She says, "Sit."

As she crosses the worn floor, steam rising from the cup she holds with both hands, she says, "I am her friend, tak? We take tea together, tak," she says as if talking to someone not in the room, as if talking to the backs of her hands holding the cup out to him, then looks into Buddy's face and resumes. "We take tea together now, you and me."

He takes the cup from her hand and his fingers are long, his knuckles covered with the rough skin of youth. There are no bones sticking through from hunger and he is blue-eyed, unlike the men, the boys that had been a part of her family. She returns to the burner and moves the lever to shut off the gas, keeping her back to Buddy, keeping remembered faces in her thoughts, but the faces are filled out now, flushed with a glow of good health, mouths full of strong teeth, full-lipped youths of her youth.

"I don't know what to do," Buddy says. He holds the cup like a butterfly he would like to release.

"Why they send you?" she asks.

"They?" he starts then stops. "I was the only one home. Except Mae. My Aunt Mae. And Jane, the boarder who watches after her. After Mae. I didn't tell them. About Mae, I mean." He says something else but Mrs. Ubreski doesn't hear; she is letting the remembered faces resettle into their graves and the countenance of her friend's nephew fill the moment. She touches her ear as she turns back toward Buddy, gives a tilt of her head to signal she has not heard.

Buddy says, "We don't mention Aunt Mae to folks, especially not strangers. Grandmother Olive wouldn't like it. Besides, she's not, you know, right. Aunt Mae, I mean. There wasn't nothing she could do."

Mrs. Ubreski nods. In a low voice she says, "Nie. My friend shares this with me. Nie, there wasn't nothing." She watches Buddy taking in the sparseness of her room, but not really giving enough time to be seeing anything the room holds. He is uncomfortable and his tea is still untouched, as is hers. She says, "Gud. It is Buddy, tak? Gud you leave this poor woman alone. My friend, she's proud of this thing you have done. My friend tells me you are hero for her."

His head makes abbreviated shakes back and forth — adamant short shakes that continue on, like a tremble, almost, that goes all the way down to ripple the tea in his cup. He says, "I gotta get outta here."

"Nie," she says, and then, "Soon."

They sit, both of them, near her open door, knees all but touching, the warm cups without saucers held in their hands like the bubbles held in the glass panes of Mrs. Ubreski's clean window; warmth dissipating little by little; steam, like a spirit stringing itself out to rise to some better place, rise to some vanishing point.

The ceiling creaks with movement. It is the big man moving, she thinks, not the small one. The small one has gone down the stairs, passed her door, returned with another man in a white coat. They are lifting Irene from the floor, placing her on a litter to take her some other place. All day they have been coming and going. They took the papa of Irene's baby away before the first light struck her window that morning. They have not brought him back.

When Buddy lifts the cup to sip, the steam is no longer rising. He says, "I don't know where to send a telegram to let Grandmother know."

"She is where?" Mrs. Ubreski asks.

"In California. With Aunt Flo."

"The pretty one." Mrs. Ubreski nods.

"Yeah," Buddy answers. "A model. You know, catalogues. Sears Roebuck. I've seen her in her underwear. Sort of . . ." His complexion goes pink under the network of freckles.

"My friend brags about this one, this beautiful sister. Not so much about the other one."

"Nobody talks about Mae," Buddy says. "Aunt Mae, I mean."

"She has trouble with men, tak?"

"I guess. I can't remember her new husband's last name."

"The pretty one, tak?"

"Tak," Buddy says. "That means 'Yes,' don't it?"

"Tak," she responds with a nod.

The man in the white coat descends the stairs. He is holding the front of the litter carrying Buddy's Aunt Irene, Mrs. Ubreski's friend. The end of the litter is carried by Liu. Mahoney carries only himself. He stops at the doorway. "You coming with us, kid?" Mrs. Ubreski says, "Nie. I make sure he get home."

"You send that telegram yet?" Mahoney says. "It's important you tell the folks that need to know about this." He lets go of the inch of moustache he's pulled at during this quiz, nods at Buddy, who does not nod back, at Mrs. Ubreski, who doesn't nod either, then continues downstairs.

Mrs. Ubreski will give Buddy the subway fare back to St. Terence Street. When he is gone, she will lumber back up those stairs and reconnoiter the space where Irene has lived. She will remove soiled areas from the floor. She will right the toppled table and reconnect the hose to the pipe in the wall. She will sit in Irene's straight-backed chair, facing the empty one where Irene will not sit again, and consider these sisters — the pretty one who has married many times, the sick one they tried to fix, and the beautiful one who was her friend. She will not cry for Irene. When her tears come, and they will, they will be for the mother of these girls, of these sons. She will cry for the mistakes women make with the best of intentions for their young, gently prodding them out to line up in front of the guns, shoveling dirt onto their graves, remembering their glazed open eyes as the dirt falls in, and, after awhile, after an ocean of salted seasons pass in the minutes of heaving quiet, she, Mrs. Ubreski, will leave Irene's room and return to her own.

WHEN BUDDY ASKED Honey for an address in Hollywood to send a message to Grandmother Olive, Wilbur said, "I'll handle that." Maybe Wil did send a wire to his mother, but Buddy sent his that same afternoon with the address Honey gave him and paid for it from his own small stash of cash. He wasn't altogether certain his uncle would send the message soon enough, or that he'd remember at all. It wasn't a matter of disrespect; it was a matter of care. Wilbur had been careless where Irene was concerned before — not that anything Buddy did now could bring his best friend, his aunt back. Still, it felt right when he paid the Western Union clerk. Not good, but right. It was the right thing to do.

Bucky was out of jail, all his gaudy bruises on display for a confession the police failed to obtain. He'd grinned a horrific grin, showing off the space where a tooth had gone missing. The tooth, Bucky said, had plagued him; even as a boy, it had rubbed wrong against the false teeth his folks made him wear for the act.

"What happened?" Buddy asked.

"Beats me," Bucky said. There'd been tears running over the green-blue swellings around both Bucky's eyes. "Beats me," he repeated.

It was crazy. All of it was crazy to Buddy. Wilbur said Bucky was not to come around. Why that was wasn't explained. It wasn't brought up — Irene's death. Buddy already knew talking about Aunt Irene was going to be like talking about Aunt Mae. If you loved Grandmother Olive, you didn't go there. You kept your trap shut. You let the dead rest — even when they weren't dead.

Phoebe and Yun Li's Legacy

WILLIAMSPORT, PENNSYLVANIA

1930

hat's this hair about?
Phoebe asks. *And these letters?*
    Moses has not seen his Phoebe
out of their bed in days; he is surprised she stands at the bureau
with Yun Li's ivory and jade inlaid box. She is transparent, of
course. It is the way of ghosts to be so. After twelve years—
Yes, he thinks, *twelve years since my journey in 1918*—Yun Li's
legacy is again revealed.

Through Phoebe's skirts, Moses sees the hatbox which
holds the bell-brimmed hat he brought home from New
York City. The hatbox sits inside the chiffarobe, narrow blue
ribbons—knotted and bowed just as the milliner's sales clerk
had made them—secure the lid. Not his gift, but Yun Li's
black box has lured his Phoebe from bed. Her hair is a fire of
red-orange, undone and scattered about her shoulders, her
face is a ruin of white. She is unearthly in her beauty. So long
as she abides, Moses may live.

"These letters?" she questions again.

How earnest she is with her questions. How innocently

earnest she is. Moses sets the tray with her breakfast on the end of their bed.

Phoebe waits. She is patient and without time.

"Don't you want to look at the hat I brought back for you? It may not be the one you so liked in the Sears book."

Phoebe tilts her head. They are worlds apart in this small farmhouse bedroom that the city of Williamsport has gradually cut away from all the surrounding land. Moses would like for her to untie the blue ribbons. He would like for her to try on the hat and, more selfishly, pose with that smile reserved only for him. There is no hardness in her, no edges, despite hollows left to her cheeks by the influenza. She is full of light. She is light itself. But no smile. No smile from his Phoebe who stands with the open box, with the hair, with the letters.

She is waiting.

Moses says, "The box is Yun Li's. He left it to me."

"Yun Li kept your letters," Phoebe says, in the way one would recount the magi arriving with gifts at the manger—believing, repeating an offered line from a story as truth.

"Yes. Letters to me. He kept them. I am not sure why."

"Yeah. He did. And now you're keeping them."

"I don't need them."

"But you have them. And this braid of hair." Phoebe holds the braid against her cheek, the dull yellow thickness a sin, like a corpse in magnificent decay when set so near to the flaming river of her red hair. She is a whisper in body of the savior who leaned over him in the boxcar years earlier, of the wife who waved him goodbye from the Williamsport platform. No longer a choir of all that is good, she is an aria.

As Moses rearranges the stems of the dried-out lilies of the valley—the ones he picked as a small bouquet for Phoebe in late spring as he had done so often during their favorite time of the year, the small white bells tremble with each careful touch he offers.

"I will destroy them," he says, knowing that he will only bury them in Yun Li's black box in the yard, or a field. Yes. A field, somewhere other than home.

"And," Phoebe says.

"And we will be done with it."

Phoebe puts the blond braid on the bureau, takes the letters addressed to Moses from the box—a small stack tied with butcher's string—then removes other separately banded swatches of hair. None as immense as the yellow braid of Ellie Bowles, none the same dull thickness, as if they came from lesser heads, as if tresses of less importance, the unbraided remains of other lives.

She says, "Will we, Moses? Be truly done with it? Will you, truly?"

"I don't know what those are."

"They are signs of love. I know all about signs of love."

"God forgive me," he says.

"What have you done, to need forgiveness?"

"I do not know. I do not . . . know."

"Then why pray? I had no use of it, not before you or after. Why pray for forgiveness when you've done nothing wrong?"

"I have done everything wrong."

"Just name me one thing . . . one thing, Moses," she says and her voice is still without time, without urgency.

"I have brought back this box full of demons," he says, watching for her to turn from the bureau with hands emptied of all the past.

"There's no such thing," Phoebe says.

"Yes. Probably not. Yes. And yet they fill this room, Phoebe. Phoebe?"

Moses is looking at the stilled bells of the little arrangement on the tray. The pillow on Phoebe's side of the bed holds the depression where her head moved in fretfulness during his absence; the coverlet here is turned back, all the wrinkles in the stale sheets finger-pressed smooth in the days since his return; the scent of death still palpable in the room. Phoebe has seemed, until this instant, as present as the unopened hatbox on the floor of the chiffarobe. When he leaves the room, which he will do in a few moments (there are children who will be waiting for him to key open the school door), the lilies will shake on their fragile stems and, in the kitchen downstairs, he will find Phoebe's tea has grown cold, once again—the pot still full and the cup unused. But for the moment, this moment, he cannot bear to look up from the flowers and know she is missing from the room, from the heavy air and the lightless place he came back to in 1918.

The trouble with demons is that they do exist; and Moses cohabitates with them, or believes, half the time and more, that he does. He finds Ellie Bowles fingering her own braid of yellow hair as often as he finds Phoebe there, and, occasionally, he finds some faceless other woman attempting to pull on the gray glove with the row of pearl buttons.

"Your tea has gone cold again," he says to Phoebe, pretending she is the one still standing in front of the bureau. He straightens his back, twists his neck as if ridding himself of some unexpected chill, and gathers the tray in hand.

In the hall, he considers locking this door, to keep his ghosts crowded into one place. But Phoebe, he thinks, might want some exercise later; she might want to walk out into the yard, visit the lilies of the valley where they will continue to bloom.

He finds his lunch in a shoebox on the counter. She is such a good wife, always making the most of leftover things.

The box is tied with a string much like the string on the letters upstairs, much like the string on the other hanks of hair.

"I will destroy them," he says. "I promise, I will."

"I know you will," Phoebe answers.

THE HOLE IS not deep. The box is small. Moses, holding
the box in his hands, might be holding a velvet case containing a string of pearls, but deeper, not velvet but ebony-black,
and inlaid with jade and mother of pearl.

"Hold onto these, will you?" he says. A strangled effort
to say her name, to say "Phoebe," fails. Phoebe is ghost and
gone; she is less here, less in the ground, less in the pine coffin lowered into the earth in 1918, than she is in his kitchen,
his bedroom, his bed. She is his great comfort. But, lately, she
leaves the house with him. She audits his schoolroom. His
skills as a teacher have suffered. The children have suffered.

A replacement might be made. He has been cautioned by
the children's laughter; he has been caught talking out loud
to his love where they only see a sparrow flown into reflective
sun on the schoolhouse windows. He needs to keep his job.

The box does not slide easily into the glove. The glove
is gray, elbow length; the buttons are gray and even when
all are unbuttoned, the box lodges there, visible through the
slit of the wrist opening. He folds the glove palm and fingers over the gap and sets the box in the hole next to Phoebe's headstone.

Moses sits back on his heels. His long, delicate fingers
dangle loosely from his wrists. He is sorry, more sorry than
anyone knows, save Phoebe, for this glove and what it holds.

He says, "This is what you want me to do. Tell me this is
the right thing. Please."

He is hatless in late October and a breeze moves against his neck, riffles his stiff black hair to lift the parted side, then set it back down. It is a motion of tenderness Phoebe often made when not totally in agreement but fully understanding whatever small nuisance of the day needed resolution — this shuffling back and smoothing his hair in place, this brush of her breath over his scarred eye and ear. She is letting him know he is close, very close to what is right, but not quite, not quite. He is a study in black for the cemetery groundskeeper, who observes his regular arrival, often with flowers, often with cones of incense brought on small glazed vessels, narrow coils of sandalwood dissolving in the drifts of air. His loyalty to a dead wife is a badge of merit, one that has served Moses in good stead so long as Phoebe stayed near their house, or here. But the classroom — Aiyee! That brought talk of "crazy." He wants her there, of course, but she can't be there. And if she continues . . . if she continues —

Moses says, "What course, what path? What is it I am to do?"

Phoebe is quiet, the passing breeze absent, and it occurs to him how utterly lost he will be if she vanishes completely, like his father had vanished all those years ago. Like his father had waved to him from the railing of the ship in 1907 and never returned in body, like she had waved to him from the platform. The platform where she stood still seems to be moving, even now, further away, Phoebe's presence smaller, tiny, a speck.

As his father had known the obligation to sail to London and retrieve the bones of Moses's uncle, Moses knows to reach into the hole and retrieve the gloved box.

He nods, takes the box out, takes the braid of dull yellow hair from the box, and says "I see the way."

"Yes," Phoebe answers.

His hands are soiled and he puts them deep in his pockets as he leaves Phoebe's grave, the hole near her headstone covered, the pieces of sod patted back into place—all as it should be again. They are, Moses and Phoebe, on a gentle swell of the green grounds, moving toward the lane where Moses has left his car, the groundskeeper doffing his hat in respect; Phoebe's weightless hand has slipped through to hold lightly at his elbow. He offers the groundskeeper a scarred smile and brief nod of acknowledgment.

It's as if the speck, his diminishing Phoebe, became whole again, as if his decision gave his Phoebe a way to reenter his world. It has to do with making things right between the dead and the living, with putting things where they ought to be, and it is as sure as her hand at his elbow, or the emptiness of her hand's absence.

Moses packs a valise under Phoebe's guidance—what he will need, what he will not. He will not travel until the week ends—substitute teachers are not easily arranged. In their room, he lays down on her side of the bed, his head in the place where her head normally rests. Her magic floats all about him; he is on the right path. Yun Li's bones have been safely in China for a dozen years, since the Spanish Flu decimated Moses's classroom, his home, his friends of the present and the past; even Yun Li—the great fatty presence of Yun Li—even him. Now Ellie Bowles must be put to rest. How like Phoebe to know this!

Moses weighs the light in the room, the twilit warm lavender displacing the rose-glow of late sun, erasing the shadows in corners. They are with him, all the demons and angels, all the ghosts. He cannot help but smile; all his old enemies, and friends, are calm.

Another Train, Another Daughter
EN ROUTE
1930

live buys a train ticket home. She is sixty-four in 1930 and her purchase is not immediate to the news of Irene's death, nor is the man behind the grille in any rush. He is lean and bald and his eyes focus on her décolletage in a way that she knows goes on even as she jerks the ticket from his hand and turns away. She has taken a taxi from Flo's. Flo's husband, Mike, had been entertaining (when were they *not* entertaining?), and Florence couldn't be spared. On the other side of the continent, according to Buddy's telegram, Irene could not be held by the coroner's office any longer. Did they have so many bodies they couldn't spare room for Irene? A charity group for has-been performers had taken up "the care of her disposal." *The care of her disposal. What a way to put things,* Olive thinks. *What an awful way to offer—a what? A kindness?*

She checks the time on the station clock and shows an idle porter her ticket, asking directions to the proper platform and where she might find a Ladies Room. She feels exposed and has the time to remedy this, tipping the porter with a dime and moving toward a suspended black sign with Ladies imprinted in elegant white. The porter will see to her bags, take them to the right platform, hold them there for her, but who has taken Irene? And why haven't they held this unmaintainable child for her? She thinks, for a moment, that she will turn back and retrieve the smaller of the two suitcases she's left with the porter, but the case is a case holding material things — the case is not the daughter Olive abandoned. She pushes her way through the door under the Ladies sign.

The train station bathroom is state of the art, smells recently remodeled, and she sets her purse on a low counter, snaps it open, and digs for a clean handkerchief she put in a side pocket before leaving Flo's. From the interior lining she removes three safety pins she keeps for emergencies: loose hems, broken bra straps, a button suddenly gone missing. She folds the square hanky diagonally and places the triangle of thin white over her cleavage, working with her mirrored reflection, leveling the straight edge of the fold, pinning and unpinning the ends from the inside, hiding the silver shine of the safety pin heads and ends.

"There," she says, patting the areas flat where the pins hold the hanky in place on the left, on the right — not a hint of silver showing through. On the bottom center there is a glint, a single stitch of pin showing. "This won't do. You're like the chrome bumper on Flo's LaSalle roadster," Olive tells the stitch of pin. She doesn't like to take in the reflection, the whole reflection the mirror offers. She is not vain; she has never been vain.

"Where Flo gets it, I'll never understand," she says. She has not checked to see if the stalls in the bathroom are empty. She assumes there are several beyond this small powder room foyer, but hasn't any need of them and doesn't explore the unnecessary.

"Well, then," she says and her eyes blink on the stitch and blink on the navy-blue cloche she wears, the triangle of white inserted to cover the plunge of the hideous navy-blue serge neckline of this perfectly awful dress Flo insisted on purchasing for her. "A comfortable travel dress," Flo had said.

"Comfortable, my eye," Olive says, but her voice has gone into a frog's croak, the "eye" not quite pronounced.

She grips the counter, lowers herself into the functional chair, a chair with arms and oilcloth upholstery, a sensible chair that could be easily disinfected by attendants who disinfected such places as these. Maybe the bathroom has not been recently remodeled; maybe it has only just been recently cleaned. Maybe the acrid scent of cut wood isn't pine at all, but a chemical imitating pine—and this is the cause for the burn in her eyes, the bumper-chrome glow of the pin-stitch just right of her heart.

She imagines Mae sitting in the chair near the window facing St. Terence Street. The window, Mae's room, is on the third floor, next door to the tenant who gets free room and board for seeing to her. The tenant's name is Jane Smith—an old friend of Oneska's, someone Nessie met in nurses' training, before the Great War, retired now, never married, and without Celibacy Insurance.

"At least you're spared this," Olive says in a whispered rush. She is speaking to the daughter she imagines back home in Brooklyn, to Mae, who proved unable to handle life and so Olive had handled life for her, let the asylum director direct her, in the best interests of all concerned, to "fix" Mae's brain. Times were hard. Food lines long. Jobs scarce. Olive couldn't afford Mae's hospital care. They might lose the brownstone.

They might all—Wilbur and Honey, their little boy Lincoln, Buddy, barely ten at the time and an orphan, Edison's widow and her two adolescent children—lose the brownstone. Was Olive meant to put them all out in the street to keep up the costs of Mae's care?

Olive stares at the woman in the navy-blue cloche, meets her eye-to-eye. "*Monster,*" she says, splaying her opened palm over the face in the mirror. But the moment is brief. She stiffens her back. *Satisfaction is overrated,* and a commodity Olive can ill afford.

She hears the first call for boarding at Track Number Twelve and snaps her purse shut. Her face is long in the mirror, what had once been very blue eyes were now a nondescript blue-gray. Irene's in the ground in upstate New York. Flo is entertaining a few dozen miles from the station with cocktails and Hollywood sunshine around an in-ground pool. Mae is in a chair three floors up in Brooklyn, unconcerned with the traffic below, her eyes on a roofline or cloud or some other thing, or no *thing* at all, with Jane Smith in the background, at the ready to pull her back into balance, should she, should Mae, slump too far into her chair.

Olive hesitates, her hand on the chrome push-plate to exit the ladies room. Her oldest sons, buried somewhere in France. Her infant daughters, buried above Yostel's Pond. Oh, but Irene! Irene . . . She straightens her shoulders, moves one foot and then the next to catch her train.

She gives the porter another dime when he stows her luggage on board. She thinks of Budd, how many years ago now? How he carried Mae through the crowds in Philadelphia, the length of his strides—how long her eldest boy's legs had been. On this rung up to the passenger car in Los Angeles, she searches the platform for signs of Edison, the

boy she left to the circus, the boy she sold with the Winton. Was that a wrong choice, too? Had she made any right
ones? Has one of the safety pins come undone? Is that what's
pricking her skin? Opportunities. Choices for her children—
that's all she'd ever wanted. Choices . . . for them.

She takes a seat, sits stiffly, bends only as required. There is
the brownstone on the other side of America. *There is Buddy,
so like his father, taking charge in her absence, handling the household, already a man,* Olive thinks. *And yes, there is the brownstone, the home, the missing income Irene had always contributed
no matter what job she took, no matter how locked those brownstone doors were to her. There is the other price paid to maintain
the home—Mae. There is death and living death.*

Olive pulls the triangle of white until the facings of the
navy-blue neckline fan to the outside, skewing the safety
pins. She tugs on the linen. She needs this handkerchief for
practical reasons—the reasons hankies are carried, to wipe
up messes when emotions take over. The conductor pauses
in the aisle, offers a white cloth napkin without a word. He
is black, the conductor, wearing a black suit; the napkin is
draped over his forearm in the way a headwaiter would carry
it. Olive takes the napkin, leaves the mess of her hanky and
dress hanging in disarray. "Nothing," she says quietly, blowing
her nose in demure and ladylike ways, "nothing is, not really,
black and white . . . the way it appears. Nothing."

OLIVE IS HOME, a mug of coffee too hot to wrap her hand
around on the table in front of her. She wraps her fingers
around it, regardless. She is in need, she's decided, of physical pain. In the brownstone's kitchen, nothing is different.
Nothing is the same. The hot mug will not leave blisters. Her

calluses are too tough, her palms too weathered, and the contents cooling, at a gallop, with her touch.

She will not go upstate to the charity plot those show
people have slid Irene into. She will cook for Buddy, Wilbur,
Honey, their two-year-old, Lincoln.

She will care for the living.

She will care for poor drooling Mae in the rocking chair
upstairs. She will launder their clothes, including the caretaker Jane's, and perfectly starch and iron every article worn,
every pillowcase and hanky.

She thinks, suddenly, of Joseph.

How convenient for him! Dying in advance of their children, in advance of Mae's unhappy undoing, in advance of
Flo's numerous husbands and (dare she think of Flo's cat-
alogue modeling of underwear as success?) career choices.
Not Irene's. He knew of Irene's choices. "Oh, you were still
alive for that, weren't you," she mumbles, then the words go
inside. *I saw how you gave her, Irene, that look of undiluted
pride, glancing to your neighbors in the audience, nodding her
way, letting them know she was your girl, yours; then, looking
at me, that shy approval of my having allowed her this tour, at
only fourteen! Fourteen, Joseph. Fourteen! You should've shaken
me by the shoulders; you should've shunned me, worried for her;
you should've . . .*

She groans, "My girl, my girl," her hands joining around
the mug and she pushes it out like the prow of a boat toward
the far side of the polished mahogany, pushes until her forehead presses and rocks against the wood. She will leave a
blur in the shine, the print of her skin leaving traces of her
tired oils on the high-rub of lemons squeezed into formulas
to feed what has been dead for eons, make the wood glow, as
if full of life.

Joseph Johns had died cutting ice for the icehouse while out with his brothers at Yostel's Pond. A hard winter had left good ice, thick ice, according to Nessie. She attended his funeral, of course. She lived in the same county; it would've been unseemly if she had not, Nessie had told Budd. Budd and Edison had attended, too. Irene, already on tour with Dottie for a year and a half by then, and somewhere with warmer waters (Was it Cuba?), had no way of knowing (Had she still cared so deeply about Joseph? She was no longer ten; she had seen so much of the world.); Florence and Wilbur, at home with Olive, were told there wasn't the money to allow them to go.

Olive, pulling herself straight in the chair, says, "How convenient for you, Joseph." Her mouth, soured as if she holds venom she can't swallow, twists. She spits into the cooled mug, scowls, spits again, and scrapes the chair back as she stands.

At the sink she empties the tainted cup.

"I have to go out, if that's OK with you," Jane Smith says from the door into the kitchen.

Olive nods. She will turn and take the stairs up to the third floor where Mae is oblivious to what she has lost, to ice hanging from branches on the tree below her window, to traffic and vehicular exhaust steaming the streets. She will attend to what precious little she can still attend to — by God, she will.

Mae's room is neither dark nor light; a gauzy curtain at the closed window diffuses what sunlight enters. A lap rug is settled over Mae's lower body and Mae's hands are loose, slightly cupped, with her unused palms facing upwards as if . . . as if, Olive thinks, *Mae has unending patience and soon, in a moment, or a year—what is meant to be placed in them, will come.*

Olive sits in a chair within reach of Mae, the chair Jane Smith occupies while at her needlework or reading. Olive thinks, *I should've let you help with the horses.* "I should've," she says out loud, deeply regretful of choices she's made. "I should've tracked down that damned Latterby Brothers' Circus and dragged Edison back by his ears. Yes," she says, watching the still profile of Mae. Olive does not say a word about the promise there'd been in each of her offspring, even this one seated beside her, who, Olive knows now, had promise back then, had gumption. Olive lowers her head, a heat behind her eyes she is wont to share with the living. *I tried, I tried everything I knew, but you, you remained true to who you were. Are you still? Mae? Are you still my Mae?*

The Return

oses straightens his tie in the Men's Room. He has left his name in block print letters on a clipboard at the sergeant's desk, several names down from the first name not crossed off. Officers in uniform and out of uniform had passed in and out of swinging doors with small wired windows about head height. The door had a sign: Authorized Personnel Only. But there was only the one sergeant at the raised counter and, "People," he'd said, "take time to process. Have a chair." And, for a time, Moses had, busying himself with a form, filling in dates and giving space to an area labeled "Complaint."

He gives the left side of his tie a tug, can't help remembering this same bow tie worn under the collar of Mr. M. Rathke, Marion, his old and dear friend. He has tied the knot wrong and the tie isn't straight at his neck. He would have Phoebe re-do the knot; she is there, her cheek leaned against his shoulder blade in the back, but, lately, on this particular journey especially, her phantom fingers have lost their ability to manipulate the material world. He will have to re-tie it himself. Can she see what he sees, tucked in behind him as she is? The loose ends of the dark blue bow tie have thickened into a long braid of yellow hair, long enough to wrap around a neck, overlap, long enough to be pulled, to strangle a woman to death—can she see this from where she stands? He pauses. "Phoebe?" he says.

"Yes?"

"I think I cannot wear a tie. Do you think it will make a difference? Do you think they, the desk sergeant, will care?"

"No, Moses. I don't think he will care."

He pulls the loosened tie from his collar and puts it in his suit coat pocket. The end of Ellie Bowles braid is there. He feels it against his knuckles, briefly—a soft coil laying in wait.

Returned to the chair where he filled out the forms, he waits for his name to be called and, in the manner he would use to call role in class, he checks off, silently, the names of those he has attended to: Yun Li; Yun Li's wife; Yun Li's legitimate daughters (four of them that he does not know by name); Yun Li's legitimate grandchildren—six nameless girls and a boy, Sing Cheung Li, named for Moses's father; Yun Li's first, second, and third concubines; their sons and their daughters; Benjamin Smith (he has posted a letter this very day to Benjamin, on the advice of Phoebe, to inform Benjamin of his great and unending sin—the sin of silence); the Williamsport School Board (Phoebe had said they should not be caught unawares but afforded some time to prepare a statement, should news reach them of consequent events). And Alice Towne. How could he have almost forgotten Sis?

But what of his father, Sing Cheung? *Aiyee!* Moses presses his eyes tightly closed. *Forgive me,* he prays to his bedeviled father. *Forgive me this failure. Please.*

His name is called. He gives the forms to the desk sergeant, an older man with broken veins in his face who glances down the form, nodding, as if in approval of Moses's clear and precise block printing. When the sergeant's head snaps up to take him in, Moses retrieves the length of braid from his pocket, the clump of Marion's dark-blue tie holding it back for an instant, then freeing, falling on the floor near Moses's feet.

"Get Mahoney," the sergeant says, calling over his shoulder to a uniformed officer who stops midway through the swinging doors.

"He's working that dead broad case down in Hell's Kitchen," the officer says.

"That suicide? Get him. Now. And tell him to bring Liu. Jesus, Mary and Joseph," the sergeant says under his breath, "Jerry'll wanna get a look at this."

"Not a suicide yet—"

"I said GET HIM. Do it now, got it?"

"You got it," the officer responds.

"Then cuff this guy," he says, jerking a nod toward Moses. "And don't be gentle about it. Got that?"

"Yes, sir."

Moses feels his arms lifted from behind, then gentled to rest his wrists on the counter; her scent is all around him, calming, soothing as the salve Alice Towne used to give her to rub into his wounds. The veins on the sergeant's face are blooming, heightening in color, deepening to a rich purple, flaring like ostrich plumes—she is there, his queen, his Phoebe.

"Wipe that dumb-ass grin off your face or I'll wipe it off for you," the sergeant snaps.

"Yes," Moses says, the bright pipes of a calliope beginning their tune.

The Undisclosed Note

**rom past experience,** Rose of Sharon has learned to tap the closed doors of hospital rooms and now gives three quick knocks before poking her head through and asking, "Anybody home?"

"We are," a woman's voice answers, followed by Buddy's low chuckle. His nurse sits at a slant on his bed, one crepe-soled shoe braced to the floor for balance.

"Don't let me interrupt," Sharon says, already retreating from her too hasty attempt to enter.

"Not at all," the nurse answers, immediately up, straightening her uniform. "He's all yours."

"You *are* interrupting," Buddy says, his mood a very good one. "But I am all yours." When he winks, Sharon looks at the nurse who is winking back, as if she, the nurse, is the one to whom he's pledged his all.

As usual, he can't seem to help but make any female within smiling range feel as if she's the queen of the moment. Why should this particular nurse be immune?

"We'll go out again, say, in an hour?" the nurse says, gripping a walker parked next to his bed.

"It's a date," Buddy says.

Two new floral arrangements crowd the sill. One card is in Bet's hand: *Come on, already! Get Well! Love, Bet & Kev.*

Kev? Bet & Kev?

Ignoring the other arrangement, white daisies with yellow centers, and its pitch-forked card, Sharon drags a chair up close to Buddy's bed. The squared cushion is dark blue and shiny like leather, but not, and when she sits, all one hundred and ten pounds of her five-foot-eight body, the chair sighs, as if accepting a grander weight.

"Well," Sharon says.

Buddy, the youth of his ninety-one years alive in his eyes, says, "Tell me."

Sharon, warming by the second, knows, *knows* there is no possible way her cousin can know anything, yet her face contorts. She is biting her lip, on the inside. On the outside, her grin is a wrench.

"*Tell me*," Buddy says, now obviously onto something he finds in her demeanor.

From the door, the nurse, who has passed behind Sharon, offers a blown kiss and, "Later, Love!"

"Love?" Sharon says, sinking her back into the dark cushion and sliding her legs out to cross at the ankles. "You do work fast."

Bet and Kevin had jointly sent, or brought, Buddy flowers and placed them on the sill where Sharon could not avoid seeing them — Bet, Sharon felt certain, thereby communicating this new twist in her love life.

"What's wrong with a little love?" Buddy offers, following the path of Sharon's gaze toward the sill and the bouquets.

"Did I say there was anything wrong?" She averts her eyes from the sill and from Buddy because, in fact, there *was* something wrong when things — passion, or whatever a body might call it — came on too fast. She believes "charm" a flimsy cause to dive headlong into whatever it was her daughter and Buddy's tenant had so obviously dived into. And to sign a card like that, so intimately, abbreviated names and all — didn't that indicate a plunge of some sort had been taken?

"Didn't you?" Buddy says. "You said *love?* the way I used to say *liver?* when Aunt Honey or some other well-meaning woman at the brownstone tricked me into taking a bite, saying it was beef or pork and not what it really was at all. Made me gag."

What Sharon hears is probably true, her gag reflex may have been triggered by the word, and then she needs to wonder about the why of that, if it's jealousy over the ease of such comings and goings and sittings on beds by the nursing staff and floral bouquets that should have her name on the card and not some tenant's.

Buddy flattens the sheet across his waist and pats down the fold. "We'll work on that," he says. "I love the stuff now."

"Meaning?" Sharon asks, remaining relaxed. Before Buddy can respond, she says, "You think I don't love — is that it?"

"Meaning I think liver is a good thing, especially with onions. And, I think you've been," Buddy hesitates, cocks his head in her direction, then looking away says, "I think you've been very recently loved and," he turns back to face her, his eyes alive with pure Buddy twinkle, "and that's what's got you all glowing . . ."

"Buddy! You think I got laid?" She chokes out the last word then bursts out laughing.

Buddy stammers, ignoring her reaction, "And it's unnatural,

or you think it should be, should feel unnatural, and so you question it everywhere—love, said or done or even thought about—and it's not a light thing for you but heavy. Almost too heavy to bear."

"You are so off the mark."

The attitude Buddy offers says, *Convince me.*

"I'll tell you what's almost too heavy to bear," she says, "is the thought of you thinking of me, picturing me even, in this *recently loved* position. And just who shared this event with me? You are too much, Buddy. Too much."

"Then what?" Buddy says, seeming to consider the possibility Rose of Sharon, Rose of the pale, icy blue, may, indeed, have not been recently laid.

"The 'What' is two Mahoneys," she says. "The old one and the old one's son. A charmer and an ass—I'm sorry—and a bastard, as he calls himself, and his son. Though, the son's really the bastard, if you ask me." She is between breaking up with laughter and some other emotion not quite anger, or, if anger, an anger not directed at Buddy or Mahoney's son or any particular person, except maybe Teddy, because if Teddy had just held onto the last liver transplant he'd undergone, if his body hadn't rejected what had been longed for and at long last given, if—

"I was thinking," Buddy says, "the younger one is more like your age and, well, things can happen, sometimes, you know, if you let them."

"What?" she shakes her head, shaking loose, perhaps, the momentary lapse into unfamiliar terrain. Anger is not an emotion she encounters regarding Teddy.

"So, tell me, Rosie. What is behind the glow you're wearing today?"

The glow, if ever she wore one, has metamorphosed from

excitement to share the news she'd found in the boxes at Mahoney Junior's place to confusion. Pulling her legs in, she lowers her elbows to her knees and lowers her forehead into her hands. "I'd be happy to tell you, if you give me the chance."

"Pity, that," he says, meaning, Sharon figures, it's a pity she didn't get laid. Or loved. But she had done, gotten loved, in a way, by chance. Or patience. Or perseverance. Or whatever had allowed her to stay with the search to uncover that number needed by the NYPD to reopen Irene's long dead case.

ALWAYS GOOD WITH tedious matters — knitting, refinishing furniture, weaving pine needle baskets — she'd been less given to matters of patience with humans, a flaw she believed sifted down from her father rather than mother. Appleonia had endless patience with humans and none whatsoever with handiwork. If "love" is an awakening, a pins-and-needles sensation that warms from the inside because of an outside influence, then Time, or History, or the Universe had rained "love" down on her in that room full of boxes at Mahoney's.

There'd been the file box dated 1930, the lid on the floor, loose papers and spiral-bound notebooks scattered from corner to corner of the room. Pages glued together from mildew and dampness, pages torn from her efforts to lever them apart. There'd been the remains of what seemed like a pigtail, perhaps, portions of a braid so tangled and mangled it might've been used by mice as a home. A curiosity, she'd set the hair aside, picked it up once again when she came upon a newspaper clipping in one of the many albums of clippings Sharon assumed had been kept by various Mahoney women down the line. In a grainy photo of an officer identified as Mahoney, the braid was held out to his side as if it were a dead snake.

It may have been late afternoon or early morning when Sharon found the clipping. The air in the bedroom at the end of the hall in Queens had the substance of changing light, of an ending or a beginning, a day opening or closing, when the significance of the photo's date hit home.

"What's going on in there?" Mahoney had shouted through the closed doors. "You OK?"

"Oh my God," was all Sharon could manage, though the door was being forced open from the hall, a half inch and an inch.

"What've you got blocking the door?" Mahoney wanted to know. "You OK?"

She managed to answer, "Go away," and he said something crude regarding her and the horse she rode in on and then there was silence — except for the sound of very old cellophane tape letting go of album pages.

HERO DETECTIVE'S 21-YEAR MANHUNT ENDS

Files Will Close On String of Vile China Town Strangulation Murders Which Occurred Over 9-year Span Two Decades Ago

Thanks to New York City Detective Jerry Mahoney's diligence, Mr. Moses Cheung, 40, has been apprehended and found in possession of an article of clothing believed to have been the glove of his first victim, socialite Ellie Bowles. In addition, the Chinaman, Cheung, carried on his person a braid of yellow hair Detective Mahoney has identified as the victim's.

The Yellow Peril Murders, as labeled by the Press, began with the discovery of Miss Bowles's body in a trunk above a Chinatown noodle house. She had been strangled and her throat had been cut.

"I knew," states Mahoney, "we had our man when I saw that hair. Mahoney was removed from the case, his first, in 1909, due to his youth and lack of experience, but, he states, "I never stopped looking for Cheung. It was his apartment and his trunk where Miss Bowles was found in 1909."

When notified Cheung was in custody, Detective Mahoney and his partner, Officer Xiang Liu, with jubilation in their hearts, immediately went to the station house. There had not been any further signature Yellow Peril Murders since 1918. Both Mahoney and Liu assumed Cheung, their chief suspect, had died in the flu pandemic, the war, or been murdered himself.

"Justice," Mahoney states, "can now be served." In addition to Ellie Bowles, twelve other women perished by strangulation, their hair shorn, and their bodies hidden in boxes between1909 and 1918. All of these murders were attributed to the Yellow Peril, according to Mahoney, however, none gained the notoriety of the first killing because of the socialite status of Miss Bowles. The granddaughter of Civil War *(continued B-9)*

"MY GIRLFRIEND," BUDDY says, "will be back. She likes to be seen in the halls with me and my walker."

Sharon has thought, and continues to think, about sharing a potentially harmful piece of old dirty laundry. "It's," Sharon begins, "a bit awkward."

He nods, shrugs, says, "I can handle awkward."

Returning his nod, she stands, walks behind the blue-cushioned chair, circles back, sits down and says, "Aunt Irene was pregnant." From her purse, Sharon pulls out an envelope with the clippings she's lifted from Mahoney's scrapbook albums.

"Ah," he says.

"You knew?" She's drawn out an inch-long scrap of yellowed newsprint with a short blurb about Irene. Whoever the Mahoney woman was who clipped all mention of Mahoney men from the newspapers, she'd snipped this one from the same dated *Long Island Press* as the "Yellow Peril Murders" story. "Hell's Kitchen Woman Found Dead" headlined the piece.

> The death of carnival worker Irene Johns is under investigation by Detective Jerry Mahoney of the New York City Police Dept. The father of the victim's unborn child is being held for questioning. Gas asphyxiation appears to be the cause of

"Yes," Buddy sighs, "I knew."

"But you didn't tell me — did you? I would've remembered that. Why didn't you tell me?"

Buddy's gaze drops to the small square of newsprint she holds. His face is hidden and all Rose of Sharon can read are the freckles on his bald head. "Would you believe . . . I knew Grandmother Olive wouldn't want me to bring it up."

"She's so-so long dead, Buddy."

"You think so?" When he says this, she has the feeling he's smiling, as if he knows something she does not.

"Some people, Olive Johns, for instance, go on. Their bodies get left behind and all, but they, who they were, sort of, *go on.*"

The lace on Sharon's shoe has worked loose. She does not bend to re-tie it. "You think Olive's a ghost?"

Buddy wags his head. "No. You *know* what I mean."

Watching Rosie come to terms with what he's said about Olive's approval or disapproval, though dead, Buddy feels she must understand. She has, he believes, her own set of lingering folks—mother, father, husband, probably friends she's failed to mention—who enter her thinking from time to time, influencing how she handles one situation or another. What's said and unsaid. He never knew Rosie's mother. Her father, Lincoln, he'd known only too well as boy.

Now there was a sad case, Buddy thinks. A lad so self-controlled he hardly knew how to be a boy. Wound up tight. Not a hint of coming unwound as Wilbur so often did. And now Lincoln's daughter, Rosie, seems much the same, though a little less so today.

"I wish," Buddy says, "you could see yourself now."

"Why? What's wrong?"

"You look fine. Sit." He pats the bed where the nurse had been seated. She hesitates and he says, "Come on. You weigh about as much as a flea. You won't hurt me."

"I might. I did," she blurts. "Oh, Buddy, I'm still so sorry about all this."

"No need. But whatever. Here's the thing, Rosie. It's over. You know? Let it go." He tilts his head one way and then the other, rocking the right words into place. "I finally did. As much as I could. But Grandmother, she didn't. And she lived a long time. Bitter. It's a bad way to live."

Sharon nods.

Buddy watches her, waits for her to look up from a long, steady stare at the back of his hand palming hers on the covers. "There was this landlady at Irene's place," he says.

Sharon looks up. "Ubruski? Or something like that?"

"Yeah, something like that. How'd you know?"

"Notes Mahoney, the detective, one of the detectives, kept on Irene's case."

He nods. "And there was Grandmother," he continues. "That landlady, Mrs. Ubreski, she's the one let me and Grandmother back in at Irene's to, well, to take what was Irene's, I guess." Now Buddy's the one staring at his hand over Sharon's, but all he can see is that room, as it was, with her things and Bucky's things crowded along the walls and into every space—and how it was still, almost precisely the same when they left.

"We brought the trunk with us from the brownstone to pack her stuff in. Bucky didn't care. He wasn't there, not when we packed up, but him and a lad he worked with brought it around to the brownstone."

Sharon says, "That trunk." She looks up, interested now, it would seem, on how sun in the window casts shadows across the toe end of her shoe.

There hadn't been shadows in Irene's and Bucky's apartment, not when he and Olive and Mrs. U. entered. The portable gas lamp had been shattered, the globe of it, at any rate, and the spigot where the hose attached was bent.

Winter sun outside had pretty well stayed outside. Irene's window let little in. And the way the room was . . . was how Buddy thought a dim dungeon might be, or a crypt, but furnished with bed, coverlets, tables, chairs, scarves, dresser, a basin and a pitcher of water, a shaving mug, shaving brush, stand mirror, a tortoise shell-backed hair brush with some of Irene's red hair.

Sharon says, "It's like a tomb, that trunk. That was it, then, of Irene, what you packed and took away?"

"Just as you discovered. Except," he pauses, "except I think Grandmother kept the old quilt. I don't know what happened with that."

Sharon starts to rise, but Buddy stays her hand. "There's a bit more," he says. "The landlady, she hung around, like she was guarding the place. For Bucky, I guess. I remember her there, big and sad, and, I don't know, angry with us, some way or another. She didn't come inside. Just leaned into the doorway, blocking our exit. You know, if we took something, if Grandmother took something she, that Mrs. Ubreski, didn't think we ought to take."

Sharon says, "Stories I've heard about Olive, that must not have sat very well."

"True." He dips his head, as if shrugging past a bit of unpleasantness.

Sharon is waiting for him to continue, waiting without pummeling him with questions or guessed-at answers, and Buddy is glad. She is a little less Lincoln-like, wound a little less tight, transformed, or very nearly, he thinks, to a woman akin to the kind of women he most admires. Blood, of course, will tell, Buddy believes, and in more ways than a pretty smile. Of course, the smile of Irene Johns was more than "pretty." It was like a flag when it came; like a pennant announcing *This is life! And I'm in it! C'mon! There's nothing to be afraid of.* Finally, this daughter of the little boy Lincoln, this granddaughter of Wilbur and Honey, and great-granddaughter of Olive and Joseph—finally, she wears that look. No, Rosie isn't smiling, but there's gumption there.

Buddy says, "It's odd."

"What's that?"

"You. I don't mean *you're odd.*" He's started off badly and knows it. "I mean how we are what we are; how we get made, like, like from the spare parts of others. Does that make any sense?"

"Sure. DNA."

He shrugs. "That, too." She is not that much younger, right now, in this moment, only four or five years at the outside, than Olive had been on that day in Irene's apartment. He would like to have a tintype of Olive to hold out next to Sharon, a portrait of Olive to compare with this girl, this young, aging, not-yet-old woman.

"And?" Sharon nudges him on.

"And, I'm not sure how to word this . . . I guess what I mean is their happiness. And misery. Parts beyond the physical stuff."

"I think that's DNA, too. The mental side. Personalities."

Buddy lifts her hand, gently, puts it back down. "That, too," he says. He is not going to get what he wants to communicate to her communicated. He sighs. "What if," he says, "I get back to that day at Irene's."

"Sure," Sharon says.

She is different, he thinks. *Any other time she'd be asking, demanding to know why I find her "odd." None of that today.*

"This landlady, she stays, like I said. We, Grandmother

and me, we just sort of stood there. There was this outline of Irene's body on the floor they'd drawn around her with chalk. I was there, in the room, when they did that—"

"Buddy, you don't have to go there, if you don't want to. You can stop, I mean, if you want."

"You'd have to be there, I guess, to get how it really was. Grandmother, she finally moved to the sink. I remember her running her fingers over the surface, like she was thinking about giving Irene a grade on housekeeping. The bed was unmade, the one Irene and Bucky shared, and Grandmother stood by it for awhile shaking her head, just shaking her head. She was holding her purse. She carried that same purse for years. Black. Shiny. I can't hardly remember a time when she didn't have that purse with her. In fact, I can't remember *any* time. Anyway," Buddy shakes his head, "she stood with that purse held by the strap, with both hands, like this, so it hung down about to her knees—just looking at that bed. Then she handed the purse to me and started stripping the sheets."

Buddy can't look at Rose of Sharon. He is watching the door, not because he expects anyone to walk through, but because the door is a flat, calm green he can look through while he retells these events. He is reconstructing them there: who moved, who did what. He feels detached in a way he hasn't felt when he's gone back to that room before— impossibly detached from the frenzy, the insane madness he'd witnessed in Olive then, there with the bedclothes.

Sharon says, "I'd heard she was tidy. Dad said I got my talent for cleaning from his grandmother."

Buddy gives a shake of his head. "No. This, this was different. She went at that bed like, like she was killing snakes, Rosie. She scared me. Not the same way that son of a bitch detective had, not like she was going to come after me, but . . ."

Sharon turns her palm up to take his hand. "Buddy . . ."

"No. Let me go on with this. There's some way of this that's not about then, but about now. I can't explain it."

"OK." She doesn't release his hand. She listens.

Olive Johns, the practical woman who ran a quasi-successful, sometimes-on-the-brink-of-failure, boarding house on St. Terence Street—she who supported an oft-drunk son she adored like her own skin, and his family; a woman who guided Buddy from as long ago as he could remember with a firm and sensible hand, who went at things stolidly but with a love that you knew, even when it was administered with a willow switch, the strapping always in good measure to the offense, the coddling afterwards, a prescribed amount to heal—that woman had gone berserk with that unmade bed.

"When she finished," Buddy says, "her hair, which she always kept neat and tidy, sort of waving back into a bun, about here," he touches the back of his head, "her hair was all over her face. Like a madwoman. Completely. And all the while . . . all the while she was—growling. Like she had this scream inside that she wouldn't or couldn't let out."

Sharon leans forward. She would like for Buddy to stop. He has old tears on his face. Fresh, but very old tears, and she wants very much for him to stop, but she leans forward, until her forehead rests on his shoulder, until she is very nearly lying down with him in his bed.

Buddy says, "When the room settled, when she settled, she looked over at me. It was like I wasn't there. She was standing in the middle of the outline, the chalk one, but she didn't know that either. I did, and I looked down. And then she looked down. And the scream, the one she couldn't seem to get out — it came."

Buddy pauses, gaze penetrating the calm green of the door. "All this time . . . the landlady woman never budged, not an inch. Well. Neither had I. Probably all happened in a minute or less. But, you know how it is? Chaos. Sort of an explosion. But, at the same time, like slow motion?"

"Yes," Sharon says. "I know that feeling." She is remembering the flurry of life-saving efforts on Teddy and the unbroken sound of a monitor once the heart's stopped beating.

"This is when the landlady stepped in. Not to help Grandmother. She walked right by her. She'd seen something fly out from the sheets, see? And it was this note to Honey, see? Like one page of a letter. And she'd looked it over, looked at Grandmother, and handed it to her."

Sharon rolls her head up from Buddy's arm. "A suicide note?" she asks, at once regretting the question.

Buddy, while he does not understand the "how" of Irene's death, has never believed, has been adamant, in fact, that Irene did not intentionally take her own life. "She would jump into life, not out of it," he has always insisted.

But why a letter, Sharon wonders, if not to say good-bye to those you love and are leaving behind? And why wasn't this letter taken with the others, the ones mentioned in Mahoney's old case notes?

"No. A letter about firing Wilbur," Buddy says.

"Oh."

Sharon's contacts with Wilbur had never been often, but always, or very nearly always, were ugly, simply by his presence. Even his non-presence left their mark: no milk in Honey's refrigerator; no washing machine so she could do laundry at home; visits to Grandma Honey's spent at the laundromat watching his vile khaki pants and khaki shirts spin; the glue lines on a lovely little figurine labeled "April." April was the month of Grandma Honey's birth and Rose of Sharon had spent her allowance on the figurine Grandma Honey had loved. Loved enough to glue back all the small chips, along with the major cracks, after *he* (she mostly referred to Wilbur as "he") threw it into a window. The resulting crack, years later, in the window *he* never replaced. But more than any of these, the perpetual bruising on Grandma Honey's wrists. God only knew what bruises she kept covered. And, one time, the cast on her arm, the one Grandma Honey *claimed* was her fault, that it'd happened when she'd slipped—which might've been true, except that Grandma Honey could not remember her lies and in one telling she'd slipped on the stairs, and in another telling, in the tub.

"I see," Sharon adds.

Buddy continues. "It's to tell Honey, this letter, the reason she must let Wilbur go is because she's pregnant. That she wouldn't fire him if it was just her. That she knew how important his wage was to her, Honey, and to Olive, to the household. There was more," Buddy says, "because the page ended on a half sentence, like 'I have' or something like that, but they, the landlady and Grandmother, never found the rest."

Sharon moves from the bed. The leg she's had crossed underneath as she sat on the bed is asleep and she's wobbly as she stands.

"You OK?" Buddy asks.

"Foot's asleep," she answers. "Pins and needles." She limps to the door and back, to the door and back, stops at the windowsill. She could keep her hands busy with recycling flowers, but her hands don't move. Little clear pitchforks with cards from people who love Buddy sprout from amidst the stems, names scrawled across the cards at various slants, probably written by florists who held a phone between cheek and shoulder while taking the orders down. Among them, Bet's name paired with "Kev." Is Bet the great-grand-daughter of a killer? Did *he*, that awful vile man, who stank always of tobacco and an uncleanness that went beyond merely not taking a bath—"did *he* murder his sister Irene?"

"My God, no!" Buddy says, and Sharon realizes what she has not intended to say, she has said.

She has said it. The damage is done. She asks, "What happened to the letter?"

"Grandmother put it in her purse."

When Sharon turns from the window, she studies Buddy in profile. He's not looking at her but at his idle hands, upturned and empty, quiet, on the rise of his stomach.

She put it in her purse! This admission, from Buddy, seems a sure indictment, to Sharon, of Wilbur. Her great-grandmother had, for whatever cause, hidden her youngest son's motive for, in a fit of anger, Sharon reasons, knocking his sister senseless, where she had then, over some minutes, or hours, died, alone on that awful floor.

Sharon wants to shake Buddy—take him by his wide shoulders and shake him until his bones rattle. What had he said? *God—no!* All Rose of Sharon can think is, GOD, YES!

"He didn't hurt her," Buddy says. "I know he didn't hurt her."

How can you know that? she wants to ask, she would ask, but she would shout it; she knows she would shout it, and she bites down hard, willing her mouth to stay shut.

"He was not a good man," Buddy says, "your granddad, I mean. He, well, he didn't know how to rein himself in—his temper, or his drinking. But he wasn't evil. If he'd, you know, lost it, and hit her, he would've picked her back up if she fell."

"Is that a little bit like *him* taking Grandma Honey into Emergency when *he* broke her arm?"

"I'd heard age hadn't improved him, but I didn't know, not about that. She was a peach, Aunt Honey."

"How could she keep that letter? It was a lead—don't you see that?"

"He didn't cause her death. I know it."

"How can you *know it*—unless you were with him . . . were you with him?"

Something vital, something palpable and so real she could very nearly feel its grip loosening, letting go, like a tangle of knots a comb comes up against finally breaks, letting the comb pull through, smooth and free, releases Sharon then. It's possible that what broke is faith. A faith in family, a faith that no matter what, we trust what we love. Buddy clearly maintains this. Sharon, in that instant, clearly does not.

"How can you know?" she repeats.

"I know because *I know*. And how could Grandmother do it? Because she'd already lost my dad and Uncle Edison to a war and he was the last boy of three that she had . . . and she loved him. She loved them all, Rose of Sharon, every last one. She loved them all."

Sharon needs to leave. He does not want her here and she does not want to be here. He knows what he knows. She knows what she knows.

"I gotta go," she says.

"It was an accident," he says.

"Right." She has not told him about the files at Mahoney's, not much anyway. The clipping, yes, but not word-one about the ongoing cases Mahoney and Liu had worked, off and on, for eighteen years, how those cases had finally resolved with a confession, taking their focus away from Irene, the same week she'd been found dead. Those multiple murders—the first, some famous Civil War doctor's granddaughter, a debutante, a member of *society*—were far more important, even all those years later, than any low-life on the carnival circuit living in a third-floor walk-up in Hell's Kitchen. Not to mention all the other Chinatown murders that had followed the first. They'd had bigger fish to fry, or gas, or hang—Mahoney and Liu. They'd been certain, by what Sharon found in the notebooks, certain, beyond any doubt, the guy who confessed had had an accomplice. He'd been slight, the confessor, slighter by nearly half than one of his nine victims.

"It was an *accident*," Buddy repeats. "Let it go."

"Whatever," Sharon says.

"I'm talking about this." He touches his new hip. "I'm talking about you, about you holding onto something you feel is your fault. I'm talking about Grandmother, how she held on to all those choices she made, for the right reasons, that didn't work out so well. We do what we do, you know? And we get on with it."

She's at the door, ready to pull it open and slip out.

"Let it go," Buddy says.

"Maybe." She wants to say more, but doesn't know what. There's a point when there's just not much more to add. A stalemate, a standoff.

"Maybe's good," Buddy says. "Maybe's a start. Look at me for a minute, Rosie."

When she turns to face him, he is beaming, a little bit forced, but still beaming. She is the queen of his attention at this precise moment. How many women, she wonders, has he made feel this way? He says, "Irene, she let go of things. Grandmother didn't. It broke her. It broke her heart."

In the hall outside 618, Sharon passes the nurse.

"Oh!" the nurse says. "I thought you might like to join us, if you were still here, for a stroll around the park." The park, Sharon is to understand by the sweep of the nurse's hand up and down the corridor, is none other than these shiny-floored grounds.

Sharon says, "Tomorrow. Maybe, tomorrow."

"Didn't he say? He goes home tomorrow." She is half Buddy's age and all-business in dark green scrubs, her face drawn with deep worry lines across her forehead that don't dissipate, even when relaxed into courteous chatter. "Fast healer, our Buddy," she says. "I'll miss him. A real sweetheart."

"He can get around that well?" Sharon asks.

The lines across the nurse's forehead move up when she lifts her brows as if she finds it extraordinary anyone close to Buddy isn't tuned in to his progress. Sharon thinks she must wear this expression often, this look of incredulousness, or awe, at the incompetent relations of her patients; wrinkles like these, deeply furrowed, indelible, must surely be the result of decades of wonder.

The nurse says, "No, not all that well, but well enough. A physical therapist will make home visits. They like to be at home, our patients. Who wouldn't?" This last seems more friendly threat than question.

"Of course." Sharon feels mildly surprised and mildly undone. "Good," she adds.

She will need to vacate the brownstone at once. Wouldn't she? Would she? Why would she need to do that? Why would she abandon him just when he needs her the most? Because he refused to abandon a belief in Wilbur?

The nurse disappears into Buddy's room. Sharon is the queen of nowhere, unworthy even, it would seem, of a goodbye nod from a middle-aged quasi-stranger in green.

im Dustman has pegged out and left Rose of Sharon's peg in the stinkhole. He stands and taps all three pendulum shades to set them swinging, sending circles of light bobbling over the tabletop, glaring off his glasses and shining off reaches of forehead on either side of a pebble-brown islet of hair still holding, for the most part, center front—a patch he keeps buzzed short.

She has chastised Jim more than once for setting the lights in motion; still, he will exhibit his gladness with every win. It seems old hat, as if she has told him to leave the damned lampshades alone, to gloat quietly, leave his ardor for winning at home for years, rather than months. She has fed one cribbage board to the chimenea, found the blue and green pegs in the ashes, hard little disks melted into misshapened tiddly winks the next day. He just brings another board. At least he's always clean-shaven; she has prevailed and won on that score. She's still working on what he calls her. The story she'd shared with him about name-teasing in grade school, about being a prepositional connector, is included on Rose of Sharon's unwritten List Of Regrets.

When the phone rings, Bet's name shows up on the small screen and she says, as she answers, "You've just saved Mr. Dustman's ass, not to mention another –"

Instead, it is Kevin. He says Bet asked him to call. He says Buddy is gone.

"*What!*"

Jim takes the phone from her hand.

Buddy had written, not five weeks ago, had said in his letter: *I would like to find a place in the park when I'm gone. Many friends there, some I haven't met. There are restrictions. If you each take a quarter cup and vary your days, I don't think anyone will notice. Forgive me if you get into any trouble. We'll settle up over there. I hope not any time soon!*

Buddy's crusty hand-writing had gone on for some pages. He was, he informed, healthy and of sound mind, with no notion of leaving any time soon himself, but, ideally, he would like, when his time came, to be like a bird he'd found once that couldn't wake up, that had died right there in its nest.

He's ninety-two, Sharon thinks. *Did I expect he would go on living forever?*

"Yes, of course. Hold on." Jim pulls the cell phone down and says, "Of . . ."

This can't be, she thinks. *Of course it can be; no—I would know . . .*

"Of! You've got it wrong. Whatever you're thinking, you've got it dead wrong."

She is ashen, gone as white as her hair. "He said Buddy's gone. Bet couldn't even call. How could I not understand?"

"He's eloped."

"What?"

"Here. Talk to Kevin."

What Sharon learns is: Buddy wed Barbara. They've gone to Barbados where Buddy has distant cousins he's always wanted to meet. Bet couldn't call because she was at a Lamaze class, one Kevin couldn't attend because of whatever (Rose of Sharon had stopped listening at Barbados) and he'd found this note from Bet telling him *Let Mom know Buddy's gone*, and he guesses he'd worded it badly (*you could say!*), but he'd had the damned note in his hand, and whatever.

She is not fond of Kevin; the history they share, to put it mildly, sucks. She had tried, had possibly gotten beyond her feelings about him witnessing her stupidity, but then, then he had lured Bet from her Assistant Art History Librarian position at Bryn Mawr. Bet, with so much potential, in some Brooklyn gallery or institute or whatever it was called. That they'd married made little difference. Nothing stays the same once a child marries.

Now this?

PIGEONS AND MORE pigeons. She is dreaming. She has her quarter cup of Buddy in a bamboo container with a cork in the top. They have all set out from the brownstone — there are cousins from upstate New York and cousins from California and cousins from Barbados. They have all taken different paths to arrive at places particular to each letting go. The breeze is brisk and the pigeons seem nervous to Rosie. Restless. Fluttering up to barely resettle before lifting themselves again. So many wings. She is startled with each repetition. Then, not. Their lift and brief flurries become expected, familiar, as familiar as the sound of shuffling cards. They bob and peck, the pigeons. She watches. She wonders what they can find to eat on this ground. It doesn't matter. She's happy

For families — those we're born into
and those we join along the way.

Arlene,
Best Wishes!
Lynn Doiron
Dec. 2018

they've found something. Then not. She is chasing them, chasing the pigeons away. They rise up. They come back. They are eating the tiny fragments of bone, Buddy's bones that had refused to burn down to ash. *Shoo!* she is strangling to say.

"Of," Jim breathes into her neck, "you OK?"

She had stayed on to help when Buddy came home from the hospital, until she'd become well and truly in the way. Barbara, returned from Umbria, was ever present with casseroles. The two unfriendly tenants from the third floor flat (sisters, as Sharon had guessed, and divorced) hardly let an hour go by that they weren't at the door, fussing with Buddy's laundry, and *Had Rose of Sharon remembered to feed the black squirrel.* There was Kevin's aunt who came by train everyday to see Buddy (it seems they had a romantic history), and friends, men and women alike, from the Yacht Club.

Moreover, Buddy himself seemed eager for his Rosie to be gone on her way. The difference was in Rose of Sharon, how she viewed her dismissal from St. Terence Street—how she understood Buddy's intent.

There was life there, but it was *his life.* There was another life, *hers,* waiting.

And there was, upon her return to Cottonwood, a note. It was in a sandwich bag duct taped to a windowpane on the French doors. Jim Dustman—the neighbor whose name she hadn't known, the neighbor whose porch light she could see late at night across the acres—had left it there.

All in all, including her time in Philly with Bet, she'd been gone since November—the better part of three months. The duct tape left an outline of glue on the window that would not let go; she had to bring out the Goo-Gone from under the sink. (She would have a word with this Jim Dustman *about that!*) He was sorry about the rake he'd borrowed without asking, the note said. He was sorry about the hose, but there'd been some nearly dead plants he'd given some water and then noticed the time and had a dental appointment and the tooth did hurt.

"Of?"

"The pigeons. They were taking Buddy's quarter cup."

"Mm. Good dream? Bad dream?" he asks, his knees at the back of her knees, his upper body curved like a shallow bowl and she, Rose of Sharon, the warm egg the bowl holds.

"He's in Barbados," she says. "I'll call him tomorrow and ask. And when are you going to stop calling me that?"

Then one of two things happened: the bowl grew smaller, or the egg grew larger, and after a while there was easy breathing.

Much, much later when she returned to the pigeons, they seemed to be waiting for her, glad with their muffled staccato conversations and start-ups and stops, pleased as she trickled more dust from the uncorked bamboo.

Maybe she knew the answer. It seemed like she knew it. It seemed like she wouldn't need to ask Buddy. Like a bit of himself in a pigeon's craw would be just the thing.

But she would call. Share her good dream.

Epilogue

BROOKLYN

2010

he trunk with the moon and
stars did not find a niche at the St. Ter-
ence Street brownstone — not, however,
for lack of space. The divorced sisters,
invited to share housing with a divorced
niece in Omaha, had vacated and Kevin, with Bet's enthusi-
astic approval, had hired an architect and contractors to
remodel the two flats into one. Bet found room for any number of furnishings, some old, some straight from IKEA's baby
department.

Among old furnishings Bet had considered purchasing
there was an antique trunk from Shanxi Province, China.
Hired to appraise any number of items prior to an estate
auction, she'd come across a collection of trunks — eighty-
two in all — many of them antiques from around the world.
There'd been Danish and Swedish trunks in far better condition than the stars and moon trunk (that had found a niche
in an adobe house out west), yet the sharp simplicity of the
trunk from Shanxi — its tell-tale red lacquer and the gilded
tip of a bird's wing — had captured Bet's interest.

The bottom of the trunk was not original to its construction

357

and she hoped this flaw would allow her to value it at a sum she and Kev could afford. This was not the case. She'd been forced, having inherited a bit more of her mother's attitudes toward honesty than her father's, to value the trunk beyond the reach of their pocketbooks.

Her research discovered the trunk's distant past, but not its more recent one, nothing of the fates of those whose hands had once passed along the trunk's simple lines, whose water-marked taffeta skirts had been straightened upon it, whose body had been hidden inside. Bet had identified the gilded wing tip as having been that of a heron—a factor in helping her price the trunk for the estate sale.

The owner of the eighty-two trunks, now deceased, had found the Shanxi specimen, the bottom knocked out and the four bottom corner brackets hanging loose, in an alley some three or four blocks inland from Coney Island. He'd barked at his chauffeur to stop, known immediately the trunk was of some age, that it could be restored, and had ordered Charles, his chauffeur, to load the artifact into his Mercedes Benz.

An attorney, one-quarter Chinese, who had inherited clients when his business partner died, located the beneficiaries of Moses Cheung. The attorney's business partner had been associated for many years with clients in Chinatown, and a paper trail, sometimes in need of translation from Chinese to English, exposed an investment made on behalf of one Sing Cheung in 1917. The investment was the purchase of various stocks, among them one hundred shares of International Business Machines. In 1930 the shares had been divided and bequeathed by the only child of Sing Cheung, one Moses Cheung, to the progeny and/or living relations of three named beneficiaries: one Yun Li of China Town, one Benjamin Smith of the Indian School in Arizona, and one Alice Towne—whereabouts unknown, but known to be employed by the Latterby Brothers' Circus circa 1909–1911.

Alice Towne's whereabouts, where she ended, remained elusive; however, records kept by the Latterby Brothers' Circus indicated her birthplace as Three Rivers, Montana. The progeny of her unwed sister had thus been traced, with some difficulty and at no small expense, to the recipient, the last remaining blood relation of Alice Towne—one Ricky Towne, a chair pusher on the boardwalk at Atlantic City.

Moses Cheung was electrocuted on May 9, 1931; his bones are interred in Williamsport, Pennsylvania, next to his beloved wife, Phoebe Cheung, the Queen of all his dreams.

BET'S FAVORITE PLACE in the brownstone is in front of the windows facing out on St. Terence Street. Baby Clymenia Mae Song's IKEA crib, clean-lined and the color of summer wheat, is within easy reach. The natural light and view to the sky above the brownstones across the way is as much as any city dweller could want, with the uppermost branches of a single tree, a tree set into an opening in the sidewalk in front of the brownstone, to give Cly leafy movements to watch.

Upon their departure from the brownstone, the divorced sisters left a rocker behind—one they claimed had been there when they moved in and consequently belonged to Buddy.

"Might've been Aunt Mae's rocker," Buddy has said. He's told Bet about Jane Smith, his Aunt Mae's caretaker who, even after Mae died, continued on at the brownstone. "She'd been such a fixture for so many years. Like a sister to Grandmother Olive. Especially after Grandmother's real sister—that'd be my great aunt Florence—and she had a falling out.

"Something to do with how Mae worked the counter at Aunt Florence's hat shop. Or something to do with husbands of clients. Mae got fired and, well, Grandmother did what she did. One way and another, whatever Grandmother did seemed to her, to Olive, as much Great Aunt Florence's fault as it was hers."

Bet shivers, she always shivers when recollecting what little she knows about family, about heroines and victims.

Rose of Sharon had wanted Bet to name her baby after Olive, but there was no way Bet could bring herself around to giving her daughter such a name. No way. For Bet, the heroine of her family's women's history was Clymenia Tabor. She'd been the one who'd tried to insure independence for her granddaughter, Olive. Of course, if Clymenia's plan hadn't backfired, Elizabeth (Bet) Appleonia Brown Song wouldn't be exactly who she is, nor would this tiny round-faced miracle asleep in the crib near Bet's rocker be exactly who she is, and will be, either.

When Bet sits in this rocker, when she smoothes the silk skin of her daughter's forehead or brushes the back of her finger along her daughter's round cheek; when she lightly tamps down her daughter's stand-up Korean-dark hair; when she hums a lullaby, knowing few of the words beyond *Sleep, my child, and peace attend thee*—then all the impatience of housewifery and mothering slip away.

For a moment Bet's gaze fixes upon the collage of old watercolors she's brought together under one pane of glass to hang in Cly's room. It's a mixed media piece with no faces, only colors — snippets of torn edges, one pastel shade next to another — all rosy to russet and gold, a sprinkle of blue every now and again. Opaque spangles scatter along what might be viewed as a serpentine river, narrow here and wider there — for balance and effect. There are no deaths, no dead babies, no dimples, no golden curls, no ginger ringlets.

There is that other picture, the panoramic photo Rose of Sharon purchased at a junk store, Mister Junque's Emporium of Collectibles — the picture with Irene posed in front of the Texaco cannon. That picture is framed under glass and hangs on a wall in Buddy's downstairs flat. Buddy is seldom there, which works out well when Rose of Sharon comes east to visit.

Rose of Sharon comes often, stays for weeks at a time.

The thing, the fling with Jim Dustman, worked out until it didn't. Bet's mother had stayed high on romance for a little more than a year, then went into the dumps again. Then not. Then yes. But not with Dustman. She'd needed, one way or another, to be more than a mere "connector." She'd needed, she'd told Bet, "to connect" in more ways than what/how she and Jim connected.

Yes, Bet thinks, when her mother's light tap comes at the door, *I wondered when Grammie would show. We take our naps; we visit our sleeping worlds of fantasy and family and keep rewriting our hopes on frosty windows.* The leafless tree outside Cly's window will have leaves again. Rose of Sharon's recent cleaning sprees will lighten up and this clucking mother-hen-of-a-grammie will find a new interest soon enough. Or not. Maybe the last time around for Rose of Sharon was *the last time around.* Bet hopes against hope she and Kevin will go the distance. Things happen, accidents happen, livers go bad, fathers and husbands die, unwed mothers with lovers who give them a chance for family and little fish swimming through their lives die. Then what? Then you hope to heal enough to step up again, climb into life again, let the force of it propel you into a moving swell, an ongoing ebb and flow of possibilities.

Bet glances at Cly in her crib, looks back to the uppermost branches of the tree beyond the window. She has wondered, more than once, that not one among them—not Buddy, her mother, or she herself—had suggested "Irene" as the name for her infant daughter. Perhaps they each, in their differing ways, thought fate might be tempted to color this newborn's life, or—

A soft tapping interrupts her thoughts. As she rises to answer Rose of Sharon's light knock, she thinks, *Why they don't ban plastic grocery bags is beyond me.* One has caught on a twig of the tree, is lufting back and forth, seems set upon freeing itself but unable.

Bet says, "Shh, she's still sleeping."

"Still?" Rose of Sharon says. "Shouldn't you wake her?"

Bet steps out onto the landing, puts finger to lips and ushers Rose of Sharon to the stairs going down. How could her mother want to wake a sleeping angel? Had she awakened Bet from her dreams when she was a two-month-old? Bet won't ask. Her mother—this woman of habits and particularities—is trying, the best she knows how, to straddle the worlds of who she's been brought up to be, who she's been trained to be: the caregiver and laundress of her father, Lincoln, her mother, Appleonia, her husband, Teddy, her daughter, Bet, Bet's daughter, Clymenia Mae, and even, Bet smiles to herself, Bet's husband, Kevin. She is, Bet realizes, not nearly so much of Granddad Lincoln now as she once had been. She has exchanged her wire-framed trifocals for glasses with glossy red frames. In the closet downstairs there is a maxi-length men's coat tailored to fit her mother's slim figure, a coat not the ill-suited pale blue, but a deep-chocolate brown.

"I don't think so; not just yet," Bet says. "I think she's finishing up on a dream."

"Ah. Well. You'll never get her to sleep tonight if you don't wake her up soon."

"Soon enough," Bet says. "In the meantime, if you're not busy, would you give that tree service a call? There's a bag hung up in the limbs and —"

"Sure. I know the bum's rush when I hear it."

On the stairs, Rose of Sharon hears the door into Cly's nursery click shut. She's been relegated to de-bagging trees. She thinks she will call the tree service, but first she will go down to the basement, find a peanut and feed Buddy's black squirrel. She wonders if squirrels are trainable, if this one could be trained to retrieve windblown plastic from trees. She will ask the squirrel.

"Come here, my little friend," she says.

The squirrel stays high and away, camouflaged by a bevy of leaves. Rosie is not deterred.

About the Author

LYNN DOIRON is the recipient of the Dominic J. Bazzanella Awards in Fiction and Creative Non-fiction and author of *hand wording, New & Selected Poems.* Her work has appeared in numerous journals and anthologies. Currently living in Baja California, Mexico, she works with retirees in honing their memoirs and is the co-founder of the Baja Wordsmiths.

READERS GUIDE

1. Doiron introduces the reader to two main families, the Johnses and the Cheungs. Discuss their similarities as well as their differences.

2. Olive Johns is convinced the only way to help her children achieve their highest potential is to abandon their rural life in Williamsport, Pennsylvania and move to Brooklyn. In doing so they leave Joseph Johns, her husband/their father, behind. What were the ramifications of her decision, physically and emotionally, not only for herself but for each child?

3. Irene Johns is the fulcrum of this novel. Discuss the impact of both her life and death on the other characters. And spend time on the symbiotic relationship between Irene and Olive. Have you seen such an entwined relationship in your own family?

4. Doiron's depictions are ever mindful of family characteristics that get passed along through generations. What traits/emotional material are being repeated in these two families? Are any traits being changed by Sharon and Bet? Is it even possible to change things that seem to be part of one's DNA?

5. Discuss the impact of phantoms on the various characters and the outcome of this story. Are there phantoms in your life?

6. The early twentieth century brought many changes to American life as it began the transition from an agrarian/rural to a mechanized/urban society. How does Doiron use these changes in developing her characters and storyline?

7. Doiron presents the reader with the behind-the-scenes life of circus performers and even goes into the cannon with Irene at a seaside carnival. Did these depictions work for you?

8. Discuss the effects of class, race and prejudice as they play out in this novel.

9. Although this novel is not a mystery, per se, there are murders and deaths that impact the resolution of the two main storylines. Do you accept Buddy's explanation of Irene's death? Do you know who was responsible for the deaths in Chinatown?

10. Does the handling of these two mysteries by the NYPD in 1918 and 1930 resonate with your understanding of contemporary police procedures?